PRAISE
THE DSI WILLIAM

'Warm-hearted, atmospheric' ANN CLEEVES

'An exciting procedural' *SUNDAY TIMES*

'A master of the genre' LIN ANDERSON

'Convincing Glaswegian atmosphere and superior writing' *THE TIMES*

'One of the best' *LITERARY REVIEW*

'Move over Rebus' *DAILY MAIL*

'Relentless and intriguing' PETER MAY

'Immensely exciting and atmospheric'
ALEXANDER McCALL SMITH

'Alex Gray unfailingly delivers' *MORNING STAR*

'Effortlessly charming, wholly engaging'
IRISH INDEPENDENT

'Suspense, twists and searing imagery . . . [Alex Gray] will have you whipping through the pages' *GLASGOW HERALD*

'It's no wonder the series has sold a million copies to date' *DUNDEE COURIER*

Alex Gray is the *Sunday Times*-bestselling author of the Detective William Lorimer series. Born and raised in Glasgow, she has been awarded the Scottish Association of Writers' Constable and Pitlochry trophies for her crime writing and is the co-founder of the international Bloody Scotland Crime Writing Festival.

www.alexgrayauthor.co.uk

ALSO BY ALEX GRAY

The William Lorimer series

Never Somewhere Else
A Small Weeping
Shadows of Sounds
The Riverman
Pitch Black
Glasgow Kiss
Five Ways to Kill a Man
Sleep Like the Dead
A Pound of Flesh
The Swedish Girl
The Bird That Did Not Sing
Keep the Midnight Out
The Darkest Goodbye
Still Dark
Only the Dead Can Tell
The Stalker
When Shadows Fall
Before the Storm
Echo of the Dead
Questions for a Dead Man

Ebook only

The Bank Job

Alex Gray

OUT OF DARKNESS

SPHERE

SPHERE

First published in Great Britain in 2024 by Sphere
This paperback published in 2024 by Sphere

1 3 5 7 9 10 8 6 4 2

All characters and events in this publication, other than those clearly in the public domain, are fictitious and any resemblance to real persons, living or dead, is purely coincidental.

A CIP catalogue record for this book
is available from the British Library.

ISBN 978-1-4087-2930-4

Typeset in Caslon by M Rules
Printed and bound in Great Britain by
Clays Ltd, Elcograf S.p.A.

Papers used by Sphere are from well-managed forests
and other responsible sources.

Sphere
An imprint of
Little, Brown Book Group
Carmelite House
50 Victoria Embankment
London EC4Y 0DZ

An Hachette UK Company
www.hachette.co.uk

www.littlebrown.co.uk

To Donnie, with love and thanks
for the start of our adventure

The people who walked in darkness
Have seen a great light.
They lived in a land of shadows,
But now light is shining on them.

Isaiah Chapter 9 Verse 2

The road to power is filled with crimes,
and woe to him who sets an uncertain
foot upon it and retreats.

Verdi: *Macbeth* Act 1 Scene 5

PROLOGUE

November

'Kohi's alive.'

The man's voice was husky, his tone urgent.

Standing in front of the prison telephone, face close to its Perspex hood, Augustus Ncube's large figure blocked out the daylight from the nearest barred window. Anyone thinking to pass by might have hesitated then retreated, the man's bulk menacing even from behind. Catching this man's eye was folly, amounting to a beating by Ncube or one of his henchmen, those amongst the prison population who had learned fast that offering some sort of fealty was preferable to silent protest. And a good deal wiser than outright hostility.

The Zimbabwean shifted his weight from one foot to the other in the ensuing silence.

'Did you hear me?' he asked at last, a bitter edge to his words.

'I heard you,' the other man replied. 'But I'm not sure I believe you.'

'You mean you don't want to believe me?' Ncube spat out.

'He's dead and buried,' came the reply. 'I've seen his grave.'

'And I've seen him face to face!' Ncube protested, moving from side to side as if readying himself to launch an attack, though his only weapons right now were words. This man would never feel the touch of his fist.

There was silence again for a few seconds. Was he digesting this information? Ncube ground his teeth, frustrated to be so helpless. If only he could see the other man's expression, read his body language.

'Listen, man, Kohi's house burned to the ground. Wife and kid with it. Headstone raised in the cemetery,' the other man reasoned. 'Besides, there was no sign of him in the township. Our boys kept an eye on his old mammy and she's still mournin' her loss, I tell you.'

'You can tell me what you like,' Ncube retorted. 'I want my father to know what I've told you.'.

He glanced around, fearful of listeners in the shadows, then turned back, white-knuckled fingers gripping the telephone.

'I'm in here because they said I tried to kill him. Shot at him in the dark. Place outside Glasgow,' he added in a whisper.

'You sure?' The voice had changed now, a note of uncertainty overlaying the doubt.

'Sure, I'm sure. Kohi's still a cop. Only this time he's working over here.'

What he did not say, what he tried hard not to think during the long stretches of the night, were those fleeting moments when he had hoped the man he'd simply known as Danny might become a friend. No one would ever know the bitterness souring his heart when Augustus Ncube had found out the truth. Or the gut-wrenching humiliation of having been so gullible. And, if he could wreak some sort of revenge on Kohi, that might give him some satisfaction.

'We'll look into it,' the voice said at last.

Then the line went dead, leaving Ncube gripping the handset with fists that trembled in a moment of impotent rage.

CHAPTER ONE

The sigh seemed to go on for ever as he rolled slowly onto his back, warmth from her body still on his skin. Brightness filtered through a gap in the curtains, light catching Molly's hair on the pillow, creating a pale halo of spun gold. Then, somewhere outside, he heard the song of a robin heralding another new day. Not yet, he thought, as if answering the bird's summons. He needed to savour this moment, bask in the peace that enveloped him.

How could one man be so lucky? He'd lost so much and yet now Daniel Kohi felt as though life had poured out more joy than he'd ever imagined. *My cup runneth over*, he thought, remembering a phrase from the Book of Psalms.

Where had that come from? he wondered. It had been a long time since he'd had any thoughts of 'the good book' as his mother called it, though in truth there had been times when Daniel had sent up a prayer to whoever might be listening. Molly was not a religious woman, declaring her lack of adherence to any faith a by-product of an upbringing by parents who'd been avowed atheists. That didn't matter, however. The important thing was their feelings for each other.

He lay on his back staring at the ceiling, its ornate plasterwork a continual source of delight. To have found such a place to live! After his refugee status had awarded Daniel an eleventh-floor flat in central Glasgow, this elegant Southside residence was a mark of how far he had come. Now established as a police officer in Scotland, Daniel Kohi's prospects looked bright. Not only did he share this spacious ground-floor flat with his elderly friend, Netta Gordon, Daniel Kohi had a loving relationship with the younger woman slumbering beside him. Perhaps the traumas he had suffered were now being offset by these good things in his life.

Daniel turned to look at Molly then his mouth twisted in a grimace of pain. That ache in his shoulder where Ncube's bullet had penetrated might not disappear for quite some time, the surgeon had told him afterwards. At least he had been fit to resume his duties sooner than anyone had expected and was now back to the regular pattern of shifts. Today was a rest day and because it was Sunday, and no critical cases demanded her attention, Molly was not required to be at the Major Incident Team's offices in Helen Street. He lay still once more, listening to the soft sound of her breathing, then smiled as he heard a clattering of pots and pans coming from the kitchen. Netta was up and about, no doubt cooking something delicious for their lunch. She had readily taken on the role of housekeeper after their move across the city but remained the down-to-earth friend he'd cherished back in their high-rise flats.

Daniel's nose twitched. Could that be the smell of scones?

In moments he had slipped from the warmth of the bed, reached for his dressing gown and headed for the door.

'Ah, you're there.' Netta grinned at him as she straightened up from the oven, sliding the freshly baked scones onto a wire tray. 'Slept well, eh?'

The twinkle in the old lady's eyes said it all. Netta Gordon welcomed Molly warmly whenever she visited their flat on the Southside of Glasgow, delighted to see Daniel so happy with his new love. There was no old-fashioned coyness about them sleeping together under the same roof that might have happened back in Harare. No, Netta was a woman of the world, content to see Daniel in a relationship again at last after the tragedy that had robbed him of his wife, child and homeland.

'Your Molly still asleep, then?'

'Aye,' Daniel replied, settling himself onto one of the kitchen chairs. 'Probably for a while yet.'

'Ach, you both work terrible long hours. Ye deserve a lie-in frae time tae time.'

'How about you?' Daniel retorted. 'Up with the lark this morning,' he added, pointing to the scones.

'Hardly,' Netta guffawed, nodding towards the big clock on the kitchen wall. 'See, it's well efter nine.'

'Still, early for doing a baking, surely?'

'Aye, well. Mr and Mrs Lorimer are comin' around this afternoon. I'll jist throw a few pancakes thegether an' a',' she declared. 'I know Maggie Lorimer likes them.'

Daniel smiled at her. 'You love being the hostess, don't you, Netta?' he said fondly.

'Well, we nivver had a place like this afore. Proper table tae sit aroon. An' no' jist paper serviettes. I brocht my ain guid Irish linen napkins frae the auld flat. Nae use in keepin' them wrapped up in tissue paper in the bottom o' a closet when we can baith get the use of them, eh?'

Netta pushed a cereal plate and spoon towards Daniel. Since her stay in hospital, the old woman had declared that once they had moved to this flat, she would no longer 'keep things for good,' as she put it. 'Life's too short,' she'd told him, avoiding his concerned expression. And that, Daniel Kohi knew, was all too true. Perhaps his burgeoning relationship with Detective Sergeant Molly Newton was part of that same philosophy: *carpe diem*. Seize the day.

Maggie Lorimer bowed her head as the minister invoked the words of the benediction. God in three persons, asked to watch over them all for another week. Then, joining the congregation in singing the threefold Amen, Maggie felt a sense of calm. All was well. Her loved ones were safe and, whatever the future held, it was in the hands of the Almighty.

It was more than half an hour later that she gathered up her coat and bag, having helped to distribute bunches of flowers to those church members who visited the sick of the parish.

'Last out as usual!' the church officer laughed as she passed him. Maggie smiled and nodded. Even the minister had departed, his presence required for a service at the old folks' home nearby.

Outside, dried leaves scurried along the pavement, swept upwards by a vagabond wind before tumbling into the gutters. She gazed up at the leaden skies and sniffed the air. Snow, she told herself. Before the day was out, there would be a layer of white covering these grey streets, Maggie decided. Still, it was not too far to drive from Giffnock to Daniel and Netta's new home in Nithsdale Drive.

As she opened her car door, Maggie Lorimer gave a shiver that was nothing to do with the bitter November day. She blinked and turned around, wondering if someone was staring at her. But the street where she had parked her car was empty.

Once inside, she flicked the door lock then stretched the seat belt and clicked it in place. Was she being over-imaginative, the cold day with its threat of snow affecting her mood?

It had been several years since Lorimer's wife had experienced the deadly presence of a stalker, something that had shaken her at the time. Yet she had sensibly drawn a line under it, focusing her energies on her teaching and her career as a children's author.

'Stupid woman!' Maggie muttered under her breath. It was her age, that was all. Some of her female colleagues were experiencing dreadful mood swings while Maggie had simply begun to feel a little more tired at the end of a working day. Her hysterectomy several years before was now an unpleasant memory, regrets about their childless status something she had come to terms with long since. Perhaps her children's stories were an unconscious substitute, as their psychologist friend, Solly, had suggested. Maggie's thoughts shifted to the idea of Gibby, her little ghost boy, and his latest adventure. Perhaps she might use that shivery feeling in the story?

CHAPTER TWO

Janette Kohi laid her palms together, mouthing the words of the Lord's Prayer. As always, she added a silent plea for God to look after her Daniel, so far away from home.

When the choir began singing once more, Janette swayed in time to the music, joining the rhythmic clapping. There was always a sense of joy when they sang as one voice, her friends and neighbours lost in that moment of praise and thankfulness, all other troubles cast aside. Daniel was safe and he was now in a much nicer place along with Netta, the lady who had become her Scottish pen-pal. There had been small hints of other friendships that her son had made and that was good, especially that nice married couple that Netta had described in her letters. He had recovered from some injury sustained during the course of his work, praise the Lord, though Netta had not gone into much detail. They wrote to one another in a sort of code, just in case anyone should discover that Inspector Kohi of the Zimbabwean Police had not in fact perished in the fire that had taken his wife and son.

So, as she flung her hands heavenwards, Janette's face was wreathed in smiles, glad to join in the final ululation.

'Keep an eye on her, Reuben,' the heavy-set man in the khaki suit said to the smaller man standing beside him sporting a red bandana around his black curls. He pointed to the woman chatting to her friends as she walked along the path that led from their church back to the township. They were sheltered from the heat of the midday sun by the shade of a massive jacaranda, its pale violet blossoms strewn on the ground, carelessly trampled by their booted feet.

'She doesn't look as if she's mournin' a dead son,' Reuben remarked, jutting his chin in Janette Kohi's direction. 'Listen to her giggling.' He spat derisively onto the dust.

'It's Sunday,' the bigger man said slowly. 'They all come out of church like that.'

'Yeah ... good folk there prayin' to God to forgive their sins,' Reuben sneered.

'Some sins can never be forgiven,' the other man whispered, edging closer to his companion. 'And we never forgive those who fail to carry out our orders,' he added, grabbing the shorter man around his neck.

'Sure, boss, sure,' Reuben squeaked, wriggling under the other's tight grip.

'Okay, so long as we have an understanding,' the big man hissed, letting him go with a shove that sent his underling sprawling onto the hard baked ground.

As he watched the man in khaki sauntering away, the man in the red bandana picked himself up, muttering curses under his breath. Reuben Mahlangu knew that the people he worked for were ruthless, and as he leaned against the trunk of the jacaranda he fingered his throat, swallowing hard.

Unbidden, the memory returned.

Out in the bush, suspended from a tall thorn tree: that body turning slowly from a noose, vultures circling in the skies above.

CHAPTER THREE

Detective Superintendent William Lorimer tucked the tartan scarf around his neck, turning up his coat collar against the biting wind. Maggie had given it to him for his birthday last February and he'd worn it on cold days ever since.

'Ready, darling?' He turned to see Maggie as she stepped out of their home, her scarlet duffel coat a bright splash of colour on this dull, grey day.

'Yes, got everything, I think.' His wife smiled, patting a tote bag with gloved hands. 'Can't wait to see them all again. And Molly, too,' she added, her grin widening. Maggie Lorimer had been one of the first to notice the growing attraction between the Zimbabwean refugee and the detective sergeant, trying to nudge them together on several occasions, and her husband was pleased to see that her efforts had borne fruit.

'Oh, I wish we could get away from this wintry weather for a while,' Maggie said as she clicked on the heated seats.

'Never like to miss Christmas here but oh, I am tempted when I see all those adverts for sun-kissed beaches!'

'I know you've got lots of plans for the Christmas break, and we have Abby and Ben's school concerts,' Lorimer said, referring to their godchildren. 'But you could always take some leave of absence in the New Year. It's been done before. Besides, you're on to a three-day week now. Maybe your young job-sharing lass would appreciate a few weeks of full-time pay.'

'Maybe,' Maggie replied slowly as they drove along tree-lined streets towards the city. 'I've never asked for anything like that. Well, not since I had that sabbatical in the US.'

'And I've got leave to take before the end of the financial year,' Lorimer reminded her. 'Maybe we could go somewhere warm?'

The thought seemed to satisfy Maggie who threw him a grateful smile. She'd put up with years of cancelled trips, crime getting in the way, he realised. Perhaps it was time to arrange something big, far away where he could not be summoned at a moment's notice.

'Your fiftieth birthday's coming up,' Maggie said suddenly. 'Maybe we could go away then?'

Lorimer gave a short laugh, remembering another birthday. A decade previously, his fortieth party had been rudely interrupted by a case that had ended tragically. Perhaps it was time to set that right as he celebrated his half century? No big celebrations, though. Something just for the two of them.

The street was quiet even for a Sunday, the big car dealership across from the tenement building already sporting its

Christmas trees, lights and tinsel. As they stepped out of the Lexus, festive banners over a line of vehicles in the forecourt were being tossed skywards by a fierce wind.

'Think we're in for a storm?' Lorimer asked. Winter in Glasgow was notorious for those freakish gusts that could dislodge slates from rooftops, bringing trees crashing down on roads and rail lines, creating havoc with schools and transport.

'I think it's going to snow,' Maggie replied, looking up into the darkening skies. There was so little daylight at this time of year and already some streetlamps were beginning to cast an amber glow.

'Come on, let's get inside,' Lorimer urged, taking his wife's arm as a particularly violent gust barrelled along the street.

'They're here!' Netta whisked off her soiled apron and hung it up on a hook by the pulley. No washing hung from the pulley on their high ceiling today, the old woman conscious of keeping the big kitchen free from any damp laundry. Besides, it had been dinned into her by her Irish mammy that such signs of a working day were not appropriate for the Sabbath.

She rushed through to the spacious hallway, fingering her white curls, then threw open the door.

'Come away in, the pair of ye,' she cried, stepping back to let the Lorimers enter. 'Oh, that's some wind that's blown ye both here.' She watched as a swirl of dried leaves danced a merry jig on the pathway.

She closed the door with a slam then turned to give Maggie a hug. 'My, that cold wind's pit roses oan thae cheeks o' yours, lass,' she declared. 'An' here's the two love birds tae see ye,' she added slyly as Daniel and Molly emerged from the lounge.

'Let me take your coats,' Daniel offered.

'We've goat this great press,' Netta told them. 'Come and see the size o' it! Walk-in cupboard, the lassie fae the letting agency ca'd it but we ayeways ca'd it a glory hole.'

She swung open a door at the end of the hallway to reveal a large space that had been fitted with shelves and a hanging rail to one side for coats. 'Ye could dae a wee dance in therr, so ye could,' Netta said proudly.

'We've put the fire on in the lounge,' Daniel told them. 'It's a big space to heat but once in a while it's worth it just to see the logs burning.'

Maggie moved towards a comfortable grey settee that had been spread with a colourful African throw, rubbing her hands as she approached the fire. 'This is lovely,' she said. 'Nice to see a real fire. Glad the owners didn't board it up.'

'Me too,' chuckled Molly. 'It's lovely to curl up here on a frosty night.'

'Aye, she's here that often I think she might be movin' in, eh?' Netta laughed.

'Oh, you know it's your home baking I really come over for, Netta,' Molly teased, grinning at Daniel, making him throw up his hands in mock horror.

'Right, who's fur tea and who wants coffee?' Netta asked.

Later, as they all sat replete from the splendours of her afternoon tea, conversation turned to the weather as the wind rattled down the chimney.

'It's blawin aff snaw,' was Netta's opening remark. 'A few mair weeks an' mibbe we'll see a white Christmas.'

'Hasn't snowed at Christmas for years,' Molly chipped in. 'Just cold and wet, usually. But you're becoming used to that now, aren't you?' she teased, nudging her boyfriend.

'Ye'll be sorry ye ever set fit in this country, eh no, Daniel?' Netta chuckled.

'Not really,' he replied, grinning and slinging an affectionate arm around Molly's shoulder. 'Scotland has a lot to offer.'

'Must be nice in Zimbabwe at this time of year, though,' Maggie suggested, a wistful note in her voice.

'Not very warm,' Daniel told her. 'A bit better later in January and February. Mid-twenties, perhaps.'

'That's no' warm!' Netta shrieked. 'That's positively tropical fur Scotland!'

'It would be a lovely place to have a holiday,' Maggie went on, turning to her husband. 'Think of all those different sorts of birds and wildlife.'

'Are you thinking of going away?' Molly asked.

'It's Bill's fiftieth next year. Seventh of February, and we thought . . . ' She raised her eyebrows hopefully.

'Zimbabwe,' he said, as though savouring the word. 'Never thought of travelling to Southern Africa. It's a place I'd love to see,' he agreed.

'A good time to visit,' Daniel continued thoughtfully. 'Tourism's picked up in recent years and there are some reputable companies that arrange safaris. So long as you are with a group, you might be okay.'

'Is it still as bad, then?' Lorimer wanted to know.

'There were roadblocks everywhere when I was there,'

Daniel admitted. 'Bent cops asking for bribes. Some tourists just paid up and then went on their way rather than get into a hassle.' His mouth narrowed in disapproval. 'It was rife, especially out of the city.'

'But if we went with a creditable company ...?' Maggie ventured.

Daniel raised his eyebrows and nodded. 'Like I said, tourism has picked up. You'd just need to be very careful.'

'Let's look into it, then,' Lorimer said, turning to Maggie with a smile.

'We could even try to see your mum,' Maggie suggested. 'Have you heard from her since you moved into this flat?'

'No, we haven't,' Daniel admitted, turning to Netta to whom all of Janette Kohi's airmail letters were addressed. 'Should be due one soon, though. If you're not travelling till late January then there's plenty of time to let her know she could be having Scottish visitors.'

'Ach, that sounds a grand idea,' Netta said. 'I'd love ye tae come back an' tell me all about Janette and where she stays.'

'And be sure to take lots of photos,' Daniel added.

'Michty me, wid ye look at thon,' Netta declared, looking out of the window.

'Oh my, it's beginning to snow!' Maggie gasped. 'I thought it might.'

Sure enough, the first small flakes whirled against the glass pane, a foretaste of more to come.

'Wee snaw, big snaw, ma mammy used tae say,' Netta observed, wagging her head.

'You're right,' Maggie agreed. 'And I think we won't stay too much longer in case it gets worse.'

'Well, take thae pancakes hame wi' ye. I'll jist wrap them up in a bit o' greaseproof paper.'

As they made their goodbyes on the doorstep, Lorimer looked out at the path, now completely covered in white. The snowflakes were indeed larger now, falling hypnotically from a sky the colour of turned milk.

'Who would have thought we'd be making holiday plans on our visit,' he joked as they settled into the car.

'Yes, indeed. And Zimbabwe. Why did we never think of that before?' Maggie mused. 'Daniel has told us a bit about it. The good things as well as the bad. And after all, British tourists must be safe enough with the companies who organise wildlife safaris.' She looked out into weather that was rapidly changing the texture of the city. Tomorrow they might wake up to smooth white surfaces everywhere. 'Right now, Zimbabwe sounds a great alternative to this.' She shivered.

'Aye, and maybe I can spend my birthday birdwatching,' Lorimer agreed. 'Let's see if you can wangle three weeks' leave, eh? It'll be a great chance to get away from everything, not just the cold weather. Work, crime . . . '

Maggie clasped his hand, a contented smile on her face.

Yet what neither of them could possibly have known at that moment were the forces already in play that would confound Lorimer's words.

CHAPTER FOUR

Looking out from where he sat on the stoep, the old man watched the winding road, a cloud of dust signalling an approaching vehicle. Usually, Joseph trained his eyes on whatever passed by their small enclave of houses perched on the hillside, only to see them drive off and disappear around the next bend. Few travellers ever turned up the track to where he lived next to a patch of derelict ground. He cast his rheumy eyes towards the place where his neighbour's house had once stood, now overgrown with weeds and thorny bushes, a rubble of bricks still jutting out from the earth. Wood ants had made short work of any blackened timbers, reducing them to dust, and it was hard to remember what the building had looked like.

Joseph remembered the child, though, little Johannes who had begun to walk, his mother, Chipo, often gathering him up against her hip in a colourful batik shawl. He'd been a happy wee fellow, his gurgling laugh always guaranteed to make the old man smile. A sigh escaped him now as he closed his eyes, the memories returning.

The noise of a vehicle trundling over the deeply rutted track made the old man start.

He blinked, to make sure he wasn't dreaming but no, there it was, a white squad car with its distinctive yellow and blue stripes. As he narrowed his eyes against the glare of the sun, he saw two men in the front staring at him through their sunglasses.

Joseph watched as they alighted from the car and slammed the doors shut. The sound seemed to reverberate in the still air, and he found himself cringing into the ancient armchair where he sat on his porch.

Police meant trouble. For most of Joseph's life their presence had meant danger, stories of beatings and torture of innocent victims still rife. It had been Daniel Kohi's stand against police corruption that had led to the tragedy next door.

The old man swallowed hard, his mouth suddenly dry. Why were they here? Surely there could be no reason for them to pay him a visit. Joseph was not a wealthy man and the few vegetables he grew out in his back garden were surely not enough for them to want to steal.

They walked slowly up the track, pausing for a moment next to the vacant lot, their voices too far away for him to make out what they were saying. Joseph could feel his heart racing. Had he forgotten to take those tablets the doctor had prescribed? No, he was sure he'd swallowed them down straight after breakfast. Yet the trembling had now reached his hands and so he clasped them together as the police officers began to walk slowly towards him.

Back then, after the fire, he had been questioned by

several officers, most of whom had been sympathetic. All of them had been spoken to by the police, every one of the neighbours living on this place at the end of a road. And their answers had been the same. Daniel, Chipo and baby Johannes had perished inside that inferno, a tragedy that had made headline news. The truth had been hidden that night, Daniel being shoved into a waiting van and spirited away. Even his mother had complied with the wishes of the church folk who had taken him, the headstone in a nearby cemetery now bearing all three names.

So why should he fear the approach of officers today? What was the meaning of that look passing between them as they'd stood in the wreck of what had once been a well-tended front garden? Or, and here the old man clenched his fingers more tightly, was it the way they were climbing the three steps up to the stoep, staring at him as he sat under their gaze?

'Joseph Mlambo?'

One of the officers had stopped, his ox-blood red boot poised on the top step of the stoep.

'Yessir,' Joseph replied, hands now clutching each side of his wooden chair.

He could not see the man's eyes behind the sunglasses, only his own reflection, an elderly man with grizzled grey hair.

'You the owner of this property?' the man asked, casting his eyes upwards at the roof of the single-storey bungalow.

'Yessir.' Joseph nodded. 'I've lived here for many years,' he added, attempting a smile that died on his lips as the other officer strode nimbly up the steps and towered over him.

'You a rich man, then?' the second officer asked, kicking the leg of Joseph's chair.

'No, boss,' Joseph replied, licking his dry lips. 'Don't have lots of money. A few dollars?' He wondered if he was expected to offer some sort of bribe for these men to leave him in peace. The most recent directive from government was not to offer bribes as this simply extended the corruption amongst the ZRP. And yet . . . if he refused to hand over what paltry sum he had, would these men drag him into the bush and beat him until he fell senseless?

'He thinks we want his money!' The second officer laughed, standing up and shaking his head. 'No, Mr Mlambo, we are not here to rob you like some bad cops you may have heard of. Goodness me, no!'

Once again, a knowing look passed between the two officers and Joseph felt a sudden need to empty his bladder. If it was not money that they wanted, then it could only be information.

'May I offer you a glass of water?' Joseph suggested, rising from his chair and signalling that the police officers might wish to enter his small home.

'Sure,' the first officer agreed. 'But we prefer to wait out here.'

Once inside, Joseph headed straight for the lavatory and closed the door behind him. He felt a sense of shame as he watched the thin trickle of urine splashing into the toilet, an old man's helpless body betraying him. His hands washed and dried, the old man tottered into his kitchen.

Once outside, a glass of water in each clenched fist, Joseph glanced over the heads of the two men whose backs were turned from him, evidently still discussing the abandoned plot next door. *Dear Lord, give me courage*, he prayed as if the blue, blue sky above was a mere curtain between the Almighty and himself.

'Your water, gentlemen,' he said stiffly, watching them turn and give him a nod as they reached out for the glasses.

'Anybody been here to dig that plot up?' one of them asked.

'No, sir,' Joseph replied. 'It's never been touched since the place burned down.'

'Is that so?' the other turned and stared at the old man. 'Who owns it, then?'

Joseph looked from one of the cops to the other. 'I don't know, boss,' he said, shrugging. 'All family dead and gone. Nobody wants to build there after the fire, I guess.'

The cop with the reflective glasses walked a little closer to Joseph and tapped the baton that was hooked on his thick leather belt. 'That so? See, we hear something different.'

Joseph felt the sweat gathering under his hairline. Was he about to be given a beating? Here on his own stoep?

He said nothing, just stared back at the man, unblinking, his heart thumping so loudly surely they must hear it.

'We hear Kohi's alive,' the other cop declared, joining his mate to tower over Joseph, his bulky figure suddenly blotting out the sun. 'What do you have to tell us about that?'

'I saw the fire that night,' Joseph began quietly. 'Nobody could have escaped from that.'

Again, a look passed between the two men and Joseph felt his body begin to shake.

'Someone tells us that Kohi did,' the first cop insisted.

Joseph shook his head. 'They're all buried in the

cemetery,' he replied. 'We were all there, at the funeral service. Pastor will tell you that.'

'Pastor's gone,' the second cop declared, bringing his foot a few inches closer to the old man, forcing him to sit down heavily in his chair. 'Overseas mission.'

Joseph's eyes flicked from one cop to the other, his mouth too dry to utter another word.

Then his gaze was drawn to the man's fingers tapping the thick wooden club.

'He thinks we're going to hurt him,' he laughed, turning to his neighbour. 'Would we do a thing like that?'

Joseph attempted a tremulous smile. It was going to be all right, after all.

The blow when it came took him by surprise, the man's fist slamming against Joseph's jaw, sending the old man flying out of his chair and onto the dusty boards.

He tried to shield his face from the booted feet but only succeeded in hearing the crack as a bone in his arm broke. Then more kicks landed on his chest and stomach, making him cry out in pain.

The assault ended as swiftly as it had begun, the men retreating from the porch back onto the track.

'That's just a reminder, Mlambo. We'll not be so soft on you next time,' he heard a voice calling out followed by a peal of laughter.

Joseph lay on the ground, afraid to raise his head until he could hear the squad car turning and heading off back down to the main road.

At last, he rolled onto his side with a groan as a sharp pain pierced deep within his chest. It was impossible to sit up, such agony as the old man had never known coursing through his body.

Despite himself, Joseph could not resist the urge to cough, and it was then that he saw the first gouts of blood spraying from his mouth.

He lay there, panting a little, his breath coming in spasms. Was he fated to lie here until death took him into its embrace? The old man closed his eyes and remembered that fateful night when death had consumed those other two innocents.

The sound of fire crackling came back to him, the scorching heat and the ashes that had almost blinded him, forcing them all back. And then Daniel had arrived . . .

Though there had been no contact with the former police inspector since that dreadful time, Joseph had heard rumours that he'd reached the safety of the United Kingdom, the church folk smuggling him out under pretence that he was one of their delegates. Truly, the man who had been Inspector Kohi's next-door neighbour had little notion of his friend's whereabouts, only the truth that he had escaped from certain death after the torching of his home.

But Joseph Mlambo had just found that even such knowledge spelt certain danger for them all.

He broke out in a fit of coughing once more, feeling the hot blood coursing over his lips.

Then the sound of distant bells ringing made the old man smile, an image of a white church tower his last conscious thought as he slipped into the darkness.

CHAPTER FIVE

'It's actually not a problem,' her head of department told Maggie Lorimer. 'Lucy wanted to have a full-time post when she applied for your two days and if she and our current probationer cover your classes for these three weeks, I can't see why you wouldn't be granted a leave of absence. Have you spoken to the boss?'

'Not yet,' Maggie admitted, laying down her coffee mug. 'I wanted to run it past you first, Suze.'

Suzette Anderson nodded. 'You've been here for far longer than I have, Maggie, and the whole department respects everything you've done. If there's a problem with his nibs, let me know and I'll put in a good word for you. You know that Manson's got a soft heart despite his fearsome reputation.'

Despite her head of department's assurance, Maggie was a little nervous as she knocked on the head teacher's study door. The Christmas holidays were still ahead, and Manson might well growl at her, suggesting she use that two week break to go overseas instead.

Keith Manson looked up as Maggie entered the room, rising to his feet and coming around his desk to greet her.

'Mrs Lorimer, what can I do for you?' he boomed. Though he was short of stature, there was something commanding about the stocky man who took Maggie's hand in a fierce grip.

Once seated beside the head teacher who had stood by her through every crisis in her career, Maggie took a deep breath then began to put forward her request.

'I've got it!' she said gleefully, stepping into Suze Anderson's warm hug. 'Three whole weeks!'

'You deserve it,' Suze grinned. 'And part of that time is February spring break, after all. What did Manson say?'

'Well, he did talk about creating a precedent but given my years of service and . . . well, what he called a high profile . . . he reckoned nobody else would mind.'

'Well, you have got a high profile, Margaret Lorimer!' Suze grinned. 'Famous children's author in our midst! Manson just loves all the kudos that's brought to the school.'

Maggie's face fell for a moment. 'I hope nobody sees that as favouritism,' she sighed.

'Young Lucy certainly won't. She's desperate for a full-time post and three weeks' pay will certainly help her.' Suze tilted her head to one side. 'You'd never take early retirement, though, would you?'

Maggie shook her head. 'Three days a week suits me fine now,' she said. 'I get enough time to write and besides, I just can't imagine not teaching.'

'Good. Well, just remember to send us a postcard from Africa. We'll want to know all about it.'

'I will,' Maggie promised, breathing a huge sigh. It seemed hardly real, permission to travel all that way with her husband granted so easily. Surely that was a good omen?

Lorimer pressed the send button and sat back at his desk. His time away was assured now that Muirpark Secondary had granted Maggie that leave of absence. They had spent the previous evening poring over travel sites before selecting the one that sounded most suitable. It was pricey, but there was a lot to be said about paying for what you got, as Maggie had pointed out. It was a well-known company that had garnered five-star reviews from previous travellers, their lavish praise giving the Lorimers a sense of confidence in their choice.

He glanced out of the window. The afternoon was already dark, street light glimmering through the continually falling snow. It would be a relief to be somewhere else for a while, he thought. By the time they came home again February would be half over, winter days hopefully less bitter.

Their itinerary looked promising. A few days spent in Harare in a five-star hotel, trips to places of interest arranged before travelling into the bush. In one safari park they'd even be staying in a tree house. Then a flight to Kariba and time spent in a remote lodge where there was reported to be an abundance of wildlife. Lorimer smiled. There had been pictures online of starry skies, so different from the thick banks of cloud that covered Scotland right now. There was an option to add on time at Victoria Falls or return to Harare, something he and Maggie were still to discuss. If things looked safe enough, perhaps they might be able to look up Daniel's mother out in the township, something that Netta Gordon had suggested. She and Janette Kohi had become penfriends since Daniel's arrival in Glasgow, their messages carefully coded to conceal news about Daniel.

It was worth thinking about, Lorimer told himself. Daniel's mother was fending for herself nowadays, according to Netta, but had always praised her small church community for their support. Still, if there was anything he could do to help, he would. British tourists were seen as fabulously wealthy in comparison to the impoverished population, Daniel had warned them, and it had shocked Lorimer to see the pitiful wages that even a senior police officer received in the Zimbabwean Republic force. His own remuneration looked like a fortune in comparison, and he made himself a promise to see what he might do for Janette Kohi.

As he turned away from the window, Detective Superintendent Lorimer could not have imagined how his inclination to assist an elderly lady in a small African village would lead to rather more than simply an interesting holiday in a foreign land.

CHAPTER SIX

December

The sound of metal against hard earth echoed through the still air. High above, several large birds wheeled, watching the activities below, their sense of smell drawing them closer.

These white-backed vultures were not often seen unless there was carrion to be had. Nature's refuse collectors, one might call them, huge birds with wicked beaks that would tear flesh from a dead creature in minutes. For now, they waited, thermals allowing them to float in circles above the small cemetery on the outskirts of Harare.

The two men digging were grunting with the effort. Rain had not fallen for several days and every tiny breath of wind in this climate, a thousand feet above sea level, came as a respite from the scorching heat.

'We'll not find anything,' one of them grumbled.

The man with the red bandana shook his head. '*He* told us to do this. So, we must,' Reuben replied testily, digging his spade into the unyielding soil.

'It's going to take hours,' the other man whined.

'And it will take the boss minutes to put a bullet into our heads,' came the reply. 'Keep digging!'

The place where they were exerting their efforts was out in the open away from a line of acacia trees that bordered the cemetery. Reuben looked at the headstone carved with an angel cradling a baby and felt a lurch in his stomach. A child was buried here. And his parents, burned to death by . . . He stopped for a moment, wondering who had really set that place alight, killing the cop and his family. Surely there could be no doubt about the fate of these victims? He'd seen the place for himself, just scrub and blackened timbers, razed to the ground. Nobody could have survived that. And yet, here they were, assigned this thankless task by the man who held so much power in the city. Power to finish me off, Reuben reminded himself, fingering the bruises around his throat.

His fingers were sore from repeated blows with the spade but at least there was a decent-sized cavity now where they'd been digging.

'I need water,' his companion complained, chucking down his spade. 'Gonna see if anyone c'n give me somethin' to drink.'

'Bring me some back, too,' Reuben told him. 'And if you don't come back, well, it'll be all the worse for you.'

He continued pushing the edge of the tool into the dried-out soil, blow by blow, muttering curses under his breath. If this other man were to cut and run, there was no way he'd be able to finish this job on his own. Bit by bit, the soil gave way to darker earth, the heap by the side of the Kohis' grave rising higher. At last, the sound of the metal clanged against something different, even harder than earth.

Wiping the sweat from his eyes, Reuben bent down and pushed away the clumps of soil, feeling something smoother beneath his fingers.

'Yes!' he exclaimed, giving a sigh of relief. Surely that was the top of a coffin?

Had they all been put into the one box? Reuben wondered. Nobody had given him any information about that. There wouldn't have been much left after being scorched to death. Hopefully they had all been laid to rest here, in a single coffin.

Reuben's eyes fell on the cloth bag laid to one side that contained his tools. He'd need them to open the damned thing.

A cloud passed over the sun at that very moment and Reuben shivered. *Damned*, he'd said, even though it was inside his mind. Looking up, he saw the vultures circling like birds of ill omen. What was he doing here, desecrating the grave of innocent people? Should he fling the soil back into the hole they'd made, make a run for it?

But the moment of doubt passed as he heard the tramp of feet and then the other grave digger appeared, a bottle in each hand.

'Gimme!' Reuben demanded, stretching out his hand and grabbing the water. He drank half of it in one long draught then exhaled slowly. 'Good. Let's get this down then keep digging. We're nearly there.' He grinned, raising the bottle to his lips once more.

The exhumation of dead bodies is a matter for the courts of law in most countries, including Zimbabwe. Neither of the men digging had been granted a licence to do so, nor was either of them an environmental health officer, but the pair were far more afraid of the repercussions from the man who had ordered this to take place than they were of the law courts. Darkness was beginning to fall when Reuben pushed the crowbar under the edge of the first wooden coffin. There was a creak then the sound of splintering and a final crack as the last nail came free.

Each man looked warily at the other. Who was going to be first to raise that lid?

'You do it,' Reuben said. 'Just see how many—'

A harsh, unnatural cry above them made the two men cower beneath the surface of the grave, hands warding off the first of the huge birds.

'Scat!' Reuben yelled, waving his hands at the vultures. 'Git goin'!'

The other man picked up a rock and flung it at the bird but missed.

'Hey, don't do that!' Reuben scolded. 'They're protected!'

His companion burst into nervous giggles.

'We're breaking the law doin' this, and you're worried about a few birds scattering their feathers? Man, I don't think you're real!'

Reuben turned to scowl at him. 'You wanna lift this?'

The other man's face fell, and he took a step backwards, shaking his head.

'You're closer,' he said. 'You do it.'

Reuben turned back to stare at the coffin. For a moment he hesitated, wondering if such desecration might lead to consequences that were out of his control.

Then, taking a deep breath, he heaved the lid sideways and put an arm across his mouth, expecting the smell of decomposition to make him choke. But there was no rotting smell. And the bodies six feet below the soil were now mere greyish skeletons.

The child was in its mother's arms, Reuben could see that, and it filled him with sudden remorse. No way should he have disturbed this grave.

Overhead the clouds had darkened further, making it hard to see the other coffin.

As the first fat drops of rain began to fall, Reuben looked up, but the birds had vanished.

It took some time and a lot of exertion but at last they heaved the first coffin out of the grave to see the other beneath. Here, if the headstone were to be believed, lay the final remains of former police inspector Daniel Kohi, beloved husband of Chipo and father of Johannes.

'What's keepin' you?' he heard the voice calling out. 'Is he there or not?'

Reuben leaned across and gave the coffin containing mother and child a small push so he could open the other one.

'Sorry, I'm sorry,' he whispered, as if the dead could somehow hear him.

Then, swallowing hard, he levered up the lid.

There was nothing. No third skeleton. Just a few slabs of stone to weigh the damn thing down.

Reuben felt a shudder pass through his body. Then he turned and looked up at the man standing above him.

'They were right,' he said at last. 'Kohi's not here.'

CHAPTER SEVEN

Ants. That was the woman's first thought as she walked past the grave, small heaps of soil surrounding the burial site. How strange. Or had the gardener been weeding around a border? A frown crossed her brow. Wasn't this the grave of that tragic family she'd read about a while back? How long had it been? Two years? More? The elderly lady shook her head. She was becoming more forgetful with the passing years. Soon it would be time to return home again, her visit to her brother here in Harare almost over. Since her sister-in-law had died, she had made this an annual trip, and today she was here to mark the anniversary of dear Jean's passing.

Looking carefully at the ground, the woman noticed other things; a faint line along one side where blades of grass had been bent over and ... what was that shining in the sunlight? Swapping the bunch of lilies into her left hand then bending carefully, she stooped down to pick it up. A tiny screw, its twisted metal glinting against a small patch of dried soil. How strange, she thought, pocketing the object. This was very odd.

The woman turned to face the narrow pathway of beaten earth where one tall white headstone loomed above the others. She walked slowly towards it and stopped, reading the inscription with a sigh. Then, placing the flowers on the grave, she closed her eyes, clasped her hands and murmured a short prayer. Whoever was up there in that lucid blue sky would probably hear her, she thought, looking up again. Then, putting a hand into her pocket to find her car keys, her fingers felt the shape of that tiny screw.

Something wasn't quite right, the woman told herself, looking towards the Kohi family's grave. She paused for a moment then gazed back towards the wide, open skies.

'Lord, only You know what's going on here,' came the whisper. 'Let these poor folk rest in peace.'

As she made to leave, the woman turned at the faint sound. For a moment it seemed as if the acacia trees on the edge of the cemetery were swaying, a sudden wind sighing through their shivering leaves.

She blinked hard then looked again. But all was still.

The old man stretched out his legs, tentatively at first, keeping the pain at bay. Sunlight spilled onto the stoep, warming his bare feet like a caress. The injuries would heal in time, the lady doctor had told him at the clinic, the dull aches inside his chest and shoulder constant reminders of his internal injuries, the punctured lung and the broken ribs, but then she had held his hand for a few moments, shaking her head and meeting his gaze. Other things took longer to heal, she'd murmured. And it was true. The fear that had followed his unprovoked attack remained as jagged now as it was when they'd left him there bleeding on the ground. He was lucky to be alive, that doctor had told him quietly. She had prescribed painkillers, giving his grandson a slip of paper to take to the clinic's pharmacy after signing his discharge papers. Nobody had questioned the old man stumbling painfully from the clinic supported by the tall gangly youth. He'd looked around, fearful that there might be police officers waiting for him in the shadows.

Now Joseph was home, the veranda in front of his open door swept clean of dust, cushions set behind the old man's back as he'd eased himself down into his favourite chair. Someone had been inside his home during the time he'd been away. Women from the church, no doubt, their Christian kindness shown in small acts like cleaning his kitchen and leaving parcels of food. Even his dirty clothes had been washed and folded, laid in neat piles in his bedroom.

'All right, Grandpa Jo?'

Joseph smiled at the sight of his grandson emerging round the side of the house. 'Campbell, come and sit by me,' he said. 'Tell me about your day.' He looked up into the boy's face.

'It was fine,' Campbell assured the old man with a shrug of his thin shoulders.

Joseph nodded. The boy was like his grandfather, a lad of few words. Joseph had played down the attack lest more trouble come to their door. He gave a quiet smile at the thought, remembering the chalk board outside church that had made him nod as he'd passed it by, wondering how many folk had been touched by the words.

TROUBLE KNOCKED AT THE DOOR, BUT HEARING LAUGHTER, RAN AWAY

There had always been laughter in the house next to his, Chipo singing to her baby son, Daniel's ready laugh as he swung the little boy around. The silence that had followed the fire had left Joseph feeling bereft of so much joy. But here was his own lad, Campbell, who had grown so tall and who could outrun every other boy in his class. A veritable gazelle, Daniel had joked when Campbell had won his first cross country race.

'Is it okay if I go to football practice, Grandpa Jo?' the boy asked. 'Mrs Gonnani said she'd call round this afternoon.' His eyes were pleading.

Joseph nodded. The boy had been a constant presence at his side ever since he'd accompanied him from the clinic, supporting his grandfather's broken arm as the bus trundled out of the city until it reached the road end where they lived. Campbell's mother had died of malaria when the boy was small, leaving his father and grandfather to bring up the boy. Richard Mlambo was a ranger out in the bush, one of several skilled trackers whose job it was to protect elephant and rhino herds from human predators. He was away for long spells and so Campbell had taken to staying with Joseph. The boy had loved playing with the little one next door, Joseph remembered, trying to teach him the rudiments of football, hoping, no doubt, that Johannes would grow up to be as keen as he was.

'Of course, lad, of course.'

'You'll be okay for a while on your own?' The boy's eagerness to be up and away was tempered by genuine concern.

No child should feel guilty to be off playing sport, Joseph told himself. 'Off you go. And remember what I told you. Keep your eye on the ball!'

Campbell gave a toothy grin and laid a gentle hand on Joseph's shoulder, mindful that hugs could hurt the old man.

Joseph watched his grandson as he ran full pelt along the road then turned to wave as he reached the corner.

He gave a quiet sigh, remembering not to inhale too deeply, the pain never very far away. The pills he'd been given were beginning to work their magic, a heaviness stealing over him.

He half closed his eyes against the brightness of the sky, aware of a movement high above. Vultures. Somewhere out there was roadkill, perhaps, and they were readying themselves to swoop down and alight on whatever hapless creature had come to grief.

Then his eyes drooped and, warmed by the afternoon sun, Joseph dozed off in his chair.

'Hello!'

A voice roused Joseph out of his slumber, expecting to see his friend, Welcome Gonnani. It was not Welcome's cheerful face that he saw, however, but a tall white woman wearing a wide-brimmed sun hat and sporting a pair of sunglasses. A tourist, perhaps? A person out for a stroll who had lost their way?

'Hello, sorry to bother you,' the woman began, coming closer to the stoep. 'This was the Kohi residence next door, I think?'

Joseph stared at her for a moment, unsure how to reply.

'Kohi,' the woman repeated. 'That terrible fire, oh, that poor, poor family!'

'Yes, madam, it was there,' Joseph replied at last, raising a hand to indicate the overgrown plot next to his home.

'I thought so,' the woman continued. Then, raising a hand, she smiled. 'So sorry, I'm forgetting my manners. I'm Pastor Carmichael's sister. You might know him from the mission school?'

Joseph thought for a moment then nodded. There had been a white pastor at the mission school for several years. Along with his wife he had brought his own particular brand of Pentecostal Christianity to the nearby village. A mild-mannered man, Joseph recalled, well respected by their own pastor. He'd probably see him at the Christmas service when several of the local churches came together.

'Joseph Mlambo.' He reached out a courteous hand for her to shake. 'I think I know your brother,' he told her. 'His wife is late.' Joseph remembered the thin, white-haired lady who had played the piano at the mission hall.

'My sister-in-law, Jean Carmichael,' the woman said. 'I was at the cemetery, taking flowers to her grave,' she explained, 'and I . . . ' She broke off with a frown, turning to look at the scorched black earth bleeding through the weed-infested ground.

Joseph watched as she continued to stare, wondering just what had brought this lady to his door.

'You knew the family?' she said at last, gazing back at Joseph.

'Yes. We were very good friends,' Joseph said, biting his lip to contain the surge of sudden emotion that threatened to spill over.

'Oh, well, perhaps you are the very person I should be telling,' she said, stepping up onto the stoep and settling herself on the ground beside the old man.

'Telling? Telling what?'

The woman shook her head. 'It's terrible, what might have been going on, you know. Utter desecration. I mean . . . ' She broke off again and looked up into Joseph's eyes as if finally deciding that he was someone she might trust.

'I think someone has been tampering with their grave.'

CHAPTER EIGHT

She looked up as a flock of weaver birds ascended from their tree into the morning skies, chattering loudly. It was not yet nesting time for these little birds, a season Janette enjoyed as she watched their painstaking efforts to build so many intricate, pendulous dwellings. There were clouds coming over from the Highlands and she took a deep breath then nodded. Yes, she could smell rain. Perhaps by this afternoon there would be the customary short-lived deluge then the welcome fragrance of wet earth, steaming as the sun dried it.

Janette Kohi stooped to pick up her trowel and placed it into the shallow basket that she used for her plants. The ground was dry and dusty but later she might manage to create a deep enough furrow for her beans. Straightening up again, she put one hand to the small of her back and uttered a groan. These aches were yet another sign that rain was on its way.

As she began to turn towards her front door, a familiar voice called out.

'Missus Kohi! Missus Kohi!'

Janette looked along the pathway at the running figure then frowned, recognising the lad. She clutched the cross she wore around her neck, suddenly alarmed by the tone of the young man's cry.

'Campbell Mlambo, what are you doing all the way out here, boy?' Janette scolded. 'This time of the day you should be at school!'

As the gangly youth skidded to a halt at her garden gate, Janette Kohi could see the sweat coursing down his face.

'What's wrong?' she asked, a tug of fear at her heart.

Campbell looked around him as if terrified that he was being followed.

'Come in, boy,' Janette told him. 'Come in and shut the gate behind you.'

Once inside, door closed, Janette ushered the lad into the main room of her small home.

'Sit here while I bring you some water,' she commanded, pointing at the comfortable settee with its colourful batik throw.

Something was wrong, that was obvious, and as she returned with the cup of water, Janette studied the boy intently. He was not wearing his school uniform today but an old pair of ragged khaki shorts and a football jersey, bare feet thrust into a pair of worn-out plimsolls. And he had run a goodly distance, surely, the bus terminal almost a mile from her home.

Campbell drank the water down in gulps then gave a sigh as he wiped his mouth. 'Thank you, missus,' he said, handing her back the cup.

'Now, tell me why you come here in such a state, Campbell Mlambo,' she said.

'It's Grandfather Joseph,' Campbell blurted out. 'He sent me to tell you. Someone's been digging up the grave.'

'What?' Janette gasped.

Campbell glanced around him once more as if afraid anyone was listening. Then, leaning forward he whispered, 'Bad cops came, missus. They came to visit Grandfather Joseph. Asked about the place next door . . . ' The boy gave an involuntary shudder. 'They told him that Daniel, your son, is alive, missus,' he added softly, shaking his head. 'Then they hurt him, missus. An' now . . . they must've dug up the grave . . . '

The boy gave a sob and covered his face with both hands.

'Oh, Campbell. What did they do to him?' Janette cried. 'Your poor, dear grandfather!'

The boy gave a moan and began to tremble. 'All bad things, missus. They beat him up, broke his bones and, and . . . ' he began to sob again, 'the broken rib punctured his lung. We thought he was going to die.' He gave a shuddering sigh and wiped the tears with the back of his hand.

'Grandpa Joseph told me to come straight to you, Missus Kohi. Just to warn you,' Campbell continued.

'Warn me, why?'

'He said to tell you get out quick. Pack right now and take your passport. Bad cops come for you next.'

'Me?' Janette gave a short laugh. 'Why should I be going anywhere? I've done nothing wrong.' Then she drew in a long breath, realising the irony of her words. Daniel had never done anything wrong and yet he had been targeted by a group of corrupt police officers before he could inform against them. And now a poor, innocent old man had been cruelly beaten for simply keeping a secret. The secret that there were only two bodies lying in the cemetery where her daughter-in-law and grandson were buried, and that Daniel was now safe in Scotland. There was every reason to fear the arrival of those wicked men who had burned their home to the ground, Janette realised.

'But where shall I go?' she asked helplessly. 'And who would want to take me in?'

She waited at the doorway until she saw the boy running back along the dusty track then turned into the house, closing the door behind her. Janette Kohi slumped into her armchair, feeling as though all the breath had been knocked out of her. Poor Joseph! What a thing to do to a good old man like that! And to desecrate the grave ... finding not three but two bodies. She swallowed hard, sudden nausea overwhelming her.

Dear Lord ... What on earth was she to do?

The thought prompted action and Janette forced herself out of the chair, her spinning mind already making a list of necessities for a hasty departure. The old suitcase behind the wardrobe was dragged out and laid on top of her bed and soon she was opening drawers, pulling out garments, rushing to the bathroom for essential toiletries.

She stopped for a moment, gazing around the bedroom. What else? Passport, the boy had told her, and rummaging in her bedside drawer, there it was, right at the bottom under old photograph albums. Grasping it tightly, Janette wondered if she ought to try to make it out of Zimbabwe somehow, flee across to the border to Botswana? But there was no money for a ticket, and she might be caught before reaching a bank.

She sat down heavily on the bed, tears forming in her eyes. It was hopeless. Daniel was gone and there was no one to protect her.

Janette's glance fell on the Bible that always lay on her bedside table. No, she was wrong. Her heavenly father would protect her. She clasped the old book to her breast and gave a long sigh.

A noise outside made her start before she had time to begin a prayer. Then a loud crash and the sound of her back door being hammered.

It was too late!

They were here.

CHAPTER NINE

The man with the red bandana now stood a few paces away from the old lady's home, a frown creasing his brow. He'd been inside for over an hour, rummaging in every drawer and cupboard, but there was nothing to suggest that Mrs Kohi had left for good. There was food in the small refrigerator with some fresh milk and an opened bag of mealie meal tied securely with twine to stop the ants getting into it. Out in the back yard several items of female underwear hung on a metal wire, drying after the rain shower. There was every sign that she might return soon and so he was keeping watch on the dusty track that led to the bus terminus. No, he'd wait here till she returned, he thought with a grin as he patted the club secured in the waistband of his shorts. Then he'd spring his little surprise.

It was dark now and there was no sign that the woman was intent on returning to her home. Yet her front door had been left unlocked, suggesting that she had not gone so very far away. The cicadas and tree frogs had set up their nightly singing now and he shivered as the shadows lengthened. *Don't come back till you've got her*, the big man had said, fixing him with a menacing glare. So, now he had a choice to make. Go back and confess that he had missed the old woman; stay here and wait for her return (which seemed increasingly less likely); or disappear into the night as far from the city as he could go. There were places in the bush where an experienced tracker might go, but Reuben had never mastered such skills.

A howl came from far off, some nocturnal creature calling out into the dark December night. He huddled closer to the tree, grasping his cold knees with both hands, staring at the house with its unlit windows like blind eyes. Perhaps she had gone visiting a friend in the city, lingered longer than she'd expected, missed the return bus and decided to stay the night? Old people talked so much, didn't they? Maybe she had lost track of time?

Gritting his teeth, he imagined how he would punish her for keeping him waiting out here all night, the rising anger in his breast the only warmth he would feel during the hours that lay ahead.

CHAPTER TEN

Netta hummed to herself as she washed the dishes in the sink. No way was she going to use that dishwasher thing on her good china plates. She looked out of the kitchen window above the café curtains with a sigh. The view from here was a back court flanked on two sides by the tenement buildings, a far cry from the eleventh floor of her high rise over on the north of the city. Sometimes she had stood looking out at the distant hills, watching as the seasons changed them from green and purple to tawny then white-peaked. And yet, here she had so many more things for which to be thankful; a good friend in PC Daniel Kohi, home comforts and easy access to the nearby shops. Since the Zimbabwean had come into her life as a refugee placed a couple of doors along from her old flat, Netta Gordon had found renewed pleasure in socialising with his friends and colleagues, relishing any opportunity to show off her excellent home-baking skills.

It was a far cry from her old life when she had been

struggling to make ends meet, a husband in and out of the jail, kids to feed and clothe as best she could. And other things that were best forgotten.

She glanced upwards at the pulley full of damp washing and noticed a frilly pale peach garment. Molly's knickers, she thought to herself. Daniel must have piled them in with his own laundry. Ach well, it didn't bother her in the least. She was a nice lassie and she made Daniel happy. Maybe there would come a day when they'd want to move in together permanently, but she'd cross that bridge when they came to it. Live for today, Netta, she told herself briskly. You never know what might happen tomorrow.

'D'you think he'll go?' David Giles asked Molly as they sat side by side in the Helen Street office.

'Lorimer? After thirty years he deserves to put his feet up,' Molly replied. 'But I can't see him joining a golf club or trying to find a part-time job to keep himself busy, can you?'

Giles shrugged. 'I've seen a few guys burning themselves out in this job and glad to retire. But then . . . ' he made a face, 'some of the best ones don't live long enough to enjoy their retirement.'

Molly nodded. It was only a week since they had attended the funeral of a former DCI, the man just short of his fifty-fifth birthday, after a sudden heart attack out on the golf course.

'And Maggie's still working,' she pointed out. 'He'd be all on his tod in their house, wouldn't he? Can't see him liking that.'

'Maybe he'll feel differently after this holiday they've planned in the new year. Three weeks away from the job might give him the taste for freedom?'

Molly smiled but shook her head. Somehow, that did not seem to fit with the man she called her boss.

'Zimbabwe? Gosh, why there? Didn't that dictator wreck the country and impoverish the people?'

Maggie gave a sad smile. 'Aye, that's true, unfortunately, but they're trying hard to restore their tourist industry and so just by going there we'll be helping them.'

'Or putting money into the coffers of a few bent politicians,' her friend Sandie snorted derisively.

'The wildlife and bird life are what really make it a place to visit,' Maggie said, deflecting the comment. 'And Bill deserves to go somewhere special for his fiftieth.'

'True,' Sandie replied. 'You've never been a pair to go for a beach-type vacation every year, have you?'

Maggie smiled. The tourist company had offered an add-on of six nights in a fancy hotel in Mauritius or time spent at Victoria Falls, but she and Bill had opted to return to Harare instead in the hope of looking up Daniel's mother. Netta had told them that there still had been no mail from Janette since she and Daniel had moved into Nithsdale Drive – though her NHS appointment card had been forwarded from the hospital – and Christmas was fast approaching. That would be a challenge for them; a white couple nosing around in the township outside the city would be easily noticed and they had hoped to enlist Netta and her regular letters to arrange some sort of meeting.

The bell rang, signalling the end of lunch break, and Maggie rose from her seat, her mind already on her next class. First years and Christmas short stories.

'Ah, African sunshine!' Sandie sighed dreamily. 'Lucky you.'

Netta frowned as she sat at the kitchen table that evening. Mrs Lorimer had asked her so nicely and, yes, she understood perfectly the risks they were taking to meet up with her pen pal. But, how to phrase this letter so that nobody would ever suspect that the recipient might be meeting up with a senior policeman from Scotland and his wife? She looked around the kitchen as if seeking inspiration. The calendar showed a snowy scene with mountain peaks that reminded Netta of that nasty business in Glencoe when Daniel and Lorimer had gone climbing and found a dead man. She hadn't mentioned that bit to Janette, only that her brave lion (their code phrase for Daniel) had enjoyed a break away in the Scottish Highlands.

She looked down at the paper on the table. *Dear Janette*, she had written. *How are you, we are all fine here.* There was never a mention of Daniel's name, her native caution making Netta choose each word carefully. Now she must impart the exciting news about the Lorimers' visit to Zimbabwe.

Netta chewed the end of her pen after signing off. It would be up to Janette now to make any suggestions about the where and the when, safer for Daniel's mother to write. Or even phone, if Janette Kohi could get hold of someone's mobile.

As she stared into space, Netta Gordon imagined Daniel's mother reading this letter and wondered what her reply might be.

CHAPTER ELEVEN

January

PC Kohi stood with his back to the pitch, staring at the rows of football fans waving their scarves in the air. Every shift brought different duties and on this cold January night his was here in Hampden Park. The pre-match noise had been full of song and laughter but now there was a tense feeling in the frosty air as every pair of eyes followed the progress of the match. Okay, it might just be a friendly, but from the amount of tartan worn by the home crowd and the way they'd belted out 'Flower of Scotland', it was easy to feel their passion for the national team.

It was one of the most frustrating jobs he'd ever done, being forced to watch the crowd instead of turning to watch the flow of play. Once upon a time Daniel Kohi had played centre forward for the police team in Harare, his turn of speed and ball skills admired by many of the younger players. He'd signed up for a trial here in Glasgow, hoping for a game with the police team, but so far nobody had asked him to come along on a training night.

There were officers stationed at the ends of each row, all eyes fixed on the crowded stadium, far enough from the turf not to impede the match. Daniel could feel the growing intensity seconds before the fans erupted in a roar, springing to their feet and cheering as Scotland scored the opening goal of the night. There was no need to turn to see the players celebrating on the pitch and shortly afterwards a voice from the loudspeaker confirmed that Andy Robertson, the Scottish captain, had indeed made the score Scotland 1, England 0.

The atmosphere of jubilation subsided a little just before half-time when VAR examined a possible handball that would have allowed the visitors a penalty, but a collective sigh of relief could be heard when the referee did not point to the spot. Daniel was close enough to the fans to hear their complaints and work out what was going on, his own relief at the decision tempered by the desire for his adopted country to win, partly out of loyalty but also wishing for the fans to behave well after the game was finished.

'Grand night, eh?' An old guy grinned at Daniel as he brushed past him on the steep aisle, heading for the exit. The score had remained the same after their captain's goal and now the fans were heading for the nearest watering hole to celebrate their victory.

'Aye. Great game, though I didn't see any of it,' Daniel chuckled, his breath clouding the chill night air.

'Aw, ye missed a rerr goal, son,' the man replied. 'Pity ye couldnae turn aroon and watch it, eh no?'

'That's our duty, sir,' Daniel told him. 'To keep you all safe to enjoy yourselves.'

'Ach well, mind an' see it oan the highlights the night,' the old man advised. 'Cheerio.'

Daniel smiled as he followed the crowd safely out of the stadium. His back was a bit stiff from standing facing the terraces, the temperature plunging to several degrees below zero, and he'd be glad to return to the flat for a hot shower once his shift was over after midnight.

Meantime there were several duties to carry out between Hampden Park and Cathcart police station before he could sign off for the night. Daniel clapped his gloved hands against his sides to ease some sensation back into his numb fingers. The floodlights were too bright to see any stars in the night sky, but he could see the moon high above, its pale aureole like singed brown parchment, a sign of deeper frost to come.

'We're in for a cold one the night,' his neighbour remarked as they finally left the stadium. Daniel had been partnered with the older cop since the turn of the year, his probationary period still in its early stages. His tutor cop, Sergeant Knight, had been off since before Christmas, leaving Daniel with Sergeant George Fleming, a veteran cop whose grizzled grey hair and ruddy complexion gave him the look of a benevolent grandfather. *Don't be fooled by his appearance*, one of the female offices had whispered to Daniel. *Looks like a big softie but he can split up a fight with his bare hands.* The older cop reminded Daniel of his former mentor in the ZRP, Sergeant Goodfellow Mbasi, a decent man who had lived up to his name, so different from those who'd given the Zimbabwean force a bad press.

'Well, at least the fans are happy,' Daniel remarked as they watched the last of them disappear towards the railway station in Mount Florida.

'Ach, there'll still be trouble somewhere, mark my words, lad,' Fleming replied. 'There's nae love lost between some of the English and Scottish fans. There'll be racist comments flying around in the pubs and broken glass shattering the peace before the night's out.'

As if to confirm his words, their radios crackled into life, demanding their presence at a bar in Victoria Road where a fight had been reported.

Daniel leapt out of the squad car as Fleming parked by the kerb. From the lamps illuminating the pub sign, he could see a mêlée of people on the pavement. Screams and shattering of broken glass as bottles were smashed made him head towards them but Fleming shouldered him out of his way, his bulky figure cutting a swathe through the crowd.

The police sergeant's booming voice rose above the riot. 'Stop this right now! I'll arrest anyone who's carrying a weapon!'

The sound died away at once, murmurs of 'polis' and 'big Fleming's here' falling into the night air. Several men had already slunk back into the warmth of the pub, a few still outside, heads hanging in shame. On the ground one man lay groaning, his forehead bleeding from a wound. Daniel knelt at his side putting his first aid knowledge immediately into practice. The man's pulse was racing, adrenalin making his heart work faster, a natural occurrence after injury. His face was ashy white beneath the glare of Daniel's torch as he examined him carefully.

Daniel breathed a sigh of relief as the fellow opened his eyes and stared into his face. 'It's all right, sir. I'm a police officer. We're here to help you,' Daniel told him in a calm and reassuring tone.

'Bloody Jocks,' the man moaned softly. 'Can't take a joke.' His English accent reminded Daniel of his arrival in the south of the country before he was sent to Scotland, so many similar voices asking him questions.

'Can you stand up?' Daniel continued, wondering how badly the man was injured or if being knocked to the ground had something to do with the amount of alcohol he'd already consumed; the smell off his breath laid claim to a night of heavy drinking, most probably begun well before the match.

Soon he had the fellow on his feet while Fleming was questioning a small group who had lingered to see if their friend needed help.

'Would you like me to call an ambulance? That looks like a bad gash on your head,' Daniel remarked.

'No, no ambulance. I'll be okay,' the man protested.

'Come over here and sit down,' Daniel insisted, leading him to the squad car and ushering him into the passenger seat. He hunkered down next to him and began asking questions, beginning with his name, Richard Trumble. Before long the story began to emerge. Insults had been bandied about across the pub, challenges made and then tempers had flared, several of the football fans from both nations spilling out into the street. When the bottles had begun to fly, Trumble had got into a fight with one of the Scottish fans.

'Must have fallen down,' he muttered, not meeting Daniel's questioning gaze.

Daniel raised his eyebrows sceptically as he was joined by the older cop.

'Right, son, you want to press charges against anyone in particular?' Fleming was bending down to peer into the car, staring at the victim of the night's outrage.

'This is Mr Trumble,' Daniel told him.

'Trumble, eh? Rumble in the jungle Trumble. Hm.' Fleming grinned towards Daniel.

'No, no ... it was just an accident,' the man insisted, his eyes flicking nervously from Daniel to Fleming.

'Looks like a knife wound to me, mister,' Fleming said. 'You carrying a weapon, by any chance?'

'Me?' The man's voice rose in a squeak of indignation. 'No, never! Search me if you like. I've nothing to hide!'

Fleming stood up and motioned to Daniel to join him.

'One of these eejits drew a blade on this guy,' Fleming whispered. 'Got a mind to take the lot of them in for the night.'

Daniel looked across at the group of supporters huddled together outside the pub door.

'We'll find nothing, though. Whoever did for chummy here has scarpered. Wan o' his pals saw the lad doing a runner as soon as we arrived.' He bent down again and screwed up his eyes, looking more intently at the Englishman.

'Ye're needin' stitches oan that, son,' he decided, reaching for his radio and calling for an ambulance. 'We'll wait here till it arrives, awright?'

The fellow nodded miserably, glowering at the big cop, any lingering defences weakened by Fleming's authority.

It was well after midnight when Daniel finally reached Aikenhead Road, his duty to see the man through Accident and Emergency and to the safety of his hotel considerably lengthening his shift. He stifled a yawn as he stepped out of the car, breath misting up the icy air.

He'd put in for overtime, of course, but right now he'd rather be safe and warm in his bed back home. The next shift was already in full swing, officers on duty, as Daniel made for the locker room to leave his kit. Once he was home, he'd have less than twelve hours till he'd be back again, he realised, looking up at the clock on the wall.

It took several minutes for the car heater to blast out any warmth and by that time Daniel was halfway to the flat, any notion of watching the game on TV long gone. Maybe he'd see the highlights on the news tomorrow, though there would be no mention of the fracas at the Victoria Bar, the fight simply par for the course on a night when the two rival teams and their fans clashed, the passion between them elemental. Or was it racist? To Daniel Kohi, a black man from Southern Africa, the feuding between Scots and English sometimes seemed absurd, though he remembered tales of fierce fighting between Shona and Matabele tribesmen in Zimbabwe. Perhaps nowhere was safe when any sort of rivalry sprang up. And yet, to be so impassioned about a game of football, and a *friendly* at that . . . well, slashing a rival fan just didn't make any sense.

By the time his head hit the pillow, Daniel was still hearing that roar from the football crowd, their pride in scoring against the more fancied team almost tangible.

CHAPTER TWELVE

Daniel was dreaming of home again, a pale sun-bleached sky above and dark smiling faces all around as he walked through golden fields of maize. Laughter and the sound of marimba music made him smile even as he slumbered, his thoughts far from the frozen January night outside his bedroom window. In his dream he saw his mother saunter round the corner of a house, several of her former kindergarten class following, their little faces beaming up at her. The field of maize was gone now. In its place, a winding road that led somewhere that he didn't want to go. And yet his feet were taking him there, the children and his mother suddenly gone.

He could smell the burning before he saw the flames. And then he heard their cries.

Daniel jumped, his eyes wide open, sweat coursing down his neck. The vision of the burning house was gone but he could still smell something drifting into his bedroom.

In moments he was out of bed, following the scent.

'Netta!' he cried, seeing his flatmate standing by the open kitchen window, waving a tea towel over the sink, clouds of smoke wafting into the cold morning air.

'Left them in too long,' she told him, tight-lipped.

Daniel tried not to grin in his relief. There on the worktop lay the empty cooling rack for her scones. The kitchen food bin was open, the burnt scones still smouldering.

'Thought I smelled burning,' he said, coming up behind her and wrapping his arms around her. 'Never you mind.' He planted a kiss on her cheek. 'Here, I'll make us breakfast, all right?'

'Wanted to give you scones to take to work,' Netta grumbled.

'You are far too good to me, Mrs Gordon,' Daniel teased her. 'Smoke's just about gone, so let me close that window or we'll freeze.'

Later, sitting at the kitchen table, Netta pulled an envelope from her dressing gown pocket.

'It's ages since your ma wrote to me,' she said. 'I've just about memorised this one by heart and written at least three since then.'

'She'll maybe be busy,' Daniel said. 'Didn't she write to say there was a school trip coming up? Sometimes she is asked to help out even though she's been retired for years.'

'That was just for a day in the city,' Netta said. 'She's never left it so long to reply to any of my letters. D'you think there might be something wrong? Or is it jist a backlog efter the postal strike?'

Daniel frowned. Work took up so much of his own time

that he hadn't fretted unduly until Netta mentioned it. There was no way for him to communicate with anyone back home, the danger of alerting the wrong people to his whereabouts too big a risk. On Christmas Eve he had waited, hoping that his mother might call, borrowing someone's mobile phone to dial Netta's number. But his old friend's phone had stayed silent.

Perhaps she was sick? Once more, that feeling of guilt. He was here, earning plenty of money but unable to do anything for his own mother, lest any suspicion fell on the woman. People everywhere were curious about their neighbours; how they managed to buy a big car, where they found enough money to travel beyond the borders. Daniel remembered the gossip that he had listened to, trying to figure out how to stop the corruption that was rotting the heart of his beloved police force. Sometimes it had been useful in his day-to-day work (and still was) but he'd long ago come to realise that ordinary folk were perennially interested in the lives of others.

If only . . . He gave a sigh. There was no point in wishing for what could never happen. He would probably never see his beloved mother again, though if the Lorimers could arrange to meet her, then that might be enough to bring some joy to them both.

What was it she used to say? *It is in the Lord's hands, Daniel. Trust in Him.*

Reuben crouched beneath the thorn bush, his dark eyes staring at the path of beaten earth leading to the old woman's home. He felt the side of his face where the bruises had swollen. Well, perhaps she would return today, and he could dish out some punishment of his own? The man in the red bandana was beginning to feel the sensation of cramp in his legs when the sound of whistling made him look up. Sure enough, a figure carrying a brown bag on his shoulder was sauntering along towards the Kohi house. Reuben grinned as the postman slowed down and stopped at the gate. He slung the bag from his shoulder and rummaged at its contents then drew out a flimsy blue envelope. Then, whistling anew, he pushed open the gate and headed towards the front door.

Don't knock, Reuben thought. Just shove it in the letter box.

The postman did not appear to heed the silent plea, however, and knocked his fist against the door.

'Ma Kohi?' he called out in a sing-song voice. 'Letter for you!'

Not a sound came from within, of course, the house having lain empty since Reuben had arrived that first day. A worried frown creased his face. Would the postman push open the unlocked door? Find the mess that he'd left there? Maybe even summon the cops? He shivered in anticipation, watching from his silent lair.

Then, with a shrug, the postman turned, paused at the letter box that was fixed onto the old lady's fence, and thrust the letter through the slot in the metal container.

Reuben watched the man as he shut the gate behind him and walked back along the pathway, whistling as he went. It was only when he had disappeared around the final bend that he unfolded himself from his cramped position and, looking cautiously around, headed towards Janette Kohi's home.

The airmail letter was the only item in the box, easily grasped by Reuben's eager fingers. He peered at the name and address, his lips slightly open, silently mouthing the words. It was hard to make out the date stamped across the top but there was no mistaking the origin of the postage stamps. This had come from the United Kingdom, he saw, the fainter printed words a mystery to the poorly educated man. Turning the letter over, however, he grinned as he saw the sender's name. Here was something he could take back to his boss! For a moment he eyed the gummed down envelope, wondering just what lay within. Pursing his mouth in a moue of discontent, Reuben knew he probably wouldn't understand the written words, anyway, unlike the woman to whom this missive was addressed. Janette Kohi had been a kindergarten teacher back in the day, a lady of much learning, respected in the community. For an instant the man recalled the small boy on the other side of the school fence who had trailed his feet in the dust, longing to join the other children. Oh, he'd done all right without the need for book learning, he told himself. And, once he'd delivered this letter, perhaps he'd be paid something, enough to slake the thirst that had built up as he'd waited for the old lady to return.

CHAPTER THIRTEEN

In the end, the man with the red bandana did not see the contents of the airmail letter, having to resign himself to the few dollars that had been thrust into his fists. He was worth more than that, Reuben told himself, ducking to avoid the blow aimed at him and then scarpering off as instructed. He threw a black look over his shoulder when he was certain the boss was no longer looking his way. Perhaps, if he could find someone to put an evil eye on the man . . . ? The thought made Reuben Mahlangu grin for a few seconds, imagining the sorts of things that might put a dent in the big fellow's overbearing manner. And yet, in spite of his current mood, Reuben knew that he was in thrall to this man for as long as he proved of any use to him.

Nelson Sibanda fingered the buttons that were straining across his uniform, unfastening the khaki shirt at the neck as he read the letter. At first it didn't seem to make any sense at all, one old lady writing from a far-off country to another.

Mention was made of Christmas and a church service, so perhaps Kohi's mother had found a penfriend through the church?

He turned to the envelope, noting that it was postmarked December, though he could not decipher the exact date.

He read on. Several times a lion was mentioned, but nothing about a safari or an incident out in the bush. Had the author of this letter been to Zimbabwe? There was nothing to suggest that, so far. He wondered about N Gordon's origin. Scotland. An address in the city of Glasgow. He'd heard of Glasgow, of course, famous for its knife crime back in the day. A lawless sort of place, no doubt, those cold-blooded northerners pulling a blade first, asking questions later. But this N Gordon appeared to be a woman, he decided. And an educated one at that.

Dear Friend, the letter had begun. Not dear Janette. *How are you, I am fine now*, it continued, suggesting that N Gordon had not been fine on some previous occasion. *Our lion is well, too, enjoying the Christmas festivities with friends here in good old Glasgow.* Our lion? Did the woman have some sort of a subscription to a zoo? He'd heard of that sort of thing where individuals might sponsor an animal. There was a cheetah enclosure out near Lake Chivero that he'd taken kids to see one time, showing off the plaque that told them how these animals were looked after. He'd even boasted about how the Zimbabwean police force had donated cash to help the place. A bit of an exaggeration but it had resulted in lots of small admiring faces looking up at him.

I have news for you, the letter went on. *The Lorimers are coming to Harare and hope to see you. It is his birthday so they are going on some safari trips. I will send you dates once I know for certain. You will like them, I'm sure. They are fond of lions, and he loves birdwatching so I am sure they will have a great time. Let me know where might be a good place to meet. Maybe the zoo?*

He let the paper fall onto the table for a moment. This was just so much rubbish. Janette Kohi had evidently agreed to some Scottish person (a woman, he was sure it was a woman) writing to her and now it seemed that she was to have visitors. From overseas. So, what? He saw white-faced tourists every day in the city with their well-pressed safari suits and expensive cameras. Just so many sheep to be fleeced, he had sniggered to one of his underlings. And it was true. They were full of pity for the poor downtrodden Zimbabweans, spending a fortune in the 24-hour tailor shops and filling their suitcases with batiks and handmade crocheted table covers before flying back to wherever they'd come from.

The word from up above was to leave them be, but such bounties were not to be disregarded. And so, like many others, he would stop them in his big patrol car, demanding to see their papers and charging them sweetly for the privilege. Nothing much was ever done to discourage this, though the top brass were forever promising the public that steps were being taken to root out the perpetrators of this practice and deal severely with them.

These Lorimers sounded just as ripe for plucking, he decided. He'd keep Mahlangu on his payroll for now, send him to keep an eye on the old lady's place. It wasn't unusual for someone to go visiting on a whim and old people were easily persuaded by the offer of a few nights' rest at a friend's home. He frowned for a moment. Hadn't he promised his own mother that he would have her to stay over Christmas? It hadn't happened. He shrugged. Well, she never held it against him, knowing how busy he was. 'Such an important man, my son,' he had heard her tell a neighbour once, the unmistakable pride in her voice.

Well, Janette Kohi would be back. And he would warn Mahlangu to make sure the place looked the same as when she left it.

He was about to crumple the letter in his fist when a thought occurred to him.

Kohi had been spotted in Glasgow. Was rumoured to be a serving police officer there. He shook his head. It wasn't possible. Ncube had a lying tongue and was out to make some sort of trouble, that was all.

And yet, it was a strange coincidence that Janette Kohi's penfriend hailed from this city. He stood still for a moment, wondering. Who were these Lorimers? And why would they want to visit an old widow living out here in the township? He gave a sigh, flattening out the letter again, wondering about the reaction of the man to whom this must be reported.

CHAPTER FOURTEEN

It was, Maggie felt as they left the airport building in Harare, like walking into a wall of heat. After so many hours confined to her aircraft seat it was bliss to be strolling out towards the waiting bus, sunlight on her bare arms.

'We're here!' she whispered to Lorimer, giving him a smile. 'Doesn't seem real, does it?'

She saw him shake his head and laugh. Then a thin man was pulling their cases from them, his words cascading in a rush as he levered them into the baggage compartment of the coach. Lorimer kept a firm grip on his carry-on bag, however.

'Not this one, thanks. I need to take it onboard with me,' he told the young porter.

Maggie whipped out some dollars from her shoulder bag and handed them to the man whose sudden crestfallen look changed to delight.

'Thank you,' she told him warmly. 'Mr Lorimer needs his binoculars for the journey.'

Then they were chivvied onto the bus and seated at a large window, the air conditioning cooling Maggie's skin.

Soon they were on a wide road lined with jacaranda trees, heading towards the city.

'Strange to think that this was Daniel's hometown,' Maggie murmured, her words drowned out by the noise of the bus. 'But then, he rarely talks about it.'

'And who can blame him,' Lorimer countered. 'He's made a new life for himself. And isn't it better to look forward rather than back?'

'Perhaps you could do that too,' Maggie suggested. 'You haven't decided if you'll retire this year, have you?'

Lorimer continued to stare out at the passing streets, many with hedges full of flamboyant red flowers, Maggie's unanswered question in his mind. He had left the job behind, no unsolved cases pending, and felt a sense of freedom now that they were in a different country, under pale, sun-washed skies. Would this be how he would feel every day if he retired from the job? Somehow, he doubted it. A holiday was just that; a break from normality, a chance to recharge one's batteries before continuing to focus on whatever awaited their return. Besides, his sort of work was not simply something to fill in whatever days he had left. What had begun as a duty to society had become more personal over the years, the drive to seek justice for victims of crime enhanced by talking to those left behind; mothers, fathers, siblings, husbands and wives whose lives had been torn apart by the blind viciousness of killers. How could he simply give that up? He still kept in touch with several family members, their need for contact with the man who had apprehended a killer continuing even after the cases were closed.

'Look, here it is,' Maggie whispered, nudging his shoulder and pointing towards a sign that said Meikles Hotel. Before them lay the elegant Colonial-style building they had viewed on several websites. Lorimer yawned, grateful that their journey was coming to an end, at least for now. They were to spend a few days here before heading off into the bush, their itinerary including some free time to explore the city. That would give them a chance to call on Janette Kohi, Daniel and Netta's concerns at not having heard from her an important part of their itinerary. Right now, though, all he wanted was a shower, a change of clothes and a long drink of something cool.

'Rock shandy,' the young waiter suggested, then began to give details of its contents.

'Sounds good,' Lorimer replied. 'Two, please, and I'll sign for them, thanks.'

'That was the drink that Daniel said all the tourists liked,' Maggie said softly. 'Called them sundowners.'

'Angostura bitters. Mm, that sounds okay,' Lorimer said. 'Anyway, if it's long and cold, that's all I want right now.'

It wasn't long before the pink rock shandies were placed on the rattan table in front of them.

'*Slainte*,' Lorimer said, clinking his glass against Maggie's. 'Here's to a great holiday.'

'I'm sure it's one we'll never forget,' Maggie assured him. 'All the birds and wildlife we've still to see.'

As they sipped their drinks and prepared to join the rest

of their party for dinner, neither could have known just how apposite Maggie's words would be, the events that lay ahead marking their lives in ways they could never have foreseen.

'She's definitely gone,' the thick-set man told his companion as they sat on the stoep of the large house, looking up into the night sky.

'How can you be certain?' the older man asked. 'What makes you say that?' he added, a tone of irritation entering his voice.

'Her passport is missing,' he said sullenly. 'But we have no knowledge of any Kohi leaving the city by plane.'

'So?'

'So, she's probably gone over the border. Botswana, perhaps. Or Tanzania. Her old man came from there, didn't he? Isn't that where she has relatives?'

'You tell me. After all, isn't it your job to investigate such things, Chief Inspector Sibanda?'

The big man's jaw tightened but he did not reply. He'd find the old woman, just see if he didn't. Having this well-dressed man cast aspersions on his ability grated in the extreme.

'She'll know the truth about Kohi,' he blustered. 'Young Ncube . . . '

'Augustus is an ass,' the older man retorted. 'Winding up in a Scottish prison. Poorest of my brood. Ach.' He spat on the ground as if to rid himself of a bad taste. 'Still, he's my son and I want some sort of retribution. Do you understand?' he asked, turning to his companion, eyebrows raised, provoking a reply.

'Yes, I understand. He was useful to us for a while till he got himself arrested with those drugs,' Sibanda mumbled. 'After Jeremiah . . . '

'That was unavoidable,' the older man snapped. 'Some people are expendable, after all.' He took a long draught of his beer then turned to the man by his side. 'Let's hope we never have to include you in that category, hm?'

The fat man in khaki shivered. Was that a threat? Or was he simply being reminded of his place in the pecking order? One false step and he might also be swinging from the branch of a dead tree, carrion for the vultures. Ncube had avoided that fate, choosing to get out. It was inevitable with his track record that he had teamed up with some drug dealers, he thought. Nelson Sibanda remembered the careless bravado of the man and how he'd dodged the vengeance of several gang members before finally quitting Zimbabwe.

Now Augustus Ncube was facing a long sentence in some cold Scottish jail. And Nelson Sibanda was tasked with finding some sort of revenge upon the man who had put him there.

Maggie was fast asleep under the fan whirring from the ceiling as Lorimer gazed out into the night sky. Here in the city, it was hard to see any stars, the street lighting obscuring them. Once they were out on safari, it would be a different matter, he thought, a smile on his lips. But first they had a duty to visit Daniel's mother, to see that she was in good health and to assure her that her son was not only safe and well, but happy. Tomorrow they would join the city bus tour, give themselves a day to recover from the journey. Then after that they would slip away from their fellow travellers and take a taxi out to the township where Janette Kohi lived.

Lorimer climbed into bed beside his wife with a yawn and closed his eyes, sleep taking him in minutes.

CHAPTER FIFTEEN

It was one of his rest days and Daniel had decided to spend it cooking. Netta was at the Queen Elizabeth hospital for a check-up and would be tired by the time she arrived home. He opened their big American-style fridge freezer and looked inside. There was some leftover chicken that would do for a curry, he thought, his mind already working on what else he might need.

A ring at the front doorbell interrupted any further thoughts of vegetables and spices and he pushed the fridge door shut again.

'Does a Mrs N. Gordon live here?'

The man standing on Daniel's doorstep looked him up and down for a moment.

'Sorry, must have the wrong address,' he mumbled, half turning to leave.

'No, don't go,' Daniel said quickly. 'Mrs Gordon does live here. But she's out just now. Can I help you?'

'*You* live here?' the stranger blurted out, then bit his

lip as though he were afraid of having committed some racial slur.

'I do indeed. Mrs Gordon and I are housemates,' Daniel grinned. 'We used to be neighbours—'

'—in Maryhill. The flats on the eleventh floor!' the stranger exclaimed. Daniel saw the man biting his lower lip and looking him up and down as if he were coming to some sort of a decision.

Then he gave a smile.

'Sorry, I should've introduced myself. Billy McGregor,' he said, shooting out his ungloved hand for Daniel to shake. 'I moved into Mrs Gordon's old place recently.'

'Why don't you come in,' Daniel offered, feeling the man's cold fingers. 'It's freezing out here.'

As he closed the door, Daniel noticed the man was walking with a pronounced limp. Whatever had brought him here, Billy McGregor had certainly made an effort to find Netta, something that pricked PC Kohi's curiosity.

He led the man into their warm kitchen and waved a hand towards the nearest chair. 'Cup of tea or coffee?'

'I wouldnae say no to a coffee, thanks,' McGregor agreed, unbuttoning his overcoat and pulling off his woollen hat then unwinding a scarf that revealed a thistle tattooed on his neck. 'Had tae wait ages for a bus tae this side of the city. But I didnae want the lady to wait for this,' he added, pulling a brown paper bag from a deep pocket inside his overcoat and laying it onto the table. 'Didn't she make arrangements for her mail tae be redirected?'

'Oh, I thought she had. How odd.' Daniel frowned. 'Let me have a look just to be sure,' he said. Then, drawing out the envelopes, he nodded. Several blue airmail letters were secured by an elastic band. He stuffed them back into the paper bag.

'Yes, these are definitely for Netta,' he murmured, his eyes never leaving the packet. Daniel swallowed hard. His own mother had written these, traces of her lingering between the pages. He looked up at the man, suddenly aware that he had offered him a hot drink and done nothing about it.

As he switched the kettle on, he thought about McGregor's tedious journey across the city.

'That was very good of you to bring these all the way here,' he told him. 'Going the extra mile, I'd say,' he added, curious to know why.

'Och, it wasnae really going oot of my way, to be honest,' McGregor admitted. 'I have a friend over in Shawlands I promised to visit, and this was practically on my way. The factor gave me Mrs Gordon's address, seeing as how I'm the new tenant in her old flat.'

'Still, it was good of you,' Daniel insisted, measuring out some scoops of ground coffee into the cafetière. 'A lesser mortal might have chucked them in the bin.'

'Och, I'd never dae that!' McGregor said, shaking his head. 'See, I was in the navy and ony mail we got from overseas wis precious. I don't like the idea of folk waiting for a letter and never getting it.'

'You're retired?' Daniel asked as he poured the coffee into two mugs.

McGregor shifted uneasily in his chair. 'No' really retired as such,' he began, avoiding Daniel's enquiring gazc. 'Goat medically discharged.' He sighed.

That explained the man's limp, Daniel thought, listening as McGregor continued.

'Had to come home and find a place to rent. The high flat's fine for now, though I'd rather have a place with a wee bit of a garden. Still, beggars can't be choosers, eh?'

'You're on your own?' Daniel asked casually.

'Aye, never married. Hard life for a wumman being married tae a merchant seaman. We're away sometimes more than a year at a time.' He shrugged, making a face. 'Naw, I'll find something soon enough, though. My pal in Shawlands said he might fix me up with a driving job. Cannae do ony heavy lifting these days, but I've goat my HGV licence from way back.'

Daniel smiled listening to the man's broad Glasgow accent, remembering his own puzzlement at Netta's speech in the days when he had first arrived in the city. Wherever the merchant fleets had taken Billy McGregor, that distinctive dialect had travelled with him.

The man gazed around the big dining kitchen then he caught Daniel's eye and grinned.

'Classy place she's goat here, eh? Going up in the world.'

'She loves her new home,' Daniel admitted. 'Especially the kitchen. Netta is a lady who likes to spend her time baking.'

'You not working yourself?' McGregor asked suddenly.

'I work shifts,' Daniel smiled. 'And it's my day off today.' For some reason he was reluctant to tell this stranger more. Was that simply a natural reticence on his part, or had the sight of these airmail letters triggered some sort of warning?

'Well, better get going,' McGregor said, draining the last of his coffee. 'Ta very much for that. Tell Mrs Gordon her wee flat wis immaculate when I moved in. I've had tae pit up wi' some right dumps in my time but that's a nice wee gaff I've goat now.'

'I'll be sure to tell her. I know she'll be grateful to get these,' he added.

McGregor fastened his coat and pulled on the hat. 'Cheery-bye, then,' he said, patting Daniel's arm and setting off once more, dragging his left leg a little as he walked.

It was some hours later that Netta returned to the pungent smell of curry wafting from the kitchen.

'Hey, how did you get on?' Daniel asked, as he turned from stirring their dinner on the hob.

'Oh, all good news.' Netta sighed, pulling off her coat and folding it over the back of a chair. 'Oh, my, let me sit down for a minute,' she added, slumping beside the table. 'My poor feet are aching.'

'Good news? Everything's in working order, then,' he teased.

'Aye, my heart's ticking over like a wee sewing machine, so it is,' Netta laughed. 'Here, can you stick the kettle on, Daniel? Ah'm fair gasping for a cup o' tea.'

'Right away, ma'am.' Daniel offered her a cheeky salute. 'And I've got some other news for you,' he added, clicking the switch on the electric kettle. 'Have a look inside that paper bag.' He pointed at the package that the new tenant of Netta's previous flat had brought.

'What . . . ? Oh, my, three letters frae Janette! Did the postie bring them this afternoon?'

'No,' he said. 'These came special delivery.' Then

he proceeded to tell Netta all about the visit from Billy McGregor.

'He was well impressed by how clean and tidy you'd left the old place,' Daniel concluded.

'Well, nice of him, I'm sure.' Netta nodded, turning over the envelopes in her hand. 'I must've forgotten tae do that redirection thingmy,' she sighed. 'What wi' the hospital and moving all ma stuff . . . ' She shook her head. 'Postmarked well before Christmas. Hm. Postal strike must've held them up. I heard that parcels were a priority, right enough.'

She laid the three letters out side by side then began to open the one dated earliest, handing it to Daniel to read once she'd finished.

He sat opposite the old lady, feasting his eyes on his mother's neat handwriting. As a former primary teacher, Janette Kohi had taught the very youngest children in their township to read and write, something that she'd instilled in her own son. All was well, apparently, Daniel saw. Preparations for Christmas were mentioned briefly, and he guessed that the subsequent letters would carry more details about Janette's involvement with the church and her local community. Like Netta, she wrote in a sort of code, referring to Daniel as 'our lion', a small reference to the Old Testament story of Daniel in the lion's den. *I hope our lion has grown a thick winter coat. He'll need it in Scotland if what you tell me about the weather has come to pass,* she had written. *I wish I could see him for myself, but his new home is so far away.* He imagined the wistfulness in his mother's voice as she had written these words. Daniel gave a small frown. She had expressed true emotion here, but wasn't that a bit too close to the truth? What if this letter had been intercepted by the Zimbabwean authorities? Read by one of those corrupt police officers who had taken revenge on Daniel Kohi in the worst possible way, robbing Janette of her baby grandson.

Daniel shivered a little before picking up the other letters. Thankfully none of them had that tone of longing but had cleverly sent out greetings to Netta's good friends and neighbours, meaning Daniel himself.

'That's good we've caught up now.' Netta sighed as she finished her tea. She leafed through the letters again, frowning at the dates. She glanced across at Daniel, questioningly. 'An' that new tenant jist brocht them roon the day? Must've been held up in the post fur weeks. Ah well, blame the government, as my mammy always used to say.'

However, the mystery of the stranger appearing on their doorstep with overseas mail only increased when Daniel returned to work two days later.

CHAPTER SIXTEEN

There were few public houses in this city that had not undergone an exercise in gentrification, pandering to the wine bar set whose money paid the wages. But the Big Yin had retained most of the elements that locals associated with bygone days of spit and sawdust, like the old-fashioned stained-glass panel above the gantry and a worn linoleum floor that no amount of scrubbing would rid of its dubious stains. It was also the place where bad business was done on a regular basis, shifty-looking young neds flitting in and out, keeking around to see who was watching their not-so-subtle handovers of folded packets.

The man in the corner was watching the door as each new figure entered, amusing himself at their antics, knowing fine well that the polis rarely frequented this howff, their preferred watering holes in far more salubrious surroundings. He raised the glass to his lips, the beer now tepid. People knew to leave him well alone, an irascible old man with a ruined face who did not take kindly to pity or scorn, his temper liable to flare up in a moment.

He was halfway to a swallow when a man with a distinct limp came into the bar, a purposeful expression on his face. Choking, the old man began to splutter then cough, bending over the scarred wooden table, one hand still clutching his pint glass.

The sound alerted the newcomer who turned to see him, a smile of recognition creasing his face. In two strides, Billy McGregor was by the old man's table, patting his back.

'Well, well, look who it is! Fancy seein' you the night! Thocht ye must be dead by now!' he declared, chuckling as though he had uttered a good joke.

'Alive as you see me,' the old man replied, gasping as he caught his breath. 'What brings you to this part of town?' he asked, narrowing his eyes suspiciously.

'Ah, well, that would be telling, eh? And you and me, we have a few wee secrets to hide, have we no?' The newcomer grinned, lowering his voice and tapping the side of his nose.

A grunt that may have been a sign of agreement was all that met this declaration.

'Drink? That looks like ye need refreshing.' He took silence for an answer and turned back to the bar.

The old man's eyes followed him hungrily. Was he over here looking for connections, a job to be done, perhaps?

McGregor soon returned with a tray of drinks, pints and drams, as welcome on a cold night like this as a warm overcoat.

They were halfway through their first pints before any mention was made of their shared history.

'You mind that night?'

'Not likely to forget it,' the old man snapped, indicating his damaged face. 'That's a constant reminder.'

'Lot o' pain, then, eh? Sorry to hear that,' his companion reflected. 'Well, maybe things will look up, you never know.'

It was then that he heard that note of optimism in the man's voice and knew there was more coming. Might take a few more drinks, but he was willing to bet that it was no mere coincidence that McGregor had found him here.

CHAPTER SEVENTEEN

'You missed all the excitement,' George Fleming told him as Daniel walked out of the police station with the older cop. 'We had a murder last night. Fellow shot dead.'

'CID covering it here?'

'Aye. Body's over at the mortuary,' Fleming said with a grimace. 'Don't suppose you fancy a wee gander over there for the PM?'

Daniel looked surprised. 'Even though I wasn't at the scene of the crime?'

'You need all the experience you can get, son,' Fleming growled. 'Besides, we've got that many off right now with this norovirus, we're hard pushed to make sure you're getting enough different things ticked off.'

Daniel hesitated from telling the man that he had in fact been to post-mortem examinations before, and not just here in Glasgow. If he did speak up, perhaps it would look as if he wanted to avoid being present at PMs. Some cops genuinely hated attending them, though Daniel was not one of them.

'Sure, what can you tell me about him?'

'Och, not a lot. His face has been battered and all his belongings were nicked, so we've not been able to identify him yet. PM's at two, can you get yourself over there on your own? I've too much to do to babysit you,' Fleming said with a chuckle.

Daniel nodded then followed his mentor along the street towards a church hall where they were going to talk to a group of senior citizens about safety in the home.

It had been a good morning and Daniel had enjoyed chatting to the older people in the church hall. Perhaps living with Netta had made him more aware of how important it was to listen to them and to be as patient as possible in explaining the different ways that they could keep their homes safe. Now he was driving across one of the many bridges that spanned the Clyde, keeping to the right-hand lane in order to turn and follow the river till he came to the Saltmarket area of the city.

He was glad to see a parking space at the rear of the mortuary and slid his red Ford Focus in beside a pale blue Audi convertible with new number plates. Did this belong to the forensic pathologist who was performing today's PM? Daniel realised he had not asked George Fleming who was on duty this afternoon. However, he did not have long to wait, and his face broke into a grin as he recognised the diminutive figure of Dr Rosie Fergusson, already in the PM room and chatting to one of her assistants. She looked up, saw him and waved a gloved hand in his direction, any smile concealed by her mask.

'PC Kohi?' A familiar voice made him turn to see DI

Miller, one of the CID officers from his own division. 'Fleming said I'd find you here.' Miller grinned. 'Glutton for punishment, are you?'

'I didn't like to tell George Fleming I'd already attended plenty of post-mortems,' Daniel admitted. 'Can you tell me more about this one? All I know is he was murdered and found last night.'

'We had a call-out during the night from a concerned member of the public who was hearing screams then gun-shots from the flat above hers in Skirving Street. When the on-duty uniforms arrived, they found the victim lying on the upstairs landing. No sign of anyone else.'

'The member of the public who called it in . . . ?'

'She was too scared to leave her own flat, but she did say that after hearing the sound of gunfire she'd heard shouts and feet thudding down the stairs. Looked out and saw a man running then turning into Tantallon Road in the direction of the park. Forensics have been all over the place, of course.'

'What about the upstairs flats?'

'Ah, he wasn't shot inside either of them. SOCOs have found evidence to show that it happened on the top landing. People directly above our elderly lady are away on holiday in the US since New Year. The man opposite works night shifts in the Victoria infirmary. So, nobody there to give us a clue. Sounds to me that they must have known these flats would be empty.'

'And the victim?' Daniel asked.

'Regular-looking middle-aged guy. They'd beaten him about the face, kicked his ribs before someone finished him off with two shots. Head, heart,' she added grimly, citing the way a trained assassin would carry out a shooting. 'Not sure if the facial and body wounds were committed before or after he was shot. We'll soon find out.' She nodded towards a body that was sliding out from the back of the refrigerated cabinet into the post-mortem room.

'You squeamish?' Miller asked with a grin.

Daniel shook his head, his eyes now focused on the activity below the viewing platform where they both stood, ready to observe.

What they could see of the man's corpse was waxy yellow, all lividity having dropped down towards his back. His face was a real mess, however, adding to the difficulty of identification. Rosie Fergusson talked her way through the examination, giving some basic pointers about the state of the wounds, particular attention being paid to the head injury. She spoke in measured tones, giving details about the man's possible age, body weight, height and general fitness.

'We'll need an X-ray to confirm this, but it looks as if he's had surgery on his right knee,' she said, her words being recorded by her assistant. 'Several tattoos across his upper arms,' she added, a flash from the camera recording these too. 'Might be able to identify him from these,' she murmured. 'Oh, and one on the side of his neck.' She smoothed the man's hair back a little, turning his head to reveal the tattoo of a thistle.

It was as if a cold hand had clutched Daniel's heart.

'I think I may have seen this man,' he muttered to the woman by his side. 'That thistle . . . the knee injury . . . ' He swallowed hard, his mouth suddenly dry.

'You're kidding me,' Miller frowned. 'How could you . . . ?'

'Dr Fergusson!' Daniel called out over the intercom. 'Can I see the clothes that this man was wearing at the time of his death?'

Later, having confirmed that it was indeed the same overcoat that McGregor had worn two days previously, Daniel was sitting opposite the DI in a room normally reserved for the bereaved.

'Tell me more about this stranger who visited your home,' Miller asked.

'He said his name was Billy McGregor and that he was now living in Netta Gordon's old flat, two doors along from where I stayed,' he told her.

'Well, that can easily be checked,' the detective said. 'And ex-merchant navy? There will be records for that too. *If* he was using his real name,' she added grimly.

'He seemed a genuine enough guy,' Daniel sighed. 'Nothing to suggest there was a scam or anything going on.'

'Tell me again what he said about his next destination,' Miller said.

Daniel shook his head. 'He only said he was heading to Shawlands to see a friend. Someone who might have a driving job for him. I think he only told me that to show he hadn't gone out of his way to bring Netta's letters all the way from Maryhill.'

'Never mentioned Skirving Street?'

'No. Just Shawlands.'

Just then Rosie Fergusson appeared, no longer in her protective clothing but a neat grey trouser suit and pink roll-neck sweater.

'You seem to have a habit of becoming embroiled with dead bodies, Daniel,' she teased him.

'Part of the job,' he countered.

'Aye, but meeting this guy just two days ago! That's seriously weird,' Rosie said, shaking her head.

'Did he know you were a cop?' Miller asked.

'No,' Daniel told them. 'I don't always give that out.'

'You didn't trust him?' Miller suggested.

'It wasn't that. I just . . . ' Daniel shook his head then shrugged. 'He was a stranger. I don't tell strangers my business as a rule,' he said quietly.

Rosie exchanged a look with DI Miller. The pathologist knew Daniel's story and how he had escaped death at the hands of corrupt Zimbabweans.

'Are you worried that this McGregor guy was some sort of threat to you?' Miller asked.

'No! Not at all,' Daniel protested. 'He seemed a nice fellow, as a matter of fact. I mean . . . why go to all the trouble to bring Netta's letters to our new flat?'

'A bit odd that you'd redirected your mail and yet Mrs Gordon's airmail letters slipped through the system,' Miller frowned.

'She might have forgotten to do hers . . . ' Daniel admitted.

'Could have been the postal strike,' Rosie murmured. 'Or using that as a convenient cover?'

Daniel sat back, mulling over this new idea. All sorts of questions were spinning round his head in the wake of the man's death and the vicious attack that had in fact been carried out before he'd been shot.

'You think the victim's visit to Daniel and Netta's flat had anything to do with his subsequent murder?' Rosie asked the detective.

'Could be a pure coincidence,' she admitted. 'If it had just been Netta at home . . . '

'She would have had the door chain on and taken the letters out of his hand. And that would have been the end of it,' Daniel insisted. 'It was just chance that was my day off and Netta was at the hospital.'

Rosie wrinkled her nose. 'Well, that's as may be. But we all know someone who doesn't believe in coincidences, don't we?'

'Lorimer,' Daniel said. 'But coincidences do happen.'

What would his friend Superintendent Lorimer make of this strange story? he wondered. Well, he was out of the country, enjoying a much-deserved holiday, Daniel reminded himself. There was no way he would text the man to inform him of this. CID in Cathcart had this in hand, and he'd be astonished if his visit from the man calling himself Billy McGregor could throw any light on the man's untimely death.

CHAPTER EIGHTEEN

'Right, time to escape!' Maggie laughed as they sat in the back of the Mercedes. The Lorimers had spent a pleasant day being guided around Harare, shown the delights of a bird sanctuary where Lorimer had befriended a pair of friendly sulphur-crested cockatoos. Then there were the ubiquitous craft shops selling a variety of handmade souvenirs patronised particularly by the ladies in their group. After lunch back at the hotel they were taken to a wide leafy park where children crowded around, their hands out, begging for whatever these white Westerners could give them. Lorimer had watched their guide closely, seeing him stroll away a little and chat to another man under a row of acacia trees. Was this a deliberate ploy to let the tourists see just how impoverished his country had become? Or were these kids planted by a grown-up to filch what they could in return for a few measly dollars? Ashamed of his cynicism, he'd handed out some money, one eye still on their guide.

Now, though, they had skipped out of the hotel before dinner, to pay a visit to Daniel's mother.

He'd given Janette Kohi's address to the taxi driver and agreed a price for the fare. It seemed far too cheap, Lorimer thought, reminding himself of the catastrophic financial crash this country had experienced in recent times. The road became narrower as they left the city behind, clouds of dust kicked up by the car's wheels. He clasped Maggie's hand and gave it a squeeze.

'Wonder what she'll make of a couple of strangers turning up on her doorstep,' Maggie murmured.

'Well, we just say we're friends of Netta Gordon,' Lorimer reminded her. They had agreed long before leaving Glasgow not to speak Daniel's name out loud. To the people here, the former police inspector was dead and buried in a small churchyard close to his old home. And the truth was a secret that they needed to hold fast.

'This is different,' Maggie remarked, gazing out of the window as they bumped along a track that was just wide enough to allow for cars to pass each other, straggly trees and bushes on either side. 'Do you reckon we might see any wildlife?'

Lorimer did not turn to reply, his nose almost up against the car window. Then, 'Look!' he exclaimed. 'A hornbill!'

Sure enough, there was the large-beaked bird sitting by the roadside, seemingly indifferent to the car passing so close by.

'Wow!' Maggie crushed up beside him to peer out at the bird. 'Look at that yellow beak.'

She gave a small yelp as the car hit a pothole, bouncing her back into her seat. 'Golly, this is a rural area right enough. Not much money spent on their roads out here.'

The track did not become any better even when a few houses came into view, their small front gardens fenced off from the path that led to the road.

'We here, boss,' the driver called out as he slowed down. 'This as far as I can take you. Want to wait and I take you back again?'

'Yes, that was what we agreed,' Lorimer reminded him. 'We'll pay you once we return to Meikles Hotel.'

'Sure, boss.' The man grinned, cutting the engine. 'It's one of these houses over there.' He waved his hand airily in the direction of a row of small homes.

They could feel the late-afternoon heat beating down as soon as they left the air-conditioned Mercedes, the wide sky above them a vague memory of blue as if the colour had evaporated.

'Okay?' Lorimer asked, taking Maggie's hand as they walked towards the little houses, their corrugated metal roofs painted in different colours, faded by the sun to shades of ochre and pink.

'Yes,' she replied, though her voice sounded doubtful. 'It's not what I expected. It looks more like a hamlet than a real village. I wonder which one belongs to Janette?'

'Ah, well, I've got a good Scotch tongue in my head as well as years of doorstepping members of the public,' he laughed. 'Ah, there's someone sitting outside their front door,' he whispered, nodding towards a house a little further along the row.

Sure enough, an elderly woman was sitting on a rattan chair in the shade of the porch, eyes half closed as though she had been watching their arrival.

'Good afternoon,' Lorimer called out politely. 'We are here to visit Mrs Janette Kohi. Please can you direct us to her house?'

The old woman nodded and raised a hand, beckoning them towards her. It was then that they noticed the pair of arm crutches resting on an angle of the wall.

'Sorry to intrude,' Lorimer told her, opening the garden gate and walking up the path, Maggie behind him. 'We are here to visit Mrs Kohi. Do you know her?'

Still the old lady said nothing but, looking beyond Lorimer, she seemed to see Maggie and motioned for her to approach.

Once she had climbed the steps to the porch, the old woman took her hands and sighed.

'You have come a long way,' she said at last, her voice scratchy and thin as though she rarely used it.

'From Scotland,' Maggie told her. 'We hoped to visit Janette. She has a friend in Scotland who is our friend, too,' she explained. 'Oh,' she gasped as the old woman raised her head and she looked into a pair of sightless eyes. 'You *heard* us coming?'

'I heard your voices.' She smiled. 'I knew someone had arrived when the car engine stopped. You want to find my neighbour?' She raised her hands then and Maggie stood very still, letting the old lady run gnarled fingers across her face.

'Yes, we do,' she said quietly.

'I see you are a good woman,' she said then gave a sigh. 'Janette, too. She was a good woman.'

'*Was?*' Lorimer broke in, alarm in his voice. 'What do you mean? What's happened to her?'

The old woman turned her head towards Lorimer who was now hunkering down by her side. 'She has gone away,' she told them. 'Someone came to her house. A young man, a friend of the family. I know his voice. Janette left not long after that.'

'Do you know where she is now?' Lorimer asked.

The old woman did not shake her head but remained motionless. 'There have been others,' she said. 'Not from around here. I feel bad things are happening in this place.'

'Who was the young man?' Maggie asked, laying one hand on top of the woman's fingers.

But the old lady shut her eyes, slumping back against the chair as though wearied by their questions.

'Which one is her house?' Lorimer asked. 'We could always take a photo for our friend.'

The old woman sighed again then waved a hand to one side. 'Last house over there,' she said.

'Thank you,' Maggie told her. 'God bless you,' she whispered.

At her words, the old woman's face lit up, smiles crinkling around her eyes. Then, leaning forward and touching her hair, she whispered back, 'Perhaps the pastor will help you.'

Janette Kohi's house resembled every other in the row, a small, terraced cottage with windows overlooking a neat garden, fenced off on three sides, a pawpaw tree casting its shadow across a row of young plants. Lorimer raised his phone and snapped a few photos.

'What do you think?' Maggie asked anxiously as Lorimer walked closer to the front door.

He laid a finger to his lips, warning her to say nothing more. The blind woman had evidently developed a keen sense of hearing, something that compensated for the loss of her sight, and he was unwilling to let her overhear what they might say. Crooking a finger, he beckoned Maggie to follow him around the side of the cottage and, as soon as they were out of the neighbour's view, he pointed upwards.

Maggie followed his gaze and saw the open window next to a huge red geranium tumbling around the back doorway. She exchanged a worried look with her husband. Janette Kohi had evidently left in a hurry, failing to close that window. Here, in Southern Africa, air conditioning might be a necessity but keeping insects and snakes from invading one's home was also a priority.

'That suggests she was in a panic to leave,' Maggie observed.

'Or was taken by somebody,' Lorimer murmured. 'We can't discount anything yet.'

He walked quietly towards the door and turned the handle. It opened noiselessly.

'Should we ...?' Maggie whispered. 'What if someone sees us?'

Lorimer shrugged. 'We'll just say we were expected. Nobody's going to question a couple of foreign tourists.'

Inside the house it was only a little cooler. They had entered the kitchen, a small, square room with a stainless-steel sink and an old cooker. Flies buzzed angrily against the windowpane, several of their kind already dead on the sill. The hum of a refrigerator showed that the electricity was still functioning. Lorimer bent down and opened the fridge where a half empty carton of sour milk sat next to a plastic bottle of water. There was a pudding dish covered in a red spotted oilcloth that he lifted to find some sort of yellow cereal.

'Mealie meal,' Maggie told him. 'It's a staple here. But it's well past its sell-by date,' she added, wrinkling her nose.

They left the kitchen, crossing a passage that led to a sitting room and the front door. Along the hallway was a bathroom, then a bedroom, its single bed carefully made, a pair of cotton slippers on the floor. On the wall opposite the bed was a framed picture of a tree, its leaves a colourful canopy of shade for the small dark bird on the ground beneath.

Faith is the bird that sings to the dawn while it is still dark, words in fine copperplate script proclaimed on the picture. To one side lay a simple ceramic ornament depicting the Nativity scene.

'He told us about his mother's deep faith,' Maggie reminded Lorimer. 'And the neighbour mentioned the pastor. D'you think he would know where she might be found? He was the one who helped him get away, remember?'

Lorimer nodded but said no more, casting a professional eye around the room before retracing their steps back to the main lounge. The wooden floor was highly polished and covered by a circular sisal mat.

'Look!' Maggie gasped, pointing to a small artificial Christmas tree with some coloured glass baubles and decorations that sat on a three-legged stool in one corner of the room.

Lorimer exchanged a worried look with his wife.

'She's been gone since Christmas,' he muttered. 'No wonder Netta hasn't had mail for weeks.'

A shelf on one wall displayed several small, framed photos and he walked across to examine them more closely. One was of a wedding party, the smiling groom their friend, Daniel, his bride a pretty woman clothed in frothy white lace, clutching a bouquet of lilies and orchids. They were flanked by a small woman dressed in pink, whom he guessed might be Janette, and a man and woman by the bride's side, evidently her parents.

'I wonder where they are now,' Lorimer murmured. Daniel had never mentioned his in-laws, only that Chipo had come from a small village near Lake Kariba, one of their destinations during this trip.

Next to this was a colour photo, its frame encircled with silver tinsel, of Daniel in his police uniform, probably from his passing-out parade. Lorimer smiled at seeing the younger Daniel, remembering the occasion at Tulliallan Castle when he had completed his initial training for Police Scotland.

He raised his phone once more, setting the camera to video and then walked around, capturing bits of the house.

'We'll take something back to show . . . ' He tailed off with a significant nod to Maggie.

'I'll close the windows, take in that washing out on the clothes line and try to make the place a little more secure,' she replied. 'Should we let him know?' Maggie turned to look at her husband.

Lorimer shook his head. 'No point worrying him when we don't know what really happened here,' he replied. 'I'll help shut these windows if you like, then we'll go and hope our taxi fellow is still waiting for us.'

The return journey seemed to take less time, or perhaps like a horse returning to its stable, the driver was anxious for his evening meal. By the time they reached the outskirts of Harare, the sun had sunk beneath the horizon leaving an ink-black sky studded with stars. Lorimer wrapped an arm around Maggie's shoulders as they gazed through the Mercedes' sunroof, the southern hemisphere a new wonder to behold.

'Africa,' he sighed, the magic of the night enveloping him, helping to dissipate the worries that had overwhelmed them on that visit to Janette Kohi's home.

'It's . . . ' Maggie began. For once she was lost for words to express the moment. Silence seemed more fitting, the only sound the purring of the car engine as it sped along the newer roads into the city.

Tomorrow they would leave for the first part of their safari, a venture into the bush where they were assured of seeing many more of the continent's natural wonders. There would be time to search for Janette Kohi on their return to the city. Someone had spirited her away to a place of safety, Maggie reckoned.

Looking up into the spread of stars scattered against the velvet sky, she sent up a prayer that Daniel's mother would come to no harm and that their heavenly father would protect them all wherever they might venture.

CHAPTER NINETEEN

February

The world was still turning as it should, Daniel thought as he looked up at the blue sky streaked with pink. January was over and February beginning, with its promise of spring just around the corner. Netta had turned the wall calendar over that morning to see a picture of a country garden, snowdrops in the foreground as if they were a herald of better days.

Then she'd chanted, 'Rabbits, rabbits, rabbits,' as she did with the arrival of each new month. It had surprised him at first, but he was becoming accustomed to his flatmate's quirky little habits. Like her insistence on hanging the washing outside on the clothes line in their 'back green' as she called it, even when there was frost on the ground. 'It's windy today,' she'd tell him, her mouth set in a stubborn line. Yet most times when he returned after his shift, there it was hanging on the pulley above the table, drying in the heat of the kitchen. No matter how often Daniel had warned about imminent rain, Netta ignored him, happy to walk down to the square of grass they shared with the other residents in their close, even if she had to bring it all back in a few hours later. He might chuckle to himself, but that was Netta's choice, and she was sticking to it.

Somewhere in this city there were people who had made very bad choices and whose behaviour now had consequences. It was his chosen profession, Daniel knew, that could sometimes make a difference in a person's life. Today he was going to visit a primary school to talk to kids about the dangers of using drugs. He would not be on his own, however, George Fleming accompanying his probationer. To show me the ropes, Daniel thought, recalling other times in a different land when he had given similar talks in Zimbabwean secondary schools. There was so much to policing, the recruits at Tulliallan had learned in their weeks of training. Not only was their job as first responders to apprehend villains after crimes had been committed, but they also had to try to ensure the safety of their communities to prevent such things happening at all. And so Daniel Kohi's days could be a strange mixture of responding to calls for help as well as teaching members of the public how to avoid dangerous situations.

It was Daniel's first visit to a school since the death of his little boy and, as he drove to meet his current tutor cop, he wondered just how he would feel. Johannes would have been at school by now, he thought, swallowing hard. Still, he had a job to do, and he must do it cheerfully, for the sake of the kids waiting for the police officers to arrive.

Janette sighed as she watched the line of small children passing by the barred window. Once, she had been that teacher at the head of the line, ushering them along, encouraging the little ones to hold each other's hands and sing songs as they walked to wherever she might be taking them. Sometimes she had let them run around the flat ground near to the school, knowing that young children needed to stretch their little legs and use up some of their boundless energy.

'Hi . . . ' She raised a hand and made to call out, but a firm hand closed across her mouth, reminding Janette that silence was obligatory here.

Soon they were out of sight, and she was pulled away from the window, a contrite expression on her face as she was led back to her small cell.

It was hard remaining here day after day, not knowing about events in the world outside these walls. Danger was everywhere. Janette Kohi knew that now. What was going to happen to her? Would she be taken to some remote place and beaten senseless like poor Joseph Mlambo? Or, was waiting here, not knowing her fate, some sort of punishment in itself?

'That was fun!' Daniel grinned as they left the playground, the children waving goodbye to them beyond the classroom windows.

'Aye, they're a diverse lot. Some from decent homes where both parents take an interest in their kids' welfare. Others, well . . . not so much,' Fleming told him.

'Some of them were interested in asking me about Africa,' Daniel observed.

'Aye, you've still got a funny accent,' Fleming laughed as they reached the car. 'Most of these wee yins from ethnic backgrounds are all second or third generation and speak pure Glesca. You were more of a curiosity to them today.'

'They enjoyed hearing about the elephants,' Daniel murmured. 'Made me picture the bush back home.'

'D'you miss it? Zimbabwe?'

Daniel paused for a moment. 'I miss my mother,' he replied. 'And others . . . a few good colleagues and friends.' He turned his gaze away from the older cop. 'But there is a lot wrong with Zimbabwe that I hated. Police corruption . . . ' He glanced back to Fleming. 'That's what brought me here in the first place, I suppose,' he said, then fell silent.

George Fleming was wise enough not to pursue the conversation and soon they were back in the station car park.

As they entered the building, Daniel saw a familiar figure striding towards him.

'DI Miller,' he began.

'Want to see you, Kohi,' the woman told him. 'We need to ask you a bit more about your visitor.' She looked at him keenly. 'The one that ended up dead.'

'I'll catch you in the canteen,' Fleming said and headed off in that direction while Daniel accompanied the detective sergeant to the CID area. Daniel had been here before and a few heads turned to nod a greeting as he entered the room. Several of the officers were busy at their computers, the need to dig deeply for information in cases a constant chore.

'Right, sit yourself down here,' she ordered him, pulling a metal chair towards her desk. It screeched across the floor, setting Daniel's teeth on edge.

He frowned. Miller's voice was colder than usual. Had he done something wrong? Or had something else come to light?

'Take me through that visit from Billy McGregor,' Miller commanded. 'Bit by bit. Don't leave anything out.'

Daniel took a deep breath and began to relate it all again from the moment the man had appeared at their door until he had left.

'He told you the letters had been delivered to his address, right?'

Daniel nodded. 'Both Netta and I had arranged to have our mail redirected to Nithsdale Drive,' he told her. 'At least I assumed she had.' He shrugged.

'Individually or together?'

'Oh, we did that separately. I didn't get much mail anyway. Just flyers and a few bills, letters from the bank, stuff like that.'

'Any Christmas cards?'

Daniel shook his head. 'No. I didn't send any,' he replied. 'And with the price of postage and the mail strike, I guess I wasn't expecting mail of that sort.'

'Yet this guy does find mail. Addressed to Mrs Gordon. From your mother.'

'Yes,' Daniel admitted. 'Netta has become her penfriend. It's a way of keeping in touch without revealing to anyone back home that I am still alive,' he said.

'And you still think this man turning up on your doorstep was just a coincidence?'

Daniel nodded. 'Of course. I mean, what has that stranger got to do with me? Apart from having moved into Netta's old flat?'

DI Miller was silent for a moment. Then she looked straight into Daniel's dark brown eyes.

'What if he had been spinning you a load of tosh?' she suggested. 'Hadn't that occurred to you?'

Daniel shook his head.

'You see, Kohi, Billy McGregor wasn't just a sailor home from the seas like he told you, though he had served in the merchant navy for a bit in his younger days.'

Miller glanced down at a sheaf of papers on her desk then she looked back at Daniel, her expression hard to read.

'McGregor was not long out of prison. We've been doing background checks and found that he had a record of being involved in several cases of assault to severe injury. He'd managed to escape prosecution on at least two occasions. Only this last time someone had got the better of him and he couldn't do a runner.'

Daniel stared into space, trying to conjure up the dead man's face when he had sat in the kitchen drinking coffee. He'd seemed an ordinary man. Friendly. But then, Daniel reminded himself, criminals rarely appeared with any physical signs denoting the wrong choices they had made.

'It seemed a nice thing to do,' he said at last. 'Taking time to deliver the airmail letters. He could just as easily have chucked them in the bin.'

'Yes, he could,' Miller agreed. 'So we have to ask ourselves: why didn't he?'

CHAPTER TWENTY

Netta shifted her shopping bag from one arm to the other. She hadn't intended buying so much in the grocery store and walking back to Nithsdale Drive was proving tiresome on her aching back. The sight of fresh bananas had been impossible to resist, and she knew how much Daniel liked those yellow plums. A brisk wind was blowing from the east, catching the ends of her headscarf and casting a fine spray of drizzle into her face.

'Too windy for an umbrella,' Netta grumbled under her breath, leaving the furled brolly in her heavy bag and steeling herself against the onslaught as she marched down the road with renewed determination.

Once she was home, she'd switch on that lovely new chrome kettle with its fancy cream handle and make a proper pot of tea. She had brought her stainless-steel teapot from the old flat as well as a hand-knitted tea cosy decorated with white woolly sheep. The dozen eggs nestling at the bottom of her bag had been the main reason for her shopping trip today. She grinned to herself as she headed along, already imagining the pancakes she'd make. 'None of yer fancy crêpes,' she'd told Molly. 'Proper pancakes. Drop scones, thon English cook aff the telly ca'd them. Naethin' like scones at a',' she'd snorted, much to the younger woman's amusement.

The tenement building was closer now and Netta stopped again to change the bag to her other hand. Despite the nice gloves she'd been given at Christmas, her fingers felt a wee thing stiff and sore. Ach, auld age disnae come alone, she thought. Between the cold wind and the onset of arthritis, Netta Gordon had to admit she wasn't as fit as she'd once been.

It was as she hefted the bag onto her left hand that it happened.

The figure running towards her was clad all in black. Netta hardly looked up, dismissing him as just another sporty type in Lycra.

Then the warning sound of a bicycle bell made the old woman turn around.

'Oh!' she cried, feeling the punch to her midriff as the runner grabbed her bag. 'Oh, help!'

She swayed to one side, the man's grip on her bag almost lifting her off her feet.

But Netta Gordon was made from hard years of toil in this city and her fingers gripped the handle tightly.

'Get aff, ye wee scunner!' she yelled at the thin weaselly-looking fellow, determined that this thief was not going to get away with her bag, or smash her precious eggs all over the ground.

There was a clatter as a bicycle fell right by her side, making Netta jump.

In that moment she felt the handle of her bag released as the thief turned around and sped off back the way he'd come.

'Are you all right, missus?'

A young boy of about fourteen had hold of Netta's arm and was looking at her with concern.

'Did he hurt ye?'

Netta saw a pair of anxious grey eyes behind a floppy ginger fringe. Jist a young laddie, but he'd come to her rescue!

'Thanks, son. Ah'm a' right, nearly hame tae ma flat. It's jist ower there,' Netta told him.

'Come on an' ah'll walk ye hame, missus. Is there anyone in tae make ye a cup o' tea? Ma mammy aye says that's best fur shock,' the lad went on.

'Aye, nae bother, son,' Netta told him.

The lad picked up his bike and walked by Netta's side till they reached the door of the tenement.

'This where ye live?'

Netta nodded. 'How about you? Should you no' be at school?'

The boy gave her a winning smile. 'Ah'm oan exam leave the noo fur ma Prelims,' he told her. 'Gonnae get a few Highers then am off tae the nautical college.'

Netta's eyebrows rose. The lad must be older than he looked. Must be about sixteen. Sitting his Highers then off tae college!

'Here, son,' she said, fumbling in her bag for the purse that was thrust deep down among the groceries. She drew out a five-pound note. 'Take this, a wee thank you fur savin' me frae thon rogue.'

'Naw, missus,' the lad said, waving her hand away. 'That's no needed. Jist think o' it as ma good deed fur today, like. Ah'm a senior in the Boys' Brigade, so ah am. Got first prize fur my Bible study an' all.' He grinned.

'Well, pit it oan the plate next Sunday or gie it tae BB funds,' she insisted, stuffing the note into his hand. 'The good Lord may jist have sent ye tae look out fur an auld wumman.' She began to laugh then and shake her head. 'But ah nivver thocht tae see a ginger-heided angel oan a bicycle!'

The laughter lines around her eyes had faded by the time Netta turned the key in the lock of their door, her hands trembling. Why had someone targeted an old woman like her in broad daylight? She shivered, replaying the incident over in her mind. What if this was something to do with her late husband or his evil associates? Would she never be able to leave that past behind? she wondered, brushing away unbidden tears with the back of her hand. And would she have the courage to tell Daniel?

'Did you get her bag? Have you got the keys?' A figure emerged from the shadows of tenement buildings and fell into step with the man who had been chased away from Nithsdale Drive.

'Some wee nyaff on a bike came and I had to scarper,' he said. 'But check this out. I think I know where she lives.'

'We knew that already, you idiot.' He came closer to the man who'd tried to grab Netta's bag. 'Suits you to do what McGregor never finished, doesn't it?'

The younger man threw him a sullen look.

'McGregor couldn't do the business, could he? We're better off without him,' he sneered, breathing hard into the older man's face and making him flinch.

'There was no need—' he began. Then his mouth opened in horror as the blade flashed out.

'Don't you tell me what was needed,' the man in black hissed. 'You did your bit as well.'

A look passed between the two men, a nod of understanding, and the switchblade was pocketed as swiftly as it had emerged.

CHAPTER TWENTY-ONE

The tinted windows of the coach made the terrain appear greener than it really was, the distant hills a streak of slate-grey under hazy skies, heat shimmering on the road ahead. When Lorimer stepped out into the warmth of the late afternoon, he looked onto flat yellow scrubland dotted with thorny bushes and strange trees that looked like something from a science fiction movie. Stretching his legs, he reckoned they had been travelling for more than three hours, waved through the checkpoint by armed police officers. Daniel had warned that their transport might be held up by bent cops intent on fleecing the tourists, demanding 'safe passage' fees, something to which the authorities turned a blind eye despite stating their opposition to such practices. He had seen the grin on their guide's face as their driver had carried on along the road, watching the man as he'd winked at the policemen. Did they know their tour guide? Lorimer had wondered. After all, he'd take tourists along this route frequently. Or had they been warned not to entrap certain of the safari companies for some political reason? Perhaps the hefty price they had already paid for this trip included a backhander of some sort?

His thoughts were interrupted by their Zimbabwean guide, Luther, who now had a small crowd around him, including Maggie. Lorimer moved to stand beside her, listening to him.

'Baobab trees,' their guide said, pointing to the thick, smooth trunks crowned with a cluster of limbs that scrabbled skywards. 'It is one of nature's miracles.' The man explained about the tree having a reservoir of water that kept it alive during even the most severe drought. 'We use it for all sorts of medicinal reasons.'

'Cream of tartar,' Maggie murmured. 'I think that comes from the baobab tree.'

Lorimer smiled. It was typical of his wife that she would know its culinary uses.

Soon they were back inside the relative coolness of their transport, bottled water handed out from a cool box as the guide continued his story about the vegetation in this part of the world. Lorimer's eyes closed, the man's sing-song voice lulling him to sleep.

The bus jerked to a halt and Lorimer sat up.

'Look!' whispered Maggie, grabbing his hand. 'Elephant!'

All the passengers were crowded at the windows, eager to watch the grey lumbering creatures crashing through the bushes, trunks waving upwards as they sought fresh leaves. Their huge feet stamped on anything in their way, young trees slashed and trampled.

There was something primeval about these massive

creatures, Lorimer thought, their only aim to feed on what they could find, irrespective of the destruction left in their wake. It was a far cry from the captive animals he had seen in zoos or tame safari parks back home. The guide warned them about the animals. They were dangerous and had killed several people venturing into their terrain, Luther said, particularly when they had young in their herd.

Once the elephants had moved past them, passengers raising their cameras before they disappeared, the bus trundled onwards along the dusty road to their destination.

'That was wonderful,' Maggie whispered, 'coming across them like that. Wonder what else we might see?' Her head turned to stare as they continued through the African bush. The edges of the grassland rippled in a heat haze, faint outlines of antelope grazing, their dun colour so like the foliage as to render them almost invisible.

At last, they turned into a wooded area and came to a halt. Lorimer could see a large tent and a circle with wooden tables and chairs set around a fire pit.

Lorimer helped Maggie alight, and they shouldered the backpacks that they would need for the next few nights, the remainder of their belongings stowed in the luggage hold of the bus.

'Where's our sleeping quarters?' an American woman asked their guide, turning around with a bewildered expression on her heavily made-up face.

The bus driver gave her a gap-toothed grin then pointed upwards.

'Oh, gee! That's awesome!' she cooed, a look of sheer delight crossing her features.

Lorimer and Maggie followed her gaze. Up in the tree-tops amongst stout branches were structures like the sort of elaborate dens a child might desire, camouflaged in shades of olive and brown.

'Tree houses!' Maggie exclaimed. 'Of course. That was in the brochure. But I thought we weren't going to stay in them just yet,' she added, turning to Luther.

'Change of plan, madam,' their guide explained. 'Tomorrow, we go into the bush. Lion have been sighted in this area, so we stay here for two nights. Take the chance to see them, then travel back to a different place. Now, just enter here and you will find a nice dinner prepared for you by our wonderful chef!' He stood aside and ushered his group into the marquee.

'Smells delicious,' Maggie said as they trooped into the huge tent.

The aroma of barbecued meat filled the tent as three teenage boys in khaki T-shirts and matching shorts dished out food for the newly arrived guests.

'Try it all, my friends,' Luther insisted, walking up and down the queue of weary travellers. 'Here is ostrich,' he pointed to a dish of succulent-looking steaks, 'and there is kudu, one of our finest antelope. Very tasty!' He grinned. 'And try our excellent sauces. Some very hot!' He gave a high-pitched giggle that made Lorimer think that there must be a fair quantity of hot spices in the large metal platters.

'Steaks, casseroles, take your pick. Fresh baked bread, good vegetables too. Yum yum!' Luther laughed, rubbing his belly.

They chose a table close to the fire that crackled and snapped, flames ascending into the gathering dusk.

'He's right,' Maggie remarked. 'This steak is delicious.' She sighed happily.

'So's this one,' Lorimer agreed. 'And plenty of different vegetables for anyone who isn't a meat eater.' However, he'd noticed that all their fellow guests seemed to be tucking into the bush meats, side plates filled with sliced yellow bread.

The sound of cicadas and tree frogs grew louder as the sun disappeared below the horizon. One moment the sky was a shade of dusky pink and then darkness descended as though a light had been switched off.

Around the campfire conversations continued, laughter growing louder as local beers washed down their meals. Several travellers had already formed close groups, burgeoning friendships that might last for the trip or continue for years. Lorimer and Maggie sat quietly on their own, watching as the stars began to spark in the velvet night sky; taking time out to visit Janette's home seemed to have set them a little apart from the others.

'You enjoy the braai?'

Luther hunkered down beside them, his dark eyes flashing in amusement.

'Braai? That's Afrikaans for barbecue, isn't it?' Maggie asked.

'Yes, madam. Many white men came from South Africa to Zimbabwe.' He shrugged as though indifferent to the part those people had played in his country's history. 'Brought many words with them. We cater for all the best tourists here,' he boasted. 'The world comes to Zimbabwe once again.'

It was true enough, Lorimer thought. There were Americans

across from their own table and they'd already been met with a 'g'day' from Australians in their group. An elderly Dutch couple also sat on their own, an occasional smile towards the Lorimers, heads raised to the night sky an acknowledgement of a shared interest. The largest group comprised of several travellers from England, most of them older than Maggie and Lorimer.

'You didn't have any trouble with the police at that check-point,' Lorimer observed casually. 'Friends of yours?'

Their guide's smile vanished at his words, and he stood up hurriedly. 'Sorry, I need to check something. Go and find your tree house. Boys here will show you where it is,' he said stiffly and walked off towards the marquee.

'Luther was in a bit of a hurry,' Maggie said, frowning. 'I think you upset him.'

There was something a little odd about the man's response, Lorimer thought, but he wasn't about to spoil the mood of this glorious night by digging any deeper.

'Probably just has a lot on his mind, having to look after us all out here,' Lorimer replied. Then, stretching out his long limbs he yawned. 'Come on, I'm bushed. Let's see what our accommodation is like.'

Yet, as they left the warmth of the campfire and headed into the darkness, Lorimer thought about their guide's reaction. *Leave it*, a voice inside his head insisted. *You're on holiday*. Had years of dealing with criminals spoiled him for enjoying moments like these? Perhaps he had developed a naturally suspicious mind when encountering strangers. Was this a warning that it was time to put that behind him and see what else life might offer?

*

Maggie clambered up the rope ladder, hand over hand, till she reached a wooden step leading into their treetop bedroom. Inside she could see a large mosquito net suspended above a double bed. On each side was a small cabinet with a single lamp, their lights attracting a variety of pale grey moths. The windows were simply gaps in the wooden structure covered by makeshift cotton curtains suspended on rods.

'Here, take that far side,' her husband insisted, crouching behind her. 'If anything clambers up during the night, it'll have me for starters.' He chuckled.

Maggie stood still for a moment. 'Surely nothing can climb up here,' she began.

'Leopards climb trees,' Lorimer reminded her. 'But there's an electric fence all the way round so we'll be quite safe, darling.'

Maggie slipped into her cotton nightdress, flicked off the night light and slid as quickly as she could under the mosquito net, gathering it securely.

It was so dark, she realised, darker than anywhere she had ever been before. Outside, the night noises grew louder, the repetitive sounds a sign of the nocturnal world come to life. Eventually sleep took her, the rhythmic sounds of croaking frogs lulling her senses.

She was dreaming of being tossed by the storm, the boat moving under her feet, waves lashing against its wooden hull.

Suddenly Maggie sat up.

What was that thumping? And why was their tree being shaken from side to side?

The noises outside had ceased, a sign of danger, perhaps, small creatures hiding from a predator.

A sound like heavy footfall by her bed made Maggie want to cry out.

Heart thudding, she reached out a shaking hand and fumbled for the light switch. Whatever dangerous beast was inside their tiny cabin, she wanted to see it.

There, its tail wound around the stem of the lamp, a small creature with huge eyes stared at Maggie.

For a moment both human and animal froze in terror before it scampered into the thatch above her and disappeared into the night.

A bushbaby! Maggie grinned at her own fright. Poor wee thing had been far more terrified of this intruder into its night-time world than she was of their unexpected visitor.

She lay back again, sensing that the tree house was motionless once more, realising the cacophony of cicadas had resumed. What a story to tell when Bill woke up! She thought about rousing him, but his soft snores reminded her of how exhausted he had looked before their holiday. She hugged the incident to herself, already playing it over in her mind. The darkness had held no danger for them, after all. Perhaps those other sounds had just been part of her dream.

Next morning, Maggie discovered that she had not been the only person to have had a disturbed sleep.

'Eland,' Luther told them at breakfast. 'They are big antelopes and can jump the fence. Rub themselves against the tree trunks. Did you feel them shaking?' He laughed as one by one the guests related the same story. Only the

Scottish lady with her tall husband had a different tale to tell, however, and they were impressed to know that Maggie had identified the bushbaby.

'Oh, my.' The American lady put a hand to her throat. 'You poor dear! What a fright you must have gotten!'

'I was scared,' Maggie admitted. 'Just for a moment, when all the noises stopped outside, I thought something big was climbing up into our tree.'

'And it was a cute wee bushbaby,' Lorimer laughed.

Just then he saw one of the young boys who had been serving them at last night's meal running up to Luther, an expression of concern on his face.

Their guide rose and walked across to talk to the lad, Lorimer watching their body language with interest. He saw Luther stiffen at whatever the young guy was telling him, the lad gesturing frantically towards the group. He watched intently as Luther took a step back and folded his arms across his chest.

Something was wrong, the detective thought, but nobody else seemed to notice as Maggie continued chatting with the others about her night-time adventure.

Luther was shaking his head now, his mouth set in a mulish expression. Whatever the boy was telling him, it had provoked a negative response. At last, the boy stopped, hands falling to his sides. Then their guide laid his arm around the boy's shoulders and walked with him along a narrow pathway that led behind the marquee.

For a moment Luther looked up and saw Lorimer staring at him. There was no smile today from the man.

'Morning!' Lorimer called, trying to dispel the moment

of tension. But the pair simply continued walking till they were out of sight.

Lorimer took a deep breath. Not your business, he decided, turning back to his wife.

CHAPTER TWENTY-TWO

It was wet and slippery underfoot but still they walked around the yard, heads down, cold air seeping into their lungs. The old Victorian building loomed up on all sides, its forbidding stones denying them any sort of view except that faraway patch of sky the colour of dirty dishwater. Ncube tramped behind another black man, close enough to talk without being overheard by the prison officers on duty. Any closer and he might hear a sharp reprimand, the nearest screw rasping out a bark, fingering the bunches of keys dangling from a thick chain as though he would like to use them as a weapon against the men under his scrutiny.

'What have you heard?' he hissed. 'Tell me.'

The other man pretended not to hear as they came around a corner of the yard, then, casting a sly grin over his shoulder, he made to stumble.

Ncube caught him as he fell, righting him at once. The guard had made to move towards them but merely nodded when he saw that the big black man had been first to grab the other man's arm.

The whispered message was given in seconds then their progress around the exercise area continued as before, sullen-faced men in a circle, some clapping their upper arms to warm up, others gazing downwards as though resigned to this pattern of their lives. If anyone had been looking more intently, they might have seen a spring in the step of the biggest one in that group, Augustus Ncube walking tall, his head held high, a gleam in his dark eyes.

Perhaps now they would believe him.

CHAPTER TWENTY-THREE

Night shifts at this time of year could be cold and miserable, as Daniel was finding out. Despite the hints of a little more daylight now that February was here, the hours of darkness still seemed to be interminable. They did not expect to see anybody about on the streets on a mid-week night as he and DS Knight, now back from sick leave, walked smartly around the block. But there was one particular area here in Cathcart that they needed to check.

In the doorway of an estate agent's office, Daniel could see the familiar heap of corrugated cardboard, an edge of tattered sleeping bag flapping in the bitter wind. They'd moved the homeless man out of this doorway several times since Christmas, ensuring he was safe, the freezing conditions threatening to hasten the old man's death.

'Andy,' Daniel called, kneeling down to examine the man. 'Hey, c'mon, wake up,' he told him, shaking the itinerant's coat collar.

'Is he okay?' the older cop asked, bending down to follow

Daniel's gaze. 'Far too cold for an old codger like him to be out.' He shuddered as the wind whipped around the corner of the street.

'Andy, can you hear me?' Daniel held his breath as he thrust his hand into the folds of rags and felt for the old man's wrist. Was he dead? Had they arrived too late this time to save the old man?

He breathed a sigh of relief as he felt the warm pulse.

'Let's get him onto his feet,' DS Knight suggested. 'We can carry him between us back to the car.'

The old man remained unconscious as they heaved him up, sleeping bag and all.

'Phew, he doesn't half stink, poor bugger!' Knight exclaimed. 'What we do for the great unwashed, eh, Kohi?'

Between them, they half dragged, half carried the old man along the street and settled him into the back of the car. Still, he did not stir.

'A&E again,' Daniel said as he released the handbrake.

'Aye, they'll need to check him over. We know how bad he was last time.' Knight cast a grim look into the back seat where the old man lay comatose.

Daniel did not reply, remembering a similar night when he and another officer had taken Andy into the Accident and Emergency department of the local hospital. They had remained there with the homeless man until a nurse had informed him that they had a bed prepared. Later, Daniel had found that they had washed the old man, laundered his clothes and kept him in for observation, his tubercular lungs a cause for concern.

'Can't fathom how he's survived this long,' Knight

remarked as they drove along the darkened streets. 'If he'd just stayed in that hostel . . . '

Daniel nodded. There was no telling someone like old Andy that being outside in this weather would finish him off for good. Perhaps that was what he wanted?

The smell off the old man wafted into the front of the car making Daniel wrinkle his nose in distaste. How the nurses in A&E managed to cope with cases like this and remain cheerful and patient was beyond him.

A rattling noise from behind made him slow down for a moment. Then the old man woke in a paroxysm of coughs that made Daniel wince.

'Nearly there, old fellow,' he promised, accelerating once more. 'Nearly there.'

The hospital canteen was a bleak place at this hour, upside down chairs resting on formica tables, only a slot machine for drinks. Knight and Daniel sat on two plastic chairs opposite reception, waiting to hear about the old man. Eventually a blue-garbed figure strode along the corridor and headed towards them.

'You're the cops who brought in Mr Allan?' she asked them.

They stood up, nodding.

'That's right, nurse. How is he?' Knight asked.

'Not good, I'm afraid. His heart's in a bad shape.' She looked from one to the other. 'To be honest, we're not sure he'll make it this time.'

'Not surprised in this cold,' Knight replied grimly.

'Will he be on his own?' Daniel asked.

'He's in a single room, not a ward,' she replied. 'They've

given him fluids and are monitoring his heart rate, et cetera.' She gave a shrug. 'We do what we can, but it probably won't be enough. Glad you brought him in anyway.'

It was their cue to leave, but Daniel hesitated for a moment before following his tutor outside. 'You do such a wonderful job,' he began. 'That old fellow . . . '

'Och, we see that sort of thing all the time,' she insisted. 'Just be grateful you got him into a warm bed for his last few hours.'

They were quiet as Daniel drove back to the police station, their shift almost over. Some nights were like this, waiting in a hospital corridor. Others could find them breaking up a domestic dispute when a neighbour called for help. And, since he had begun his probation, he'd had even worse experiences. Finding that drug addict and her little baby was one that Daniel Kohi would never forget.

That case had brought him into professional contact with his friend, Detective Superintendent William Lorimer, the strange link between their respective cases overlapping. Well, Lorimer was away in Zimbabwe for a much-earned holiday with his dear wife, Maggie. As they approached the junction at Battlefield, Daniel wondered if they had managed to meet up with his mother. He had heard nothing, though Maggie had promised to text Netta Gordon the moment they took a photo of Janette Kohi. He had never once dared to make contact with anyone back home, fearful of the repercussions. If they knew he was here, working once more as a cop, well, what nastiness might these people inflict on his own mother?

No, she was surely safe in her own home, Daniel decided. Though it would ease his mind if a letter were to arrive addressed to their Southside flat.

CHAPTER TWENTY-FOUR

'His name is William Lorimer,' the man said, standing under the shade of a jacaranda tree opposite Meikles Hotel. 'That's right. Yes, I can wait,' he added into his mobile phone, shifting impatiently from one foot to the other, body language at odds with his words.

The letter was crumpled and sweat-stained now, Netta Gordon's spidery writing blurred where the fine blue airmail paper had been creased. It was mostly innocuous, one old biddy writing to another about stuff to do with weather and what happened at Christmas in the city of Glasgow. He'd looked it up on the internet, remembering that was where Ncube was incarcerated. One short video showed a bleak, industrial town, with litter-strewn pavements, rain sweeping across grey streets and a muddy-looking river that split the place in two. He'd also glanced at a tourist video, the city bathed in sunlight, old buildings etched against a bright blue sky, art galleries and fancy restaurants displaying what might tempt a visitor to venture to this place on Scotland's west coast. Glasgow was evidently a place that wore different faces.

And, if Ncube was correct, that was where Kohi was right now.

'You still there?' a voice asked.

'Yes. What can you tell me?'

He listened, standing still now, shadowed by the overhanging branches of the tree.

'And he's gone ... where?' he asked, eyes widening in surprise.

A few minutes later he slipped the mobile into his shirt pocket and crossed the road. Meikles Hotel was where the Lorimers had begun their trip, he had been told. And so that was where he must begin to ask some questions.

Reuben sidled up to the deserted house, scuffing his sandals in the dust. After the job at the cemetery, keeping an eye on this place was no big deal. He whistled softly as he walked by the same houses that he'd strolled past several times now. The old blind woman was out on her stoep as usual, arm crutches by her chair. Couldn't see him, Reuben thought, poking a childish tongue out in her direction.

'You there! Boy!'

Reuben jumped. Surely she couldn't have seen his rude gesture! Wasn't she blind after all?

'Come over here!' she demanded in a tone that brooked no refusal.

Reuben gave her his most ingratiating grin as he stepped towards the gate, just in case she was indeed watching him.

'Are you going into Mrs Kohi's house again, boy?' she

asked, raising one of her crutches and bringing it down with a decided thump on the tiled floor of the porch.

'Yes, missus, I am,' Reuben replied, hovering at the end of her garden path. 'Got to make sure everything is okay while she's away.'

There was a forbidding silence then, as the woman's sightless eyes stared in his direction, making the young man shiver. Did she know anything about the Kohi woman?

'Maybe she'll be back soon?' he ventured.

'Surely you would know,' came back the tight retort. '*If* you are looking after her place?'

Reuben backed away. This old person was sounding far too perceptive for his liking.

'Got to collect the post,' he mumbled.

'Oh? And why is that? Who has asked you to do this?'

None of your business, Reuben wanted to call back but there was something about this lady that reminded him of all his teachers at school and of his long-suffering grandmother who had tried so hard to keep him on the right path. They'd cowed him back then, but he was his own man now, wasn't he? Money in his pocket, doing a job of work for the big man in Harare. Bunching his fists, he felt a sudden urge to pick up a stick and batter the blind woman till she lay senseless on the ground.

But the moment passed in a wave of shame. She was just an old lady, looking out for a neighbour.

'See ya around, missus,' Reuben called, slamming the garden gate behind him and running the last few yards to the house at the end of the row.

He rattled the front door handle, but nothing happened.

Slipping around the back, Reuben tried the back door. But it was the same.

Someone had been here and locked the place up.

There were no longer any clothes hanging on the metal washing line, just a row of empty plastic pegs. And all the windows were shut fast.

He could attempt a break-in, Reuben thought, but that might not be such a good idea. Anybody could catch him as he climbed through a broken window and besides, the noise would alert that damned old woman.

He peered in the windows at the back, rubbing the glass with sweaty fingers, and then came around the front again but could see no changes inside. Had Janette Kohi returned, and he'd missed her? But her neighbour would have told him. Turning to look down the street, he saw the old lady still sitting on her chair. Did she know about this? Had she been messing with him?

This time, he strode along determinedly and pushed open her gate, letting it swing behind him.

'You saw anybody at the Kohi house, missus?' Reuben asked, tilting his chin as if to express a new-found bravado.

A dry cackle came from her cracked lips.

'See?' she laughed. 'I see nothing, young man, but I can hear the fear in your voice.' She paused then leaned forward a little. 'Who's pulling your strings, boy? What mischief have you been told to do?'

'Who's been here?' Reuben whispered. 'You know something, don't you?' he continued, creeping closer to the stoep.

And then he stopped, his heart thumping.

Her ancient face was full of wrinkles. Just like

Grandmother's had been at the end. *Wisdom lines*, the pastor had called them at the funeral.

Her smile and that shake of the head were all he needed to back away.

He could tell them that the elderly neighbour hadn't seen anyone. She'd not actually said so, but he could make that bit up. She *did* know something. He was certain of that.

Someone else might beat it out of her, but it wasn't going to be Reuben Mahlangu.

Meikles Hotel had retained all the glamour of its colonial past. Overlooking the nearby gardens, this famous hotel was a favourite with tour operators and catered for the needs of those visiting from Europe, the US, Australia or other parts of Africa. Despite the many white faces, it was no longer the preserve of those who had kept sway over the country until its indigenous people had toppled British rule. These days it was not just the waiting staff who were black, but most of the dignitaries sitting in the restaurant or enjoying sundowners at the bar.

Reuben's boss strolled into the foyer, admiring the wide space with its potted plants placed discreetly in break-out areas, screening guests from the gaze of passers-by. Then, slipping his sunglasses into his shirt pocket, he strode towards the restaurant for his meeting. Today Nelson Sibanda was dressed in casual clothes, smart enough to be somewhat invisible amongst the diners here. His usual uniform might draw a few speculative glances and that was something he wanted to avoid. The clink of glasses and the explosive *pop* as a sommelier drew the cork from a bottle was followed by a few muted cheers and genteel laughter from three well-dressed couples around a table. This was not the sort of place for rowdy behaviour, no matter who was in a celebratory mood. He passed them by, noting the elaborate hairstyle of one of the women and the waft of something floral. Another time, another place, he might have made eye contact with her. But not today.

The thick-set man in the crisp white shirt and scarlet tie looked up as he settled into the seat opposite, his deep-set eyes flicking over the newcomer. His once dark curls were grizzled with grey now, a constant reminder that his best years might be behind him.

'You're late,' the man snapped. 'You know I don't like to be kept waiting, Mr Sibanda.'

Nelson Sibanda inclined his head just sufficiently to indicate courtesy. He would not be dominated by this man, no matter what favours he was about to ask. The old politician was as wily as a coyote but his glory days were fading, and he needed the big man seating himself at the dining table just as much as Sibanda needed him. Indeed, Sibanda had smoothed the path for the old man's wayward son, ensuring he'd been kept out of trouble before seeing him off at Harare International Airport.

'I wanted to let you know about the latest developments,' Sibanda began, looking up as a waiter arrived to hand him a menu.

'A drink, sir?' the fellow asked, bending forward a little.

'Just water for me,' the politician said, covering his empty wine glass with one hand.

Sibanda stifled a sigh. He had a thirst that had been

growing all morning, yet to ask for alcohol might be seen as less than polite. Then he remembered the words he was about to say to this old Zimbabwean and flicked his hand up.

'A beer,' he said. 'Make sure it's chilled.' He grinned at the waiter. So, what if that was a faux pas, he thought, stretching his legs under the table and ignoring the other man's sniff of disdain.

'Well, what can I suggest for lunch, Nelson?' the older man asked.

Nelson Sibanda's eyes widened at the use of his first name. That suggested an intimacy which boded well for this meeting between two men.

'The ostrich is always good here,' the politician added, as if Sibanda were unused to dining in the prestigious hotel restaurant.

'I know,' Sibanda said testily, irked by the implication. 'Especially with their house sauce.'

The man opposite smiled and continued reading the menu in silence as if he had scored a point in a game that was only just beginning.

Later, Sibanda would find out from reception about the man and woman called Lorimer and where exactly they were heading. But for now, he was content to eat a good meal and make conversation with the man whose influence had once extended far beyond the limits of Harare.

Each of the two men studying their menus shared different sorts of powers in this country, powers that had been twisted for their own ends and which might well lead to the misfortune of innocent people.

The politician picked up his water glass as Sibanda's beer

arrived. 'Your good health,' he said, tilting his head a little and giving a wry smile. 'May you live long enough to see your fortunes succeed.'

'And yours, sir,' Sibanda replied, clinking glasses with Wilson Ncube.

'Do you want to know your fortunes?' their guide asked as they swept along the rutted paths between clusters of thorn bushes and straggly trees. Maggie frowned, looking across at her husband and the other two passengers in the open-topped Land Rover.

'What do you mean?' she asked.

'Wise man up ahead, missus. He throws the bones for you, tells you what will happen in your life,' he said, chuckling.

'I'm up for that if you are,' the white-haired lady sitting behind Maggie said, tapping her shoulder. 'Probably just a bit of fun, something else to relieve us of our dollars,' she whispered. Maggie turned and smiled. The older Australian couple had been good company, their quiet manners and keen appreciation of wildlife endearing them to the Lorimers since the beginning of their trip. Dinah had been a teacher in Tasmania, her husband Fred a civil servant.

Like me, Lorimer had offered, hiding his profession behind that catch-all title, glad that neither Fred nor Dinah had probed further. After all, working for Police Scotland could be seen as a governmental post. Though afterwards Maggie had chided him for describing himself like that. It was stretching it a bit far, she'd told him.

Holidays were about seeking new places and seeing as much of the world as they could now that they were both retired, Dinah had declared, as if firmly putting their past careers behind them.

'Why not,' Maggie agreed, wondering if their guide was cashing in on this particular diversion. A visit to a fortune teller might be a good tale to relate once they were home. She wasn't superstitious and, besides, the poverty in this country demanded that any decent tourist would put their hand into their pocket at every opportunity.

Up ahead, their guide had declared but so far all they could see was scrubby landscape and dun-coloured foothills dotted with small bushes. It was, Maggie thought, a far cry from the Scottish landscape with its pine forests and sweeps of heathery moorland. At this time of year, the hills back home were blanketed in coppery bracken, its winter foliage protecting any new shoots that might be emerging from the ground. As the vehicle bumped across a rutted track then slowed down, a movement made Maggie grab hold of Bill's arm.

'Look!' she whispered.

A troop of baboons was casually strolling across their path, faces turned towards the Land Rover.

'Dangerous creatures,' their guide said quietly. 'They can give a very bad bite. Just look at the teeth as we come closer.'

Maggie clung to Bill's arm as a bigger animal appeared to be turning in their direction. What if it jumped right up onto their safari Land Rover?

The guide threw them a conspiratorial smile then, reaching down by his seat, he drew out a rifle.

The instant that he raised it and aimed for the baboons, the whole tribe fled, screeching in alarm.

Luther turned back to the four Westerners, a gleam in

his eyes. 'They don't like it when I do that,' he said. 'Don't even need a real gun, though this one is kept loaded just in case. If they see a long stick being pointed at them, they'll think it's a gun.'

'They know as much as that?' Maggie was astonished.

'Learned behaviour,' Dinah told her. 'I saw it on a wildlife documentary. Animals are clever. Pick stuff up really fast.'

'That's right, missus,' Luther agreed. 'But we're the top bosses of the animal kingdom.'

'Not lion, the king of the beasts?' Lorimer asked.

'Well, maybe,' their guide conceded, starting up the vehicle once more.

Soon they were approaching a small village surrounded by trees, thatched mud huts and chickens scratching the dry ground – exactly what had been depicted in their travel brochure. Three women sat cross-legged on a mat, their hands full of great bunches of white crocheted material. Behind them on a wooden fence hung several finished tablecloths; evidently this was a regular stopping-off point for tourists. The women's delighted smiles at the sight of the newcomers made Maggie vow to buy something to take home.

'You can see them later, ladies,' Luther said, as if anticipating this, then jumped down and offered a hand to Dinah then Maggie. 'But first we keep an appointment with the fortune teller.'

'Don't believe a thing you're told. It's all done for the tourists,' Dinah whispered to Maggie with a giggle.

The two women were led around to a larger hut at the rear of the village shaded by a huge msasa tree. Maggie glanced behind, but her husband was looking skywards, his binoculars trained on some bird or other she'd no doubt hear about later.

Luther stopped at the entrance and motioned for the women to wait. He laid a finger across his mouth, indicating a need for respectful silence. This was a solemn affair, or at least part of a well-rehearsed act, Maggie thought.

It was a few minutes later that they heard a voice from within, speaking a language quite unknown to them.

Luther bowed his head and replied in the same tongue.

'Follow me, ladies,' he said and beckoned them into the darkened interior.

There, sitting cross-legged on the beaten earth floor was a wizened elderly man whose thin arms and legs belied the sharp intelligent expression in his rheumy old eyes.

Maggie stood very still, wondering what it was about this man that, as he smiled directly at her, gave such a feeling of serenity.

He did not speak yet but raised a hand to motion that she should come closer.

'Sit opposite, missus,' Luther told her. 'Keep the mat between you. We will wait out there,' he added, leading the Australian woman away from the hut.

Maggie noticed the brightly woven batik mat on the floor and wondered what significance it had, if any. Surely this was just so much mumbo-jumbo? A way to earn a few dollars from unsuspecting tourists. And yet, as she placed herself onto the ground and crossed her legs, she had a peculiar sense that the shaman's eyes were seeing more than simply another white woman to be fleeced.

It was as if he was deliberately trying to mesmerise her, she thought as their eyes met and he kept his gaze upon her. A trick used by professional hypnotists and conjurers, no doubt. It was not until she heard the rattle that Maggie saw the small bag that the medicine man held in his hand.

Of course, she remembered. The throwing of the bones. That was the ancient source of divination and healing that had been practised amongst rural tribesmen for generations.

She looked down as the bones scattered onto the mat between them. Animal vertebrae, she saw, yellowed with age.

'You come to me today to find out your future,' the man said slowly, still gazing into Maggie's face. It was, she realised, a statement not a question, and she was unsure how to reply or indeed if any reply was expected.

'Your children are all gone,' he said simply, raising a hand and letting it fall again in a sweeping gesture as if he were casting the past away.

Maggie nodded, suddenly too full to speak. She had lost so many babies, born before their time. And tiny David, who had breathed for such a short while after she had given birth to him. How could this old man know something so personal as this?

He waved his fingers above the bones as if divining something from the pattern they had made on the mat, eyes now intent on seeing what they might tell him.

It was all part of the act, Maggie tried to persuade herself. Nothing to cause that shiver down her spine.

Then she heard a small cry, like an animal in pain, and the old fellow was rocking back and forth, his face contorted.

'What is it?' she asked, grasping his gnarled fingers. 'Are you all right?'

The hand that she caught suddenly had hers in a vice-like grip.

'Be careful, good lady,' he implored, opening his eyes and staring into Maggie's face. 'There is danger coming.' His voice had become rather more anglicised than at first, as if he had dropped the act and was genuinely trying to communicate something to her.

That was a generic sort of warning, Maggie thought with a small qualm of disappointment.

Or was it?

'I see a man with a red scarf around his throat,' he added, looking back at the scattered bones. 'Do not trust him, nor the big man in khaki. He means you harm.'

'How do you know this?' Maggie whispered, leaning forward.

'The bones tell me many things, good lady,' he said. Then he looked down and, gathering them up in his gnarled old hand he let them tumble back into the little cloth bag.

A shadow passed the doorway and stopped. Someone was outside, listening. Was it the guide, Luther?

At once the old man's demeanour shifted and he spoke more loudly. 'You should live a long and happy life,' he said, in the sing-song voice of a carnival fortune teller picking up their act once more.

Voices sounded outside the hut and the shadow vanished.

There was a moment of silence then he looked up into Maggie's eyes once more and she saw an expression of sorrow as if the old man regretted having to use these throw-away words. He laid down the bag of bones and grasped her hand again.

'You and your husband need to take great care,' he warned her, his voice serious. 'These people mean mischief.'

He looked past Maggie Lorimer then, his eyes vague as though he were in a sort of trance.

'I see flames, and death. They are searching for a man,' he whispered in an unearthly tone. 'But they must not find him. You may have to walk the paths of darkness. But you will find the light.'

Then, with a sigh, he bowed his head, a gesture that indicated their session was finished.

Maggie scrambled to her feet, hands already dipping into her shoulder bag to find the dollars.

The old man sat up straight and shook his head.

'No charge, good lady,' he insisted. 'The truth is free. Now go and enjoy our beautiful country.'

The smile he gave her was beatific, as if he were some ancient seer who had been divining these bones for centuries within this modest dwelling.

Maggie felt a peculiar sense of lightness as she rose, then inclined her head in a courteous gesture. Something had happened here that defied explanation. And yet, despite the man's anxious warnings, it felt as if some burden had been lifted.

Once outside the sun hit her full in the face, making Maggie realise that she had been shivering. Even as she basked in the warmth of the day, she wished she were still sitting opposite that old man, asking him more questions about the strange things he had said. And the reference to searching for a man? Did he mean Daniel? Yet, how could he have known . . . ?

As she watched the Australian woman enter the hut, Maggie was certain that Dinah would be regaled with stock phrases and empty promises, the sort of flattery meant to deceive rather than the earnest words she had been given. Later, she might pretend to have no faith in this tourist attraction but would ponder all that he had told her and keep it close to her heart.

'Lorimer,' the desk clerk repeated. 'Lorimer, yes, of course. Husband and wife from Scotland. They are with Wildlife Tours,' he added. 'Luther Khumalo is their guide. You know him, I think?'

Sibanda nodded. The safari guide was known in and around the same places in Harare that cops and their touts frequented and Sibanda had used the man for information before now. So, he was leading this particular party, was he? Well, that suited him just fine. Having a man like that already in his pocket might be better than having to dispatch an idiot like Reuben Mahlangu out into the bush.

As he walked out from Meikles Hotel, Nelson Sibanda whistled softly through his gold-capped teeth. Things were looking up, he thought. And if he found that these Lorimers were here to cause any trouble, well, a little accident out in the wilds was not unknown for strangers, was it? Once he had found the whereabouts of Janette Kohi and disposed of her, he might rest a little more easily, his orders from Wilson Ncube carried out to the letter.

Sibanda was feeling that sense of well-being following his

rather sumptuous lunch, and a new-found confidence that his agreement with the old politician would finally put his worries to rest.

Daniel Kohi had threatened to stir up a proper hornet's nest, but he was gone, the fire a deadly warning to any who chose to challenge the ways that Nelson Sibanda conducted himself within the Zimbabwean Republic Police. Things would continue as they always had, those too feeble to protest being subjugated by those who enjoyed power over them. Wasn't it just the same as out in the bush, after all? Natural selection kept the strongest safe and the weakest as their prey.

Lorimer, he mused, rolling the word around his tongue. An unusual name. William and Margaret Lorimer. He would look them up on the internet once he was back in his office, just to see a little more, and have the advantage of knowing about these Scottish visitors whilst they were completely oblivious to his very existence.

Sibanda turned away from the kerbside where the line of taxis idled, awaiting their next fares. So, these Lorimers had been driven out to Janette Kohi's home, had they? That might explain why Reuben had found the place locked up. They'd been snooping around, looking for the woman but had failed to find her. And his trawl of the internet had given him quite a lot of information about the couple who had hired a car to take them out of the city. He was a cop back in Glasgow, pretty senior by all accounts, with a reputation for getting to the bottom of difficult cases.

Well, it was up to him now to stop William Lorimer from

solving the mystery of where Kohi's mother was hidden. His mouth curved in a cruel smile. It was a simple matter to issue an order to eliminate them.

And Nelson Sibanda was a man accustomed to having his orders obeyed.

CHAPTER TWENTY-FIVE

'You'll walk it,' Daniel told her, slinging an arm around Molly's shoulder as they sat on the settee.

'Oh, I don't know,' Molly replied. 'It might lead to lots of changes.'

'You wouldn't want to leave the MIT,' Daniel murmured.

'No. I'd rather stay a DS than have to be transferred to a divisional headquarters.'

'Even if it was Cathcart,' Daniel teased.

'*Especially* if it was Cathcart,' she laughed, giving his arm a playful slap.

'But Detective Inspector Newton, it has a certain ring to it, don't you think?' Daniel sighed. His colleague in CID, Diana Miller, had recently been promoted to DI and there was a feeling that female officers were having a well-deserved moment of success, particularly as Police Scotland was currently being led by Chief Constable Caroline Flint.

Molly cuddled closer. Daniel had lost so much, and it was a credit to his sense of purpose that he was starting his career in the police all over again. Once he too had risen to the rank of inspector in his homeland, but it would be years before he might attain the same pay grade here. It didn't seem fair that she was on the brink of promotion. But then, a lot in his life had been unfair to Daniel Kohi.

'Tell me about your mum,' Molly said, deliberately changing the subject.

'Mum? What do you want to know?'

Molly didn't answer but laid her head on his shoulder as if expecting Daniel to tell her a story.

'She's quite small,' Daniel began, a smile hovering on his lips. 'Likes to wear lots of orange clothes. That's her favourite colour,' he added, giving Molly's arm a squeeze. 'Always smiling. A happy sort of lady. Her Christian faith means so much to her, of course.'

'Were you brought up to go to church?'

Daniel looked down for a moment. 'I was. And I loved being part of our church family. It was those good people who helped me to come here,' he said softly.

'I'm glad they did,' Molly whispered in his ear.

'Well, I'm always going to be grateful to them,' Daniel continued. 'But I struggle to believe in a God who allowed . . . ' He stopped with a sigh.

'But, your mum,' Molly said, turning the conversation once more. 'Tell me more about her.'

'Okay, well she was born in a wee village outside Harare and went to college in the city. Trained as a teacher and taught in primary school till she retired a few years back.'

'A life in two sentences!' Molly teased. 'There must be more to her than that?'

'She met my dad in the city. He was still working for a mining company and had to spend a lot of time away from home, but it was a happy marriage. I remember Mum singing a lot back then. She has a lovely voice. Sings in the church choir.'

'And your dad?'

'He died in an accident at work when I was seven. Mum brought me up pretty much on her own after that. She has a brother in Botswana, but we hardly ever saw him when I was growing up. As I said, she was a primary teacher till her retiral. By that time, I was in the police force and earning enough to help her out.'

'She's quite old?'

Daniel paused for a moment to think. 'I think she was thirty-five when I was born,' he said. 'So . . . goodness, my mum will be seventy this year!'

'That's a big one,' Molly murmured. 'What did you used to do for birthdays?'

Daniel took a deep breath before continuing. 'Always had friends round on the day,' he answered. 'Friends and family. The house would be full of noise and Mum would be in and out of the kitchen, giving orders to whoever was tending the barbecue. We didn't have much,' he sighed, 'the economy went to pieces long before I was born but there was always food in our house. Mum's wages and then mine, till I got married . . . ' He tailed off, a shadow crossing his face, and Molly felt ashamed that her question had led back to the tragedy that had robbed Daniel of his homeland.

'She sounds a great lady,' she said.

Daniel smiled once more. 'Oh, Janette Kohi is well

thought of by all her old pupils. Best teacher in Zimbabwe, they called her.' He chuckled.

'And she loves to cook?'

'Oh my, how she loves to cook!' Daniel nodded. 'I can imagine her and Netta swapping recipes for their favourite cakes.' His face fell again and he turned to Molly with a frown.

'I'm worried about her, Molly. Why haven't we heard anything since before Christmas? My mum is a strong woman, independent, but ... ' he bit his lip and sighed, 'it isn't like her not to write to Netta. And after all, she should have had our new address by now.'

'Don't worry,' Molly soothed. 'I think the mail strike resulted in a huge backlog of letters. One of our officers only got her Christmas card from a sister in Canada this week.'

Daniel gave her a squeeze. 'I suppose so,' he conceded, but the worry lines between his large dark eyes remained even as he spoke.

CHAPTER TWENTY-SIX

'Lions!'

Lorimer raised the field glasses and stared into the distance. At first all he could see was a dusty pale brown hillock. Then, as their vehicle drew closer, he made out the shape of two huge beasts.

'Young ones,' Luther told them. 'Brother and sister. We've been aware of them since they were cubs.'

'Neither of them has a mane. How can you tell which is which?' Maggie asked.

'The male is a bit bigger,' their guide replied. 'He's still to develop his mane and will stay with his pride till he's about three years old.'

'What happens then?'

Luther shrugged. 'He has to find a mate initially and then begin his own small pride.' He shot the Scottish couple a grin. 'What you might call a clan.'

'And the female stays with all the other females and young ones,' Maggie suggested.

'Unless she is killed or taken by another male. She'll remain in the same pride with a dominant adult male until he is challenged by a younger and stronger male, having cubs and raising them. She also does most of the hunting and teaches her cubs how to creep up on prey.'

'What do they hunt?'

Luther turned and pointed into the distance at a herd of grazing animals.

'Wildebeest are a favourite, but they'll often stalk different types of antelope; kudu, impala or perhaps a duiker, one of our smallest antelope. Or zebra, perhaps. You'll see skins for sale back in the city if you want to take some home for rugs,' he added carelessly.

Maggie shuddered. She'd read about the big game hunters and their obsession with bagging game for trophies, the sable antelope, Zimbabwe's national symbol, particularly prized.

'No thanks,' she replied crisply. 'I'd rather see them alive and wandering freely here.'

'And we surely will, madam. Perhaps not many little duiker, they are very shy. But now that pair are on the move, and we will see where they go.'

Fortune, their driver, proceeded slowly, the four tourists watching the lions' every move. Slowly but surely the great beasts lumbered closer and closer until they were walking parallel with the Land Rover.

At last, they reached a copse of trees and stopped just as the first of the pair lay down a little way off.

'That other lion does not seem at all bothered by the proximity of humans,' Lorimer whispered to their guide.

Luther smiled and shook his head. 'They've fed already. We keep in touch with other guides and rangers who let us know such details.' He chuckled. 'If we did not, then you might be their dinner for today.'

Lorimer gazed at the huge, tawny animal as it stretched up one massive paw towards the trunk of the nearest tree, its claws tearing scratch marks down the bark. It reminded him for all the world of their own cat, Chancer, using one of the trees in their garden as a scratching post. For a moment he felt as if he were seeing aspects of their pet's behaviour, magnified in this magnificent creature.

And then it turned and looked straight at him.

Golden eyes stared unblinkingly, forcing the tall man to stare right back.

How many villains had his blue gaze stared down over the years? And yet, this wild animal had him ensnared in its powerful eyes.

He looked away first, impossible to maintain eye contact.

It was humbling. A sign that the lion knew its place in the order of things, a place above the frail humans seated in the safari vehicle.

At last, the great beast yawned, showing fangs that might tear a man limb from limb. Then, rising to his feet, he ambled off into the bush, soon hidden amongst the dusty brown terrain.

He turned to see the others in the Land Rover, their eyes following the pair's progress, Maggie now lowering her digital camera, having captured the scene on film.

Later they would surely relive these moments here and back home, chattering about how wonderful it had been, but

Lorimer knew that this encounter, and the silent awe he had felt, would stay with him for a lifetime.

'Only thing to make your son feel better is what landed him in jail in the first place.'

Wilson Ncube clenched his jaw – knowing that these words were right didn't help. Not in the least.

'My boy wants Kohi to hurt,' he seethed. 'Idiot ought to have killed him when he had the chance.'

'But he didn't,' Sibanda pointed out, his tone infuriatingly reasonable to Ncube's ears.

'So, what happens now?'

'Oh, we're making progress. And I'll let you know the moment we get hold of his mother.' Sibanda's voice dropped to a whispered chuckle. 'And Kohi will hurt then, all right, once he finds out what we have in mind for her.'

'Don't let it be quick,' Ncube snarled softly. 'Make sure she suffers. And I want to know every last detail, understand? My boy deserves that at least.'

'How could he know about Daniel?' Lorimer asked her.

They were sitting a little way from the campfire, most of the other guests having retired to their tree houses for the night, flames still flickering brightly enough to give off some heat.

Above them the stars were wheeling across the night sky, tiny diamonds strewn on a jeweller's case of black velvet.

'I don't know,' Maggie sighed. 'But he was different when he talked to me about personal things. He sounded more like an educated man who was used to speaking English, not a tribal chief.'

'How would you know how a tribal chief speaks?' Lorimer laughed, teasing her.

'You're right. Maybe they just drive out here from the city to fleece the tourists,' she said glumly. 'And, if he did, then that might explain how he knew about Daniel?'

Lorimer frowned, trying to work out a logical explanation.

'But? I sense a but coming on.'

'But he was specific in his warnings,' Maggie said slowly. 'And he refused to take any money!' she exclaimed. 'I forgot to tell you that bit.'

'How would anybody know that we were connected to Daniel?' he asked, staring into the distance as though directing his question to the universe. 'That old blind lady?'

'It can only be her,' Maggie agreed. 'And she seemed very, very cautious. Would she know that Daniel is alive? Could she have some connection to the medicine man?'

'Shhh!' Lorimer laid a finger across his lips. 'Don't utter a single word, not even out here.'

He turned his head, looking in all directions as if afraid someone might be lurking within earshot.

'We'll make more enquiries when we go back to Harare,' he told her. 'It's important that we find out where Mrs Kohi has gone. Meantime, let's enjoy these unique experiences.'

'Kariba the day after tomorrow.' Maggie sighed longingly, rising to her feet. 'Come on, time we went to rendezvous with that bushbaby.'

Lorimer linked hands with her as they strolled away from the fire and headed into the shadows by the huge trees. The cicadas and tree frogs were beating out their nightly rhythm, a texture to this country that was becoming familiar now. He waited at the foot of their ladder, letting Maggie go first.

A crack behind him made Lorimer swirl around.

Had someone stepped on a twig, their presence concealed by the dark?

But then he noticed that the fire was shooting sparks up into the air. No, he decided, just a log falling into the dying embers.

It was not until Lorimer had climbed into the tree house and pulled the curtain over that the figure stepped out of the darkness, staring upward, a thoughtful look on his face.

CHAPTER TWENTY-SEVEN

Bush telegraph worked in different ways, Richard Mlambo thought as he trained his binoculars on the line of sage green Land Rovers heading across the plain. He grinned at the thought of so many foreigners gawping at the herds of elephant that they would find at the watering hole half a mile ahead. Hidden by a line of trees on the hilltop, Richard had a perfect view of the safari wagons as well as the elephants splashing in the shallows. It was still early morning and very cold, the sun yet to crest the horizon. Morning and evening were the best times to see a variety of wildlife at these particular spots. With the arrival of dusk came the dangers of possible predators and Richard Mlambo was always prepared with a fully loaded rifle.

He had been listening to the different conversations on the tour guides' radios, their talk back and forth mainly about the whereabouts of big game. Richard had apprehended elephant poachers in this way before, unscrupulous men tipping them off for whatever money they could get.

More than once it had been a member of the Zimbabwean Republic Police Force that had operated a nice little sideline in alerting big game hunters to the best places to shoot whatever they wanted. And, of course, the illicit trade in elephant ivory had gone on for decades, rangers like himself fighting a battle against those who threatened the very existence of the Zimbabwean herds.

His brow wrinkled in a frown under his bush hat as he heard a crackle then a hum. That was a different sound and Richard was always on the alert for someone hacking into the wavelengths.

'This is leader N for Luther,' he heard a faint voice say. *'Do you read me?'*

That was a voice he had hoped never to hear again, Richard Mlambo told himself, gritting his teeth as he trained his gaze on the tourist Land Rover. So, Sibanda was in touch with young Luther, was he? That didn't bode well. And why was he trying to speak to the guide at this time in the morning when he must know that Luther was currently escorting a tour group?

Richard had come across Luther several times, a small, shifty-looking fellow who had given off bad vibes, as his son, Campbell, would have put it. There was something a bit too ingratiating in his manner, Richard had thought on the occasions when he had to deal with him. Plus, the fact that he seemed to enjoy a rather too cosy relationship with the cops.

Ever since the deaths of Daniel Kohi's family, Richard had been wary of anyone in uniform apart from his fellow rangers. Daniel had been a good man, a good neighbour to his father, Joseph, and worth the secrecy that they had maintained about his demise in that fire.

'Can't talk now,' he heard Luther reply. *'Call me later. Over.'*

Then there was radio silence.

The ranger sat and stared at the small fleet of Land Rovers until they disappeared into the trees. He was well trained in tracking, his senses attuned to every little change in the terrain that he saw and in the sounds that he heard.

And what he had heard in the safari guide's voice made Richard Mlambo very curious.

Fear.

Luther slipped the radio into the pocket in front of him, glancing sideways to make sure Fortune, the driver seated beside him, had not heard anything.

It was one thing to send him messages via the new boys who tended the Treetop camp but quite another to contact him on his radio. Whatever Nelson Sibanda wanted, it could only be bad news.

'Lookee here!' he cried out as the waterhole came into view. 'Lucky morning for you, my dear visitors!' He turned and grinned at the two couples behind him, the Scottish Lorimers and the Aussies, Fred and Dinah. It was easier now with just these four tourists, the others having been driven to the airfield and on to the pleasures of Victoria Falls.

'See! We have hippos right there. Elephant, too. And over there, giraffes, zebra and wildebeest! We wait quietly here now till sunrise and watch them.'

*

Lorimer noticed how Maggie shivered, pulling her collar higher around her neck. Daniel had warned them to take plenty of layers as the pre-dawn mornings here could be so chilly. He had also advised keeping a scarf in their pockets to cover their mouths at dusk, when so many flying insects batted across their faces in an open-topped vehicle. Lorimer slung an arm around her, pulling her close, his hand rubbing her arm.

She smiled up into his eyes, grateful for the cuddle, then extricated herself gently from his grasp, nodding towards the view ahead. He handed her the glasses, letting her have first sight.

The animals did not seem to be worried overmuch by the proximity of the vehicle, though it was a decent distance away, in good enough range for those with binoculars to see the details around the waterhole. Luther and the driver sat crouched low in their seats, protected from the cold air by the windscreen, the tourists seated higher up behind them. He watched their guide as he fiddled with his two-way radio, but Lorimer was unable to make out any voices giving information. He smiled. This was out in the middle of the bush and yet the modern technology of Luther's earpieces allowed no sound to disturb the tranquillity of the moment. There would be no mobile phone signal for miles, he guessed, and so these devices were of the utmost importance for guides like theirs.

The man's face changed for a moment and Lorimer was curious to know just what was being related to their guide. A storm brewing, perhaps? Unlikely, the skies above them clearing into a pearl-pink dawn that presaged yet another fine day. There was a problem of some sort, Lorimer thought, their guide's jaw clenching suddenly.

And then he turned and stared right at Lorimer, flinching for an instant as their eyes met, then quickly turning back.

What was that all about? he wondered.

'Here. Have a look at this,' Maggie whispered, handing him the field glasses.

Lorimer took them from her and raised them to his own eyes, the guide's strange reaction not entirely forgotten but tucked away for future consideration. The panorama before him was illuminated by the first rays of sunrise, another of those moments that would stay in his memory for ever, Lorimer thought, a sudden pang in his soul. Observing these animals in their natural habitat, the small sounds around them, dawn clearing away the last grey clouds from the sky, was so different from all the wildlife programmes he had watched on television. Here it was for real.

There was danger all around these creatures compelled to come here and slake their thirst, so many of them alert to predators that might take this opportunity to hunt and kill. And yet they came, heads down to drink their fill before the scorching heat of the day dehydrated them. What lay ahead for such animals as the wildebeest or zebra was anybody's guess, since lions might stalk them for hours, seeking one that was old or weak or even one that strayed that little bit further from the herd. Nature was cruel in that respect, he thought. No mercy given when it was a matter of survival for them all.

How different were humans? Lorimer had come across a few that he considered cruel, brutal even, in the way they dispatched their victims. But most deaths happened in the heat of a drunken moment rather than as a carefully planned execution such as they might well witness here should one of the larger mammals make a kill.

As he watched a giraffe bending its long legs in order to reach the water, Lorimer marvelled at the sight of them all, aware of how privileged they were at this moment.

'Your turn,' he whispered to Maggie, handing over the glasses with a soft smile.

Richard lifted his glasses once more, but the distance was too great to make out any details of the people in the back of the nearest vehicle.

The ranger frowned. It might not be part of his remit, but something told him that he ought to keep his communications channels open a bit more often. Nelson Sibanda was bad news for Richard and his family. The man had created a sense of fear within the Zimbabwean police force ever since the dreadful night of that fire. Everyone suspected who had been behind the atrocity that had burned that mother and son to death, Inspector Kohi also presumed to have perished with them. Though there were some who had kept Daniel's secret safe, until now.

The beating his father, Joseph, had received at the hands of those cops could only have come from Sibanda, Richard thought. But trying to prove it would only lead to more trouble for his family.

Out here in the bush, protecting the country's precious herds of elephant and other endangered species wasn't just a job that he loved but one that he needed to support his father and Campbell, back home. Some days Richard yearned to be there on the stoep with them both, telling his bush tales. But right now, his curiosity was aroused sufficiently for him to find out exactly what sort of hold the police chief had over one of the tour guides. He had called himself 'leader N', as if he wanted some sort of anonymity. But it also suggested that Luther would know who that was. N for Nelson. Nelson Sibanda, the corrupt senior officer said to be in line as the next chief of police, the start of whose meteoric rise had coincided with the arson attack on the Kohi home.

The sun had risen now, and Richard laid aside his binoculars, lest glints from them be perceived by anyone looking in his direction. And, though the heat was shimmering above the grasses, the ranger shivered where he stood, watching and wondering.

CHAPTER TWENTY-EIGHT

'DI Miller wants to see you,' DS Knight told Daniel as he entered the building.

'Now?'

'Soon as. Better get up there,' his tutor told him.

He took the stairs two at a time then paused outside the DI's office door, straightening his jacket before knocking.

'Kohi, come in. Take a seat,' the woman commanded, fixing her eyes on him. 'I want to talk to you again about McGregor. And why he took the time and trouble to visit your flat and deliver those letters.'

Daniel waited, frowning. Hadn't he offered an explanation at their earlier meeting, suggesting that a man inclined to get into fights also had a decent side to his nature?

'What if . . . ' Miller continued to stare at Daniel, 'he came to find Mrs Gordon?'

'Netta?' Daniel smiled and shook his head. 'What on earth would any ex-con want with my flatmate?'

'You know her husband was inside?' Miller continued.

'Yes, she mentioned that one time,' Daniel admitted. 'I think she was glad to be a widow, to tell you the truth. It must have been a hard life bringing up kids when your husband was in and out of jail.'

'She never told you what he'd been inside for?' Miller asked.

'No.' Daniel clenched his teeth, suddenly ill at ease to hear what this detective was going to reveal.

'Armed robbery,' she told him. 'And there were rumours at the time that one of the getaway drivers was a young guy by the name of Billy McGregor.'

'Oh.' Daniel's mouth fell open in astonishment.

'So, even though he wasn't caught after the raid, we don't think it was a coincidence that he turned up on Mrs Gordon's doorstep.'

Daniel could hear voices from the lounge when he arrived home, but it was just Netta watching her favourite soap opera on television, the sound changing to familiar jingles from repeated adverts. He stood for a moment behind her armchair, wondering what to say. The old lady had settled into their flat share so well and it seemed suddenly cruel to rake up the life she'd left in Maryhill. Netta had also been harassed by unscrupulous moneylenders, something Daniel had managed to stop. She'd had surgery just a few months ago, too, and was recovering so well . . . how could he disturb her peace of mind by asking all sorts of questions?

The programme returned after the intermission and Netta watched as a family get-together in a pub turned into a loud and angry brawl.

'Go get him!' the old lady told a character who was

brandishing a chair leg. Netta's own arm was raised as if to encourage the ongoing fight scene.

Yes, it was fiction, Daniel mused. But Netta's reaction was that of a feisty, battle-hardened woman, not a shrinking violet. He came and sat beside her, tucking a cushion behind his head as they watched the events continue until a dramatic drumroll and crashing discordant music signalled the end of the episode.

As the credits rolled swiftly down the screen, Netta turned to Daniel with a grin.

'Ye're home,' she said, patting his arm. 'Have ye had anything for your tea?'

'I'm fine,' Daniel lied. He had anticipated a microwave dinner after his shift but that could wait.

'There's a pot of soup on the stove,' Netta said, making to rise.

'It's okay. I'll get it later,' Daniel told her. 'Sit down, Netta, dear. There's something I need to tell you.'

The old lady listened as Daniel began. 'Do you remember that man who came to bring your airmail letters from Mum?'

'Aye, dead nice of him, so it was. Sorry I wasnae here tae see him and say thanks,' Netta said.

'His name was Billy McGregor,' Daniel said slowly. 'Does that name ring any bells?'

Netta shook her head.

'I didn't tell you this, Netta, but he died not long after his visit here.'

'Aw, no, the poor laddie! Whit wis it? An accident? A' that ice on the streets . . . '

'No, Netta, this was not an accident,' Daniel said carefully, making sure he held his friend's gaze. 'Billy McGregor was murdered.'

'Oh!' Her hands flew across her mouth in a horror far more real than any emotion that had flitted across Netta Gordon's face during the television programme.

'I'm not really part of the murder investigation,' Daniel continued, 'but I've been asked about the man since he had visited us here.'

'How did the polis know he wis here?' Netta demanded.

Daniel hesitated for a moment, reluctant to divulge any details of McGregor's post-mortem examination. But then, he was sitting beside a woman who had suffered far worse experiences.

'I was at his post-mortem,' Daniel began. 'My tutor wanted me to have more experience and so I saw him . . . '

'Aye, go on,' Netta frowned.

'His face was badly disfigured by the attack, but I noticed a tattoo on his neck that helped to identify him,' Daniel explained.

'And you telt the polis about him comin' here?'

'Aye, I did. I thought it was just a strange coincidence but . . . '

'But what?'

'Turns out that the victim of this murder, the man who'd brought your letters here, had a criminal record.'

'A bad yin, then?'

'He didn't seem so when he was here,' Daniel had to admit.

'But whit's that goat tae dae wi' us?'

'This Billy McGregor . . . you're sure you haven't heard of him before?'

'No,' Netta said, then her brow creased in a frown as she stared at Daniel. 'There's something else, isn't there?'

'Billy McGregor did some jobs for your late husband. Things that got him imprisoned,' Daniel said softly.

The old lady's face blanched as she sank back against the cushions, her mouth open in shock.

'The police are wondering if McGregor knew who you were and had come here deliberately to see you. They think the letters were just a way of making contact.'

Netta's head was spinning, sounds from the television a blur of noise. She gazed at Daniel and could see that he was speaking as his lips were moving but all she heard was a buzzing in her head. Her fingers reached out to clutch Daniel's hand and then he was gone, leaving her sitting there on her own, her chest tight with sudden pain.

She closed her eyes and thought about what he had told her, memories that had been banished for years flooding back into her brain, things she had never wanted Daniel to discover.

'Here, drink this, Netta,' she heard Daniel's voice telling her.

Slowly she sat up, his arm guiding her gently until she felt the room slow down once more.

'Tea,' he insisted, holding the china mug to her lips. 'You need to take it, dear,' she heard him say, his tone gentle and persuasive.

The old lady choked on the first sips then, blinking away tears, she grabbed the mug and took a few swallows of the hot tea.

'Ye've pit sugar in it!' she grumbled. 'Ye know ah dinna take sugar in ma tea.'

'It's good for shock,' Daniel said firmly. 'Remember who won the trophy for first aid at Tulliallan.' He laughed.

'Oh, laddie, you're too good tae me, so ye are,' Netta whispered, tears running down her pale cheeks.

'Nothing to what you've been to me, Netta, dear,' Daniel reminded her. Their friendship had blossomed into something very special from that first kind offer of a cup of tea from the elderly lady to the Zimbabwean refugee two doors along from her small flat on the eleventh floor.

'When you're ready, we need to talk about your late husband,' Daniel told her.

'Aye,' Netta nodded. 'I c'n see that, right enough.'

She took the last of the sweet tea and made a face as she laid down the cup. 'Well, where do I begin?'

Daniel sat quietly as his friend began to relate her story. He had made a second pot of tea and now they were sitting side by side on the settee, the television switched off.

'I should never have married him,' Netta said with a rueful laugh. 'Mammy telt me often enough that Mickey Gordon would come tae a sticky end. But then, she wanted me to marry a nice Irish fellow called Peter McCredie. Ah, where wid ah be the day if I'd listened tae her?'

'Was he a good guy, this Peter McCredie?'

'He wis all right,' Netta conceded. 'Dead strait-laced like his maw and paw. Not much get up and go about him. A steady sort, which is what Mammy liked, I suppose. But he couldnae dance like Mickey Gordon.' She nodded, a wisp of a smile on her lips. 'Mickey wid fair whirl ye aroon the flair in a Strip the Willow.'

'A what?'

'It's a Scottish country dance,' Netta explained. 'Get your Molly ta take ye tae a ceilidh some time, an' teach ye a few dances. The Gay Gordons is aye a favourite at weddings. We had that at ours.' She smiled, her eyes misty with nostalgia.

'So, you married him.'

'And lived tae regret it,' Netta said at once. 'Mammy wis right. He was a nae user. Had a job on the railways, or so he telt us, but that wis jist a front for his other activities.'

'Care to enlighten me?' Daniel suggested.

'Ach, nae point in goin' ower them all. Jist tae say he wis done several times for robbery with violence. Hit a bloke with a crowbar one time and nearly killed the fellow. Got fifteen years for that one.'

'But he stayed with you when he was released, didn't he?' Daniel asked, remembering the good coat that Netta had given him from the back of her closet. A coat that had belonged to her late husband.

'Aye, more fool me.' She sighed. 'He never laid a hand on me, mind. Or the bairns. And, when he wis at hame he'd aye have money for groceries and wee treats. I never asked where it came from,' she said, hanging her head. 'Mibbe I jist didn't want tae know.'

'Did you know about his criminal activities, though?'

Netta heaved another sigh. 'I never asked questions,' she admitted. 'Think I was too feart tae know the answers. See, when he wis inside we were as poor as church mice. It wis that hard trying tae feed and clothe the weans. I had a few cleaning jobs that helped but at the end of every week there never seemed to be anything left in my purse.'

'Didn't you qualify for benefits?'

Netta snorted. 'Me? Go wi' ma hand out tae the social? Nae fear. I had mair pride than that, son.'

Daniel did not reply. He'd seen enough in this city to realise that there were the wee fly men who milked the system for everything they could get, in direct contrast to the pensioners living on their own, an ingrained sense of pride or humility stopping them asking for the help to which they were entitled. All too often these old folk ended up in care homes, far more comfortable in their later years, the council giving them a warm room, plenty to eat and the companionship that they may have lacked previously, alone in a cold tenement.

'So, you never met Billy McGregor?'

Netta shook her head. 'Mickey didn't bring any of that lot home. He knew how I felt about it, even though I didn't say much. A wee look when he came in at three in the morning might have given him a clue,' she added with a sniff.

Daniel tried to imagine the life his friend had endured. What use would it have been to upbraid a hardened criminal like Gordon when his presence at least put food on the table for her family? Yet he could envisage Netta throwing a scowl her husband's way. She was a strong woman, he reminded himself. And it may have taken more courage to stay with the man than to flee with her children.

'Was there anything you can think of that might have made McGregor want to link up with you, Netta? Any reason why he tried to see you?'

Netta was silent for a few moments, her brow furrowed in thought.

'There was something that Mickey said, in the hospital. Just afore he passed away,' Netta said slowly. 'He said I'd be looked after. That he'd made arrangements.'

'What do you think he meant?'

She shrugged. 'I don't know. Life insurance policies were all paid up. The man frae the Pru came roon every month and it wasnae a lot tae pay out. Enough tae get him buried,' she said. 'I thought that wis what he meant.'

Daniel was silent as he pondered her words. Criminals like Gordon could accumulate plenty of stolen goods, or even cash. Had Netta's husband squirrelled some of that away, dying before he could tell her where it was hidden?'

'His last spell inside,' he began. 'Can you remember what that was for?'

'Bashed that pair van driver, the one I telt ye aboot,' she said.

'Driver of . . . what, exactly?'

'Oh, that company, the wan that takes cash tae the different places. Canna mind its name. Ye'll find it on yer computer mair than likely, son. It wis a' ower the papers at the time.'

'And did any of your husband's gang get away with the money?'

'Oh, aye. But it wis never found. That wis a mystery, see. Mickey and four o' the others got time wance the polis caught them but wan o' them managed tae scarper. No names were ever written in the papers and none o' the rest of them wid ever say who it was. Honour amang thieves,' she added with a bitter laugh.

'Was Billy McGregor one of those imprisoned for this particular robbery?'

'Naw. Never heard his name till you told me he'd brought yer mammy's letters. Why?'

Daniel wondered about the man who had escaped justice on that particular night. He'd look up the archives back at the station and read through transcripts of the trials to see if he could find out more. What if McGregor thought that Netta knew the whereabouts of that missing money? Had Gordon expected his wife to be looked after by his fellow criminals?

'Your husband never said anything about stashing a lot of money somewhere? Gave you any idea where it might be found?'

Netta roared with laughter. 'Son, see oor auld place in Maryhill? D'ye think ah'd hiv been there a' these years if there had been any money coming my way? Naw, I'd hiv bought a wee bungalow ower in Giffnock, near Rouken Glen. I aye loved that part of the city,' she sighed. 'It's jist a coincidence, Daniel, that's all.'

But Daniel Kohi was not so certain. A man had been brutally murdered shortly after his visit to this flat. He felt a shiver down his spine. Perhaps, on his release from prison, McGregor had hoped that Mickey Gordon's widow might have some idea where the missing money had been hidden. And he may not have been the only one with that idea. Whoever had killed the man might well turn their attention to the elderly lady sitting by his side.

CHAPTER TWENTY-NINE

Molly twirled a strand of blonde hair round her finger. She really ought to make time to have it cut but Daniel had told her recently how much he liked it. A small smile flitted across her face. No man had ever influenced DS Newton before to the extent that the handsome Daniel had. Oh, she'd had several youthful flings, times when she had even fancied herself a little in love, but there was something different about Daniel Kohi. He made her feel . . . how could she describe it? Safe? Yes, that was part of it, certainly, but being with him felt as though she had come home at last after a very long journey. For a woman whose job had involved danger at various times, and who was not afraid to confront different types of criminals, it surprised Molly that she was so happy to enjoy this feeling of contentment since she and Daniel had finally come together.

The office was quieter than usual today; outside could be heard the rhythmical ebb and flow noise of traffic skimming over wet ground. Molly was clearing up some paperwork that had piled up in the wake of a drugs haul out in the west coast. *The wild west*, one of the detective constables had quipped and she had laughed along with the rest of them. But reading over some of the case notes was sobering, statistics showing the numbers of deaths from drugs and the quantities that had been shipped into their country. She gazed over at the steamed-up window, daylight mere blocks of milky brightness as the rainclouds blotted out the sun. Thousands of miles away her boss was no doubt enjoying higher temperatures, swapping his winter coat for a T-shirt and shorts.

It was odd not seeing the rangy figure of Lorimer pacing along the corridor, one hand trying to smooth his dark hair (that always seemed to need a cut, like her own), the other holding a mobile to his ear as he answered calls that kept coming from all parts of Scotland. Life in the MIT demanded a readiness to drop everything at a moment's notice and head off to wherever a major crime had taken place. With Lorimer away on holiday and no imminent jobs away from the city of Glasgow, Molly felt as if the office were holding its breath, awaiting the next call to action, but today was different, just the drudgery of paperwork, a dull necessity till going home time. Her smile broadened, anticipating her next visit to Nithsdale Drive once she was off duty for the night.

As the man in the red jacket turned into Nithsdale Drive, he took a sideways step, an automatic reflex on spotting a cop car coming in his direction, the female officer at the wheel chatting to the woman sitting beside her.

That was . . . his head turned to watch their departure, clenching and unclenching his fists. If he was not mistaken, that was the Gordon woman. But why on earth was she being taken away by the police? He hesitated, gazing until the car had disappeared around a corner. Then, straightening his shoulders, he made his way towards the door from where, moments ago, the pair had emerged.

It was strange being driven in a police car, Netta thought, as she looked out at the streets passing them by. She had walked from the flat up to Pollokshaws Road plenty of times now but had never yet ventured further south. The traffic slowed them down and so she was able to see when they took a left then accelerated for a bit before turning into Victoria Road. Daniel had talked about taking her to Queen's Park once springtime came and, as the car approached a junction, she saw a mass of tall bare-branched trees flanking the park then, straight ahead, a wide gateway with a path beyond. She'd like to walk up that path right now, Netta decided, clenching her fists.

'All right, Mrs Gordon?' the young female police officer beside her asked.

'Aye, hen. Is it much further to go?'

'No, we'll be there in a few minutes,' the woman replied, patting the back of Netta's hand.

Nice lassie, Netta thought, turning to see the edge of the park sweeping past.

'That's the auld Victoria Infirmary, isn't it?' she asked, pointing to a drab, forbidding building towering above them, its curved balconies like arms folded across the bosoms of a scowling maiden aunt.

But then her eye was caught by a different sight.

'Oh, it's still there!' she gasped, looking at the green and white striped edifice shaped like a pagoda. 'The auld Battlefield Rest!'

'It's well named,' the woman said. 'It's a lovely restaurant. My boyfriend took me there for my birthday.'

Netta stared at the iconic place in wonder. Memories drifted back of standing beneath the clock waiting for a bus in the rain, alone in the dark, wondering if she had enough money for her fare. Mickey Gordon had left her there that time with nothing but empty promises and a bitter feeling that she had made a dreadful mistake in letting him back into her life.

The Battlefield Rest that Netta remembered had changed, though. Its colours were brighter, the balustrade and tiny flagpoles all clean and white, fancy planters with miniature trees lining the entrance. Everything had changed since she had been a young woman, she mused as the car set off once more.

Netta looked up at the corners of the tenement buildings as they passed, Battlefield giving way to Prospecthill Road then finally swinging into Aikenhead Road where she saw the familiar blue chequered sign, indicating their destination.

'This is it, Mrs Gordon,' the police officer said in a cheery voice. 'We'll get you in for a nice cup of tea and a chat with Detective Inspector Miller. Okay?'

Netta sniffed in reply. She didn't have much choice after all, did she, but a cuppa would go down fine, her throat already dry with nerves. The young officer dropped her at the front entrance then drove off to park around the back of the building, leaving Netta to climb the stairs. She paused for a moment, looking up at the towering floodlights of the national football stadium, then stepped up towards the main doors of the police office.

Inside it was like every police station Netta Gordon had ever seen during her married life, the big, polished counter separating the public from whatever went on beyond that glass partition. Posters were pinned to the wall intended to advise the public about crime prevention. One colourful sign caught her eye. WE ARE ALL THE SAME, it read, in different colours. She browsed the huge pinboard more closely, noticing a few more anti-racist messages. ONE SCOTLAND. MANY CULTURES, another proclaimed. How had Daniel reacted to seeing that day after day in this place? she wondered. It wasn't something he had ever mentioned. Netta regarded the rest of the crime prevention posters with a cynical eye; some folk sat on these benches would have more notion about crime than the officers in their smart uniforms. It was the weans that needed telling, she'd said to Daniel the day before his visit to talk to primary schoolchildren.

'Hello, can I help you?' A woman with long fair hair stood on the far side of the reception counter, smiling at Netta.

Before she had time to reply, a side door opened and the constable who had driven her here emerged.

'Mrs Gordon to see DI Miller,' the girl called out. 'Come this way,' she told Netta who followed her obediently through the door.

Soon Netta was being led up a flight of steps, a whiff of something lemon lingering in the air. Well, the cleaners kept this place nice, she thought approvingly, looking at sparkling windows devoid of cobwebs.

'In here, please,' her escort said, making Netta turn with a start. 'Here' turned out to be a small cosy room with a few easy chairs, a potted spider plant on the window sill and a circular table set in the middle. A box of paper hankies was open and Netta wondered, correctly as it happened, if this was a place where bad news was perhaps relayed to relatives.

'Tea with milk and sugar?'

'Oh, jist milk, lass,' Netta replied, gathering her good coat under her as she sat gingerly on the edge of a chair.

'Be right back,' the officer told her and then disappeared, leaving the door ajar.

Netta stood up again and walked towards the door, listening to the murmur of voices from the next room. There was a peal of laughter then a phone began to ring, and the noise subsided. Maybe there were several polis in there having a meeting, she thought, scurrying back to her seat as she heard footsteps approaching along the corridor.

A woman with short-cropped hair wearing a beige trouser suit entered, a lanyard swinging around her neck. Smart but not fussy, was Netta's first impression of the newcomer. Sharp, too, the way she was looking down at her with those bright eyes. No eyeshadow. In fact, no make-up at all, Netta saw. Not like Daniel's Molly who always had a nice lip gloss and whose perfume reminded her of old rose gardens.

'Hello. Mrs Gordon? I'm Detective Inspector Miller,' the woman said, introducing herself and then sitting down opposite Netta. 'Thanks for coming in today and sorry for the inconvenience. Oh, here's our tea.' She turned as the lassie from the cop car came in with a tray with two plain mugs and a plate of foil-wrapped biscuits. 'Thanks, Jennifer.'

'Daniel said you'd been in hospital recently,' Miller began.

'Aye,' Netta said. 'Took a bad turn on the stairs in our old place. Ended up in the hospital fur a while. But ah'm all right now.'

'Good.' Miller nodded, picking up the plate and offering the biscuits to the old lady.

'Ta,' Netta said, taking one and unwrapping its green foil. A chocolate mint biscuit, one of her favourites, she realised, sitting back a little more comfortably into the chair.

'Sorry to rake over a past that you might not like to revisit,' Miller said, in a cheerful tone that held absolutely no trace of contrition. 'But we'd like to establish whether there was any link between McGregor's visit to your current address and his association with your late husband.'

'Cannae see that, myself,' Netta replied. 'Hadnae heard o' any o' those toerags fur years. Hadnae seen ony wan o' them since his funeral,' she added. 'So why wid he come lookin' fur me?'

Miller gave her a smile that did not reach those intelligent eyes.

'That's just the sort of question we've been asking ourselves, too, Mrs Gordon. First of all, how would a new tenant up in the Maryhill flats know where to find you?'

'Well,' Netta frowned, 'wid the factor no' huv telt him?'

'Apparently not,' Miller replied crisply. 'Our officers asked the staff at the factor's office, and it is their policy not to divulge the addresses of previous tenants unless those tenants have specifically instructed them.'

Netta frowned. 'Daniel says that's whit the man telt him. That the factor gave out my address.'

'Well, either he was lying or the factor didn't tell our officers the truth.'

'The post office knew tae redirect oor mail. An' I think I meant tae arrange that, though ah'm not sae sure now,' she admitted. 'But, if ah did, why's that no' happened, eh?' Netta cocked her head to one side and gave the detective a keen look.

'We've also been investigating why those letters were overlooked,' Miller told her. 'Unfortunately, all that seems to have happened is a big backlog of mail before and after Christmas that was not dealt with as speedily or efficiently as it ought to have been. Computer problems added to that... you'll have heard about the serious problem with hackers, no?' she asked as Netta shook her head. 'Well, all sorts of problems arose and so quite a lot of mail that was meant to be redirected was simply delivered to the address on the outside of the letters.'

'Jist a whole load o' nonsense, as per usual,' Netta snorted. 'Wouldnae have happened back when I wis young. Nae computerised systems then, jist the local postie that everyone knew, an' we goat two deliveries a day an' all!'

DI Miller did not attempt to hide her amusement, a wide smile making the faint lines around her eyes crinkle. She looked more human, Netta thought, returning a grin of her own.

'See this fella, the wan that Daniel brought intae the hoose? Hiv ye's ony idea who killed him?'

The woman's face darkened in an instant. 'Our enquiries are ongoing, Mrs Gordon, and you being here today is part of them.'

'I see,' Netta said slowly. 'So, this man, McGregor, he knew my late husband when he wis a youth. But efter that he wis banged up?'

'Correct,' Miller said. 'PC Kohi has told us that the man asked for you by name, easy enough since it was written on three airmail letters, but how he knew you were living in the Southside of the city intrigues us since the letters were all addressed to Maryhill.'

'Me too,' Netta nodded. 'See this line o' enquiry,' she began, 'is it no' possible that it wis Daniel they were efter? Ah mean, ah'm jist an auld done wumman but he's a refugee wi' a past. Had tae flit frae some richt bad yins where he came from.'

Miller screwed her eyes up against a shaft of sunlight that had suddenly flooded the room with brightness. She made no reply to Netta's suggestion, however the old lady thought that she could discern a pensive expression on the younger woman's face. Had she planted the notion that had been rattling around in her old brain ever since Daniel had mentioned their visit from a stranger? The Lorimers would be visiting Janette while they were on their holidays, see if she'd sent any more letters. Netta had written to her penfriend, telling her about their change of address, after all. She took a deep breath, an idea taking shape in her mind.

'What is it?' Miller leaned forward. 'You look as if you've remembered something.'

'Aye, but it's naethin tae dae wi' the late Mr Gordon,' Netta said, her jaw firming. 'It's mibbe a simple enough thing but ye'll nae be able tae check if it's right or no'.'

'What do you mean?'

'What if . . . ' She paused for a moment or two, trying to put her thoughts in order. 'What if Daniel's maw disnae know our new address? See that place ower there? Fu' o' corruption so it is. Wouldnae pit it past onyone tae nick ma letters and read them. That's why Janette and me write tae yin anither in a sorta code. So naebody kens that Daniel is ower here.'

Miller nodded slowly. 'If that is the case, then we would have to see if McGregor had any links to Zimbabwe,' she replied.

The meeting at Cathcart police station had continued, Netta being grilled for almost another hour about her relationship with her late husband. By the time she was escorted to the main entrance by DI Miller and handed into the back of a police car, Netta felt grubby and tired. Too many things had been picked over, things that she'd prefer to forget. The life she'd had to live when he'd been in jail had been scrutinised, her three cleaning jobs a juggling act to keep clothes on her kids' backs and food on the table. Yes, Netta had to admit, there were times that her children might have been neglected, left for hours at home while she scrubbed floors and polished glasses late at night in a public house. And yes, perhaps that was why her eldest had run off to sea at an early age, the middle boy setting his mind to travel to Perth. (The one on the other side of the planet, no' the one in Scotland, she'd told Miller.) Only the youngest had remained in Glasgow, married to a lassie from Cumbernauld, two snotty kids who turned up once a year to feast on her Christmas pudding and take away their gifts. They only wanted money nowadays, she'd grumbled to the DI. And even when she did see them, they never spoke, just stared at their phones the whole time.

She hadn't seen them since moving in with Daniel, however. Excuses had been made this last Christmas, but Netta knew fine that it was because she now lived with a police officer that her son was disinclined to visit. Terence was always that bit vague about how he earned his living and Netta had stopped asking years ago, too afraid to learn that her youngest had followed in the footsteps of his reprobate father. She'd shared none of this with the detective, but the past seemed to have swept up on her like a high tide covering a previously calm seashore.

CHAPTER THIRTY

Richard Mlambo frowned then lowered his field glasses. Rumours of poachers in this area had thankfully come to nothing but at that moment he was more concerned about the safety of the visitors to his country than the big game he was protecting.

It was past time for them to make for the next waterhole then set up camp for the night, the light beginning to fade. Richard had watched the progress of Luther's vehicle for most of that day, listening out for further calls from the city. But so far Sibanda had not poisoned the airways with his voice. The ranger's mouth twisted, remembering how badly hurt his father had been. It had taken him three days to return from where he had been, on the southern border of the country, and reach the hospital in Harare.

Sibanda's men, someone had whispered to him that night as they had gathered on the stoep, listening to the night noises under a canopy of stars. It had been Daniel's attempt to pin a corruption charge on the man that had led to the slaughter of his wife and child and his exile from home. And now Sibanda was stirring up trouble once more. What had young Luther got involved in? he wondered. He'd known the fellow for some years, remembered him from Sunday school when Richard had taught the boys. Campbell had just been a toddler then, his mother still alive. Richard sighed, a longing for the days when he and his neighbours had lived peaceably together. Yes, times were hard, money always tight, the government doing little or nothing to ease the burden on ordinary people. But they pulled together while men like Sibanda lined their pockets at the expense of others.

A noise made him look up at the same time as a kudu, whose sensitive ears had also heard the sound. The antelope strolled away but Mlambo picked up his earphones and listened intently.

He knew that voice at once. And then, *'Yes, I'm here, boss,'* he heard Luther say, an eagerness in his tone that caused his heart to plummet.

'I want you to do something for me, Luther,' Sibanda said smoothly. *'And you'll be well rewarded for it, never fear.'*

'Sure thing, boss,' Luther replied.

'The couple called Lorimer . . . '

There was a pause and Richard tensed.

'Boss?' Luther said at last. *'You still there?'*

There was a crackle on the line and Richard wondered if the connection had been lost. But then he heard some whispered words that chilled his blood.

'Don't bring them back. Understand?'

*

'What a beautiful sunset!' Maggie whispered as they sat in the back of the Land Rover, Dinah and Fred behind them. Their driver, Fortune, slowed right down then cut the engine, turning his head to grin at his passengers.

The sky had darkened to a shade of blue that defied description. Perhaps there might be a word for it in Gaelic, Maggie thought – someone had told her once that there were fourteen words for blue. Now the colour seemed to be changing even as she gazed, the horizon a line of fire, daylight's last embers burning most brightly; it was the blue of sapphires one moment, then the colour of ink. The last creatures were mere outlines on the edge of the waterhole, large shapes of elephant and water buffalo.

Nobody uttered a word, all staring at the sight, the first stars sparking high above them.

It was something she would always remember; that moment when heaven and earth seemed to wheel together, creating a feeling of how small she was.

And then, as if at a signal, the night noises began, their driver switched on his engine and the moment was over.

Maggie felt her husband's fingers entwine with hers and squeeze softly, a gesture that told her more than any words. He had experienced it, too, that moment of revelation. Even their young guide, usually so talkative, appeared to have lapsed into silence after turning as if to check that his four passengers were still there.

The journey to their new camp was over a bumpy track and as they gathered speed, Maggie could feel the heat disappear from the day. Her mouth was covered with a gauzy scarf, and she pulled down her bush hat to prevent the night-flying insects becoming tangled in her hair. With each lurch along the potholed road, they seemed to be travelling further and further into the dark, the only lights those from the Land Rover illuminating the way ahead.

Then, as they turned a corner, she could see a faint line of smoke beyond the trees, a sign that the camp was not too far off.

'Here we are!' Dinah exclaimed cheerfully behind her as they drove towards a clearing, in the middle of which a fire pit had been lit. They could see several tents a little further away, the entire camp surrounded by a high wire fence for protection. A wooden gate swung open as the vehicle slowed down, a couple of lads pulling it back to let them in.

'Oh, I'm so glad we did that!' Dinah said as she stepped down after Maggie, Lorimer reaching out a hand to help them both. 'Now for some dinner!'

'Smells good,' Fred agreed. 'I'm ready for my tucker after that.'

Maggie turned to their young guide, Luther. Fortune, their driver, was covering the vehicle with a tarpaulin, to prevent the night dews from soaking the seats.

'Thank you,' she told him. 'That was very special.'

The guide looked at her as if startled for a moment.

'It's not every day we get to see a sunset like that. And I really appreciate how much you've been doing for us all,' she said warmly.

'It's okay, missus.' He shrugged, lowering his eyes as if embarrassed.

'I mean it,' Maggie continued. 'We'll never forget this safari. Or you,' she added with a grin.

‘Come on,’ she heard Bill say. ‘They’ve been waiting for us to come back to serve us dinner.’ She saw him turn to the guide and their driver. ‘You two deserve a good meal too,’ he chuckled. ‘That was a long day for you both.’

Luther watched as the Australians and the Scottish couple headed for the braai. The smell of roasted meats was making him hungry, but he would wait until the guests had filled their plates before he and Fortune took their places in the queue.

Sibanda’s words echoed in his brain as he watched the lady walk hand in hand with her tall husband. She was a nice lady, a good person, and did not deserve to be harmed.

He shivered as he thought about what sorts of things might happen to him and his family if he were to defy the man whom he had called ‘boss’.

Suddenly his appetite disappeared, and Luther slunk away from the warmth of the fire into the shadows, head hung low.

CHAPTER THIRTY-ONE

Netta Gordon was worried. The dead man, Billy McGregor, had stirred up some memories from her past that she had thought were gone for ever. Standing by the graveside of her late husband, Netta recalled the murmured condolences of so many men that she'd never wanted to see that day nor ever again. They had all worn their smartest suits and black ties as befitted the occasion, one of them, Kenny Lafferty, holding a large umbrella over Netta's head as she watched the coffin being lowered into the damp earth. She had shed no tears for her husband, staring blankly at the scene around her, feeling her sleeve being tugged at last by one of her boys, indicating that it was time to go to the purvey. Sandwiches and sausage rolls, fancy cakes courtesy of the local hostelry and as much drink as they could pour down their throats, she thought now with a spark of anger. There had been very little left once she'd paid the undertaker and the publican.

They had all drifted away eventually, with their wives and girlfriends, assurances to *see her all right* and *call whenever you need us*, hollow promises not one of them had ever fulfilled. Where were they now? Still in the nick, perhaps, or six feet under like her husband and Lafferty, Netta supposed. A right bad lot. All she wanted after that day was to shut the door behind her and get on with life. And so she had, working to pay her rent in a variety of cleaning jobs then managing on her widow's pension somehow when that became too hard.

Billy McGregor. She savoured his name for a moment, trying to recapture the scene in the pub that rainy afternoon. He'd have been just a lad back then. Maybe he'd been with one of the older men and she'd never given him a glance, supposing him to be someone's son. Lafferty's boy might even have been there, too. Netta shook her head. No, she simply could not remember Billy McGregor. What had brought him to her old flat in Maryhill? That wasn't a coincidence. Someone had arranged it deliberately. But who? And how could she find out?

That DI Miller didn't seem like the one to ask, even though she was in charge of the man's murder investigation. Besides, Netta was done with police stations, even if that was where her dear friend worked these days. She gazed at the hail battering the kitchen window, its insistent drumming note like something unearthly trying to get in, making her shiver. No, she wanted to talk to a different detective, one who might take the time to ferret out whatever was behind the man who'd been living up on the eleventh floor and had somehow got a hold of the missing airmail letters.

Molly would be here tonight after work and Daniel was on day shift. She'd make them apple crumble and custard for pudding, Netta decided, a smile on her face. The fruit bowl on the kitchen table was full and the pears had ripened nicely now. She'd slice one and add it in as a wee treat. That would go down well after the rich beef stew that was simmering gently on the hob.

'Netta, you spoil me!' Molly declared with a sigh, laying down her spoon after scraping the last vestige of crumble from her plate. 'One day you'll need to teach me how you make that!'

'Och, it's nae bother, lass. Jist rub the flour and butter between your fingers then add the sugar.'

'But that crunchy topping! And the spicy taste?'

Netta laughed. 'A wee bit o' demerara on top an' some cinnamon. Or nutmeg. Ginger if it's a rhubarb crumble, mind. And never stint oan the butter.'

'I'll be as fat as a puggy,' Molly protested, patting her stomach.

Daniel laughed. 'I doubt that very much,' he told her affectionately. 'Slim woman like you!'

'Well, you aye seem tae work it off, the times ye go tae that gym,' Netta observed.

'Police officers are meant to keep a certain standard of fitness,' Molly said, grinning. 'You never know when you might have to sprint after a villain.'

'Speaking of villains,' Netta began, 'I wondered if I could have a wee word with you?'

Daniel caught his old friend's glance and rose from the table. 'I'll clear these up and make a pot of tea. You ladies retire to the lounge,' he said with a mock bow.

*

Molly sat opposite the older lady, intrigued by her sudden change of mood. Something was bothering Netta Gordon, she thought, watching her fidgeting with her watch strap. She was sitting on the edge of her armchair, too, not sinking back, relaxed after that delicious meal as she normally did.

'What is it, Netta?' Molly asked quietly. 'Has anybody been following you again? You know we told you that should have been reported.'

'No, no, it's nothing like that.' Netta shook her head. 'It's jist . . . ' She paused, frowning, but not yet meeting Molly's enquiring gaze.

'Thon bloke that got killed. McGregor,' she began. 'I cannae fathom how he goat intae ma auld flat in the first place.' She looked up and blinked. 'No' sure if ah'm supposed tae ask ye, Molly, but ye're sich a clever yin, goin' fur yer inspector's exam an' all that. And bein' in the MIT ye c'n find oot sich a lot o' things . . . '

Molly smiled at the old lady and leaned forward, taking her hand. 'Oh, Netta, I'm sure DI Miller has all that sort of thing taken care of already.'

'Really?' Netta looked doubtful. 'How c'n ye be sure?'

Molly gave a deep sigh. It was not perhaps the done thing for an officer like her to interfere in another person's case, but if it put the old lady's mind at rest?

'Let me see what I can do,' she said. 'No promises, mind. And it is best to keep Daniel out of the loop. If he mentioned this to a senior officer, it might not go down well on his probationary record. Might be seen as criticism.'

Netta let go of her hand and settled back in her chair.

'Thanks, lass. It would put my mind at rest, so it would.' She looked up as the door to the living room opened and Daniel came in with a tea tray.

'Ah, thanks, son. Ah see ye've pit oot ma ginger biscuits,' she remarked as he put the laden tray onto the coffee table. 'New recipe off the telly,' she told Molly. 'That nice Nigella wumman. Hope ye like them.'

If DI Miller was surprised to see an officer from the MIT she did not show it.

'Well, well, Molly Newton.' She grinned. 'It's a while since our paths crossed.'

'Must be five years at least,' Molly agreed, sitting down opposite the other woman in the staff canteen.

'You look different,' Miller observed. 'Being in the MIT suits you.'

'I looked different for almost every job I did back then.' Molly laughed, remembering the times they had been undercover, Miller finally deciding that CID was her preferred career route. 'I hear you're married,' she added, glancing at Miller's wedding band.

'Aye, and she's not a cop either.' Miller smiled. 'Keeps me sane not having to talk shop after work.' She gave Molly a quizzical glance. 'What brings you over here to Aikenhead Road? Something big brewing?'

'Not really,' Molly said. 'I'm doing a favour for a friend. Mrs Gordon, PC Kohi's flatmate.'

Miller's eyebrows rose. 'I interviewed her recently,' she said. 'Was there something else she wanted to tell me?'

Molly shook her head. 'No, she's just a bit worried.

Wonders how McGregor got the lease for her old flat. Do we know anything about that yet?'

Miller scratched the back of her neck for a moment. 'Actually, that line of enquiry didn't amount to much. Seems he was eligible for a flat there after he'd been released. There are a few asylum seekers up in the Maryhill flats, as you know, and his probation officer had found that there was a vacant one in that block after Mrs Gordon moved away.' She shrugged. 'It was just the timing of it. Pure coincidence, nothing more.'

Molly wanted to ask, *Are you sure?* but something held her back.

'Any further forward with the case?' she asked instead.

Miller pursed her lips and gave her head a slight shake. 'Nothing. Nobody saw a thing, forensics found hee-haw and we've been trawling through the man's associates before, after and during his prison sentences. None of his cellmates have reason to cause us any concern.'

'No luck, then?'

Miller shook her head more vigorously. 'Sometimes it's a wee bit of luck that we need, isn't it? I'd hoped Mrs Gordon might have come up with something, but she told me she didn't remember the man at all. And I believed her.' Miller frowned and gazed into Molly's eyes.

'Is there something she isn't telling us, do you think?'

'I don't think so,' Molly replied. 'But I do think whoever sent McGregor with those letters hasn't finished with her.' She went on to describe the incident with the attempted mugging. 'And I for one don't think that is just another coincidence,' she finished.

'But she didn't report that, so what do you expect us to do?' Miller asked.

'I don't know,' Molly sighed. 'There's something odd about that entire episode. It's as if McGregor was seeking out Mrs Gordon but I'm beginning to wonder if that was the intention all along.'

'Oh?' Miller seemed surprised.

'What if he'd not been sent to see Netta Gordon at all?'

'You mean . . . '

Molly nodded. 'What if it was Daniel they really wanted to find?'

CHAPTER THIRTY-TWO

Luther thrust the rifle deep into its place in the door of the Land Rover. He'd been trained, like all the other guides, in using the weapon, warned repeatedly not to fire unless it was absolutely necessary. And, so far, there had been no need to discharge it. Baboons would race off, screeching, if he as much as pointed it at them, behaviour that made him laugh every time it happened. He would need a real reason to fire this gun, Luther had protested, and not the one that had been suggested to him. An accident, Sibanda had said with a lightness in his voice that belied the deadly act. Say you were firing at a leopard or a jackal, he'd said. But it wasn't as easy as that and nothing Luther could say would convince him otherwise.

He was being asked to take the lives of two innocent human beings. Two guests who were supposed to be in his care, not subjected to murder, he had argued. And, if it all went wrong, what then? He'd end up in jail, for years and years, never seeing these wide open stretches again.

But had he made a mistake, refusing to carry out the man's orders? Luther shuddered, imagining the carnage that could follow. That policeman, Kohi, had been warned not to blow the whistle and look what had happened to him. And his family.

The smell of roasting meats from the evening's barbecue wafted across to the guide, reminding him of the consequences of disobedience.

It was the noise of someone retching that made Lorimer turn and walk towards the treeline.

He saw a dark shape bent over before recognising the young man being very sick a few yards from the catering tent.

'Luther! Hey, are you all right?' He was by the guide's side in moments, holding on to his shoulders as he tried to straighten up.

'You . . . ?' Luther looked up at him with bloodshot eyes and burst into tears, gulping in air as though he were having a fit.

'Hey, hey, come on, lad, let's get you cleaned up,' Lorimer said, one arm supporting him as he headed towards the standpipe nearby. 'Hope that isn't something you ate, or we'll all come down with it.' He tried to lighten the situation. He'd handled many a drunken person back in his uniformed days, cajoling them into a semblance of sobriety, even as he'd looked carefully for any injuries. But there was no smell of alcohol here. Just the stench of vomit and a buzzing sound as night insects descended upon it

'Go away! Don't talk to me,' Luther gasped, arms around his stomach as if he were in some degree of pain.

'Can't do that, lad. Not when you've been so sick.'

Lorimer turned on the tap and let the water soak into his pocket handkerchief. Then he leaned towards Luther to wipe his forehead.

'No! Please, don't touch me!' the young man cried, cringing away from Lorimer, an expression in his eyes that the policeman knew only too well. Fear.

'Luther, what's wrong? Why are you so upset?'

The young man sank to his knees, covering his face with his hands, moaning incoherently.

'Go away. Please, just go,' he gulped. 'You and Mrs Lorimer. Go!'

'What's wrong, son?' Lorimer frowned, hunkering down beside the younger man. 'Is this something to do with that shaman?'

There was a long silence broken only by muffled sobs and the repetitive chirping of cicadas and crickets, part of the texture of the gathering dusk.

'I can't do it, boss, I can't do it,' Luther whispered at last, letting himself slump to the ground as if in defeat.

'What is it, Luther? You can tell me,' Lorimer said quietly. 'I can sort things out for you, I'm sure.'

In the darkness the lad's eyes were ghastly white as he turned to stare at him.

'How can you help me? You're just a visitor, here one day, gone the next,' he whined.

Lorimer sighed. He'd been so reluctant to give away his identity, hoping that this trip would be as far from his job back home as possible.

'Back home in Scotland I'm a senior police officer, Luther,' he said quietly. 'And there are probably quite a few things I can do to help you.'

The lad's mouth fell open, a certain sign of shock.

'No!' he cried, backing away from Lorimer, eyes wide with terror.

Then, to Lorimer's dismay, Luther scrabbled away on all fours and disappeared into the night.

The detective stood up, squeezing the handkerchief in his fist, his frown deepening.

The fellow was clearly terrified of something. And mentioning that he was a police officer seemed to have made whatever strange situation Luther was in far more difficult.

Best not to pursue this, Lorimer decided, tucking the sodden hanky into one of his safari jacket's pockets. The firelight flickered ahead, and he could hear muted laughter as Maggie and their new Australian friends socialised around the fire pit. Whatever sort of trouble their guide was in, he had just made it worse, he thought.

Behind him a shadow flitted past, unseen. If he had turned at that moment, Lorimer might have seen a small movement, glimpsed the moonlight shining on something metallic. But his mind was already on the next part of their holiday.

Tomorrow would bring a new dawn and a different leg of their adventure, a flight across Lake Kariba and the promise of even more wildlife. Luther would remain with the other guests, the Lorimers having elected to do this excursion on their own. A guide from the Kariba area would be waiting to greet them, Luther no doubt glad to see these visitors depart.

What had caused their young guide's upset would have to

remain a mystery, something that irked the tall man walking out of the darkness towards the halo of brightness.

You're on holiday, Lorimer reminded himself, the familiar feeling that something was far from right nagging at him. *Not your business*, a small voice insisted, as he took a seat by the fire.

The unseen shadow lingered for a moment as it watched Lorimer's progress then, as swiftly and silently as it had come, disappeared into the trees.

'Okay?' Maggie smiled up at him and he nodded, his fingers touching hers, unwilling to spoil the pleasant atmosphere. He'd pretend that nothing had happened, keep the young man's strange behaviour to himself.

Lorimer's resolve to forget the incident was sincere.

But events in the darkness were soon to cancel out his good intentions.

CHAPTER THIRTY-THREE

'What's that!'

Maggie sat up in bed, grabbing her husband's hand.

Lorimer was awake instantly, the noise reverberating in the still night air.

A scene of carnage came to his mind like the fragments of a nightmare, where a father had slaughtered his child then turned the gun on himself. There was no mistaking that sound.

'Gunshot,' he murmured, already out of bed, scrabbling to find his shoes.

Seeing Maggie pulling a shirt on over her nightdress, he caught her hand.

'Stay here. Don't venture out of the tent,' he commanded, picking up the torch beside their bed. 'Whatever's going on, you're safer here.'

He bent to kiss her then unzipped the flap and ducked low, looking in the direction of the gunshot.

He could hear other feet running across the hardened ground, voices calling in their native tongue.

Lorimer followed the beams of torchlight, careful to aim his own in their wake. It was too dark to be certain of where they were heading, trees and bushes on either side of a narrow path obscuring the view. Was he still within the confines of the camp? Lorimer wondered, risking a quick glance upward into the canopy of trees. Or was he being watched by some nocturnal creatures from their position high above? Snakes, slithering down towards him, a leopard, intent on hunting?

The night was split by a high-pitched scream then other voices began to cry out, one of them a long wail of despair that chilled his blood. That meant only one thing, no matter the language.

He broke into a run, following the torchlight, heedless of any danger that might be lurking in the undergrowth.

There, in a small clearing in the forest was a huddle of figures. They looked up as Lorimer approached and he recognised three of the catering boys and Fortune, their driver, standing over something lying on the ground.

Not something. Some*one*.

As Lorimer directed his torch beam onto the fallen man, Fortune caught his arm.

'It's Luther,' he said, pulling him away. 'It m-must have been a-an accident, boss,' the man stammered, aiming his torch downward to reveal the slick pool of blood under the guide's head.

Lorimer shook him off and knelt down beside the guide's body, feeling for a pulse. Luther's skin was still warm but there was no sign of life.

'He's dead,' he confirmed, looking up at the four men staring down at him. 'I heard a gunshot.' He stood up and looked at each of their stricken faces in turn. 'But where is the gun?'

'I picked it up, boss,' one of the boys said nervously. 'See, there it is, against that tree.'

Lorimer swept his torch around to look. Sure enough, the rifle that Luther had kept inside the Land Rover door was propped carefully a short distance away.

'Who else touched it?' Lorimer asked.

'No one, boss, just me,' the lad told him. 'Luther must have set it off by accident.'

'Maybe he was cleaning it and it went off,' one of the others suggested.

'Out here? Away from the camp in the middle of the night?' Lorimer's tone was heavy with scepticism.

'M-must have been s-stalking something,' the driver muttered. 'Only e-explan-ation.'

Lorimer bent down once more to examine the body of their guide. He had fallen forwards, his head turned to one side. He let the torchlight play across the man's tight curls then stopped when he found the entry wound.

Looking up, he saw them all watching him.

'This was no accident,' he told them. 'Somebody shot Luther in the back of the head.'

All of them turned as other heavy footsteps approached.

'What happened?'

Lorimer turned, relieved to see Fred, the elderly Australian, lumbering towards them.

'Oh, my God!'

The older man put his hand across his mouth, eyes fixed on the body lying on the ground. 'Oh, no . . . '

'Luther's been shot,' Lorimer told him, gently. 'Someone needs to secure this place and call the police.'

'No po-lice out here, boss,' Fortune explained. 'Just the rangers. N-nearest police office is at Kariba.'

'Well, we need to do everything we can to protect Luther's body,' Lorimer decided. 'The smell of his blood might attract all sorts of predators to this place.'

The other men looked at Lorimer, his height and the authority in his voice commanding instant respect.

'We can carry him to his tent,' one of the boys suggested. 'Poor Luther . . . ' he added, shaking his head.

Lorimer felt as though every one of his senses was heightened in the darkness, each nuance of speech instantly examined. Had one of these lads shot the guide? Or was it the nervous, stammering driver? Up until now he had never heard Fortune utter a single word, his response to anything a simple grin, his stammer doubtless making him the silent member of their safari party.

This was no ordinary crime scene, Lorimer realised, with no facilities to take prints or specimens for forensic analysis. He was in a wild place with no authority and only the good will of these men to assist him.

And the possibility that one of them might be a killer.

'Okay, let's get him back to the camp,' he sighed.

'I can help,' Fred told them.

'No, boss, we'll do it,' Fortune insisted. 'You don't want b-blood on your hands.'

The two visitors watched as the young men carefully

lifted Luther's body and carried him slowly back along the pathway. Lorimer pulled out the scarf that was in his jacket pocket and stepped back into the shadows.

'Where are you going, man?' Fred called out anxiously. Then, as he caught sight of Lorimer's hand around the rifle, the scarf between the weapon and his fingers, his mouth fell open in astonishment.

In one swift movement, Lorimer cracked open the gun and let the remaining bullets tumble into his palm. Then, pocketing them, he closed it once more, still using the scarf to prevent his own fingerprints from contaminating the weapon.

'Poor young man. What happened? Did he shoot himself by accident?' he whispered to Lorimer as they followed a few paces away, their torches snaking beams of light on the ground.

He did not reply at first, merely shook his head.

'This wasn't an accident, Fred. And I think the sooner we can find a ranger to take over here, the better,' he said at last.

Fred gave him a strange look. 'You sound like you know what to do,' he said at last, a light dawning in his eyes. 'You've handled things like this before, haven't you?'

Lorimer nodded. 'Aye,' he admitted. 'Sad to say, I'm all too familiar with murder victims in my particular job.'

'Not just a civil servant, then. A cop?'

Lorimer nodded but said no more, the two men walking side by side towards the camp, the figures ahead bearing their sorry burden.

*

'We need to protect his body,' Lorimer told the four men once they had laid Luther on the ground inside his tent. 'Fortune, go and bring the tarpaulin from the Land Rover. We'll wrap him in that till he can be transported away from here.'

'The p-plane can t-take him when you go to Ka-Kariba, b-boss,' their driver said.

Lorimer nodded. 'Aye, that is the best idea. Meantime, can any of you get onto the radio and alert the nearest ranger? Sooner the authorities know about this incident, the better. And I think I'll hold on to this for safe keeping,' he added, tapping the rifle. 'It's no longer loaded.' He looked at each man in turn.

There was no flicker of unease, though each of them dropped their gaze, looking away from his stare after a few moments.

'Right. Who's going to call that ranger?'

He watched as the young men shuffled their feet, still looking at the ground, no one willing to take that initiative.

'I'll do that, b-boss,' Fortune said. 'I think Richard Mlambo will b-be in this area.'

The remainder of that night was like a vigil, the men taking turns to sit in pairs outside Luther's tent, guarding the guide's body. The ranger had responded and was on his way but could not be with them for at least two hours, Fortune told Lorimer. And the plane from Kariba was not due until midday. Till then, Lorimer must remain watchful, hoping that with daylight he could hand over the responsibility of this situation to the ranger, Mlambo.

*

Maggie's face was ghastly white in the torch beam as they sat side by side on the low bed.

'I couldn't see any more in the dark,' Lorimer explained after breaking the dreadful news. 'There may have been footprints, who knows? But with six of us congregating there it will be impossible to take any sort of evidence from the crime scene.'

'Maybe not impossible for a ranger,' Maggie said slowly. 'Aren't they trained in bushcraft? Tracking animals is their special skill, surely?'

Lorimer nodded. 'You're right. This Mlambo guy might find something that nobody else would notice.' He looked out of the tent. There was a faint blur of light on the horizon, dawn not far off.

Clasping Maggie's hand, he gave it a squeeze, wondering what this new day might bring.

CHAPTER THIRTY-FOUR

Today was Molly's final interview out at the Police Training and Recruitment Centre in Jackton. Daniel smiled as he thought about her back in her West End flat. He'd insisted that she return there last night, despite his own desire to wrap her in his arms till morning. *You need your sleep*, he'd joked as she'd drawn him a knowing look.

He hummed a tune as he sauntered into the bathroom, a song from his boyhood that reminded Daniel of a time when he'd be sitting cross-legged with other small boys at Sunday School. What had put that old refrain into his mind? He grinned at his reflection in the bathroom mirror. A man now, grown so far from the skinny little lad who had run barefoot around the playground near his home. For a moment he paused, remembering another child, his own Johannes.

The humming ceased abruptly as he swallowed down his grief.

Molly might become a detective inspector today, he told himself. Was that the pinnacle of her ambition? Or was there still something else that the slim blonde woman wished to achieve? They had never talked about it, Daniel too afraid to ask. But was there a latent desire in Molly Newton's life to be a mother? He was too wise to assume that was every woman's aim in life, especially those who had so many other skills to offer. And yet, couldn't she have both? There were female officers who worked beside Daniel, juggling their childcare and still dedicated to the job.

He stepped into the shower and turned it on, wincing as the first spray of cold needled his skin. He'd find out later whether the woman he loved had stepped up a further rung of the ladder, though he had every confidence that she would. One day he would join her there, Daniel vowed. Meantime, PC Kohi had a job to do, too, and he'd better not be late for his shift.

Two figures slunk around the back court of the tenement, hugging themselves into the shadows. Silence was of paramount importance, though any spoken words might have been muffled by the masks around their faces. The black man had departed for work, the old woman alone in the ground-floor flat.

A dog barking in the next back court made the pair freeze. And then a distant male voice called out to the animal, a door slammed, and all was silent once more.

They could see a light from the kitchen window, several feet above the patch of drying green. Steps led up to the heavy door leading to the close, the basement beneath Netta Gordon's ground-floor flat making it hard for anyone to access the windows on this side.

'What now?' one of them whispered.

'Need to wait till she's gone,' the other replied, hopping from one foot to the other as the cold seeped through his thin-soled trainers.

Once the kitchen light had been switched off, they crouched next to the door, listening intently.

At last came the sound they had been waiting for: the thump of a ground-floor door closing and a faint rattle as a key was turned in the lock.

The tall grey-haired woman slipped her front door keys into a pocket of her shopping bag and zipped it shut. Her bus into town was due soon so she'd better get a move on if she were to make it to the stop on time. She glanced across at her neighbour's front door with a small nod of approval. An unlikely pair, the older lady and that young policeman, but they were proving to be good neighbours and Mrs Gordon kept the brasses on their front door immaculate. She hurried out of the close, letting the outer door slam as a gust of wind caught it, then stepped smartly along the road.

One of the men raised a warning finger to his lips as the other rose to his feet.

A shake of the head was all that was needed. *Wait*, the unspoken command.

Only when there were no further noises did they make their move. The slimmer of the pair was hoisted up towards the kitchen window, feet scrabbling against the sandstone wall, gloved hands grasping the window sill.

'Double glazed!' he hissed, dropping once more down onto the damp path. 'Never going to get intae it that way!'

'Need tae be the front door efter a',' his companion sighed. 'C'mon. See if we c'n jemmy it open.' He patted the bulky shape beneath his anorak.

The heavy door to the close opened with a creak, making the men cringe at the sound. Then, on silent feet, they headed towards the front door of the downstairs flat which they assumed was now vacant.

Netta paused as she headed along the corridor, her arms holding a basket full of garments to be ironed. Was that the postie? A letter at last from Janette?

She laid the ironing basket on the carpet and made for the front door just as the screech of metal sounded against wood.

In moments she was at the door, grabbing the safety chain into place before the splintering wood was forced open.

'What the . . . !' she gasped at the sight of two black-clad figures in masks and balaclavas staring at her, alarm in their eyes. 'Get to blazes, the pair of ye! I'm going tae call the polis!' Netta screamed, slamming the door shut once more and bolting it fast.

The sound of running feet and the storm door slamming shut made the old woman head for the front room and push her net curtains aside, only to see the men disappearing around the corner.

Breathing heavily, Netta walked back into the hall and stood for a moment, wondering whom to call. 999? The local cops? It was a moment of indecision that gave the two would-be thieves time to make good their escape. At last, sitting down on the chair next to the telephone table, Netta decided her best course of action was to call the lassie from Cathcart. The wee card DI Miller had given her was somewhere in her handbag, Netta remembered.

Once the call had been made, Netta might have gone next door to her neighbour for a restorative cup of tea, but she'd heard the woman going out a little earlier. She'd make one for herself, settle the nerves. But in truth, Netta Gordon was feeling a sense of outrage rather than any fear or trembling. Wee nyaffs trying to break into her home! The cheek! And yet, remembering the pair running down Nithsdale Drive, she felt that one at least had been labouring in his flight. Not a youngster, as she would later tell the detective.

DI Miller sighed. There was more to this than met the eye. Mrs Gordon had finally admitted to the attempted mugging when she'd called to report the damage to her door, two men in black trying to force their way into her flat. Was it Kohi they were after? Or was Netta Gordon some sort of target? One way or the other, the detective was certain that it had to be linked to the death of Billy McGregor.

CHAPTER THIRTY-FIVE

Richard Mlambo turned the wheel of his vehicle and felt the tyres trundling down a rutted slope. The encampment near the forest was one he knew well, herds of elephant skirting its perimeter in search of food. It had been a hideout for poachers in the off season at one time when few tourists had made the journey there, but Richard had not seen any trace of them in this part of Hwange National Park for several years. Could young Luther have been shot by a poacher? His brow furrowed as he considered the idea. Fortune had suggested that it had been an accident, but his tone had betrayed the older man's anxiety, his stammer worse than Richard remembered.

And then there was Lorimer, the man whose name had recently cropped up. A police officer in the Scottish police force, or whatever they were called. Fortune had spoken his name in a breathless whisper as if he was someone to be feared. Well, Richard Mlambo was not afraid of any white man, no matter who he was or where he had come from. He'd helped put several of them behind bars in his time, made sure that others paid hefty fines for their criminal activities out in the bush, destroying the precious game. No, whoever he was, Richard Mlambo would listen to what he had to say then send him on his way. No interference from an outsider, he told himself, swinging the truck around as the encampment came into view.

Lorimer stood up as he saw the vehicle arrive, its wheels kicking up swirls of dust. Already the sun was warming the air, the sound of crickets subdued, clouds of gnats swarming beneath the trees. The soft kurrr, kurrr of a pair of doves came from a branch above the tent where the guide's body lay. Mourning doves. Appropriate, Lorimer thought, recognising the birds' yellow eyes ringed in red.

He saw the ranger spring lightly from the truck and lope towards the high gate that separated the camp from the narrow road. There was a clang as he unfastened the bolt at the top, swung it open then pulled it shut behind him before walking towards the camp.

Lorimer stepped forward, hand outstretched.

'I'm Lorimer,' he said simply.

'Richard Mlambo,' the other man replied, scrutinising the tall police officer. At six foot four, Lorimer was easily head and shoulders above most of the Zimbabweans he had encountered, but Mlambo had sufficient height to look him straight in the eye as their hands met in greeting.

'I'm sorry to drag you all the way out here,' Lorimer apologised. 'But the lads seemed to think that was the best thing to do. Under the circumstances.'

*

Richard nodded. He warmed to this fellow's voice, its soft tones quite unlike the many visitors he had met from South Africa or the United States of America. And he had such piercing blue eyes, the likes of which he had only seen in a young male lion. The similarity made him assess the man a little more. There was something about this Lorimer that demanded respect, and that was authority, Richard decided.

'There's a plane taking my wife and me across to Kariba today and over the lake,' Lorimer told him. 'Fortune, our driver, suggested that we take Luther's body onboard.'

'He said as much to me,' Richard said. 'And the police will be waiting there to transport it to a mortuary.'

'Will you come with us?'

Richard nodded. There were things he wanted to ask this man, and where better than the privacy of a small aircraft, its engine noise masking conversation?

'Where is the body?' he asked, looking past this Scottish policeman to the cluster of tents beyond.

'Over here,' Lorimer told him, breaking into a walk and pointing to a tent where an older white man was sitting on a chair.

From what Fortune had told him over the radio, there were just two couples in residence now, the Lorimers and Australians by the name of Bridges who were being taken back to Harare later today for their flight to Johannesburg. As they approached the tent, the man rose to his feet and Lorimer introduced him.

'Fred, this is ranger Mlambo.'

'G'day,' Fred said, grasping Richard's hand. The

Australian's strong grip indicated a man who enjoyed rough outdoor work, Richard noted with approval.

'Terrible thing t'have happened,' the Australian went on sorrowfully. 'M'wife and I have been having a great time out here. Love the country, its people ... never expected somethin' like this.'

'Let me see the deceased, if I may,' Richard asked. He would be questioned later and needed to have the facts ready, though he reckoned that Lorimer might already have garnered plenty of evidence.

Inside the tent the smell was already bad, the decomposition accelerating in the heat of the morning. By the time they got this corpse aboard the light aircraft, it would be a thoroughly unpleasant journey for everyone concerned.

He hunkered down and untied the cords that held the thick tarpaulin closed, the sickly smell wafting out.

Khumalo seemed smaller in death than he remembered, his eyes closed, lips just slightly parted to show the gleam of white teeth. Someone had laid him on his side, Richard noted as he leaned to examine the head wound.

'He was face down when they found him,' Lorimer explained. 'We heard a gunshot and ran in its direction.'

'And you saw this,' Richard murmured, pointing at the matted blood on the back of the victim's head.

'I'm guessing he was shot in the back of the head as he was running away from ... whoever it was,' Lorimer offered. 'His rifle was nearby, though one of the boys had lifted it and put it aside.'

'That was the murder weapon? His own gun?' Richard frowned.

'Yes. I removed the bullets,' the Scot told him. 'There is no doubt in my mind that it was the weapon used to kill him.'

'Hm,' Richard murmured. It would all blow over, in that case, the Zimbabwean police calling it an unfortunate accident. *Guide shot by accident while handling his own rifle*, no doubt the headline of a small article inside their local paper. He was cynical enough to know their ways by now. No hint of murder would taint the tourist industry if the powers that controlled the country could help it.

'I thought you might like to see where it happened,' the tall man continued.

Richard nodded, pulling the tarpaulin around the guide's inert body once more. 'Sorry to bid you goodnight like this, Luther,' he murmured quietly then, standing up, he turned to Lorimer.

'How far is it?'

The forest clearing looked quite different in daylight, Lorimer thought, looking up as the *wurk, wurk wurk* call of a yellow-billed hornbill alerted him to a couple of birds taking flight and disappearing. Sunlight filtering through the leaves left a dappled pattern on the floor beneath, the baked earth a dull ochre, apart from one darker patch.

'There,' Lorimer said, stopping and pointing. 'If I was at home, this whole place would be secured as a crime scene. Forensic specialists would be combing every inch of the track for clues.' He turned a quizzical eye on the ranger. 'I'm told you have the sort of expertise that could pick up things that ordinary folk might not see,' he began, a smile tugging at the edges of his mouth.

Mlambo was already studying the ground, his eyes examining the foliage. What could he see? Lorimer wondered, fascinated by the sort of bushcraft he had only read about.

Mlambo took a few paces backwards, along the track, searching for something that only he would know.

'I can see that Luther ran fast along here last night,' he said at last. 'He was being pursued by someone who did not run, but rather stalked him.'

'You can see all that?' Lorimer marvelled.

Mlambo did not enlarge on what he was discovering, simply keeping his eyes to the ground, occasionally crouching down to examine a clump of leaves or what looked like grass.

'Let me go a little further,' he said at last and set off beyond the clearing, following the narrow track that led deeper into the trees, Lorimer following close behind.

At last, the ranger stopped and held up a hand to prevent Lorimer walking past him.

'His attacker came this way,' he said, almost to himself, his eyes looking all around, taking in not just the terrain but the bushes and saplings that skirted the path too.

'See?' He turned to Lorimer.

'What am I supposed to be looking at?' Lorimer answered, confused.

'There.' Mlambo pointed at the branch of a tree. 'See how it is bent a little. Now, look down,' he continued.

Then Lorimer saw it, the dusty outline of a heel print, almost invisible to anyone other than a keen-eyed ranger.

'He came this way. And in a hurry. That way leads to the river,' Mlambo explained. 'You heard no sound of an engine? A motorboat, perhaps?'

'No. Just the gunshot and then the scream when they found his body.'

Mlambo nodded. 'It may have taken him a few minutes to reach the river. And if they rowed away in a small boat, you would have heard nothing.'

'But they left the gun,' Lorimer said. 'Why do that?'

Richard Mlambo was looking at him with what Lorimer could only describe as a pitying look, something that the Scottish detective rarely saw in another man's eyes.

'To make it look like an accident.'

'In the back of his head? Come on, you're kidding me!'

Mlambo shook his head. 'You do not know the ways of our Zimbabwean police officers, my friend,' he said. 'That is what they will claim, no matter the evidence to the contrary.'

Lorimer tightened his lips, sighing softly.

'I do know something about police corruption in your beautiful country,' he admitted. 'A friend of mine had to flee Harare after a dreadful incident.'

Richard Mlambo took a step towards him, catching Lorimer's arm.

'Are you talking about Daniel?' he asked, staring into the detective's eyes. 'Daniel Kohi?'

Lorimer did not answer immediately.

Was this man a friend? Or a foe? Could he trust him?

'He was our neighbour,' Richard whispered, turning his head as if afraid his words might be overheard. 'Before the fire.'

CHAPTER THIRTY-SIX

They were sitting by the fire pit, Mlambo clutching a mug of water, Lorimer and Maggie beside him. The catering boys had made breakfast for the four remaining tourists and then taken themselves off to clear up the dishes at the standpipe behind the big tent.

'I saw Luther last night,' Lorimer began, his tone deliberately low. 'He seemed agitated to the point of being very sick. It was clear to me that something was troubling him.'

'Or some person,' Mlambo added quietly. 'I have overheard a few things on my bush radio recently.' He turned to look pointedly at Lorimer. 'Things that I was not meant to hear.'

'Go on.'

'Has Daniel ever mentioned a man named Nelson Sibanda?'

Lorimer shook his head. 'No.'

'He doesn't speak much about his life before . . . ' Maggie swallowed hard.

'I can imagine he would want to put it all behind him,'

Mlambo whispered. 'Anyway, this man, Sibanda, is a senior cop. Like you, I guess,' he said, offering Lorimer a thin smile. 'But he isn't cut from the same cloth, as you say.'

'Did Daniel work with him?' Maggie asked.

Mlambo nodded. 'He was well above Daniel's pay grade but even that could not explain how the fellow could drive a new Mercedes or afford a villa out in Richmond.'

'Sounds like corruption,' Maggie said.

'Daniel had tried to infiltrate a particular group of cops who were undermining the government's strategy on corruption. He was what you call a whistle-blower.' He leaned forward, lowering his voice. 'Or, he would have been until that fire.'

'Are you telling us that this guy Sibanda orchestrated the deaths of Daniel's wife and child?' Lorimer asked.

Mlambo nodded. 'Almost certainly. And the other morning I overheard him trying to speak to Luther.'

'On the radio?'

'Yes. Occasionally I tune in and get someone else. It happens. This time I heard Sibanda talk to Luther, but the guide told him he couldn't talk as he had his guests with him. Do you remember anything like that?'

Maggie turned to her husband. 'No, do you?'

Lorimer shook his head. 'I guess Luther was just avoiding any talk to the guy, what do you think?'

Mlambo was silent for a moment, as if considering the question. 'In this job we rarely talk to others on the radio, usually our small group of rangers, sometimes the safari tour guides. But when we do listen in, it is easy to pick up any sort of emotion in their voices. Excitement if a particular pride of lions is sighted, for example. I listened to Luther's voice that morning,' he continued. 'And he sounded very afraid.'

'Do you think this Sibanda was trying to put pressure on Luther to do something illegal? Helping poachers in return for a bribe, perhaps?'

'Yes,' Mlambo replied. 'I've never been one hundred per cent happy about that young guide, may God rest his soul.' He gave a deep sigh. 'It is wrong to speak ill of the dead, I know. But Luther Khumalo was a sly individual. One that I found difficult to trust.'

He looked from Maggie to Lorimer. 'I heard Sibanda talk to Luther later that same morning,' he added slowly. 'And I heard him tell the guide . . . ' He stopped for an instant, turning to see if anyone was within earshot. 'Sibanda appeared to be ordering him to harm you both,' he said at last.

'Us? But why?' Maggie's eyes widened.

'Well, perhaps you were not the only one who couldn't trust Luther,' Lorimer said thoughtfully. 'If he had been ordered by this man to do something bad and refused, would that be a reason for killing him?'

Mlambo sighed again. 'We may never know who exactly was behind his death,' he said. 'It will be covered up as an accident, his family sent a small amount from the tour company in recognition of his short term of service. And it will all be forgotten.'

'But can't we do something to *make* the police look into his death? I mean, it is so obviously not an accident,' Maggie protested. 'And you overheard him being asked to do something to hurt us!'

Richard Mlambo gave her a sympathetic look. 'It doesn't work like that in our country,' he told her. 'And that is something you had better know right now,' he added, giving Lorimer a meaningful look. 'An outsider like yourself, no matter how high ranking you may be, sir, will find that your cases are packed, and your return tickets dated far sooner than you would like. And that may well be preferable to whatever alternative Sibanda has in mind.'

Lorimer and Maggie exchanged worried looks then he nodded. 'Okay, so we just go about our business, pretend this never happened. Look at the wonderful animals and birds . . . ?'

Mlambo smiled and nodded. 'Yes, act as if nothing had happened. That might help.'

Maggie caught the man's grin. 'Help? Help what? Help who . . . ?'

Mlambo's smile widened. 'A certain lady who is attempting to leave our lovely country. I think you may know her name?'

'You mean Janette Kohi?'

'Shh!' Mlambo put a finger to his lips. 'I cannot say too much except that she faces danger from the same people who killed these innocent neighbours of ours. If it is possible to fly her to the UK, I may need your help at some point.'

Maggie's mouth opened in astonishment. 'Goodness!' she exclaimed quietly. 'Where is she?'

Mlambo's face fell. 'We don't know. My son, Campbell, was sent to warn her. But since then, we have heard nothing.'

'Do you think she's been abducted?'

'I do not know, but in here,' he tapped his chest, 'I feel

that she is still alive. And if she had come to harm, then I think that news would have filtered out.'

'We should go back to Harare and find her!' Lorimer insisted.

'No, do not go back,' Mlambo told him sternly. 'That is what Sibanda would want you to do. Once in the city, you will both be very vulnerable to his orders. At best, you'd be bundled onto a plane and sent home. At worst . . . ' He gave a shrug.

Lorimer shook his head and sighed. 'I hate this feeling of being useless,' he said. 'Not my style at all.'

'Don't worry. I think the good Lord has sent you here to Zimbabwe for a purpose,' Mlambo told him. 'You are a believer?' he asked, directing his question at Maggie.

'I am,' she answered. 'And I think Daniel was too before he lost so much.'

'The Lord is with us every step of our journey,' Mlambo said firmly. 'We may not see Him, but we know He is there.'

Lorimer listened to the frank exchange between the ranger and his wife. Maggie's faith was a mystery to him most of the time, but he could not deny that it had served her well in times of trouble. Sometimes he could almost feel a sense of joy emanating from his wife as she sang around their home, or when she spoke about the wonders of creation. It was something he could not quite bring himself to share, though he occasionally felt a mysterious force working above and beyond the everyday world. And there was that medicine man, with his strange insight into Maggie's personal life. What was it that she was fond of quoting from Shakespeare? *There are more things in heaven and earth . . . than are dreamt of in your philosophy.*

'Come,' Mlambo said, rising from his place as one of the catering boys drew near. 'We need to load that poor fellow into my truck and drive to the airstrip. We can talk more on the way.'

CHAPTER THIRTY-SEVEN

'Inspector Newton, congratulations.' The blonde woman shook Molly's hand, smiling up at her.

Molly beamed back in her elation at having passed this final hurdle.

'One more female inspector,' the examiner added with a wink. 'And perhaps something even higher in years to come!'

'That would be nice,' Molly agreed.

What was left of the morning was spent in conversation with the examiner and her team, though Molly (Inspector Newton!) had declined their offer of lunch, eager to return to Helen Street and share her good news with the rest of the team. The afternoon would be spent clearing her desk and moving into the same room as the other detective inspectors.

If only Lorimer were here to share her good news, Molly thought as she began to sort through the items in the cardboard box. The other officers had crowded round to congratulate her, someone bringing in a box of doughnuts, arrangements made for an evening in the pub.

'I'll miss you, Newton, or should I be calling you ma'am?' Davie Giles said, grinning from ear to ear. She could see he was pleased for her but there was something a little sad about shifting from the DS room where she'd sat next to Davie for so long. They'd made a good partnership for lots of cases, and it would be odd not having him by her side now that her duties could find her leading an investigation, delegating tasks to colleagues like Davie. Davie Giles had been one of her most supportive colleagues when Molly had first spoken of trying out for promotion. He'd grinned at her and given her a hug before she'd left him behind in their old room, offering a mock salute. No bad feelings there, then, and how could there be? Theirs was a close friendship that would continue despite her new rank.

And how would Daniel feel about this? He'd seen his share of difficult cases back in Zimbabwe, reaching the rank of inspector. Now he had taken the brave step of beginning all over again, a necessity for a foreign national joining Police Scotland. Soon, PC Kohi would be taking his own test, that of British citizenship in order to be more firmly established here. They'd pored over sample tests, amazed at some of the questions, particularly obscure ones about English history. But Daniel had an advantage over most candidates in that he had been born with that rare gift of eidetic imagery, a photographic memory that was both a blessing and a curse.

No, she'd never let her beloved call her ma'am, Molly decided, lifting out a framed photo of Daniel taken on the day of his passing-out parade. Oh, but he was handsome!

Perhaps one day there might be a different photo on her desk, Molly sighed, a flickering image of her dressed in white standing next to the man she loved. Was that too much of a dream? Would the police officer who had seen his home burn to the ground, his wife and child perishing within, ever be ready to commit to another woman?

'Penny for them, DI Newton,' John Turnberry said, looking up from his laptop.

'Changes,' Molly said, briefly.

'Aye, well you'll find the work is still the same, but you may have to make a lot more decisions on your own,' DI Turnberry replied. 'Welcome to the gang.' He swept a hand around the room. The seven other desks were empty, DIs out and about investigating ongoing cases. What, Molly wondered, would be her first assignment as a detective inspector?

As she emptied the remaining contents of her box, she wondered if there might be time to ferret around on Netta Gordon's behalf. Not that she wanted to upset DI Miller over in Cathcart, but with Lorimer away and nothing in her schedule for the rest of the day, it might be an opportune time to see just how Billy McGregor had come to be placed in that flat on the eleventh floor.

Michelle Struthers stood up as the tall blonde woman entered the office, suddenly aware of the clutter of papers on her desk. DI Newton had called ahead to see if it was convenient to speak to the probation officer and Michelle had invited her over to the office, curious to know what could not be said over the telephone. She ran fingers through her curls, wondering what sort of impression she was making on this willowy figure, smartly dressed in a navy trouser suit and red silk shirt. There had been no time this morning for make-up, the kids dragging their heels as she chivvied them from breakfast table to teeth-brushing then into the car, Michelle flinging dishes into the dishwasher and taking a damp cloth to the kitchen table. Her husband had been snoring his head off in the spare room, his night shifts at the hospital allowing him a decent eight hours before he was supposed to collect their kids from school.

'Mrs Struthers? DI Newton,' the officer said, striding forward and taking Michelle's hand. She was cold, Michelle noticed, not wearing gloves despite the horrible weather.

'What can I do for you, Inspector?' Michelle asked, waving a hand to indicate the seat across from her desk. This was her domain, she had decided, and she was determined to show this police officer that she could not simply swan in and begin to ask her questions. So, no offer of tea or coffee. She was a busy woman and whatever was to be said had to be done as speedily as possible, was the message she wanted to convey.

'You mentioned one of our former clients, Mr William McGregor,' Michelle began. 'I was under the impression that his death was being investigated by DI Miller at Cathcart police office?'

'You are correct,' the blonde replied smoothly. 'I just wanted to check a few things, myself,' she added.

No real explanation as to why she was there, Michelle thought. Odd. However, this DI was with the Major Incident Team and perhaps there was a link with a different ongoing case? Not hers to know, she decided, feeling a slight sense of pique.

'Billy McGregor was given a flat that had been vacated by a Mrs Gordon,' DI Newton began. 'Was there any reason why this particular flat was allocated to him?'

Michelle frowned. It had been a busy period and she had been rushing about trying to help a lot more clients than Billy McGregor.

'Let me have a look.' She sighed, wondering how much time this woman was going to take of her precious afternoon. If her husband didn't pick the kids up after school, she'd be in trouble again with their head teacher. He'd forgotten more than once to do his parental duty and Michelle was too often left to take the ensuing flak.

She scrolled back to the date of McGregor's release. No, it had happened before that, she frowned, letting the pages flip past more slowly.

'Here we are,' she said at last, conscious of the other woman's eyes upon her.

'The housing association gave us a selection of places where he might stay,' she said, raising her eyebrows as she remembered. She bit her lip, not wishing to admit that she had forgotten the details.

'And did you choose that flat for him?'

Michelle shook her head. 'No,' she sighed. 'Mr McGregor asked specifically for that one.'

'Why do you think he did that?'

Michelle felt herself go hot under her Aran sweater. 'I don't know,' she admitted. 'I think maybe I showed him a list of possible addresses. We do try to let clients have accommodation that suits their needs. Near family, for instance,' she said, trying to defend herself.

'And did he have family nearby?'

Michelle shook her head. The inspector's question was quite reasonable, but did she detect a slight tone of scepticism?

'No, he had no family at all in Glasgow,' she admitted. 'But he jumped at the chance of that flat since it was high rise and he'd have a good view. After being incarcerated that was understandable.' Michelle had said as much to DI Miller and that had been accepted. But now, in light of the man's death and his visit to the address of the flat's previous resident, the probation officer began to wonder if she'd been duped by the ex-con.

'It was just a coincidence that Mrs Gordon's flat became vacant when my client needed accommodation,' she insisted.

'And yet he chose that flat from a list . . . of how many?'

Michelle turned her screen to show the detective inspector. It was a fairly long list, encompassing several areas of the city and Greater Glasgow, none of them very salubrious.

'I don't always trust coincidences,' DI Newton said, more gently now, a certain sympathy in her eyes for the probation officer who was now perspiring under her heavy jersey.

'Perhaps you might go back a little further,' she added, looking at the screen. 'Who was McGregor's co-pilot before his release?'

'Why do you want to know that?' Michelle asked, surprised to hear the term. It was usually only inmates themselves that referred to their cellmates as co-pilots.

The blonde threw her a disarming smile. 'Just indulge

me for a bit,' she said. 'It's something I've been wondering about.'

Michelle pursed her lips and scrolled further back in McGregor's case notes.

'I don't have a record of that, but he was an exemplary prisoner,' she insisted. 'One of the foreign inmates even benefitted from him being a literacy buddy.'

'Oh, and do you have any background about this other guy? Where he was from, perhaps?'

Michelle looked up, surprised. 'Africa,' she said. 'Zimbabwe.'

'Augustus Ncube was Billy McGregor's pal before his release,' Molly told DI Miller. 'McGregor was his literacy buddy. That is significant, don't you think?'

'Good lord,' Miller exclaimed. 'Does your Daniel know this?'

'No,' Molly replied. 'And I do not aim to tell him without your say-so.'

'Thank you, Detective Inspector Newton,' she heard the other woman chuckle. 'Nice of you. Congratulations on your promotion, by the way.'

Molly laughed. 'I've hardly had time to get used to it,' she admitted.

'Well, this does put a new slant onto things,' Miller continued. 'Ncube and McGregor, hm, interesting combination, even though they weren't cellmates. And poor old Billy hardly out the nick before he ends up dead.'

Molly took a deep breath, wondering what the other woman was thinking.

'Don't say anything to your beautiful boyfriend just yet,' Miller told her. 'I think we need to speak to someone in Barlinnie before we think of talking to Ncube. Leave it with me for now, okay? And you can tell old Mrs Gordon not to worry.'

Molly clicked her phone off and sat back in the car, thoughts whirling. Augustus Ncube had shot at Daniel, intending to kill him. His case was due to come up in court and there was every likelihood that he'd be sentenced for a very long stretch. It was unusual for a convicted prisoner to be linked with one on remand, but not totally impossible either. Perhaps because McGregor was due for release, he had been appointed Ncube's buddy for a short while, his literacy role part of his rehabilitation?

'Curiouser and curiouser,' Molly murmured to herself.

There had to be something significant behind McGregor selecting Netta Gordon's address from all these others. And as for his association with Ncube . . . ?

She shivered for a moment. Why had they heard nothing from Daniel's mother for so long? What had really happened to her letters?

And, had the danger that Daniel had fled somehow found its insidious way right here to Glasgow?

CHAPTER THIRTY-EIGHT

Reuben put a finger under his red bandana, swallowing hard. The sweat was trickling down his chest now, the heat of the day suffocating in this airless van. The flight from Harare had landed on time and now he was heading to the hills above Kariba to take up his new post as temporary cook boy at a prestigious country residence that catered for wealthy tourists.

Hilltops it was called, though it was far beneath the sprawling hills that overlooked the lake. An abundance of wildlife and the attention of expert guides, coupled with luxurious accommodation and fine cuisine, attracted mainly overseas visitors, the price for even one night's stay well beyond even the most affluent Zimbabweans.

'You'll have a nice holiday,' Sibanda had told him with a laugh. 'Make the most of it, won't you?' He had added a nasty leer, taking a finger across his throat, a warning to Reuben of what might happen if he failed to carry out the man's instructions.

Khumalo was dead, he had been told. An accident, of course. Though Reuben suspected that the young guide had met with a different sort of fate after his conversation with Sibanda. They'd all run about as kids, he, Luther, Jeremiah and Augustus, though Reuben and Luther had kept themselves a little apart from the politician's son, particularly when he'd indulged too often in the drugs he'd boasted about selling. Now Luther and Jeremiah were both dead and Augustus was rotting in some British jail. Reuben felt himself shudder in spite of the heat.

Kariba was going to be a challenge, he realised. The terrain was different up there and perhaps the opportunities for carrying out Sibanda's orders might present themselves quickly.

Don't take too long about it, Reuben had been told. *Just make it look like an accident, okay?*

Another accident, he thought gloomily. But the man behind the deaths would get away with it, regardless.

White folk, Sibanda had told him with a toss of his head, as if these tourists were somehow expendable.

Reuben repeated the name, *Lorimer*, under his breath, wondering why he could not stop shivering.

Their pilot grinned at them from under her khaki bush hat. Clad in shorts and a matching shirt, the girl looked to Maggie as if she were scarcely older than her sixth formers.

'G'day,' she said, her Australian accent reminding Maggie of their friends, Fred and Dinah, who were now on their way to Harare airport for the next leg of their trip. 'I'll be flying you over the lake today,' she added.

Maggie looked past her at the tiny aircraft sitting on a runway that was scarcely more than a strip of tarmac surrounded by dried earth. A short distance away she saw a group of hornbills, apparently unconcerned about this large flying object nearby.

'Anyone want to sit up front with me?' the pilot asked, looking from Lorimer to Maggie and across to Richard Mlambo.

'I'd love that, if nobody else minds?' Lorimer asked, sweeping a glance at the others.

Maggie nodded, a sick feeling in her stomach. What were they doing, flying in this miniature plane, a slip of a girl at the controls? Nobody seemed to share her concern, however, Mlambo more worried about where to store the dead guide's body, Lorimer already walking around the aircraft, eyes gleaming in anticipation.

She watched in a mixture of fascination and alarm as the pilot pulled a screwdriver from the pocket of her shorts and began to undo the fastenings of a metal plate on the side of the plane. In one casual move, the Aussie pilot lifted it off and laid it against the wheel.

'That's our hold,' she explained, glancing at the makeshift body bag. 'Think you'll need to take your luggage onboard this time.' She pointed at the Lorimers' two small cases. 'Only enough room to fit that poor fella in,' she said, shaking her head.

Maggie moved away, not wanting to watch as the ranger and the man who'd taken their tickets heaved their burden into the hold.

'Okay?' Bill turned to catch her hand in his. 'Not worried about this flight, are you?' he asked, concern in his eyes.

'Course not,' Maggie lied, tossing her head. 'Rather grim to be taking a dead body with us, though.'

'Mlambo has contacted the police. They'll be there when we arrive, and that,' he said with a twist to his mouth, 'will be that.'

'You don't like it, though, do you?'

Lorimer shook his head. 'It stinks,' he said. 'And I don't mean the corpse.'

Maggie turned as she heard a clang. Their young pilot was bent forward, screwing the panel back onto the side of the aircraft. It was just a heap of metal, Maggie thought, defying the logic that told her unscientific brain how impossible it was for it to take off, fly across a stretch of water and land successfully on the other side.

Lorimer shot a smile at the young woman by his side. Did she have any inkling that this was a boyhood dream come true? His younger days had seen him haunt the local library with his parents, old-fashioned stories of flying ace Biggles a firm favourite with his dad who had introduced him to the books. Now, as the engines roared, blotting out any possibility of conversation, he felt a thrill through his body.

'All right back there?' the pilot shouted, turning to catch Maggie Lorimer's eye.

His wife looked uncomfortable, a bit pale, perhaps, Lorimer thought.

'Don't worry,' the girl called out. 'My mum's just the same. Hates flying with me!'

Lorimer glanced over his shoulder, giving a sympathetic smile. Was that intended to reassure his wife, or was Maggie wondering at this very moment just how old and experienced their pilot might be?

The girl turned back to the controls and waited for a moment. Then the small plane began to roll forwards, gathering speed so quickly that Lorimer hardly had time to see the ground flashing past, hornbills left in their wake.

Below them columns of steam spiralled up from the forests, heat being released as the day progressed. It was hard to forget about the inert passenger in the hold, the man whose eyes would never gaze out of an aeroplane window again, as the landscape became a child's version of a toy jungle. There, ahead, a sheet of water shimmered beneath them, pale blue like the sun-bleached sky. Kariba, the lake that bordered both Zambia and Zimbabwe. Khumalo may have kept some dubious company, but there had been no doubting that genuine love for his country.

They had not risen all that high, Lorimer realised, able to pick out details in the landscape, brown shapes that must be hilltops as the plane flew closer to its destination. This was far better than the huge commercial aircraft that had transported them from Scotland then London, though he had enjoyed one early morning moment seeing a mountaintop rising from a mass of clouds and realising that he was seeing the tip of Mount Kilimanjaro.

Now the plane's engine note was changing, and Lorimer felt his ears fill up a little as their descent began. The magic of the experience was wearing off, the thought of what awaited them at Kariba airport taking over.

He turned to give Maggie a thumbs up sign but saw that she had her eyes closed. The ranger caught his glance and shot him a sympathetic look. There had been no chance to talk on the flight, but there was little else Mlambo could have told him. *Stay vigilant*, the ranger had advised. *Keep to a group, if possible. And lock your doors at night.*

Lorimer had listened and nodded. There would be a police presence down there already, waiting to relieve them of their deadly burden. He peered down as the ground came into view, questions turning in his mind.

What else might be waiting for them as they came in to land?

CHAPTER THIRTY-NINE

The sound of a heavy vehicle crunching over the gravelly track made the old woman lift her head and listen intently, gnarled hands clutching her rosary beads. There was the slam of a door and then that unmistakable tread of heavy footsteps drawing nearer. A big man, she decided. One full of his own importance. What was it her Tanzanian uncle had called it, the girth of those self-important men swelling before them? Their 'public opinion', that was it! She smiled to herself, but the smile faded as the footsteps suddenly stopped, replaced by heavy breathing.

'Good morning, sir,' she called out, wondering if her unexpected visitor would announce his name.

'You Mrs Paul?' a man's voice demanded. 'Kristine Paul?'

'I am,' the old lady replied, tight-lipped at the casual impertinence. 'And who may you be?'

She heard a laugh then felt the tread of feet on her wooden steps as the man climbed up to the stoep.

'You can't see me, of course. Blind, aren't you?' His words

were accompanied by a sneer, something she did not need eyes to see.

Kristine declined to answer, merely offering the tilt of her head.

'You don't need to know my name. Just that I'm a po-lice officer and I want you to answer my questions.'

Not a polite police officer, she decided, but a bully used to getting his own way. She imagined an overweight fellow perspiring in the heat of the day. Someone who threw his weight about but usually got others to do most of the work.

'How can I help you, officer?' she asked in a sweet tone that was cloying to her own ears.

'That Kohi woman, your neighbour along the end of the row. Where's she gone?'

'Oh, I don't know,' she said slowly. 'Perhaps to Botswana? She has family there, I think.'

There was a silence as the man digested her words. She would offer no more, better to remain in apparent ignorance than garnish more untruths. That visit by the Scottish couple was one secret that Kristine Paul would keep firmly to herself.

'She didn't tell you where she was going?'

Mrs Paul heard the first trace of doubt in the man's voice. Putting on a sympathetic smile she shook her head.

'Hm, you see nothing, of course, but that doesn't mean you aren't aware of what goes on round here. Or so I've been told.'

She felt his breath on her face as he leaned forward. But that did not intimidate the old lady in the slightest.

Then he turned and made his way back down the steps.

'We'll be watching you, lady,' he warned, his boots crunching on the ground.

That was something she did not doubt. It did not necessarily mean the police would do anything to a harmless old blind woman, however.

Clasping her hands as the vehicle roared away, the old Zimbabwean woman took a deep breath and began to pray.

'Lord, protect Janette and surround her with your love and strength,' she whispered.

There was a fluttering sound as a pair of doves alighted on the tin roof above her then a familiar cooing, the gentle bird call soothing her spirit.

All would be well, Kristine Paul told herself. There was, after all, a greater force for good at work banishing the darkness.

The first thing Maggie saw as she alighted from the tiny plane was a group of women dressed in colourful frocks, sitting on the ground. Behind them, draped along a fence, were the elaborately crocheted table covers like the ones she had seen on her visit to the medicine man, hand-made by these women who were waiting patiently for the tourists to arrive. It was no use buying one to take back home, Maggie thought sadly, the small hand luggage she had with her quite inadequate to hold anything as large as that. She had already bought some batik table mats which were in her other luggage, to be transported back to Harare once this part of their trip was over.

'Sorry, too big for me,' she told the ladies as they rose as one at her approach.

Either they did not understand English or were determined to push their wares at her, Maggie realised.

A voice behind her called out and the ladies lowered their hands, tucking the cloths back over the fence.

'They try it on everyone.' The pilot chuckled as she joined Maggie. 'Do a good job here, mind you, nice product but far too big for most visitors to pack,' she added, voicing Maggie's own thoughts. 'C'mon and have a cool drink while we wait for your transport.' She picked up Maggie's case and strode towards a nearby building. A quick glance behind her revealed the men pulling something from the side of the aircraft.

'Let's leave them to it, hey?' the pilot said.

Inside, the building was cooler, fans suspended from the ceiling attempting to waft away some of the afternoon heat.

Through a window Maggie could see a white van with the crest of the Zimbabwean police force, two men seated inside. Soon the body of the dead man would be their responsibility, she told herself.

It was not the way he would have gone about things, Lorimer thought, frowning as the police arrived. He stood at the side of the perimeter fence in a patch of shade, fists clenching and unclenching as he watched every move of the uniformed officers. Two men in buff-coloured safari suits emerged from one car, shortly followed by four others from a white truck. His eyes followed the first pair as they strolled casually from their vehicles and approached the ranger. One of them was the senior officer in charge, Lorimer decided, reading his body language. He had stopped now, close to Mlambo, hands on hips, booted feet coming to rest on a small rise of ground so that he looked down on the ranger.

Even if he could have heard what they were saying, it would have made no difference, the language being that of the Shona people. The boss was waving his hands about now, expansive gestures that somehow conveyed the man's displeasure, and Mlambo was shaking his head, protesting at something. From the expression on the ranger's face, Lorimer could see he was not best pleased at whatever accusation this police officer was making. He bit his lip, the effort not to intervene increasingly frustrating. If Mlambo were to look his way, try to catch his eyes, then he would take that as a signal to step forward, offer to tell what he knew about the dead guide.

But Richard Mlambo studiously ignored the tall Scotsman standing in the shadows, then, with an exasperated sigh, began to walk back to the aircraft.

It was no use. Despite the ranger's warnings, it was impossible just watching from the sidelines, letting the dead man be returned under a false story. He took a deep breath, jaw tightening as his policeman's instinct for justice kicked in.

Lorimer strode forward until he reached the Zimbabwean officers.

'Can I have a word, please?' he asked, looking directly at the two men who turned and stared back at him with undisguised disdain.

'I'm Detective Superintendent William Lorimer of Police Scotland,' Lorimer told them. 'I may be on holiday, but I have many years of experience dealing with sudden deaths. And I can tell you that this man,' he pointed to the body being carried from the plane, 'was definitely murdered.'

The pair exchanged a worried look then one of them shook his head and stepped closer to Lorimer as though to intimidate the taller white man.

'You have no business in our affairs, *Mister* Lorimer,' he sneered. 'We know who you are,' he added, his chin jutting upwards defiantly. 'This was an accident, pure and simple.'

'It defies the laws of physics for a man to shoot himself in the back of his head,' Lorimer growled, 'never mind any other sort of law. I may be a tourist to you people, but I can still make a report to your superiors in Harare.'

'I wouldn't do that,' the officer returned with a cold smile. 'It might be seen as political interference and our leaders do not take kindly to anything like that from the UK. We are a republic and have our own independent ways of running this country. You would do well to remember that.' He stepped a little closer to Lorimer, who caught the smell of nicotine from the Zimbabwean's breath.

The Scot stood his ground, glaring back at the man until the Zimbabwean dropped his gaze and retreated to stand by his fellow officer, arms folded in apparent defiance.

There was clearly no more to say or do in the face of such intransigence. Daniel's reminder about police corruption was being played out here, not hidden but blatantly displayed for all to see. Those who dared defy this sort of regime were brutally punished, like his friend, or cowed into submission.

Lorimer felt his face growing hot with anger as he turned on his heel to the sound of malicious laughter from the two men. He had been trained to believe that police officers had a duty of care for their fellow citizens and, despite what he had read about corrupt regimes, it still hurt to see this denied in practice.

He saw the ranger in conversation with the two police officers once more, but from the way Mlambo's head was bowed and the glances towards him, Lorimer guessed that they were telling him to keep this interfering Scot out of their business.

There was silence from the line of women as the body was carried from the hold and taken to the waiting truck. Only when the vehicles drew away and the dust had settled did the sound of ululation begin, a shrill, gut-wrenching noise that was meant on this occasion to signal grief. It was a ritual, Lorimer knew, this outpouring from a small group of people to show their sorrow at the appearance of death.

'I'm sorry,' he heard the ranger say as he came to stand beside him. 'There was nothing much I could do except allow them to take Luther's body.'

'Did they ask anything about the circumstances of his death? Anything at all?'

Mlambo shook his head. 'No. They said to me that they had been told about "the accident".' He raised his fingers to make the shape of speech marks in the air, his expression glum.

'Nobody asked for a report? Or a time of death?'

Again, he saw that sorrowful shake of the ranger's head. And Lorimer knew that was the end of the incident as far as he and Mlambo were concerned.

'Go to Hilltops now, Mr Lorimer,' Mlambo said quietly. 'Enjoy the next few days before your return to Harare.'

'That's it?'

Mlambo nodded, then a faint smile appeared on his face. 'Well, maybe you will see me again, who knows? Our paths may cross before you see your homeland once more.'

He clasped Lorimer's hand. 'Be careful,' he warned, glancing from Lorimer to Maggie, then giving him a keen look before turning towards the small building where the pilot awaited him.

Lorimer nodded back, wondering if he would indeed meet Richard Mlambo again. Would this man whose life was dedicated to the elephants and other precious species take time to see a couple of tourists who were passing through his country? Or was there something else on the ranger's mind that he was holding back?

Maggie squeezed his hand as they watched the tiny aircraft take off, its wings tilting a little as though bidding them farewell.

'Shouldn't be more than another half an hour,' she whispered. 'They're sending a safari van to pick us up. The itinerary was quite clear about that.'

'Oh, I think it may be a lot less than that,' Lorimer replied, pointing to a small cloud of dust approaching, then the shape of an olive-coloured SUV. 'Come on, let's go and see if this is our transport.'

He picked up their bags and Maggie followed him from the building out into the sunlight. Shading her eyes, she watched as the vehicle slithered to a halt and the driver and a second man jumped out.

'Next stop is meant to be the best place for birdwatching,' she said, in an attempt to lighten the tense expression that she could see on her husband's face. 'And it'll be your birthday while we're there.'

Lorimer gave her a lopsided grin. 'So it will. I'd almost forgotten about that.'

He frowned as Maggie gave a gasp, hand clutching her throat. 'What is it? What's wrong?'

He followed her stare but there was nothing untoward that Lorimer could see, just a young man from the safari truck sauntering towards them, a red bandana tied across his brow.

CHAPTER FORTY

The sky was full of leaden clouds that presaged snow, Daniel noticed as he drove through the city streets. Even at eight in the morning the pavements were puddled with yellowish reflections from the street lighting, any signs of the sun hidden from view. It might last like this for days or even weeks, he knew from the time he had lived in Scotland. February was said to be the least favoured month with only St Valentine's Day to alleviate the general depression, he had read somewhere. Perhaps that was why it had been shortened to a mere twenty-eight days when calendars had been constructed. Even Netta had been in a grumbling sort of mood at breakfast, bemoaning the darkness and incessant rain that prevented her from hanging her laundry out of doors.

'Ah cannae be bothered wi' days like this,' she'd lamented. 'Jist as well we hae thon pulley,' she'd added, pointing at the long wooden strips that were secured below the kitchen ceiling. Daniel had insisted that she use the indoors washing lines, afraid of allowing his old friend to step into the shadowy back court. The attempted burglary, if that was what it had been, had not shaken Netta in the least but Daniel was concerned that something in the old lady's past might have attracted unwanted attention here. The stranger who had visited their home in Nithsdale Drive had been brutally murdered and until the perpetrators were found, Daniel was uneasy at leaving the old woman in the flat on her own.

He would take her shopping on his next rest day, Daniel promised. To Silverburn, if she fancied a look around the Southside shopping mall, or to Braehead beside the River Clyde.

He stopped at a set of traffic lights and looked around at the other commuters, men and women staring straight ahead, lost in thoughts of their own. Molly would already be at work, her day beginning way before daylight. They would celebrate her promotion soon with a nice dinner in the West End. She had sounded happy when they had spoken on the phone last night before joining her colleagues in the pub for a few drinks. Detective Inspector Newton had a good ring about it, he thought, smiling, before releasing the handbrake and setting off once more towards Cathcart police office.

Diana Miller read the message from her old friend at the MIT. It wasn't really her case, and she might have taken umbrage at the interference, but she understood why Molly had gone to the trouble to find out more. The attempted break-in at Nithsdale Drive was just one more headache in this case but there were specific leads that she must follow and not be sidetracked by. Billy McGregor had been close to Ncube, the fellow who had put a bullet in Molly's boyfriend, the lovely Daniel Kohi, she thought grimly. That was a piece of information that she should have unearthed but the probation officer had obviously been less helpful to Diana and her team than she had been to DI Newton. Ah well, no point in feeling sore about it, they were all in this job for the same reason, to stop these people getting away with their crimes.

Now it was up to her to talk to the officers in Barlinnie Prison and arrange a visit to Ncube himself.

HMP Barlinnie, or the Bar-L as many Glaswegians called it, was famous for a host of reasons, some of its previous inmates having spent time in what had been called the Special Unit. A dark grey Victorian building in Riddrie, a part of Glasgow's East End, it was Scotland's largest prison for male offenders and those on remand. Fearfully overcrowded, its days were numbered, plans to replace it dragging on for years. The old Special Unit was just a memory now, though DI Miller had read many of the stories about how art therapy had been used for just over two decades in the previous century in an effort to rehabilitate offenders. It was something for which the DI had some sympathy. Rehabilitation was essential if society were to make any sort of progress away from the current trend of criminality and recidivism. Not all officers agreed with her, and she knew that prison officers were themselves divided on just how much good these schemes could do.

She handed over her mobile phone to the duty officer and waited to be screened then ushered through the metal turnstiles. Security here, as in other Scottish prisons, was formidable and any visitor, police officer or not, had to undergo a rigorous inspection.

At last, she was at the other side and heard footsteps coming down the nearby staircase.

'DI Miller, good morning.' The grey-haired man smiled at her as he reached the foot of the stairs. It had been a surprise when the governor himself had offered to meet her but here he was, taking time to greet her, a benign expression on his face as if he were welcoming an old friend for morning coffee.

'Ncube is a worry,' the governor said at last when Diana had finished her story. 'I'll make no bones about it. The man has upset a fair few of our officers with his bully-boy tactics. Hasn't quite gone as far as assaulting anyone, at least not anything we've been able to pin on him. Yet,' he added with a grimace.

'Has he had any visitors recently?'

The governor nodded. 'Yes, his lawyer has been in to see him several times.' He frowned. 'We can't stop private conversations between a client and his lawyer, of course, though I often wish I could hear what some of them talk about. Would make our lives a lot easier.'

'Let's talk about McGregor,' Miller said. 'This buddy literacy scheme? How did that come about?'

The governor nodded. 'It's a good scheme. Helps those poor souls who have had very little education. You'd be astonished how many are unable to read when they come in here. Skipping most of their schooling is one aspect leading to that, but there is a considerable amount of low intelligence in a sector of our prison population as well. Poor souls far too easily led by others, for the most part. And other problems like dyslexia that were never picked up when they did attend school.'

'And Ncube?'

'Lacked basic skills to read English. Speaks it well enough, mind.'

'So, he finds himself paired with McGregor who was due for release?'

'Correct. McGregor was an amiable sort of chap, didn't seem intimidated by Ncube at all and it was considered that they were a good pairing. They were never cellmates, though. Ncube's co-pilot was a sleekit wee bloke from Inverclyde who was out not too long after Christmas. He's got an older fellow with him now.'

'Is there any way we might find out how McGregor really came to live in that Maryhill flat?' Diana mused.

The governor smiled. 'You could try asking Ncube, but I doubt if he will tell you anything but lies.'

'We were wondering if he had any phone calls from abroad?'

'There were two,' he said, nodding. 'He was permitted to speak to his father's aide not long after he arrived. You do know that Ncube's father was a prominent politician in Zimbabwe? Yes? Wilson Ncube. And the same man called again . . . ' he frowned and pulled his laptop from the side of his desk, 'let me see . . . '

Diana Miller waited as the man laid a hand on his mouse, wondering just what he was about to find from the recorded transcript.

'Ah yes, well, that's interesting, hmm. The call came from

this fellow just a few days before McGregor was released. He was out by Christmas.'

'And I suppose you have a name for this man?'

'Wilson Ncube's aide? Fellow by the name of Sibanda. Nelson Sibanda.'

DI Miller had a determined expression on her face as she entered the police office. She had called ahead to DS Knight, asking if he could release Daniel Kohi from duties that afternoon. Needed to speak to him as a matter of urgency, she told Daniel's tutor cop.

She clutched the transcript of the calls that the prison governor had printed off for her, recalling the man's words.

'One thing he did mention early on was that Kohi was alive. Guess he feels sore that he only winged your constable,' he'd chuckled.

The transcript showed quite clearly the disbelief on the part of this aide, Sibanda, who evidently held that Daniel Kohi was dead and buried in Harare.

There was no need to wait for Kohi to return, Miller found as she slipped through the doors to the CID base; the uniformed officer was leaning against a wall, looking at his mobile phone.

Daniel straightened up immediately and pocketed the device as soon as he caught sight of the DI.

'You wanted to see me, ma'am?'

Miller nodded and pointed to the door of her tiny office. 'My room, now, please,' she said crisply.

Daniel followed the woman into her office and waited till she motioned for him to sit opposite. He stared at her intently, a slight frown puckering his forehead as if he were anxious to know what had brought this meeting about.

'Nelson Sibanda,' Miller said shortly, meeting Daniel's gaze. 'Tell me everything you know about him.'

Daniel's lips parted in a moment of astonishment then he closed them again tightly, his frown deepening. Sibanda! A name he had hoped never to hear again.

His eyes flicked to her fingers drumming an impatient tattoo on her desk. This was serious, Daniel thought.

'Sibanda was the man who was responsible for the deaths of my wife and son,' he said at last, his voice husky with sudden emotion.

Miller gave a slight nod, but her eyes were steely, not permitting Daniel to do more than swallow hard as she waited expectantly for more.

'Nelson Sibanda was a senior police officer whom I believed to be very guilty of corruption within the Zimbabwean Republic Police Force,' Daniel told her. 'I had accumulated enough evidence to take to the most senior officials that I believed would punish him.'

There was a pause as Miller scribbled into a notebook then looked up once more.

'Many of the officers I worked with were decent, honest people who wanted to make a difference to our society,' Daniel went on, 'but Sibanda and his thugs had warped the minds of others, either forcing them to accept bribes and do unspeakable things to men and women or cowing them with threats of serious repercussions if they didn't do his bidding.'

'Go on.'

'I resisted his overtures,' Daniel sighed. 'I did not believe the threats against my person or my family.' He shifted uncomfortably in his seat. 'After all, I was a police inspector and,' he shrugged, 'people thought well of me. I was wrong, of course,' he added softly, looking down at his hands.

'There was an incident that brought it all to a head. A fellow who had been good at bringing information to officers, a tout, you would call him. He was found hanged from a tree out in the bush,' he said. 'Everyone knew Sibanda had authorised it but of course there was the usual cover-up, the official verdict being suicide.'

Miller nodded, catching his eyes again.

'That was the last straw for me,' Daniel admitted. 'Jeremiah was a good enough fellow, ran about with a few druggy types but generally kept his nose clean. His family were devastated,' he said. 'Not just that he had passed, but that the story of suicide had gathered momentum. They were a good Christian family, and it was a sorrow to them that Jeremiah had become a bit of a lost soul.'

'What did you do?'

Daniel put his head in his hands and breathed out a long sigh.

'I went to my overall boss, a man I trusted. He was in charge of corruption, and I thought . . . I believed . . . that he would do something about Sibanda.'

'But you thought wrong, I guess?'

Daniel nodded. 'Sibanda had infiltrated far further up the chain of command than I realised. And one day I came home . . . ' He shook his head, too full to speak further.

'It's okay,' Miller said more gently. 'I know your story, Kohi. And I am sorry to ask you these questions, but I needed to know more about Sibanda as it impinges on a current case.'

'Oh?'

'We were given to understand that this Sibanda is the aide to a former politician. Is that correct as far as you know?'

Daniel frowned and shook his head. 'That doesn't make sense. Sibanda wasn't involved in politics ...' He paused for a moment. 'Well, I didn't think so but perhaps he had connections ... there was so much that was wrong ...' He sighed heavily.

Miller's expression was serious as she replied. 'It turns out that Nelson Sibanda has been in touch with a certain inmate in HMP Barlinnie. Augustus Ncube.'

Daniel's eyebrows rose in surprise.

'We are beginning to piece together the facts that led Billy McGregor to your flat that day,' she went on. 'And your Molly has been doing a little digging to help us.'

Daniel's eyes widened. Molly had said nothing to him about this. Was the MIT involved in the case now?

'Does the name Wilson Ncube mean anything to you?' Miller asked.

'Yes, he was a politician a few years back. Held a post in government but has retired now. Why do you ask?'

'You don't know then?' Miller asked.

'What ... ?'

'Augustus is his son.'

Daniel sat back and blinked. 'I never made the connection,' he said slowly. 'Ncube is a common name back home. And Augustus never seemed the type to have an important person for a father.'

'Seems he was slipped out of Zimbabwe before he could stand trial for drug offences,' Miller explained. 'And his road to Glasgow led him into similar circles.'

'And, to me,' Daniel added.

Miller nodded. 'When we asked you to undertake covert duties last year, we had no idea about Ncube's background. And now it seems as if there is a lot more to learn.'

'How does McGregor fit into all this?' Daniel asked.

Miller explained the dead man's connection with Ncube in Barlinnie and the possibility that information from Netta Gordon's letters had come into the Zimbabwean's ears.

'We've still some investigating to do but at the moment we are building up a picture of how Mrs Gordon's letters to your mother might have been intercepted by anyone trying to find you. There is nothing in the transcripts of his phone calls to back this up, but information can find its way into prison in all sorts of different ways.'

'But people thought I'd died in the fire!'

Miller shook her head. 'Not any more, Daniel,' she told him. 'Ncube has seen to that. And now we have to find if McGregor was deliberately set up in Mrs Gordon's old flat with the express intention of trying to target you.'

'But . . . why was he killed?'

Miller's face was grim as she answered him. 'Why, indeed?'

CHAPTER FORTY-ONE

'I'm Reuben,' the man with the red bandana told them, heaving their bags into the back of the truck as an older man came around and shook Lorimer's hand.

'We'll be driving through the hills, and I'll keep an eye out for any interesting wildlife on our way,' their driver said, with a grin. 'Reuben here is our new cook boy plus general helper,' he added, pointing at the younger man. 'Let's get going. You like to sit up front with me, Mr Lorimer?'

'Yes, thanks, if it's okay with you, Maggie?'

Maggie gave him a tremulous nod and allowed the driver to assist her into the back seat of the vehicle. It was surprisingly spacious inside, windows allowing her to see everything as they drove along.

'Hello, Mrs Lorimer.' Reuben swung into the truck, leaving a space between them. 'Here's a cushion if you want to make yourself more comfortable,' he said, pulling a faded red cushion from the luggage space behind them.

Maggie took it from him and shoved it behind her just as

the truck set off, rumbling along the narrow road that led from the airstrip, several wild turkeys flapping out of their way. A quick glance showed that the young man beside her wore the same sort of uniform as the driver, a brown shirt with *Hilltops* embroidered in gold, matching shorts that showed his knobbly knees and thin legs. But it was that red bandana, the warning sign the shaman had mentioned, that gave Maggie a sick feeling in her stomach, rather than the truck bouncing over the potholed track.

In her capacity as a secondary school teacher, Maggie Lorimer had met all sorts of troubled teenagers, some who had had a poor start in life and whose subsequent behaviour was challenging. Yet there was something in their English teacher that softened many of these tough kids, her manner towards them both kind and respectful. Perhaps this young man was not so very different from the boys she'd taught over the years? And rather than show any signs of fear, maybe a friendly approach would win his trust?

'That was a dreadful tragedy at our last camp,' she whispered to Reuben.

'Ah, missus, these guides, what a risk they take handling big weapons,' Reuben said, his face assuming an expression of sadness. 'Many of them have no real training. Not like the rangers.' He shrugged, as if that was an explanation that put an end to any discussion of the incident.

'I see,' Maggie said stiffly, turning to look out of the window. But she did not add that such an explanation was unlikely to satisfy her detective husband. Luther had been shot dead by another's hand, albeit with his own weapon. If that was what these newcomers wished their guests to think then it was best to go along with it. For now.

'Look!' Lorimer lifted his binoculars and turned his gaze upwards.

There above them Maggie saw a flock of birds, their blue-green plumage dazzling in the afternoon light.

'What are they?' she asked. 'Some sort of parrots?'

'They're Cape glossy starlings,' Lorimer replied.

'Oh, my, what a sight!' Maggie exclaimed.

'Lots of birds where we're going, Mr Lorimer,' the driver giggled. 'Wait till you see some of them!'

Lorimer lowered the glasses and turned to speak to Maggie.

'Surprised we haven't seen any of these types of starlings before now,' he told her. 'They're the commonest species in Southern Africa.'

'Seen them in the cemetery,' Reuben confirmed, then he frowned and looked away as if wishing he hadn't spoken.

It was a throwaway remark, nothing to make anybody else in the truck wonder, but Maggie was puzzled at the young man's change in demeanour. Had he lost a relative recently? Her writer's imagination made her think more closely about Reuben and begin to make up a story about him. What if he was new here because he needed a fresh start after some tragedy? What if that red bandana was a sheer coincidence despite what the medicine man had told her?

'You had a bad experience recently?' she asked, laying a kindly hand on Reuben's arm.

He turned swiftly, mouth open in a moment of

astonishment. She watched as he swallowed hard and shook his head. 'No, missus, what makes you say that?'

'You mentioned being in a cemetery,' she said, attempting a smile. 'I thought maybe you had suffered a bereavement?'

Reuben gave her a puzzled look. 'Just worked there, missus,' he muttered. Then he turned away and stared out of the window, leaving Maggie with the instinctive feeling that her question had not been truthfully answered.

Their arrival at Hilltops took both the Lorimers by surprise. Rising out of a fold in the landscape, its tent-like brown roofs blended into the colours of the hills behind, wooden balconies supporting individual decks. Each bungalow resembled a huge mud hut but on closer inspection their walls proved to be made of some modern materials painted to look like more traditional African homes.

'Welcome to Hilltops!'

A large man with close-cropped dark curls and wearing a light tan shade of uniform strode forward as the Lorimers jumped down from the truck.

Lorimer noticed the name badge, *Francis, manager*, as he shook the big man's hand.

Behind him two young women in brown skirts and yellow blouses grinned shyly at the newcomers as they held out trays of bright orange drinks.

'Mango and papaya, very refreshing!' the manager proclaimed, taking them from the girls and handing them first to Maggie then to Lorimer.

And so they were, Lorimer thought, taking his first sip through a paper straw, glad of the cool drink.

'Let me show you to your accommodation, dear guests,' he boomed, raising a hand and waving it proprietorially towards an open doorway into what looked like a reception area. 'Have a rest now and then I will send someone to show you around our beautiful Hilltops.' He beamed, ushering them through the doorway into a circular area where ceiling fans whirred to produce some sort of coolness.

Lorimer and Maggie followed the big man past a reception desk and out into a wooden-floored corridor that encircled a vast area full of tropical plants, alive with the sounds of small birds that looked like warblers.

'Here is one of our three restaurants,' Francis told them with an airy wave of his huge hand as they passed a smoked glass doorway. 'And now, come down and see where we have prepared your bungalow.'

Maggie smiled as she saw her husband leaning over to get a closer look at the little chattering birds. This was the perfect holiday for him, she realised as he trailed behind them, entranced by all these new species.

The manager led them down to a stream and across a rope footbridge that swayed as they stepped across it.

'It's like something out of *Indiana Jones*,' Maggie giggled softly, turning carefully to catch her husband's eyes.

'Let's hope there are no hazards ahead,' he quipped.

Maggie could not contain a gasp as the manager threw open the double doors of their bungalow. Inside was a polished floor of parquet, no doubt made from locally sourced types of timbers, with a pale cream sisal mat of intricate design. The walls were hung with colourful batiks of birds, she noticed, as she strolled through the lounge, an unlit wood-burning stove placed in a purpose-built stone niche to one side.

But it was the bedroom that really took her breath away. At first sight it seemed perched on the edge of turquoise water, so close was it to an infinity pool just outside a wall of glass. The bed itself was enormous, swathed in curtains of creamy muslin to serve as mosquito nets, with flower heads of frangipani and hibiscus strewn across the coverlet.

A candle in a tin lay on each bedside table, no doubt extra protection to ward off flying insects at night, though Maggie did wonder if they might not attract moths.

'Anything you need, just call me on the telephone,' Francis said, giving them a small bow, his podgy hands clasped in apparent satisfaction at the reaction of his newest guests.

Their luggage was already there, placed on a couple of stands, and Maggie was glad that she had packed a couple of wrap-around cotton skirts as well as some light tops for the evenings.

'This is posh!' she said, taking her husband's arm. 'You never told me this safari lodge would be quite so grand, especially all the way out here!'

Lorimer bent and kissed her cheek. 'It's fantastic, isn't it,' he agreed. 'A change from the tents and tree houses. Well,' he added, looking around, 'I don't mind spending my birthday here.'

What a fool he had been letting the word 'cemetery' drop from his lips! Your big mouth will get you into deep shit one of these days, he told himself crossly. And yet he seemed to have got off with it, the white woman all solicitous and nicey-nicey to him. She was the fool, he decided, listening to the creaking of the bed and the white woman's giggles as they lay down. He was just out of sight, the walls of the lounge masking his shadow as he crept away from the bungalow.

That was the first hurdle passed, and Sibanda would approve, he thought, slipping the empty glass jar into his tunic pocket. He had to go now and do the chores for which he'd been hired. But hopefully by morning the little friend that he'd carried all the way from Harare would have done its work.

CHAPTER FORTY-TWO

It was not as straightforward to see the prisoner as DI Miller may have anticipated, Ncube's lawyer making all sorts of noises about police harassment and client confidentiality.

'Load of rubbish,' Miller seethed under her breath. McGregor's death was still her number one priority and finding the link with Ncube and the deceased having been literacy buddies was a step in the right direction.

'I will be interviewing your client in connection with a murder enquiry,' she told the lawyer. 'Harassment may be the least of his worries,' she added drily.

The man on the other end of the telephone line hummed and hawed but reluctantly agreed to the detective inspector's request to meet at Barlinnie.

'I've seen the governor and spoken to the lawyer, so I'm meeting Augustus Ncube tomorrow, at last,' Diana Miller told Molly. 'Let's see if we can tie him to McGregor's demise. There is definitely a link there and I mean to find it.'

Molly put down the phone, a thoughtful expression on her face. To tell Daniel, or not? Miller had not given any indication that Daniel was to be kept out of the loop and, after all, his very future might depend on the outcome of Miller's visit to the big Zimbabwean prisoner. But Netta would worry if she believed that there was still a threat to Daniel's life. The men lurking around their flat had not returned and Molly guessed that they would not attempt a return trip since Netta had reported the incident.

No, she decided, better to keep this development to herself for now. Wait and see what the next day would bring. If there was time, she might drive over to see Netta and Daniel before going back to her own flat in the West End. She gave a sigh, glancing at the paperwork on her desk. There were new crimes being committed all the time and she might be asked to take on the role of senior investigating officer now that her rank had been elevated to that of detective inspector.

As if her thoughts had prompted that very thing, her phone rang again.

In minutes, Molly had gathered up her coat and scarf, grabbed her bag and was out of the office.

'Davie! With me,' she called to her colleague, DS David Giles, who rose to his feet at once.

'An incident over in the Asda car park in Ibrox. One man with a firearm, two others lying unconscious at the scene,' Molly told him as they sped down the stairs. 'Uniforms were on the scene almost at once. Seems they've disarmed the guy, so no need for armed response.'

As they drove down Helen Street in the February gloom, Molly was glad that whoever had been first responder had managed to arrest the man. A quick result would be the best possible outcome, especially if those affected were not badly injured.

There was an ambulance just drawing up at the scene, its lights flashing, as Molly parked her car. Under the neon glare from the front entrance, she could see two uniforms holding the suspect who was standing between them, head hanging down. Beyond them people were crammed close behind the entrance, gazing out.

'Someone's had the sense to keep the customers inside, these doors are locked,' DS Giles observed.

'Store manager, maybe. Once we deem it safe, you can begin to take statements from any witnesses,' she told him.

Molly approached the uniformed officers who had a good grip of the perpetrator and showed them her warrant card.

'What happened?' she asked.

'We were called after a shot was heard,' one officer said. 'We were just on Edmiston Drive so got here in less than five minutes.'

'This one had a gun,' said the other, nodding at the unkempt-looking individual in his grasp. 'Name's Robert Lennox. We know you well, eh, Robbie?'

The suspect raised his head and stared mournfully at Molly through bloodshot eyes. She tried not to sigh, already wondering what sorts of substances would show up in a blood test.

'He was still here when you showed up? Armed?'

'Lennox was on his knees. Offered absolutely no resistance.'

Having seen the state of the man, Molly was not wholly surprised.

'Where's the firearm?'

'Here, ma'am,' the other officer said, reaching into his coat and drawing out an evidence bag which held a dark pistol.

'Hold on to that for now. I'll sign for it once we get this chap up the road,' she said, wondering how on earth a drugged-up tramp had come into the possession of what looked like a 9mm Glock.

Turning now, Molly saw an old lady being assisted by a female paramedic into the back of the ambulance.

'Think she fainted when she saw the gun, ma'am,' the first officer explained. 'Other chap's bleeding, though.'

The man on the ground was being tended to by another paramedic and Molly joined him, hunkering down by his side. The victim was dressed in a red anorak and jeans, thick-soled boots, not trainers, she noticed.

'DI Newton,' she told him shortly. 'This fellow's critically injured?' she asked, staring at the pool of blood darkening the forecourt where the incident had occurred.

'We won't know for sure till we get him to hospital,' the paramedic replied. 'That guy with your two officers apparently fired a gun at him. He's still breathing but that's a nasty head wound he's got. Need to get him in as quick as possible.'

Soon the prone figure on the ground was stretchered carefully into the ambulance and in moments the sound of the siren whined up to an ear-splitting crescendo, lights flashing as the vehicle set off. The Queen Elizabeth University Hospital was mere minutes away, an advantage if this victim were to receive immediate attention.

Having heard that Lennox had been cautioned, arrested and already charged with possession of a firearm and attempted murder, Molly saw him bundled into the police car and called ahead to Helen Street to alert the others at the MIT. She would follow the ambulance and see if she might find out a little more from the old lady, but first she needed a word with the store manager who was hovering at the glass doors, waiting for a signal to open them again.

She strode towards the glass entry doors and nodded, watching as the manager turned a key and the doors slid open with a noise like a sigh.

Customers had been crowded up against the glass, many gawping in unabashed curiosity at the ongoing situation. She'd need to talk to a few of them, too, Molly thought. There were just too many possible witnesses for David Giles to tackle on his own. Already she needed more bodies down from the MIT, she realised, raising the phone to her ear and calling the office.

Any notions she might have had about dropping in to see her friends in Nithsdale Drive were rapidly banished.

It was going to be a long night.

CHAPTER FORTY-THREE

William Lorimer was a man of few fears, his life of fighting crime having toughened him up against most dangers. There were two things he personally detested, however. One was being in a cramped, enclosed space, especially in the dark.

The other was spiders.

When he saw the movement above his head, Lorimer's first instinct was to leap out of bed, dragging Maggie with him.

'What . . . ?' she protested sleepily, blinking the sleep from her eyes.

'Spider,' Lorimer told her grimly. 'There.'

He pointed at the small creature high above the muslin curtain descending on an invisible thread. It was hard to see much, the illumination from their bedside candles casting feeble shadows across the walls.

'It's just a wee spider,' Maggie protested. 'Okay, so it's bigger than the ones we get at home,' she added, looking up as the spider made its way down inside the pale mosquito netting, 'but remember what Daniel told us. There are almost no dangerous spiders in Zimbabwe.'

Lorimer nodded, suddenly feeling foolish.

'Come on back to bed,' she cajoled. 'It'll probably scuttle out of sight now that you've made a move.' She yawned.

With one eye on the spider, Lorimer crept back under the thin covers. Sure enough, it did seem smaller and a bit further away now, no doubt scared off by the human commotion. Maggie rolled onto her side and in moments he could hear her snoring softly.

He stared upwards, refusing to close his eyes. Perhaps he was making a fuss over nothing, he thought, feeling a bit ashamed of his reaction.

Then, just when he felt a little less afraid, the spider began to move again.

Downward it scuttled, straight towards his head.

'Maggie! Get up!'

He had pulled her out of bed again just as the spider reached his pillow.

'Sorry, love, but I am simply not spending the night with that thing on our bed,' he said firmly.

'Do you want to look it up . . . oh, of course, we haven't had our phones charged for days,' Maggie said, stepping a little way from the bed as she peered at the offending creature.

He swallowed hard. Was this a childish reaction, something for which he would be laughed at by the staff? And yet . . . the way that creature had descended, straight towards him . . .

'I'm calling the manager,' Lorimer decided.

'Is that really necessary?'

He did not reply but lifted the telephone and dialled for reception.

'It's Mr Lorimer. I'd like someone to come to our room,' he said, once a voice asked who was calling.

'It's a spider in our bed,' he said, in answer to *'What seems to be the trouble, sir?'*

Lorimer listened, feeling more and more foolish as he was given a short run-down on Zimbabwe's spider population which seemed to harbour only two dangerous species amongst thousands of harmless ones.

At last, he heard the manager heave a sigh, assuring his guest that yes, he would be over directly.

Maggie continued to yawn, her head resting on his shoulder as they sat together waiting for the manager. Was he being silly? Would this be an embarrassing moment to spoil their holiday here?

It seemed to be ages since he'd called but at last a knock at their door signalled the man's arrival.

'Oh, dear, I am sorry you've had a fright.' The man grinned, rolling his eyes at Lorimer. 'You people from colder countries are just not used to seeing so many spiders.' He laughed. 'We get them all the time. And as I said there are only two ...'

He stepped closer and stared at the spider on their pillow. Then, whipping off his shoe, he darted forward and struck out at the spider with a yell.

In moments it was dead, dangling by one leg from the manager's fingers.

'What ...?' Maggie's mouth opened in astonishment.

'That was one of the two,' he said, no longer smiling. 'Not

a common button spider – this,' he raised the dead spider up to the light, 'is *latrodectus renivulvatus*.'

'Does it have another name?' Maggie asked, drawing closer than her husband to inspect it.

'Oh yes. It is called the black widow,' the manager said. 'Just as well you called me – their venom can be fatal.'

Later, once a couple of staff members had scoured the room to ensure there were no further unwanted visitors, Lorimer slipped into bed, holding Maggie tightly.

'Sorry I made such a song and dance about that,' he said.

'I'm glad you did,' she whispered. 'That was the last thing we would have expected here after all they do to keep insects out. After all, it's hardly a tree house with thatch.'

'Think I'd rather have your bushbaby than a black widow, any day,' Lorimer replied drily.

That would be another story to tell once they were home, Lorimer thought as sleep finally took him.

Next morning Maggie woke to sunshine pouring into their room. She rubbed sleep from her eyes, recalling the incident in the night, then heaved a sigh. Today was a new day and they would be going on a walk to see more of the birds and animals for which this area was famous.

Lines from a Joni Mitchell song came into her head, sunshine compared to butterscotch, sticking to all her senses. She smiled then rolled over, breathing into her husband's neck.

'Are you awake?' she whispered. 'It's a glorious day out there.'

Lorimer opened his eyes and smiled at her. 'Good morning, gorgeous.'

Reuben clutched the large plate of sliced meats more tightly before it slid dangerously from his hands.

They were still here!

He swallowed hard, quickening his pace and setting down the platter of fresh food on the buffet table. The tall man and his dark-haired wife were not simply alive but smiling and chatting to another pair of white guests, laughter bubbling up amongst them.

Whatever had happened to the small creature that had been intended as a murder weapon? Sibanda's idea, of course, to make it seem like an unfortunate accident. He cursed the big cop under his breath. This would not go down well for him, Reuben thought, fingering the red bandana tucked inside his shirt. What to do now? He'd been given a warning not to return to Harare unless the Lorimers were dead.

'Washing up time, man!' one of the staff members told him, pointing to a pile of dirty dishes stacked up beside a huge sink. Reuben nodded. He had to carry out such duties while the Scottish couple sat and ate their breakfasts, blithely unaware that they were the subject of Nelson Sibanda's murderous thoughts. Would he have another chance to create some sort of accident while they were here? Reuben's hands slid into the soapy water, grasping a pile of cutlery, thinking hard.

The veldt shimmered at the edges, waves of heat blurring the distant hills. Lorimer and Maggie followed their guide, a local man from Kariba named Patrick, along with five other guests who made up their small party. Before they'd left the hotel complex the Zimbabwean had given them a short talk about the terrain and the types of wildlife they might see. He also ensured they were all wearing bush hats and sensible footwear before handing out cold bottles of water and spare binoculars.

'This is what I've been waiting for,' Lorimer whispered to Maggie as they stopped to look at some birds perched on a bare-branched thorn tree.

He raised his binoculars to bring them into focus.

There, its plumage glistening in morning sunshine, was a carmine bee-eater, one of the most spectacular birds he had ever seen. Its deep turquoise cap contrasted with the bright pink breast and darker pink wing feathers, long thin tail stretching downwards. Lorimer gazed, enraptured, reluctant to take his eyes off the bird. Beside him Maggie was doing the same, Patrick whispering details about the birds, pointing out the curved beak that searched out its prey, mainly bees but other insects too.

At that moment the bird took flight, its wings a fan of deep pink, the bright blue head and back vivid spots of colour as it rose to capture some insect.

'Look at that!' one of the others exclaimed admiringly.

Lorimer followed the bird's flight, the tail feathers spread out like twin rudders, one long, elegant feather streaming behind.

'I've always wanted to see that,' he murmured as the bird flew further away and the party moved on.

It was to be a day he would never forget, stopping to admire the secretary bird whose long-legged gait and disdainful expression did indeed remind them of a person full of their own importance, as Patrick suggested. There were others, too, less spectacular than the bee-eater, like the terrestrial brownbul and an immature blacksmith plover with its speckled brown plumage. And, of course, the huge wingspan of those soaring fish eagles, a common resident, Patrick informed them with a shrug as if he saw them every day, which, Lorimer guessed, he probably did. Still, they were magnificent birds, their white heads and tails unmistakable against the blue African skies.

As the day wore on, Maggie was congratulated for spotting a jackal in the distance, almost invisible against the brown terrain. A few ostriches in the distance posed no threat, Patrick assured them, the birds more inclined to keep their distance from humans than to attack. Though, if they did, the intensity of their kick could be fatal.

'We farm them here, as you know,' he said with a grin. 'Have you had ostrich steaks yet?' He licked his lips then rubbed his belly, making them laugh.

Lorimer looked up at the sky and frowned. Where it had been blue some hours before, the colour had changed to a strange pinkish hue. Their guide had noticed it too and stopped them, pointing up.

'Storm coming,' he said. 'I think we will have rain soon.'

As they turned to make their way back to Hilltops, there was a rumble as if a distant herd of wildebeest were approaching. The heat was intense now, sweat coursing down their bodies, the haze around them thickening.

A crack resounded making Maggie jump and clutch Lorimer's arm.

'Thunder,' he told her, though it had sounded like a sudden gunshot.

Then streaks of lightning split the crimson skies above them. And in that same instant the rain began.

In moments they were drenched, the full impact of the storm hitting their heads and shoulders, everyone's bush hats sopping within seconds.

Patrick hurried them on as fast as he could, though sudden puddles forming on the previously dry-baked earth impeded their progress. It would be hours before they reached Hilltops again and there was absolutely no shelter between these flat open plains and the luxury complex. Thunder continued to rumble ominously, the skies flashing around them as they struggled back.

Then, as suddenly as it had started, the rain stopped, and the sun began to peer around the edges of those menacing pink clouds.

'Thank goodness that's it gone,' Maggie cried. 'I've never been so wet in all my life.' She laughed, taking off her cotton hat and wringing it out.

It was a weary group that climbed the last few yards up to Hilltops, Patrick encouraging them with the cool drinks that would be awaiting their arrival. Sure enough, the girls were there, trays of fruit juice ready for the guests. No giggles this time, but sympathetic looks at the state of their wet clothes and bedraggled hair.

Lorimer clasped his arms around Maggie as they showered together, the flow of warm water a welcome relief.

He felt her body sink into his as she relaxed, and held her more tightly. The storm had been as unexpected as that deadly spider, but with one difference. Recalling the threatening remarks from those corrupt cops back at the airstrip, Lorimer was beginning to think that he and his beloved wife might now be a target. How had that dangerous spider come to be in a room that was meant to be deep cleaned and free from insects?

Maggie shifted beneath his grasp and smiled up at him. 'Need to shampoo my hair,' she told him, reaching for the travel-sized bottle.

'Are you okay?' She frowned, shaking the water from her eyes. 'You look serious all of a sudden.'

'It's nothing. Just thinking about that spider.'

'You think it was put there deliberately?'

His mouth twisted for a moment.

'I had the same thought,' she said, massaging the shampoo into her hair. 'In fact, I wanted to talk to you about the fellow who came with us from the airstrip. Reuben.'

They were dressed now and sitting by the infinity pool, legs dangling in the cool water, watching the sun drop lower towards the horizon.

'So, your witch doctor told you to beware a man with a red bandana? That is kind of specific,' Lorimer mused.

'And there's something else,' Maggie said, relating the conversation that had brought up the mention of a cemetery. 'It was odd. As if he had said something he regretted and was trying to cover it up. I've heard loads of kids do just that, I'm good at picking up all those sorts of nuances.'

'You think we ought to investigate this chap? Reuben?'

Maggie shook her head. 'I think you'd terrify him,' she said. 'Let me speak to him instead. See what I can find out after dinner.'

'Be careful,' Lorimer warned.

'Don't worry. It's your birthday tomorrow. I promise I won't do anything to spoil that.'

CHAPTER FORTY-FOUR

Molly rubbed her eyes, feeling the last vestiges of mascara crumble beneath her fingertips. Davie and several other officers had taken statements from scores of shoppers at the Asda superstore, letting her proceed to the Queen Elizabeth University Hospital to see the elderly lady who had fainted at the scene.

Catherine Fairlie was sitting in a side room when Molly entered, the uniformed officer on watch stepping aside with a deferential nod. She was still dressed in her own clothes, lying back against a bank of pillows, a single sheet spread across her body. Molly saw her white hair, the tight curls testament to a recent perm, the hands across the coverlet veined but fingernails manicured in a soft shade of pink.

'Hello, I'm Detective Inspector Newton,' Molly began, the new designation slipping more easily from her lips after repeating it so often these past few hours. 'How are you, Mrs Fairlie?'

The old lady gave her a tremulous smile and an apologetic eye roll. 'Hello, dear. Oh, I feel so much better now. These nice nurses gave me painkillers. They say the bang on my head isn't serious. Sorry to have been such a nuisance. It just . . . well . . . gave me such a fright.'

'You are not a nuisance at all, Mrs Fairlie. In fact, you may be quite important in helping us piece together exactly what happened.'

'Well, I can do that easily enough. Still got all my marbles,' she chuckled. 'Not like some folk my age, poor souls.'

'Why not tell me all you remember,' Molly suggested.

The old lady described how she had left the supermarket, lugging her shopping trolley behind her just as the gunman had lunged past her towards the man in the red anorak.

'The sound was horrendous!' she exclaimed. 'I never knew that it was so loud. I've only ever heard a starting pistol at the London Olympics when I went there to watch the athletics. Anyway, I saw the man fall down then . . . ' She shrugged. 'I must have fainted after that.'

Molly took her through the necessary details about Lennox and what the old lady recalled of him. Yes, he looked a bit like a tramp, she remembered thinking it odd to see him alone outside Asda with no shopping bags. And then, when he'd brandished the gun, she thought at first it was some sort of joke. Till the bang.

Catherine Fairlie screwed her eyes shut as she tried to bring the scene back to mind.

'I think it was in his pocket,' she said at last. 'That's right. He was quite close to me when he pulled it out of his coat, the inside pocket where men keep their wallets, and then . . . ' She grinned at Molly as she made a gun from her bony fingers and pretended to shoot.

'You are a marvel,' Molly told her. 'Passing out and yet you remember all of that,' she said.

'You should get it all on CCTV,' Mrs Fairlie replied tartly. 'Isn't that what they do on all these TV dramas?'

'Nothing to beat a good eyewitness,' Molly assured her, rising from beside the bed. 'We'll be in touch asking for a written statement, but meantime I'll let you have a good rest.'

'He's saying nothing,' DS Davie Giles told Molly as she stood beside him in the incident room. 'Out like a light as soon as he was in the cells. Loaded to the eyeballs with something powerful. Frankly, I'm surprised he was even capable of firing that pistol, never mind hitting his target.'

Molly nodded. As SIO she had already handed out actions about examining the weapon as well as a background check on Robert Lennox, and reports on both were beginning to filter back.

'Lennox's got form but never for carrying a firearm,' she told the members of the assembled team. 'At least as a civilian. He was injured out in Afghanistan where he'd been deployed as sniper. So, he knows his way around a weapon or two. Since then, his life's been on a downward spiral. Petty thieving, small-time drug dealing at one time, but nothing that would suggest he'd ever been hired to fire a gun. Where did he get that weapon? Was his target known to him or was this just a drug-crazed random act? These are questions that have to be answered.'

She stopped for a moment, listening to the officers as they offered such reports as they had for now. Until Robert Lennox was capable of answering questions, they might not make a lot more progress. Ballistics took time and so did trawling through the CCTV footage. The latest news about the victim was that he was out of surgery but still unconscious.

'He has been identified as Matthew Dobbie,' Molly told them. 'Aged sixty-four, lives alone over in Govan Road.'

Dobbie, she went on, had no criminal record, unlike the man who had tried to kill him. He'd been on benefits since being the victim of a serious assault some years back and there appeared to be no link whatsoever between the man and his assailant.

'Just because there's no criminal record doesn't mean he's squeaky clean,' she warned them, 'so we must not make any assumptions based on his background just yet. This may be a personal matter between Lennox and Dobbie. We have to wait and see what Robert Lennox has to say once he is compos mentis.'

The surgeon was not at all surprised to find a police officer waiting to take the bullet away in an evidence bag. Sadly, his career to date included having to extract bullets from several victims in the big Glasgow hospital, not all of them survivors, unlike Matthew Dobbie who was now recovering in the high dependency unit. Whatever the forensic experts out at Gartcosh Scottish Crime Campus might find apart from residue of flesh and blood, he would not find out unless the time came for him to be called as an expert witness for the

Crown. That, too, was something that the consultant neurosurgeon had experienced in his lifetime, and he pondered what the outcome might be in this particular case.

Robert Lennox woke with a groan. His lips were dry, tongue sticking to the roof of his mouth. Blinking, he frowned at the cramped cell, that small square of window on the grey metal door shut fast.

Why was he here? What had he done to bring him back to the nick? His head hurt, his stomach heaving as he tried to sit up. There was a fuzzy sensation that made it difficult to focus, as if he had been knocked out cold and was just coming round.

The sound of the cell door opening made him look up to see a uniformed police officer.

'Mr Lennox? Ready for some breakfast?'

Detective Inspector Newton strode along the corridor, wondering if she was right to take control of this interview, something that could have been adequately handled by a DS. Lorimer sometimes waded in, though, she told herself, not pulling rank so much as eager to deal with certain types of suspects. And he was the best, his reputation legendary for remaining calm and controlled while assessing people during interview with those piercing blue eyes of his. That was why she was here, Molly reminded herself as they approached the interview room. To emulate the man who had taught her so much in her career.

Robert Lennox looked dreadful, his complexion drained of colour, eyes bloodshot and puffy, the pupils still like pinpricks. Lots of drugs would have been found in his bloodstream, Molly reckoned, though the lab was still to return their results. A mixture of heroin and alcohol could have impaired the man's judgement and a physical examination had shown the familiar tracks of a junkie, the stink of booze on his breath a real giveaway. Molly hesitated a moment, wondering if it was too soon to question the man who raised his head at that moment, giving her a bewildered look. What, she asked herself, would Bill Lorimer do?

'Happy birthday, darling,' Maggie whispered, climbing back into bed. She had brought his cards with them, hidden inside a pocket of her backpack. Hers was a funny card, not one with champagne and hearts, but with a big 50 on the front and some penguins cracking jokes, the nearest she could find to a bird motif.

Lorimer turned and smiled, blinking those blue eyes as he emerged from sleep.

A kiss later he took the card and read it, his smile breaking into a laugh. 'Thanks, love, this is perfect,' he chortled.

'Fifty,' Maggie murmured, snuggling into his side. 'Half a century.'

Lorimer gave a fake groan. 'Oh, dear! What's a nice lady like you doing in bed with an old geezer like me?'

Maggie wriggled closer and smiled up at him. 'Let me show you, shall I?'

Later, as they sat side by side, feet dangling in the turquoise waters of their own private pool, Lorimer breathed a sigh of contentment. He had everything a man of fifty could wish for. Here he was with the woman who had put up with so much over his years as a cop, not minding when he dropped everything at a moment's notice (sometimes in the middle of the night) to attend a scene of crime. Sure, a family would have been good, but they had two beautiful godchildren, Abby and Ben, whom they adored. Aye, he was a lucky man. So many great friends and colleagues. And Maggie, most of all, he thought, giving her hand a squeeze.

Maggie sometimes expressed her belief of how blessed they both were, as though their happiness together was God-given. They'd weathered patches of darkness in life, like all couples, but right now, feeling the water lapping on his legs and seeing the sun rising above those ochre hills, Bill Lorimer was almost willing to join his wife's faith in a higher authority who had given them so much.

'Penny for them,' she murmured.

'Ah, just feeling grateful,' he replied, smiling. 'I'll never forget this birthday, that's for sure.'

'Well, there are still some surprises waiting for you,' she told him, with a mischievous grin. 'But now I think we need to go and get our breakfast, don't you?'

'But I don't remember any of that!' Lennox protested as the tall detective opposite sat staring at him.

'I think my client is saying that the charges against him have come as a genuine surprise,' the lawyer observed with a nod.

Molly gritted her teeth. The problem was she believed Lennox. The poor man had been agitated when he'd been told of his crime, protesting that he'd never fired a gun in his life. A lie, of course, that they soon corrected. But the former soldier was a wreck of the man he must have been out in that dreadful war zone. Now, having questioned him for almost an hour, Molly was beginning to consider that Lennox had been set up in some way to fire that gun. She imagined his shaking hand being directed at the victim, a whispering voice in his ear moments before he had stepped out onto the forecourt of the supermarket.

CCTV footage, the old lady had insisted, and Molly knew that she had been right. This guy was someone else's puppet, she guessed, drugged practically out of his mind but lured by an offer (of money? More drugs?) to commit this crime. Lennox must be remanded in custody meantime, but she would endeavour to see that he was given proper medical help in the hope his memory might return. And that he would name whoever had really been behind the plan to murder Matthew Dobbie.

'He's awake,' the nurse told her as Molly hovered on the edge of the high dependency ward. It was a cold but sunny day outside, February seventh, still a long way from springtime but here it was warm and almost pleasant, the whirr and beep of machines a soothing background noise, the room half lit to aid patients who were still asleep.

'May I talk to him?'

'Just for a few minutes. He's been given morphine so might be a bit sleepy. It was major surgery,' she reminded the detective sternly.

Molly sat beside the bed, nodding at the patient whose head was swathed in bandages. These were old scars, she thought, glimpsing the deep lines running down to the man's jaw. A face with a history. What, she wondered, had caused someone to attack this man all those years ago? And had that anything to do with the shooting?

'Matthew, I'm Detective Inspector Newton,' she told him. 'I hear you're making good progress.' She smiled.

Dobbie blinked at her but did not reply, though Molly could see the movement in his throat as he swallowed.

'You were shot outside Asda,' Molly went on. 'Have you any idea who might have wanted to do that?'

Dobbie's eyes closed once more, and she saw his hand move restlessly beneath the covers.

She might have told him that they had a man in custody for the attempted murder, but Molly wanted to play her cards right with Matthew Dobbie. If he thought he was still in danger, they might have more chance of finding out who was really behind this.

Her eyes flicked across to the doorway and the uniformed police officers outside, there for the protection of a victim who was undoubtedly meant to be dead.

'Who wanted to kill you?' she murmured aloud, focusing once more on the injured patient.

There was a moment when he opened his eyes again and stared hard at the detective, lips opening as if to utter a name. Then the moment passed, and Dobbie turned away with a small groan, his fingers scrabbling to one side as he pressed a buzzer.

In a flash the nurse was back, cutting off the sudden noise of the call and bustling around the bed.

'You'll have to go,' she told Molly firmly.

Molly rose from her chair and stared at Dobbie. 'Hope you get better soon,' she told him with a nod. 'You'll see me again, though.' She glanced at the nurse before leaving the ward and beckoned to the uniformed officers waiting in the corridor.

'Someone tried to have this man shot,' she said quietly. 'Make sure nobody gets in here who might present a danger to him.'

CHAPTER FORTY-FIVE

Breakfast at Hilltops was giving Reuben Mahlangu a headache. Do this, go there, stop and pick up these dishes! Instructions from the older waiters and the head chef seemed to fly at him from every angle.

'Look at you!' The big burly man grabbed Reuben's shirt. 'That won't do at all. Get changed this minute,' he demanded, thrusting the young man from him so hard that Reuben fell against the edge of a steel cabinet.

'Where . . . ?'

'Laundry room,' a passing waiter whispered, hearing the new recruit's reprimand and glancing down at the stains on his tunic. 'You'll find clean ones there.'

Steam from the big industrial washing machines was almost overpowering as Reuben opened the laundry room door. Sweat had already been coursing down his brow in the kitchen but in here the fug made him gasp.

Still, it was a small respite from his duties as he searched the cupboards for a fresh tunic, turning his mind once again to his immediate problems. Staying here in this luxury resort was not an option, Sibanda's arrangement with the management had been for just one week, or, as he'd told Reuben, until the Lorimers had met with an accident. Disappearing into the bush was foolhardy at best, a boy raised in the city no match for the wild. Besides, with no friends to help and little money, he was stuck until Sibanda's men came to fetch him back to Harare. Would they know by now that he had failed to kill the tall Scottish man? Probably. Bush telegraph was a mysterious thing and bad news travelled as swiftly as a herd of kudu. No news would mean that Sibanda might even now be thinking of ways to punish him.

Reuben shut the cupboard and pulled off the offending shirt, slipping on a clean tunic in one easy movement. Better to stay put meantime, he told himself. See what happens next.

'You, boy, take this to table three!' one of the chefs demanded, thrusting a large tray into Reuben's hands as he emerged into the passage between the kitchen and dining rooms.

The breakfast room was a large area, floor-to-ceiling glass windows on one side with a view of the hills, tables set far enough apart to allow the guests some privacy from their neighbours. Table three was at the far end, close to the windows, and Reuben saw with a sinking heart that this was where the Lorimers were seated. A spurt of anger against these white people made him grip the tray handles fiercely but then the sound of the woman's laughter changed everything.

'Oh, breakfast! Thank you so much. Reuben, isn't it?' she asked, turning to him with a smile.

Reuben nodded, setting down the plates of fruit and glasses of pink guava juice.

'Yes, missus,' he mumbled, reluctant to meet her eyes.

'It's my husband's birthday today,' she said quietly. 'We had a bit of a fright with a spider last night but thankfully the manager killed it. Otherwise, I might be the widow this morning.'

Her quiet tone made Reuben look up and he saw at once the understanding in the woman's face.

'God is good,' she said simply then nodded slowly.

Reuben felt his face hot with shame. She knew what he had done and yet here she was, allowing him to serve her breakfast!

'Aren't you going to wish Mr Lorimer happy birthday?' Maggie asked, a smile playing around her mouth.

The tall white man was watching him too, Reuben noticed, but there was no sign that he had any suspicion about the attempt on his life, just a calm stare from those strange blue eyes.

'Happy birthday, boss. Good life to you,' Reuben murmured, swallowing hard as he picked up the now empty tray.

As he scuttled back to the kitchen, Reuben felt dazed, as if the ground were shifting beneath his feet. He had wished this man a good life, words that had scarcely ever fallen from his lips. And he had meant it. Something burned inside him at that moment, the sense that he had almost done the worst thing in his life, killed another human being, and yet had been spared.

God is good, the woman had said, words that pounded in his brain as he went about his duties, no longer resentful for the demands of his superiors; instead, he was glad to be busy doing useful but menial tasks.

'God is good,' Reuben repeated, hugging the phrase to himself as if to ensure it was not lost in the clashing of pans and shouts from the chefs. If they saw the tears streaming down his cheeks, perhaps his colleagues might think he'd been made to peel onions, but everyone was too busy to notice the slight figure whose face had taken on an expression of bewilderment.

Maggie sat back and looked at her husband. It had been more than thirty years since they had met at university, Bill dropping out to pursue a career in the police while she had continued with her plans to become an English teacher. She took a sip from the guava juice, marvelling at how far they had come together.

Here they were now, in the bright sunlight of Africa, celebrating his fiftieth birthday and yet still surrounded by elements of darkness. It was, she mused, almost as if death and despair had followed them all the way from Scotland. Instead of casting off the toils of his working life, Bill had become embroiled in a murder case that was to be covered up by a corrupt regime. And yet . . . the sunshine glinting on the silver cutlery and crystal glasses seemed to mock her thoughts.

The light shines in the darkness and the darkness can never put it out.

The verse of scripture came to her unbidden. It was like a voice telling Maggie Lorimer that all would be well.

'What shall we do today?' her husband asked, stretching out and taking her hand across the table.

'What do you want to do?' she replied. 'It's your birthday.'

'I don't mind,' he replied. 'So long as it doesn't involve spiders!'

The seventh of February was the date DI Miller had been instructed to visit HMP Barlinnie once again, this time to talk to Augustus Ncube. She had been awake since five a.m., the dark morning chilly as she made her breakfast then headed to Cathcart police office in Aikenhead Road. Meetings first, to assess her team's duties and hear reports from the night shift – always more work to do than she could sensibly handle but then that was a feature of this job. Crime and criminals did not work to any systematic timetable, nor did the need for officers to attend incidents lessen in any way. More bodies in uniform meant more money coming from the public purse and those strings seemed to be tightening year on year, Miller told herself as she set off at last for the big prison over in Riddrie.

HMP Barlinnie loomed across the winter skyline, a darker grey than the snow-filled skies above. For years the place had been a subject of discussion, its overcrowding and old-fashioned facilities a thorn in the sides of the prison service. And yet here she was, parking outside this Victorian heap, the promise of a new facility still to be fulfilled.

It was warm indoors, inmates assured of that, at least; their brief sojourns for exercise in the cold air a contrast to their stuffy cells. Diana Miller looked out at the walls from where she sat alone in the governor's office, the man having excused himself for a moment to speak to one of his staff. It was a bleak outlook, no matter which way you viewed it, the towering slabs of granite firmly enclosing the prisoners who had the misfortune to be here. How did Ncube feel? she wondered, a man used to sunshine and big African skies. Would he have preferred incarceration in his own country to this old building? She gave a mental shrug. She was unaware of conditions in a Zimbabwean jail. Or the treatment Ncube might face, despite his connections with higher authorities.

'Sorry to keep you waiting.' The governor smiled, sitting opposite the detective inspector and waving a hand in the direction of the open door. 'New education policies don't seem to be doing as much for the lads as we'd hoped,' he explained, though Miller had no idea what that meant. Changes didn't always make for improvements, she thought cynically. 'Coffee?'

'I won't, thanks,' she replied. 'Need to see our man as soon as I can today.'

'Know how you feel,' he replied with a rueful smile. 'There are never enough hours in a day. I have a meeting with inspectors of prisons later on that I could well do without.'

We're all the same, chasing our tails to finish the next task, Miller thought, as she rose to accompany the governor down to the room where she would at last see Ncube.

He did not stand up when the door opened and the prison governor entered, accompanied by a woman with short fair hair. For a moment he looked up, hopeful to see another face he might recognise, but there was only his lawyer. There had been no messages from home, no encouraging signs that anything was being done to facilitate his removal from this horrible place, and Augustus had gritted his teeth as he saw the prison governor entering the room.

'This is Detective Inspector Miller,' the governor said, waving a hand towards the woman sitting down opposite Ncube's lawyer who was busy shuffling papers out of his briefcase. 'She wants to ask you some questions about a friend of yours.'

Ncube looked up, a frown beginning to draw his thick brows together. What friends did he have?

'Good morning, Mr Ncube,' the woman began. 'I believe you were part of the literacy programme here, is that correct?'

'Yes,' he replied shortly, wondering where on earth this was going. What had his reading skills to do with anything ... and then, as he remembered the man with the tattooed neck, his lips parted and he shifted uneasily in his chair. McGregor had chickened out. And been dealt with. Or so he had been told in moments of whispered messages. But surely nothing could come back to him here? Wasn't being incarcerated the perfect alibi, after all?

'I believe you had dealings with another inmate here before his release a few weeks ago – Billy, that was his name, am I right?'

Ncube swallowed hard. They knew, dammit. Billy must have opened his big mouth. He remembered the finer details of Billy's delight in accessing that flat over in Maryhill, then the bribes promised to the postal worker who was losing so much pay during the strikes in order to find out where Kohi's old lady friend had gone.

*

The scene came back to him vividly, Billy McGregor smoothing the papers on the desk in front of him, setting a folded piece of paper carefully to one side. He recalled how Billy had looked up as he sat down with a grunt, smiling cheerfully at the arrival of his literacy buddy.

'Awright, son?' Billy had asked, a big grin on his face.

'You're in a good mood,' he had remarked, as though McGregor's breezy air was some sort of affront.

'Out soon, remember?'

'Okay for some,' he'd grumbled. 'Is this our last session, then? When do you leave?'

'Not long now. Got a good reason to be happy,' McGregor admitted. 'Probation officer got my accommodation sorted. And you'll never guess ... ' He looked both ways, leaning forward as his voice dropped to a whisper. 'I know the place I'm going to. Got to choose it, so I did. Rented flat in Maryhill, eleven floors up. Smashing view I'll have ... '

'Like to rub it in, do you?' he had snarled.

'No, no, it's not that, son. See ... ' He paused and glanced around again. 'I happen to know that flat. Old lady who's moved out was married to an old pal of mine. Guy's dead now but we did a few jobs thegether, know what I mean?' McGregor's grin seemed to split his pale face as if he was remembering some ploys.

He had unfolded the paper and turned it towards Ncube.

'Here's the address. Let's see how your reading's getting on.'

He had picked up the sheet of paper and mouthed the words written in pencil. For a moment he had sat very still then gazed across at his buddy.

'This is where you are going to live?'

'Aye.' McGregor's grin faded under his stare.

Ncube remembered how he had tapped a thick finger at the paper. 'The old woman's name,' he'd said huskily. 'Tell me.'

'Och, cannae right mind. Mickey Gordon's missus, let me think.'

'It begins with N,' Ncube had stated, his mouth hanging open slightly as if he was in a daze. It was as if Sibanda's information had been memorised for this very moment.

'Aye, Netta . . . Here, how do you know this?'

McGregor had sat back, shocked.

'There's something you may be able to do for me,' Ncube had told him. 'And I can make it worth your while.'

'C'mon, son. I'll soon be oot o' here while you're . . . well, whit c'n ye do in here, eh?' McGregor had spread his hands wide as if to gesture the futility of such a claim.

Was that when he'd leaned forward and grasped a handful of McGregor's sweatshirt?

'I have friends in high places,' he'd sneered. 'Very high places. They'll look after you. If you can do as I ask, then you'll be sitting pretty in that new flat, no money worries.'

He'd let McGregor go suddenly as one of the prison officers turned to stare at them.

Ncube blinked as the images faded, realising it was a different person facing him now.

He looked across at the woman who was eyeing him with some amusement. He could pick her up and choke her in one easy move, he thought, fists bunching at his sides. He ground his teeth in frustration, acknowledging that it was this detective with her pert smile who was in charge here.

'Let's begin with another man you know, shall we?' she asked sweetly. 'Daniel Kohi.'

He blinked twice, unsure how to reply.

'You met Daniel Kohi in October last year,' she continued. 'When you were walking your dogs.'

Her words were confirmation of what had been churning in his mind all these months. Danny had been set up to meet him, infiltrate his group. And the bastard had succeeded, yet not before Ncube'd put a bullet in him, one that had been intended to kill. He felt a cold fury rise in his gut and tears filled his eyes as he remembered how he had been duped. Even his dog, Simba, had been taken by the cops.

'Daniel is fine now, in case you wondered,' the officer said.

'Not interested,' he replied gruffly, swallowing down the disappointment of betrayal he had experienced. Daniel, a police officer whom everyone thought was dead and buried, had transformed himself into Danny, a fellow Zimbabwean Augustus had seen as a new friend. How stupid he had been! And how he had burned to punish the man for making him look like a fool.

'We know your links to drug crime in Zimbabwe and how you managed to dodge the authorities there,' she went on. 'Friends in high places, right?'

Ncube said nothing, just staring at this small white woman who was exercising such power over him and clearly enjoying it.

'Your father must have paid a few people a tidy sum to get you out of Harare,' she remarked. 'And we believe you are still hopeful that he can pull strings over here. Well,' she leaned forward, a grim sort of smile on her face, staring into his eyes, 'let me assure you that absolutely nothing of the sort that went on in Zimbabwe will help. No bribes, no back-handers, nothing. You will remain here in a Scottish prison for as long as our law sees fit. So, you might as well begin to cooperate with us, Mr Ncube. Only that way can you help yourself. Do you understand me?'

It went against everything that he was used to doing. In here he'd enjoyed a modicum of influence over some of the feebler inmates, but he'd always believed that somehow he'd be released and sent home, a foreign national regaining his own country.

'If I help you, will you send me back home?' He swallowed hard, cursing the whine in his voice as he posed the question.

For a moment she looked down at her notebook as though consulting something, then shook her head.

'I cannot guarantee anything,' the detective told him. 'But cooperation on this case might well do something to reduce your sentence, who knows? That's up to a judge to decide. And, before you get any daft ideas, they are incorruptible over here.'

'What do you want to know?' he asked dully.

'First of all, why did Billy McGregor want to access Mrs Netta Gordon's mail? Was it to locate the whereabouts of Daniel Kohi?'

He nodded, dropping his head and rubbing his eyes with both hands.

'McGregor, the man whose death we are investigating,

visited Mr Kohi's new residence and spoke to him. Was that the plan?'

Ncube's jaw dropped.

Spoke to him! Was this true? Had Kohi actually been living with the old woman? Billy had never been able to tell him that. What exactly had happened to the man after he'd delivered the letters?

Ncube was silent for a moment, remembering good-natured Billy and the jokes he used to make. How could he ever have believed that this man would carry out a killing? And yet, he had gone along with the plan. He knew that Billy had found the flat in Maryhill and passed on the letters from Janette Kohi, a few stolen moments during recreation enough for whispers of information to be passed on. After that it ought to have been simple; a matter of finding Kohi's location from the Gordon woman, sticking a knife in his guts then running off.

Ncube put his head into his hands with a stifled groan.

McGregor had come face to face with Daniel Kohi, after all, might have carried out his part in the plan there and then . . .

But that hadn't happened. And it had been the man who had helped him with his reading who'd been killed instead.

Friends, he thought, with a cynical twist to his mouth. First Danny then Billy. No, he'd messed up big time ever since he had made that call to home, telling the man in Harare that Kohi was alive. Was there any point in trying to avenge himself now?

There is still the mother, a little voice reminded him, lighting a flicker of hope in his brain. And it was up to the man who had given the orders to slay the rest of Kohi's family to finish the job at his end.

'What do you want to know?' he asked again, sitting up a little straighter and looking the woman in the eye. They'd want the names of McGregor's killers, but he could shrug off that question easily enough, his ignorance perfectly genuine for once.

'Did you send Billy McGregor to find Police Constable Daniel Kohi?'

'That went well,' the governor said as they strode along the corridor together. 'You have the knack of prising information out of the most unlikely fellow. And it gives me pause for thought about our current buddy system,' he added with a shake of his head. 'Rehabilitation is what we set out to do but we also need to safeguard our inmates, that's our duty.' He sighed. 'I suppose we won't come out of this too well once you've made your report?'

DI Miller did not reply. She could understand the fine line between giving inmates some freedom to discuss things with one another and keeping tabs on their every utterance. Britain was not a police state, nor ever would be so long as she had breath in her body. But questions had been answered now about how McGregor had inveigled his way into Netta Gordon's old flat. As for the people who were behind his death, was that something that Ncube pretended not to know? He'd been frank enough about trying to find Kohi, hoping the old lady might reveal his whereabouts, wanting to do him some mischief in return for him having infiltrated Ncube's gang the previous year. She remembered the genuine shock on Ncube's face. Nobody had known that he and Mrs Gordon had moved in together and it had been sheer luck that Kohi had answered the door to McGregor.

'Wasn't shooting him enough?' she'd asked sarcastically, watching Ncube slumped in his metal chair. That was something that Molly Newton might like to follow up, Miller told herself. Meantime, she was intent on finding out a lot more about exactly who might have dispatched McGregor.

CHAPTER FORTY-SIX

'That was good,' Lorimer said, heaving himself out of the turquoise water of the swimming pool. Water glistered down his skin, now turning a decent shade of brown. What a way to spend his fiftieth birthday, he thought, sun beating down on his bare shoulders as he towelled his hair and gazed towards the hills.

'See!' Maggie caught his arm, pointing towards a herd of zebras. 'I knew we'd see them here!'

Lorimer picked up his binoculars and followed her gaze. Sure enough there they were, tails twitching as the flies swarmed across their patterned skin. High above, the sky was palest blue, as if the sun had melted all its earlier colour. Vultures were circling in the distance, too far away to be identified as a particular species but their hypnotic movements signified their patience in searching for a kill. Nature's dustbin men, he remembered young Luther calling them. For a moment a frown darkened Lorimer's face then he drew in a deep breath, reminding himself yet again that this was not his country, and he had no official jurisdiction in the matter of the man's death. Still, it rankled that he'd been helpless to do any more than protest to those two burly cops back at the airfield.

'Fancy a walk? Just the two of us?' Maggie suggested.

Lorimer smiled at her. 'Great idea. Let's see what else we can find here in the grounds, eh? Should be safe enough with these electric perimeter fences everywhere.'

Soon they were strolling hand in hand through the snaking pathways, flamboyant shrubs on either side, some already bursting with red flowers. It would be a birthday to remember, Lorimer thought, feeling relaxed after his swim, glad to be taking time to soak up the African sun. The air was filled with the repetitive hum of insects, and the occasional tree full of chattering weaver birds but there was no human voice to spoil their afternoon walk, Lorimer and Maggie, alone on the dusty trail that led around the extensive grounds, down into a shallow valley below the hills. He glanced at his wife, sighing with pleasure at the sight of her; a wide-brimmed straw hat shielded her face from the sun, then she turned and gave him a special smile, squeezing his hand, no need for words to express how special this moment was.

It was as they ventured into the valley that it happened.

A sound like an angry mob coming over the hill made them both look up to see a troop of baboons watching them from the crest of the nearest rise. And then the animals began to charge towards them.

'Bill!' Maggie screamed, grabbing his arm and starting to drag him back towards the hotel.

It was then that Lorimer realised just how isolated they were, the hotel buildings now out of sight, a long way back. The baboons were racing downhill now, some larger males to the fore, females with babies clinging to their backs. They would reach the humans in minutes, their vicious teeth capable of tearing into flesh, killing them in a bloody frenzy.

A whistle to their left made them stop. There, clad in shorts and singlet, was a young boy, running towards the primates as if to chase them off. Lorimer watched in amazement as the boy raised a plain metal rod and aimed it at the troop, just like a small boy pretending to fire a gun.

With yelps of anguish, the baboons turned and fled, their anger turned to fear as they disappeared over the crest of the hill.

Lorimer waited as the boy strolled over the dusty ground to join them.

'Thank you, oh thank you,' Maggie told him, shivering suddenly, when he stopped and smiled shyly at them. 'You saved our lives!'

'Oh, I was always there, missus.' The boy grinned. 'Boss says to make sure you do not go out alone. You don't see me out in this part of the estate, but I am always nearby,' he said, shrugging. 'That's my job.'

'How did you . . . ?' Lorimer pointed to the thin metal rod the boy carried.

'Ah, the baboon, he is a clever one, learns quickly,' the boy replied. 'He has seen a gun and knows what it can do so he learns to fear it. But he is not so clever that he can tell a real rifle from something that looks like it, see?' He took the rod and aimed it as if to shoot. 'That is why guides like me always have these with us. Baboons are bad news, boss,' he added seriously. 'Teeth as sharp as a leopard, tear you to pieces.' He shuddered. 'But now we go back, have something nice to drink?'

'Thank you again,' Lorimer said, silently vowing to reward the lad once they'd returned. True enough, that was a story they had been told, but he had never expected to see it put into practice, especially with him and Maggie as prey to those savage animals.

'Where you from, boss?' the boy asked.

'Scotland,' Lorimer told him.

His reply was met by a frown. 'Where is that?'

'It's part of the UK,' Lorimer explained.

'North of the English border,' Maggie chimed in. 'It is very cold there just now, maybe even snowing.'

The boy's eyes lit up. 'I have never seen snow,' he admitted. 'Only in pictures. Or on television. Tell me, please, what animals do you have in Scot-land?'

'Oh, well, we have rabbits, hares, foxes and deer, not so many antelope species as there are here, badgers, beavers and, well, quite a lot of animals in the sea.'

'You live by the sea?' The boy's eyes widened.

'Yes, Scotland is part of Great Britain which is a very large island nation,' Maggie told him, her voice taking on the informative tone she used in the classroom.

'The sea!' he sighed. 'I would like to visit that one day.'

Lorimer was well aware that few people from Zimbabwe could afford to travel from their landlocked country but talking to this boy was giving him a new perspective on just what that must be like.

'There are seals and otters, whales and lots of seabirds,' Maggie continued.

'What other animals do you have?' the lad asked, his curiosity apparently still not satisfied.

'Oh, horses, cows and sheep. Goats, chickens, pigs . . . '

'And monkeys,' the boy chimed in.

'No, no monkeys. At least, only in the zoo,' Maggie laughed.

The boy drew them a look of disbelief as though these white folk were teasing him.

'But you must have monkeys!' he exclaimed, waving his arms expansively. '*Everyone* has monkeys!'

The hotel was in sight now and Lorimer gave Maggie a nod, dropping her hand and picking up speed to return to their room so he could find some money to give to this lad, leaving his wife in delighted conversation with this Zimbabwean boy who was finding out so much more about a cold land far, far away that was devoid of monkeys.

'I didn't think my birthday was going to be memorable for another narrow escape,' Lorimer told Maggie as they changed into fresh clothes for dinner.

'Never did like baboons but that lad did make me want to see vervet monkeys. They sound rather sweet from the way he described them to me,' she replied.

'Well, we still have time to spot them before we return to Harare. And other creatures too,' Lorimer reminded her. Their safari adventure was almost at an end and the final days suddenly seemed precious.

CHAPTER FORTY-SEVEN

A quick glance at the calendar showed no red rings signifying the dates of a murder, Molly saw with a grim smile. Another few millimetres and the guy might have been lying in the mortuary rather than in high dependency. The date sparked something in her subconscious. Lorimer's fiftieth birthday! Of course. Maggie had taken cards with her from Daniel and Netta as well as the team here and Molly gave a brief thought to a day of sunshine in a far-off land where she supposed the Lorimers would be having a lovely quiet time together.

Her reverie was interrupted by a knock at her door as Davie Giles appeared, his eyes gleaming with excitement.

'Ballistics report!' he exclaimed, sitting down opposite without being asked. 'You're going to love this!'

Molly looked up at once, her friend more animated than she'd seen him for a while.

'Have a look,' he told her, handing over a sheet of paper. 'Just printed that off one minute ago.'

Molly scanned the page, blinked then began reading again.

'That gun, the Glock 26, is the same one that was used in the Shawlands murder? Good lord, that's hard to believe, isn't it?'

'Not so very many deaths by gunshot wounds in Glasgow, despite what the popular opinion of our city might be,' Davie countered. 'But this is immense! I mean, do we really think that Robert Lennox has been involved in McGregor's killing?'

Molly sucked her lower lip thoughtfully. Lennox had struck her as a poor creature, somebody's patsy for the shooting outside Asda, but now she had to reassess the man in the light of this new evidence.

'We need to talk to Lennox again, this time with a lawyer present, not just a medic,' she told him. 'By tomorrow he'll have sobered up from whatever cocktail of drugs has been circulating in his system. Maybe we'll see a different side to the man.'

But first it was her duty to speak to the SIO in the McGregor case who would undoubtedly be reading this same report back at Cathcart.

'I saw Ncube again this morning,' Miller told her. 'He's admitted being involved in trying to locate Daniel. He clammed up when we spoke about McGregor's murder, but I'll be mightily surprised if he didn't have some hand in that too, despite being banged up in the Bar-L. The governor is going to ask his officers for the names of any other inmates like McGregor who got to know Ncube and who have been recently released.'

'You think he's got someone on the outside doing his bidding?'

'Could be.'

'Okay, thanks.' Molly heard the click as DI Miller ended the call. That was interesting. She'd like to be by her side as the SIO in Cathcart spoke to Daniel, to see his reaction to this latest development, but her main concern now was Robert Lennox and where he had obtained the weapon that had killed McGregor so soon after his visit to Daniel and Netta's new flat.

'Did I ever tell you about Pastor John?' Daniel's face lit up as he spoke the man's name.

'I don't think so,' Molly replied.

'He's our parish minister back home.' Daniel's face became suddenly serious. 'It was Pastor John who brought me here,' he explained. 'The night of the fire . . . ' He paused for a moment then shook his head as though to rid himself of a sudden image. 'He took me away with a missionary delegation that were attending a UK conference. How he managed to pull enough strings, I will never know. But we boarded the aircraft and once in England I was taken to see the appropriate officials . . . ' Once more Daniel stopped and sighed, the memories of that time still painful. 'Lots of people far worse off than I was in that place,' he murmured. 'And Pastor John stuck with me as long as he could. Made sure I was being properly cared for and then I was put into the care of another church until the Home Office sent me to Scotland. And here I am,' he finished, turning to the DI with a sad smile.

'One of the good guys, then,' she replied. 'Do you keep in touch with him?'

Daniel shook his head. 'No. I haven't heard from my pastor since I came here. I was advised to make no contact with anybody from home in case there were any repercussions.'

'Well, someone seems to know more than we would like,' Molly said, making a face. 'I think Ncube's people back home have been working for him to try to get at you.'

'We've been so careful,' Daniel groaned. 'Even my mother has just that penfriend arrangement with Netta,' he said.

The DI nodded. 'And it looks as if that was their way of finding you, I'm afraid. That, and the fact that Augustus Ncube found out who you really are. So,' she said, meeting Daniel's dark brown eyes, 'who is it in Harare that wants you dead?'

Daniel gave a sigh. There was only one answer to that.

'A policeman called Nelson Sibanda,' he said.

Robert Lennox was shaking the following morning as he was led from the cell, along a corridor and into an interview room. Inside, the heating was on and the window ghosted with condensation, but he could see large flakes of snow falling outside from a pitch-black sky. There were times he'd been glad of a prison cell for the night, a warm breakfast assured, but since his arrest, he'd been unable to eat much, a sour taste of dread in his mouth.

Arrested for attempted murder, a gun in his hand, a man shot and fighting for his life ... the words from that officer rang in his ears as Lennox sat opposite the detectives, a duty solicitor by his side, some tired-looking female he'd never set eyes on before.

After the customary preamble of reciting date and time (was it really that early in the day?), Lennox stared at the man and woman across the table as the man read out the charge and asked him to identify himself.

'No fixed abode,' he muttered, in reply to the question of his address. One hostel was as good as the next and occasionally he'd have the luxury of some guy's broken-down sofa for the duration, companions in a drug-induced haze. Where he had been the night before that incident outside Asda was a bit of a mystery, and he shifted uneasily in his seat, wondering if the sharp-eyed female would believe him.

'Who sent you with that gun?' she began, straight to the point, no messing about or trying to soften him up.

Lennox shook his head.

'Please speak for the audio recording,' the male detective commanded firmly.

'I don't know,' Lennox whispered. 'Truly. I can't remember much about it at all.'

'What do you remember?' the woman asked, her blonde head tilted to one side as though she were really interested to know what he would tell them.

He heaved a long sigh.

'I've been thinking about that,' he admitted, clenching and unclenching his fingers, the desperate need for a hit of nicotine making him jittery. 'I do remember a bloke talking to me outside the garage.'

'What garage would that be?'

'The wan at Asda,' he replied, feeling more comfortable now that he was recalling the moment. 'They do petrol there dead cheap.' He gave them a weak grin. 'Guess youse lot go therr an' a', eh? Cheap petrol . . . '

'Tell us about this man.'

Lennox pursed his lips in concentration. There had been a man, of that he was sure. And the same man had given him 'something to keep out the chill', as he'd put it. But what had he given in exchange? His mind began to fog over once more, the details hazy.

'It wis that cold,' he began. 'He asked me wid ah like tae sit in the car.' He shrugged. 'Thocht naethin' of it, jist a nice fella offering me a wee bit warmth fae the weather, know whit ah mean?'

'And your purpose of meeting this . . . fellow?'

Lennox gave her a watery smile. 'Nae flies on you, hen, is there?' he said. 'Aye, we wis daein' a wee bit o' business. Drugs. Naethin' more,' he said, giving her a wide-eyed look. For a moment the woman seemed to be on the verge of laughing out loud at his pretence of innocence, but she gathered herself quickly and put on a mock-serious expression.

'So, you meet this fellow . . . name?'

'Naw, nae name, hen.' He smiled, feeling a little better now that he was on safer ground.

'What happened then?'

'Whit d'ye mean?' Lennox frowned at her.

'Did you remain in the car? Take any substances while you were sitting with this nameless person? Or did you make your way back to the supermarket?'

The smile faded from his face as quickly as the snowflakes landing on the window sill.

'I cannae remember how I goat therr,' he admitted. 'Mibbe he took me in his car, mibbe ah walked . . . it's aw a bit o' a blur . . . '

He could see from the exchange of looks between the detectives that they believed him. That weird nightmare when he staggered out into the cold and then found his arms pinioned behind him by two uniformed cops . . . was that what they wanted to know?

'Were you given the gun by that man in the car?' the woman asked, leaning a little towards him as if they were having a quiet tête-à-tête over a coffee and cinnamon bun instead of here in this smelly wee room.

Lennox put his head in his hands and gave a groan. 'Ah cannae remember! Ah telt yese that a'ready. Mibbe . . . ?'

'What do you remember about being outside Asda that night?'

He drew a deep breath, hearing the shudder in his chest. 'Tubercular lungs,' the doctor had said. 'No' long fur the big goodbye then,' he'd replied with a wee laugh.

'Ah remember it wis strange . . . lights everywhere . . . the pain in ma back . . . naw, that wis a different night . . . ' He broke off, his head swimming with so many images, fragmenting into a mad mosaic that made no sense.

'Go on,' she said softly.

'Ah had something in ma haun, an' the man in red wis in front of me . . . ah cannae remember whit happened after that . . . mair lights, a lot of screaming . . . then someone grabbed me and hurt ma shoulder . . . ' He looked at the male detective and wagged his head. 'It hurts when they dae that ... stick yer wrists in thae cuffs, pull yer arms till they're near oot o' yer sockets.'

He winced at the memory, rubbing his wrists as though the chafing pain was more than a memory.

'Why did you shoot that man in the red jacket?'

The question thundered in his ears now, the woman's voice echoing in his brain.

'I didnae know I'd done that,' he whispered, hands raised in supplication. 'Honest. Ah widnae dae something like that tae anither innocent person. Ah'm no' that sort of guy!'

'And yet you were a professional marksman in the army,' DS Giles commented.

'Are you claiming that you were so under the influence of a cocktail of drugs – we have the toxicology from your blood test, incidentally – that you were unaware of having possession of a weapon nor of discharging that weapon to the grave bodily harm of another?' the woman butted in before Lennox had time to think.

Robert Lennox looked from one of the detectives to the other, blinking as he realised the import of that question.

'Aye,' he replied.

Later, after some long and involved story about a fella called McGregor whom he'd never even heard of – (*Any relation o' Callum McGregor?* he'd quipped, citing the name of a Scottish international footballer, only to be met with a cold stare) – Lennox was escorted back to his cell.

It wid be a shame tae be given a sentence fur somethin' that wisnae his fault, he'd telt that lawyer, still protesting to her that he'd nae idea where that gun came frae nor why he'd apparently shot a defenceless man from behind. Still, if he were inside, there wid be a prison doctor and he'd mibbe leave this auld world in a wee bit mair comfort than whit he wis used tae.

'What do you think?' Davie Giles asked Molly as they closed the door behind them.

Molly sighed. 'I still think someone might have put Lennox up to this. That garbled story about the man in the car has a ring of truth about it. What has the team found on CCTV? Specifically around the area of the petrol pumps?'

'Check your inbox,' Davie advised. 'I'm sure they were working overtime on them.'

It was later that day before they saw for themselves the footage that had been scrutinised by a couple of detective constables, their report emailed through to DI Newton. A few new facts had emerged after their colleagues' painstaking work.

There was Lennox emerging from a white Škoda Fabia, its plates easily seen in the glare from the overhead lights of the supermarket.

'And there,' Molly said, blinking back tiredness. 'Exactly what is in that report. Someone else was in that car.'

Sure enough, they saw a figure slide in behind the tramp, steadying his arm at one point as Lennox staggered forwards.

'Face obscured by a hood,' Molly said irritably, as they watched the recording. 'No, wait, see, he's looking up!' She glanced at the written report for confirmation. 'That's what we were meant to see. Our guys froze that image as soon as they saw it.'

It was a moment of revelation, the man's face turned to see something that was out of sight.

'Gotcha!' Molly grinned, her weariness vanishing. 'Now let's see what you're up to, pal!'

As they watched the pair turn towards the corner of the building, the detectives saw the black figure thrusting a gun into Lennox's unprotesting hand. For a moment they stopped, and their heads were close together as the man who had been in the car seemed to be speaking to Robert Lennox, motioning him to put the gun into his pocket.

Then Lennox was on his own, staggering to the front of the supermarket, raising the gun as a man in a red jacket appeared through the automatic doors.

'How the hell did he manage to fire a shot in the state he was in?' Giles commented, shaking his head.

'Once a sniper, always a sniper.' Molly sighed. 'Whoever is really behind this knew who Lennox was, what he had done in Afghanistan. He's not the first man to come home from carnage like that and be unable to cope with life. Nor will he be the last, God help them.'

Davie nodded his agreement.

'Let's find out the owner of this Škoda and the identity of our hooded friend,' she said. 'Wonder if he knows a certain Mr Ncube,' she added softly to herself. Things were slowly fitting into place, the two shootings evidently linked in some way. Perhaps they were about to find answers to several interesting questions.

CHAPTER FORTY-EIGHT

Nelson Sibanda let loose a stream of curses. First that upstart, Luther, now Reuben, the man he'd hoped to control by putting the fear of death into him. Okay, so he'd come good with digging up old bones and keeping watch on the mother's house, but this latest plan had ended badly. An image of a figure dangling at the end of a rope came back vividly. Jeremiah had been a lesson Sibanda had wanted them all to learn but it seemed now that the test of their loyalty needed to be reinforced. He still had control over some of the cops out in the bush country, the two who had taken a successful shot at Luther and escaped by boat, the same officers who'd brought his body back to Harare. They were keeping an eye out for the Kohi woman, too. Somebody had her, but who?

The big man paced up and down, sweat rolling off his massive brow despite the fan whirling its stale air from the ceiling. Old Ncube was a spent force, the former politician no use for his purposes now. Once Wilson Ncube had wielded such power that Sibanda had become little more than his lackey, but those days were long gone. Disposing of Kohi's old lady and the Lorimers might have been Wilson Ncube's idea, but the fact was that Sibanda needed to be rid of both these elements to retain his own credibility with the current regime. If it ever came to the attention of those way above his pay grade that he had ordered the arson attack on that house, then his career would be over, and he had better think of which border to cross.

He stopped and gazed out of the window of his office. The day had begun like every other February day, a cool eighteen degrees, pleasant enough until the afternoon humidity rose and the torrents of rain began to fall. That was his favourite time, when the streets dried swiftly, and he could step out to slake the thirst that had built up all day. He wiped his brow, aware that it was his own excessive weight that made him perspire like this. Too many dinners with people of influence, his mother had scolded him. Until now it hadn't mattered much, the grunt work done by younger, fitter men who were under his command, not just those in uniform but others; lowlifes that he'd recruited and used for his own nefarious ends.

Gritting his teeth, he continued to stare but all he could see was the man with the red bandana grinning as he'd agreed to the plan to kill that white detective.

Reuben Mahlangu had to go.

And this time he would be the one to finish the job.

CHAPTER FORTY-NINE

'Report's just come in about a stolen white Škoda found abandoned, ma'am,' one of the detective constables informed Molly. 'Matches the registration plates we've been looking for.'

Molly rose to her feet. 'Where?' she asked, grabbing her sheepskin jacket from the coat stand and following the woman out of her office.

It was dark as they drove from the main road into the wooded area out past Bishopbriggs, mist gathering over the bare treetops. Molly and Davie squelched through a muddy track towards the squad car and peered down into the ditch, blue and white tape already sealing the site from public view. Perhaps the driver had thought it ideal to hide the car, imagining only dog walkers and the occasional mountain biker venturing into this bleak place, although the proximity to a bus stop, a couple of hundred yards along the road, might have been the reason to choose this location. Trash the car, catch a bus back into the city and disappear into the night. Had that been the plan? She would need to hand out an action to investigate every bus that had stopped along the main road to see if they could find a match for the man caught on Asda's CCTV.

Luckily for the team, a well-meaning member of the public had called to report the ditched car, stopping to jot down the Škoda's registration as he passed by on his bike.

'Right, let's have a look, shall we?' Molly said to Davie, as they slipped on pairs of blue nitrile gloves.

A few minutes later her detective sergeant exclaimed, 'Ha! See what I've found.' He picked up a piece of paper half-hidden under the passenger seat and handed it to Molly, letting the DI examine it closely under the beam of her torch.

'Shouldn't have left his petrol receipt in the car.' She chuckled. 'And didn't pay cash, either. Don't think this one was too bright, do you?'

'We'll find him soon enough,' Davie Giles agreed. 'Credit card details can be traced pretty quickly.'

House-to-house enquiries had been made all along the street where McGregor's body had been discovered, though not every resident had been questioned, some away from home, according to neighbours, others working shifts. One such door knocked in the wee small hours had been visited several times before with no success, the flat in Skirving Street a mere fifty yards from the scene of crime.

'Another link to McGregor,' Molly murmured, her breath clouding white as she stood at the entrance to the close. 'Up there.' She pointed to a light from a bay window. 'Someone's at home.'

There was no back way out of this third-floor flat so no need for stealth, several pairs of feet belonging to officers from the MIT thudding up to the suspect's front door.

'Police! Open up!' came the yell along with fists thumping against the door.

Somewhere inside, a light was extinguished.

'He knows we're here,' Molly said. 'One more warning, then we burst the door.'

More thuds and shouts through the letter box were sufficient to bring the sound of chains being rattled and keys turned in locks.

The door opened to show a thin-faced man, barefoot as if he had just got out of bed, wearing hastily donned joggers and matching black sweatshirt.

'Kevin Lafferty?'

The man nodded, a sullen expression on his unshaven face, his eyes flicking from Molly to the other officers looming behind her. A small sigh escaped him then, a sign of resignation to his fate, perhaps, as DI Molly Newton read Lafferty his rights and had him handcuffed before escorting him down to the waiting police car.

As she drove across the city, Molly Newton was thinking hard. That visit to Netta and Daniel's flat by McGregor had been no coincidence. And the subsequent attempt to mug and rob the old lady was surely part of something much, much bigger. She had a hunch that Netta Gordon might well have a small part to play in this case.

*

Dogged police work, Molly told Daniel much later that night as she slid into bed beside him then promptly fell asleep. He'd listened to her account of the Major Incident Team's search for the man in the hooded sweatshirt and their success in tracing the owner of the white car. Stolen from outside a house in Bishopbriggs, the vehicle had ended up driven into a ditch on the outskirts of the city.

It had been a mere two hours ago that Molly and her team had banged the door of that flat in Skirving Street. Now the driver who had brought Robert Lennox to the Asda compound was being held in the cells at Helen Street overnight.

Tomorrow Daniel had a rest day and so he was content to lie here now and gaze at Molly's face as she slept. Light from a streetlamp outside shone on her blonde hair, so pale against his dark skin. They were a handsome couple, Netta had declared one evening, nodding her approval. He sighed, thinking about how his mother might feel if she ever came here, to find a beautiful white woman in his arms. After her love for Chipo and little Johannes, would she have any affection left for a stranger in a cold, cold land?

CHAPTER FIFTY

Night-time noises were something he would miss once this holiday was over, Lorimer thought. They were part of the texture of this fascinating country full of colourful birds and the animals who lived from one day to the next, seeking the all-important waterholes while ready to flee from any predator. And yet there was a serenity to the wild places, too. The herds of zebra and antelope grazing calmly, hippos wallowing in the mud, the most dangerous animals of all looking playful amongst their own kind. And giraffes, such grace in these strange creatures whose calves could not just stand but also run mere hours after being born.

Lorimer frowned, the pictures in his mind disappearing. It was quiet, far too quiet, and that signified something. He looked up through the fine mesh of their mosquito net but could see no eight-legged creature crawling down towards him. He turned to see if Maggie was awake, but she slumbered on, a waterfall of dark hair spilling over the pillow, obscuring her features. Silently he slipped from the bed and grabbed his trousers, his policeman's instinct telling him that something was amiss. It would be cold outside, February nights here warm by Scottish standards but still chilly after the heat of the previous day. Pulling on a hooded fleece and his walking boots, he looked around for the small torch he'd brought and pocketed it.

Outside it was still quiet and he took a moment to gaze upwards at the skies. This southern hemisphere with its myriad stars scattered across the heavens was a sight to inspire a poet, he thought. How could he begin to tell those back home what a sight this was?

There was nothing out here that he could see, no large animal entering the compound, no troop of baboons infiltrating this place. And had there been an intruder, surely there would be guards around, some sort of night-time security patrolling the perimeters? He was about to retrace his steps over the swinging bridge and go back inside his bungalow when a muffled sound made him stop and listen.

Was that a human cry? Or had he imagined it? Something mechanical, a generator starting up?

Then a different sound, this time most definitely human, voices coming from beyond the main building, and what might have been a door slamming shut. Curious, Lorimer crept along the wooden pathway towards the source of these noises, stopping only when he caught sight of a large police vehicle parked close to the main gate.

Something had happened, he felt sure, but what? Hesitating, Lorimer reminded himself that it was none of his business what the Zimbabwean police were doing here, but a memory of that shot in the dark and Luther's inert body drove him on.

He did not need his torch just yet, solar lights picking out the path around the main block, petering out towards the staff quarters, the place from where he'd heard those voices.

Just as he left the path and plunged into a darker area, he saw them.

At first it looked like a large moving shape but then as his eyes adjusted to the dark, Lorimer could pick out two men who were holding someone between them, followed by a large, bulky figure who looked as if he were carrying something in his hand. He watched closely, frowning as they walked towards the gate, ignoring the big police car and leaving the compound. For a moment they halted as a security light flared up and Lorimer saw, to his horror, a figure with a sack over his head, tied with a dangling rope and struggling between his two captors.

For a brief moment he saw this menacing tableau, then the light went out.

Walking swiftly around the building, Lorimer headed for the path that would take him to the gate. First, he had to pass the back door of the staff quarters and risk that light coming back on and capturing him. Hugging himself close to the wall, he crawled under where he had caught sight of that beam, edging nearer and nearer to the staff annexe.

A yell ahead made him freeze and stare in the direction of the sound, hoping that nobody would come running out and find him there. He'd pulled down his hood, obscuring his paler complexion, something that might make him stand out against the darkness of the night. But no running feet came his way, and he could see the men who had left the compound heading towards a wooded area beneath the hills, close to where that troop of baboons had emerged.

Head bowed to hide his face, Lorimer noticed something lying on the path a few feet away from where he stood. As soon as he felt safe to move, he hurried forward and stooped to pick it up, recognising it straight away. Reuben's red bandana! Looking towards the group who were taking their prisoner away, Lorimer realised with a pang that the slight figure struggling in the grasp of those thugs was the young man whom he'd suspected of planting that deadly spider in their room. Were these men cops? He swallowed down the bile that rose from his stomach, the thought that those who ought to be responsible for law and order in this country might be carrying out some foul deed of their own under cover of darkness. He watched until they had disappeared around a corner and out of sight.

Stuffing the bandana in his pocket, Lorimer looked around for something that might do as a weapon should he need it. It was impossible to see much so he switched on his torch, casting its beam around till he spotted a familiar narrow shape. It was the metal rod the young lad had used the day before when he'd chased off these baboons. That would have to do, he told himself, cutting the torchlight and following the same path the men were taking out of the compound and into the dark.

'Remember Jeremiah?' Sibanda sneered, picking up the end of the rope and giving it a tug. Beneath the sacking, he could hear Reuben's muffled sobs. 'Not long now. Soon put you out of your misery!' he cried, making the two cops laugh as they half-carried the man between them further and further into the woods.

'Need to find a big enough tree,' one of them declared, loudly enough to make their victim moan aloud.

'Bit further on,' the other said. 'Then we'll hang him high!'

All three laughed as their prisoner began to scream.

'No, please, no! Don't . . . !'

But his protests were cut off in a scream of pain as Sibanda aimed an accurate kick into the back of his leg, making Reuben buckle to the ground.

'There!' One of the cops pointed ahead. 'See!'

They picked up the quivering man and hauled him, sobbing, towards a baobab tree, its arms outstretched as though in supplication against the horror to come.

'That'll do,' grunted Sibanda. 'String him up now!'

The moon above was waning, hardly more than a pale crescent as Lorimer saw the men under that tree.

'Stop or I'll fire!' he yelled, aiming his stick in the direction of the culprits.

For a moment everything was still, Lorimer waiting to see if one of them might pull a real gun from his jacket. Had he gambled too far with this? And was he about to make a widow of his wife?

Then, as Reuben began to struggle against his captors, Lorimer saw the two of them drop their burden and begin to race away under cover of the woods.

He came closer now, still clutching his makeshift weapon and pointing it at the big man who was hesitating, hand still grasping the end of that rope.

'Let the boy go!' Lorimer shouted. 'Or I'll fire this!'

He saw the man turn and stare at him, a puzzled expression on his flabby face.

Then, before he could do anything more, Lorimer heard a rumbling sound, the very earth shaking under his feet. As if from nowhere a herd of water buffalo appeared, charging straight towards them.

Nelson Sibanda dropped the rope and began to run, his breath coming in huge gasps as the animals drew nearer, their hooves kicking up a dust cloud.

Lorimer ran towards the boy on the ground, hauling off the rope and sack around his neck, and pulling him into the shelter of the tree just as the herd galloped past.

One anguished scream was all that they heard above the noise of thudding hooves and then, as Reuben and Lorimer watched, the huge horned animals vanished over the crest of the hill.

'Stay here,' Lorimer whispered to the terrified young man. 'I need to see what happened to that man.'

'It's Sibanda,' Reuben quavered. 'He sent me with instructions to harm you. They were going to kill me . . .'

Lorimer took his torch and walked slowly towards the area where moments before that herd of wild creatures had thundered past. He could see a shape on the ground, the rounded back of the heavy man who had tried to run. There was no movement, but he knelt by the body and took hold of his wrist. A faint pulse, so the man was not yet dead.

In the weak torchlight he could see that Sibanda had suffered several blows to his chest, and one where those lethal curved horns had pierced him, blood gushing from his side.

For one moment he saw the man's eyes flicker and the two men stared at one another.

'I'm Lorimer,' he said.

There was no answer, just a look of sheer hatred that Lorimer would find hard to forget.

Then, with a sigh, Nelson Sibanda's eyes closed for the last time.

As they made their way back to Hilltops, Lorimer and Reuben heard the sound of an engine starting up.

'They're getting away,' the younger man said in alarm.

'They won't get far,' Lorimer assured him. 'Once we reach the hotel, I'll make a call to the ranger service to track them down.'

Reuben stopped then, under that starlit sky, and turned to face Lorimer, clasping the hands of the tall white man. There were tears streaming down his face, but he did nothing to wipe them away.

'You saved my life,' he wept, 'after I tried to take yours. How can I thank you?'

Lorimer gave him a lopsided smile. 'I guess deep down you're not a bad man, you've just made some bad choices, eh?'

'Your missus, she knew, didn't she?'

Lorimer nodded and they began to walk again. 'Aye, she can see the good in folk.'

He put an arm around Reuben's shoulders. 'You can turn things around, you know. Make a new start.'

Reuben encircled the older man's waist and hugged him tightly, no more need for words between them.

*

The next morning dawned bright and fair as the Lorimers bade farewell to Hilltops. Outside, a minibus with the hotel logo on its side was waiting to take them back to the airport for their flight to the capital. Waiting by the perimeter gate was a young man in the uniform of the luxury hotel, his hand raised in salute.

Maggie Lorimer smiled at him as they followed the other tourists towards their transport. All that had needed to be said had been said, Reuben talking to them almost until dawn in the safety of their room. It had been Maggie who had suggested that the young man remain here at Hilltops, learning his trade under the watchful eye of the management who had been told the story of all that had taken place the previous night.

Though there was never another mention of spiders.

'He'll be all right,' she said, turning to give one final wave from their seat on the minibus.

'Aye, he will. After what he went through . . .' Lorimer gave a sigh and yawned. 'Think I'll sleep all the way to Harare,' he joked. 'Wake me up when we arrive.'

CHAPTER FIFTY-ONE

'I know you don't fancy coming into another police station,' Molly told the old lady, 'but I really want to see if you can identify a man we arrested last night.'

'Wan o' they toerags that tried tae smash in oor guid front door?'

'Could be,' Molly replied. She had given no name to Netta, following the police code of practice. If Kevin Lafferty turned out to be the old lady's attacker, Netta's identification might prove to be another piece in the jigsaw puzzle of this case.

It was still early, daylight yet to break through the grey Glasgow skies as she helped Netta into her winter coat. Daniel had fussed a little, making them both toast and tea, insisting he would drive behind them and wait at Helen Street to bring his old friend back home again.

Netta shivered as she was taken into the room with the glass wall. Through it she could see the line-up comprising of six men of around the same height, all dressed in black.

'It's okay, Netta,' Molly soothed. 'You can see them, but they are unable to see you watching them. Just take your time and tell me if you recognise any of these men.'

Netta let her eyes travel from left to right, blinking as she came to the third man.

'Aye, that's him,' she sniffed. 'Nasty wee guy that tried tae nick my handbag. Right bad-looking lot, so he is! Has he gone and robbed another poor wumman?' she asked, turning to Molly.

'Thanks, Netta,' Molly smiled. 'Can't say any more right now. I'll let Daniel know you're finished here.'

Molly sat in the same interview room where Lennox had been quizzed the day before, curious to know more about Kevin Lafferty, the Škoda driver. He was sitting opposite her now, a cocky-looking individual in black joggers and sweat-shirt, his jaws working as though he were chewing a wad of gum. Gone was the air of defeat from the previous night, the man having had time to talk to his lawyer. Lafferty was a known drug dealer, one of a gang who had so far managed to slip through their net. That much Molly knew from her early morning briefing, the team's collaborative efforts bearing fruit. And now, thanks to Netta Gordon, she knew a bit more.

Lafferty was looking her up and down in an obvious sort of way, his eyes resting on her blouse then slowly licking his lips suggestively. Behaviour of this sort was not uncommon in young louts who believed they could embarrass a female officer and Molly Newton had seen enough of it to find it tiresome at best, the showing-off from an arrogant youth who had only a vague idea of what trouble they were in.

The tape was running, Lafferty had confirmed his name and address (home owner, not tenant of the flat, he'd sneered, as if that gave him some kudos) and Molly had read out the charge against him.

'Mr Lafferty,' she began, distinguishing the young man by the use of his surname, 'please will you tell me what you were doing outside Asda supermarket in Ibrox on the evening of February sixth.'

For a moment the chewing stopped, and Lafferty made a quasi-comical show of pressing a finger to his forehead as if to consider the question.

He hummed a little then shook his head, grinning stupidly. 'Sorry, can't remember. What day was that?'

Okay, thought Molly, *this one thinks he's a funny guy. Let's just cut to the chase.* Her tone was brisk as she continued.

'We've found your fingerprints on several places of interest, one in particular the door frame of a flat rented by a Mrs Netta Gordon.'

'Rented?' The young man's mouth fell open, an expression of disbelief on his face.

Wiped that smile off quickly enough, Molly thought with a grim flicker of satisfaction. But what was it about Netta's status as a tenant that bothered this guy?

'What have you to say about an attempted break-in to this home?' she continued.

'Ah . . . no c-comment,' he stammered, shifting in his seat and then wrapping his arms around his body in a protective gesture.

'Okay, we can go down that road if you like, Mr Lafferty. Or would you prefer if I addressed you as Kevin? That's what Mr Robert Lennox called you, right?' Molly looked down at the papers on the table. '*And* Mrs Gordon has identified you as the man who attempted to mug her,' she added sweetly.

She watched the young man swallow hard and glance nervously beside him at the older white-haired gentleman in a grey suit, the on-duty solicitor whose job it was to provide legal aid for him.

'No comment,' he replied gruffly, dropping his gaze as Molly continued to fix him with the sort of steely look she had seen Lorimer employ on many occasions.

'We have ballistic evidence that proves the gun you gave to Robert Lennox is the same that was used in the shooting of William McGregor,' she said quietly. 'It would be a good idea if you gave us details of where you obtained that gun and your movements on the night McGregor was killed in Skirving Street. Where you appear to own a flat nearby. That way we either eliminate you from a murder charge and one of attempted murder and you find yourself in prison for possession of a firearm or . . . ' and here she paused to ensure that Lafferty looked up at her, 'we charge you with the lot. It's up to you. Tell us the truth, admit your full part in both these incidents and any sentence that is forthcoming will be a good bit less than if we have to provide a judge and jury to determine your guilt.'

The picture this young man presented was so different now, all his previous swagger gone.

'It was all McGregor,' he began, his plaintive tone that of a young man who had suddenly realised the gravity of his situation.

And then it all came out, a torrent of words, stumbling over each other, blame laid upon the dead man who had sought him out.

'He wanted me to help him find this African guy,' Lafferty insisted. 'Said he'd get paid by this inmate's family to do him in.' He spread his hands in a gesture of innocence that did not wash with the detective inspector.

'You shot Billy McGregor,' Molly said, fixing Lafferty with a cold stare.

'No comment,' he whispered, glancing away to the side.

'We've spoken to Augustus Ncube,' Molly told him. 'Do you think he wanted you to kill McGregor? Wasn't this his way of locating the police officer who resided with Mrs Gordon?'

'Didn't know any of that,' Lafferty mumbled, his face reddening.

'We have CCTV footage of you handing a gun to a man outside Asda,' Molly continued, shifting the focus of her interrogation. 'Same gun you used to kill McGregor.'

The young man shrugged, as if taking a life was no big deal and that Molly ought to understand this, a gesture that gave her a strong desire to reach out and shake him. By the time this was over she was determined to wring a confession out of this man.

'You gave him that gun and instructed him to shoot Matthew Dobbie. Now, why was that, Kevin? What part did Dobbie have to play in all of this?'

'Ask him, why don't you?' Lafferty sneered, a flicker of his former bravado on his weaselly features.

You bet I will, Molly thought, gritting her teeth.

'Now,' she took a deep breath before continuing, 'you are going to tell me all about your association with the man named Robert Lennox.'

It was as she had suspected, the opiate-befuddled ex-soldier a mere pawn to the drug-dealing Lafferty. Ncube's plan had been to employ McGregor to seek out Daniel Kohi and kill him, Lafferty claimed. McGregor had told his old friends that there was hit money to come from this rich African's family if they helped him. But McGregor had changed his mind, and Dobbie had shot him.

Molly Newton had listened and watched, the man's body language convincing her that what he said was only a sliver of the truth. Money was at the root of this, she believed, but how would Ncube have transferred funds from Zimbabwe? Something didn't sound right.

No wonder Dobbie had been reluctant to speak to her from his hospital bed, Molly thought as she had listened to Lafferty's confession. Yes, Lafferty admitted, he had been with Dobbie when he'd shot McGregor, but he'd had nothing to do with it, he'd assured her. That might be for others yet to decide, Molly thought as she made her report.

She'd listened intently as Lafferty had poured out his version of the story, one she believed was peppered with lies. Dobbie had got greedy, Lafferty claimed, wanted all the cash for himself.

What cash? she had asked but then Lafferty had clammed up and Molly realised she had made a mistake. There was more to this case than they knew.

After some discussion with his lawyer, Lafferty had

admitted giving Lennox the gun. Yes, the former sniper had been known to Lafferty, his serious addiction making him an unwitting accomplice, expertise with a gun his only currency to exchange for drugs.

Ncube would probably never acknowledge his association with these men who had been taken into the plot with Billy McGregor. Money, Molly thought. Had these men really expected some recompense from Ncube's family? Or had Lafferty been referring to something else? And would he admit that the plan to have Daniel Kohi killed had gone so awry that it had ended up with trying to eliminate two of his own accomplices?

More background checks were being carried out on Kevin Lafferty right now, as well as on his putative victim, Dobbie. And she must go back and question this man in the Queen Elizabeth hospital, see what his side of this story might be.

It was time for Diana Miller to hand over her part of this case to the MIT, though Molly suspected that the DI would be keeping a watchful eye over one of her probationers.

CHAPTER FIFTY-TWO

'Cannae imagine that wee laddie turning oot like that,' Netta remarked as Molly filled her in about Kevin Lafferty being one of the masked intruders to her flat.

'You know him?' Molly gasped in astonishment.

'Oh, aye. Huvnae seen him since he wis a wean, right enough. His faither wis wan o' my late husband's ne'er-do-well associates,' Netta sniffed. 'Wan o' the gang that raided the Securicor van that night. Did ye no' find that oot?' she added in surprise. 'Sure, auld Iris Lafferty's in a home now but she wis a canny auld besom in her day.'

'Don't suppose you ever heard the name Matthew Dobbie?'

Netta pursed her lips, a shadow crossing her face. 'Aye,' she said at last. 'No' a name ah'm likely tae forget. Poor soul Mickey Gordon battered half tae death.'

'He was the driver of the Securicor van?'

Diana Miller confirmed all that Netta had said. Lafferty's late father had indeed been one of Mickey Gordon's henchmen and the myth about hidden money from a robbery had evidently been passed down the generations.

'Both Lafferty and McGregor had no doubt been anxious to trace Netta Gordon to see what she knew,' DI Miller concluded. 'Ncube's involvement was quite separate, by the looks of things. Sometimes coincidences really do happen.'

'Lafferty seemed to think that Netta had bought the flat in Nithsdale Drive. McGregor must have assumed she'd stumbled upon the hidden money,' Molly told her. 'The idea of a cache of stolen money plus McGregor's association with Ncube made for two separate operations. One, a plot to find Daniel Kohi, and two, the search for stolen loot.'

'Culminating in McGregor's death and the attempted murder of Matthew Dobbie,' Miller agreed. 'Looks to me as if they were all becoming too greedy, each of them desperate to have the money for themselves.'

'But the question remains. Where is that money now?'

Molly left her friend with that question unanswered. It was time to talk to Matthew Dobbie.

Winter sunlight filtered through slatted blinds in the ward to which Dobbie had now been transferred, though he was still in a private room, a uniformed officer seated in the corridor outside.

DI Newton sat beside Matthew Dobbie's bed, listening to the rise and fall of his breath. He looked like any other old man who had been through major surgery, his face pale even against the dressings across his skull, the livid scars a testament to what he had suffered so many years ago. A victim, it had been said, but as Molly Newton watched him sleeping, she wondered about that now. The ferocity of his beating had exonerated the man from any thoughts that he may have been working with the gang of armed robbers, newspaper reports that she had read showing public sympathy for the Securicor driver. And yet . . . he had known McGregor and young Lafferty all these years later. His story was not yet at an end, Molly thought as she saw his eyelids flicker.

'You again?' he growled.

'How are you, Matthew? Feeling a bit better? Are they looking after you all right?'

The man in the bed gave a sigh. 'Cannae complain. Nurses are fine. Jist wake me up too much. Temperature, blood pressure, pills . . . it nivver ends,' he said, unaware that he was indeed complaining, contrary to what he had said at first.

'You are on the mend, though,' Molly assured him. 'I spoke with your consultant and he was happy to tell me that.'

'Ah well, he'll know best, eh?'

'And you know rather more about the man who wanted to kill you,' Molly said softly. 'A man who put a gun into a drug addict's hand so that he wouldn't be blamed for your death.'

She saw Dobbie's lips tighten, then his head turned away a fraction.

'We have Kevin Lafferty in custody, you'll be pleased to hear,' she continued in the same calm tone. 'So, he is no longer a threat to you. Well, except that he claims it was you who shot Billy McGregor.'

'What?' Dobbie tried to sit up, his mouth falling open. 'Lying wee bastard! It wis Lafferty shot Billy. I've never handled a gun in ma life. Is he tryin' tae pin that wan on me?' His eyes snapped with rage. 'Ah wis there that night, telt Billy no' tae be sae saft. But wid he listen? Naw. Didnae want tae get involved in doin' a polis. Jist wanted tae find the money . . . '

He glared at Molly. 'Wance he'd shot him, Lafferty said we'd split it twa ways, it wisnae me that wanted Billy deid.'

'Oh dear,' Molly soothed. 'You were all looking for the money from that raid. The one where Mrs Gordon's husband attacked you so viciously?'

'Aye.' Dobbie sank back against the pillows with a defeated sigh. 'Auld besom didnae deserve tae find it, buyin' a posh hoose on the Southside. Billy telt us that big kitchen wis fu' of fancy gadgets.' His eyes flicked across to Molly for a moment. 'She must've plenty left over, though, eh?'

Molly laid a hand on the old man's arm. 'Sorry to be the bearer of bad tidings, Mr Dobbie, but Netta Gordon is just a tenant in the flat in Nithsdale Drive. A flat she happens to share with Police Constable Kohi.'

The shock of her statement robbed Dobbie of any colour that was left in his chalk-white face.

'You mean . . . ?'

Molly nodded sympathetically. 'Looks like you have all been chasing an illusion, Mr Dobbie. And now,' she added, straightening up in her chair, 'I think you had better tell me your side of the story. From the beginning.'

CHAPTER FIFTY-THREE

Laburnum Lodge was a pleasant care home surrounded not by the yellow blossoming trees for which it was named but a stand of ancient oaks, bereft of their foliage on this crisp February day. Molly had called ahead to ensure that she might speak to one of the elderly residents, Mrs Iris Lafferty, before picking up Netta who was wearing her best winter coat and a thick woollen scarf.

'Nice enough place, I suppose,' Netta conceded as they waited in the porch of the lodge. 'But ye'll nivver get me intae wan o' thae homes, nae fear,' she shivered.

After Molly had shown her warrant card to the manager and introduced Netta as an old friend, the pair were escorted through to a bright, airy lounge where about a dozen residents were seated around in a semicircle, being entertained by a string quartet.

'Fancy,' Netta whispered to Molly as they waited by the doorway. The music finished to a smattering of applause and the manager led them towards an old woman in a wheelchair who was still clapping in obvious delight. She was dressed in a pink cashmere jersey, Molly noted, a warm rug across her knees.

'Iris, visitors to see you, dear,' the manager said. 'Come and we'll take you to one of the break-out areas. You'll be more private there.' She grasped the handles and wheeled her resident from the lounge, Netta and Molly following closely behind.

The walls of the home were brightened with prints by Jolomo, one of Molly's favourite Scottish artists. It might be, as some called it, God's waiting room, but she had seen far worse places in which the elderly spent their twilight years.

'There now, I'll leave you to have your chat,' the woman said with a nod to Molly. 'Just ring the wee bell when it's time to leave and someone will let you out.'

'Well, Iris, do ye remember me?' Netta began, sitting opposite the old lady. 'Oh, and this is my friend, Molly. She's a polis. Detective inspector. Sorry to trouble you, but she wants tae rake ower a few things in our past.' She grinned, taking the woman's gnarled hand in her own.

Molly's eyes were drawn to the large diamond rings sliding around the old lady's arthritic fingers. If these were the genuine article, then someone had spent a small fortune at one time on Iris Lafferty.

'Hello, Mrs Lafferty. I'm Detective Inspector Newton but yes, you can call me Molly.' She smiled, shooting an exasperated glance at Netta.

'I remember you, Netta Gordon, sure I do. Don't know how ye managed tae stick thon Mickey fur as long as ye did. Mind you, same could be said fur me. Saw them baith deid and buried though, eh?' she cackled, showing a mouth full of gaps in her teeth.

'Mrs Lafferty, I wanted to ask you about that armed robbery,' Molly said, her tone serious once more.

'Ach, all water under the bridge, hen,' Iris Lafferty replied. 'Whit wis it ye wanted tae know?'

'There was a story about a cache of missing money,' Molly began, shifting in her seat. 'We have your son in custody right now and it is our belief that he and his associates were attempting to find it.'

'Associates? They're a' deid, hen, naebody left tae tell the tale,' Iris laughed.

'What aboot Billy McGregor and Matthew Dobbie?' Netta countered, ignoring Molly's frown.

'Aw, McGregor. Right enough, their young getaway driver, could aye bob an' weave, that one. And Dobbie?' The old woman began to laugh again. 'Your Mickey damn near killed him and naebody ever guessed it wis an inside job. Dobbie was as guilty as the rest of them.'

'It is our belief that these three men were after the missing money,' Molly told her.

Iris Lafferty shot the detective a sympathetic look. 'Aw, hen, if that's true, then they've a' been on a fool's errand.'

'How's that, Iris?' Netta asked.

The old woman heaved a sigh, but her eyes were twinkling as she replied.

'Oh, dearie me, that money's long gone, hen. Kevin's daddy had it all stashed away. Wis canny enough tae leave it fur a year till he dug it up, mind.'

'A million pounds?' Molly asked.

'Like ah said, it's long gone, hen. Bought oor wee place in Skirving Street and well, you know whit ma man wis like, Netta?'

Molly's eyes flitted from one to the other, two elderly women who had been the wives of serious felons.

'Ye don't mean . . . ?'

'Aye.' Iris Lafferty shook her head. 'I managed a wee nest egg fur a rainy day but what he didn't spend in drink went tae the bookies.' She turned to Molly. 'It's amazing how quickly a man can get through that amount of money. Drank himself tae death in the end. And good riddance.'

'So, there's nothing left at all?' Molly asked, her mind whirling. Had McGregor, Dobbie and Lafferty been chasing shadows? And had the darkness of their greed led to death?

'Did Kevin no' remember that drunken sot he had for a faither?' Iris murmured. 'Ah, well, he wis jist a wee lad then, efter a'. And his auld man aye filled his heid wi' nonsense aboot buried treasure.'

It was as they drove back through the city that Molly reflected on the old woman's words. What an irony, she thought. Such a waste of lives chasing a pot of money that did not exist.

Iris Lafferty had shown no remorse for her husband's misdeeds nor for the benefit to herself that the stolen money had provided. Would this cold case ever be brought to a court of law? Perhaps not, but at least some answers could be filed away for closure.

As for Lafferty and Dobbie, Iris had not shown any surprise at her wayward son's crimes nor any sympathy for the shootings. That old woman, hardened by the sort of life she had led, was quite a contrast to the lady sitting beside her, gazing out at the familiar streets. Netta had escaped from her past life, had kept a special brightness inside her that shone in her dealings with other people, especially with Daniel, whose friendship she treasured.

CHAPTER FIFTY-FOUR

DI Diana Miller was waiting just inside the corridor as Kohi appeared. There was a satisfied smile on the woman's face as she remembered the conversations with her superior officers regarding the Zimbabwean police constable. Daniel might not have been aware of the focus of their interest, even before he had been allocated his division, but the deputy divisional commander had pushed hard for him to come to Cathcart, in an effort to show a willingness to flag up inclusivity. They had wanted a diverse combination of officers, he'd told Diana, not just to be seen to be politically correct but because their own part of Glasgow was a genuine cultural mix. That had boded well for the DI's request. And now, as he strode along the corridor, backpack over one shoulder, Diana Miller stepped out to greet him.

'Someone said I was to report to you, ma'am?' Daniel asked.

'Yes,' she replied with a smile. 'You've been noticed in some high places, Daniel Kohi. Our chief constable also seems to hold you in high regard. Mentioned she knew you before you joined up. Why's that, I wonder?'

Daniel managed to keep a straight face as the DI stared at him, obviously curious to know the answer to her question. But that was one secret he would keep to himself. Having risked his refugee status at Lorimer's request, Daniel had been a vital part in saving the city from a dreadful terrorist attack. He had met Caroline Flint, then the deputy chief constable, in strange circumstances as he had rescued a young boy and handed him over to the safe keeping of police officers. Flint had remembered him thereafter, a special smile on her face as she'd presented him with the First Aid award on his passing-out parade at Tulliallan Police College.

'No? Oh, well, I guess some things are not meant to be aired,' Miller said, giving Daniel a quizzical look. 'I'd like you to attend a briefing this afternoon. CID muster room at four p.m. I've squared it with DS Knight.'

She walked away, chuckling to herself at the bemused expression on PC Kohi's face.

Later, as Daniel drove back to the station and parked, he was curious to know why he was being summoned to attend this briefing and what it was all about. DI Miller had not mentioned any particular case to him, and Daniel knew that she still had some involvement in the murder of Billy McGregor, the man who had visited their flat. Was he being invited to join the investigation team? Or was there something else afoot?

*

If he was surprised to see Deputy Divisional Commander Holland sitting beside DI Miller, Daniel tried hard not to show it. The muster room was where the detectives assembled daily for briefings on specific cases but right now only the broad-shouldered figure of Commander Holland accompanied by Diana Miller were there, seated behind a table.

'Take a seat, Kohi,' Holland said, waving a hand to the solitary chair opposite.

Daniel removed his hat, laid it on the table in front of him and sat.

'You have any idea why you are here, Constable?' the man asked.

'Not really, sir,' Daniel replied.

'Well, it's like this, Kohi. We've had our eyes on you ever since Tulliallan. Well, maybe even before that,' Holland added with a grin that told Daniel the man had been speaking to the chief constable. 'An officer with your experience and skills is exactly what we need when it comes to investigative duties. DI Miller here,' he raised a hand and turned to the woman by his side, 'assures me that your service to date has been exemplary and, to be honest, I see no reason for you to plod on with your two years' probation when you have already had the sort of experience here and overseas that would be ideal for a fast track.'

'What exactly does that entail, sir?' Daniel asked.

'Means we send you to train in all the necessary skills a detective will require.'

'It also means that in the next few years you are quite likely to stop calling me ma'am,' Miller told him, a sardonic smile on her face. 'Fast tracking jumps you from being a police constable through DS to a DI pretty quickly. If you have the talent.'

Daniel's mind whirled. Molly had been a serving officer for a good number of years, and she had only just been promoted.

'How would other officers feel about me being promoted over their heads?' he asked.

Holland chuckled. 'Lots of them hate it,' he admitted. 'The old guard don't like to be given orders from someone they feel isn't ready to take command. But it's largely up to the men and women who are given this chance to make it work. Not just for themselves, but for the entire department to which they are assigned.'

'You'll take this chance, Daniel?' Miller asked, a small frown deepening the line between her brows.

'Thank you,' he began, clearing his throat before continuing. 'It was my ambition to return to the role of detective inspector when I joined Police Scotland, but I never thought . . . ' He swallowed hard. 'Thank you for giving me this opportunity, sir, ma'am.'

'I don't think you'll let us down, Kohi.' Holland rose from his seat and thrust out his hand for Daniel to shake. 'Right, I'll leave this with you now, Diana,' he said, raising a hand to bid them both farewell.

Daniel was already on his feet and watched as the deputy divisional commander left the room.

'Wonder what DI Newton will make of this news?' Miller chuckled as she escorted Daniel from the room, a grin on her face.

CHAPTER FIFTY-FIVE

As Molly Newton stepped into a puddle of sunlight, she reflected on how her conversation with the man sitting next to his bed might proceed. In some strange way, she felt almost sorry for Dobbie, who was now a prisoner as well as a patient in this hospital room.

'Good afternoon, Matthew,' she began, watching the man as he narrowed his eyes, clearly unhappy about her arrival.

'I've been to see an old lady today,' she told him, standing so that she cast a shadow over Dobbie. 'And she told me a rather interesting tale. About a large sum of hidden money.'

Dobbie's eyes widened as Molly related the truth behind the stolen money, shaking his head in disbelief as she reached the end of the story.

'You mean . . . ?'

Molly nodded. 'Kenny Lafferty, Kevin's late father, had it hidden all the time he was inside. Pretended not to know where it was but once he was out, well, I've told you the rest.'

Dobbie blinked back tears, but were they tears of rage

or tears of sorrow? Certainly, from the way he pursed his cracked lips, Molly thought she was observing a degree of unspoken frustration on the part of the man who had nursed such bitterness for decades, only to have his last hopes snatched away.

He swallowed back the words that wanted to stream out of his mouth, words to express his deep dismay and, if he were to be honest, a feeling of regret.

Billy need not have died.

The scene in the close came back vividly as he stared past the detective. Billy had been his usual cocksure self, slapping young Lafferty's back as he told them how he intended to spend his share of the money once they had found it in the old lady's flat. He was certain she wouldn't have risked banking a big sum like that, Billy had laughed as he and Lafferty had exchanged dark looks behind Billy's back.

But there would be no third share for McGregor. Lafferty had made that clear. A quick couple of shots and scarper, the dealer had said.

If he hadn't turned around ... Dobbie swallowed hard, remembering the shock on the man's face as he'd seen the gun in Lafferty's hand. Then, that scream ...

When Lafferty had forced him to batter the dead man's face to a pulp, he had done it willingly, almost in a frenzy, as if it would cancel out his own years of suffering.

Matthew Dobbie closed his eyes and felt the first trickle of tears escaping.

'He wanted it all for himself,' he whispered huskily. 'That's why he tried to kill me.'

The detective's voice was not unkind when he heard her speak again.

'I think it's time you gave us another statement, Matthew.'

'It's never straightforward, is it?' Daniel said, one arm around Molly's shoulder as they lay in bed that night, discussing the outcome of the murder case.

'Nope, it rarely is. And,' she added with a shake of the head, 'it so often involves drugs, doesn't it? Lafferty and Robert Lennox, the addict he used as a hit man.'

'That was what brought Augustus Ncube to Glasgow,' Daniel said. 'Poor guy. He had the chance to do something different but dealing was all he knew, I suppose.'

Molly looked at him with a frown. 'You almost sound sorry for him,' she said.

'Well, look what he's lost. Home, country, his freedom . . . '

Molly made no reply. Daniel Kohi had also lost far more but there was no way she could voice that right now.

She felt his arm drawing her closer to his side.

'Whereas I've got you,' he said softly, bending to kiss her. 'And I have something rather interesting about my own career to tell you, Detective Inspector Newton.'

CHAPTER FIFTY-SIX

POLICE SUPERINTENDENT FOUND DEAD

The body of Police Superintendent Nelson Sibanda has been found near a safari lodge in the Kariba district by rangers. It is thought that the officer may have been on some sort of solo mission out in the bush when he was trampled to death by a herd of water buffalo that are known to frequent that particular area of grassland. Sibanda, who was well known in the capital, had been the subject of recent allegations of corruption which were being investigated. Former senator Wilson Ncube has admitted that he had grave reservations about Sibanda's appointment as head of Criminal Investigation and that the superintendent had attempted to bribe him in the past. A post-mortem examination will take place, however preliminary signs are that this was no more than a tragic accident.

'Well! What do you make of that!'

Father Peter McGlinchey took back the newspaper that he had given the older woman to read.

Janette Kohi shook her head. 'He was not a good man,' she whispered. 'Daniel tried to . . . ' The priest laid a kindly hand over hers as she stifled a sob. Some things were difficult to remember, tragedies that never really left a person the same. How to live after losing a beloved grandson and daughter-in-law was hard to imagine for a man who had neither. And yet, despite his single status, Father McGlinchey was a man of deep understanding, having seen much suffering throughout his role in the church.

'God rest his soul,' he murmured. For, he reasoned, this man, no matter what evil he had committed in his life, had still been a child of God.

Janette looked at him and nodded, though her mouth was fixed in a thin line as if it were a waste of breath to bestow any mercy on the man who had destroyed innocents like little Johannes and his mother.

'Perhaps now it will be a little easier for you to leave,' the priest suggested. 'I think we've kept you here with the good sisters long enough.'

Janette frowned. 'How? Why do you think that, Father?' She had become used to the confinement of her small cell within the abbey, a sanctuary from danger. How could she face being out in the world once more?

Father McGlinchey smiled and patted her hand. 'Till now I think this man, Sibanda, has been watching for you, waiting for a moment to pounce. But with this,' he pointed to the newspaper, 'I wonder if his stranglehold on so many corrupt police officers will loosen for good. You've read this report. Accused of corruption. I think now that has been said publicly, there will be few who will want to be associated with this man's memory.

'Let us say a prayer,' he went on, and, taking Janette's hands in his own, the kindly man asked for guidance in the coming days and for the good Lord's strength to overcome any obstacles that might still lie in her way.

It was amazing to be sitting in the back of a car watching the world speeding past, Janette thought, her eyes taking in every familiar piece of her city as they drove to the office building where she would have to collect her visa. It felt strange to be back in normal clothes once more, a nun's habit that had been her disguise all these long weeks laid aside temporarily, though a headscarf pulled forward kept her face hidden for now. The big Mercedes taxi was such a ubiquitous vehicle in the city, something that did not immediately draw attention to anyone watching, which was why Father McGlinchey had insisted on hiring one for the woman whom he had kept closeted with the nuns. So many weeks had passed since his parishioner, Kristine Paul, had called for him to help, the old blind lady keeping her neighbour's whereabouts a secret from all but a select few.

First thing this morning, he had taken Janette to a lawyer's office on the outskirts of the city to complete the transaction that had been decided between Richard Mlambo and Janette. The ranger had secured funds from his savings to buy the plot of land beside his father's home and the money would be in Janette's account in three working days. She had sat silently, letting the priest do most of the talking until it had been time to sign the paperwork. There had been no qualms about letting the place go. Chipo and Johannes were long gone to their place in heaven, and it was to the living that Janette Kohi now owed her duty. Afterwards, she had experienced a slight sense of release and gratitude. Relinquishing Daniel's plot of land marked a loosening of ties with the past as well as enabling her to be with him once again.

Now she was back in the bustle of the city, the noise of traffic and people shouting so different from the calm she had become used to these last few weeks. The taxi drew up outside the building where Janette was required to go and collect her visa.

'I'll be waiting here for you,' Father McGlinchey told her, leaning back and clasping her hand for a brief moment.

Janette hurried up the steps of the building and stepped from the heat into a cool, air-conditioned lobby. There was a small queue at the reception desk, a family of South Asians, the mother wearing an emerald-green sari, father in a pale beige business suit and two small children hanging onto each of their mother's hands. Janette hung back out of politeness. It was no business of hers what they were saying to the man behind the desk though she began to smile at one of the little boys as he turned and gazed at her, one finger in his mouth. She raised her eyebrows at him and grinned, making him giggle and turn closer to his mother's skirts. Ah, she hadn't lost the knack with children, Janette thought as the little boy caught her eye again and pretended to be shy.

She could see the Asian man nodding now and raising

a hand, signalling the end of his discussion with the man behind the desk. Then, with hardly a glance at his family, he swept along, his wife and children scurrying in his wake.

'Yes?' The man in the short-sleeved white shirt gave Janette an appraising look.

'I am Mrs Janette Kohi,' she began, holding out the letter she had been sent. 'I have come to collect my visa.'

The man took her papers and appeared to read through them quickly before handing them back.

'Take the lift to the top corridor. Then it's the second door on the left,' he said, pointing in the direction of a bank of elevators.

'Have a very nice day,' he added, already looking over Janette's shoulder to see who was next in line. He would not remember the small woman wearing a dark brown headscarf knotted beneath her chin, just one more person in a day full of forgettable faces.

Soon Janette had stepped out of the lift, glad that it had been vacant to take her to the top floor. Then she followed the receptionist's directions.

There was nobody waiting outside in the row of seats and so she approached the door and gave a tentative knock.

A disembodied voice called 'Come in' and Janette pushed the door open to find herself in a pleasant room overlooking the city streets.

'I am Mrs Janette Kohi. I've come for my visa,' she explained to the middle-aged lady sitting on a comfortable high-backed chair behind a dark wood desk.

It was over almost as soon as it had begun, the authorisation of her visa stamped with the date a simple matter after all, and Janette found herself descending to the ground floor before she had time to admire the view from that office window.

As she stepped out of the lift, Janette caught sight of two armed police officers standing on either side of the entrance, their eyes scanning each person as they passed out into the street.

She stopped, frozen for a moment, heart pounding. Were they looking for her? Waiting to arrest her? Put her in jail on some trumped-up charge?

The sound of laughter came from behind her, and she felt something soft wafting against her leg as the Asian family swept past her, the woman's colourful sari picking up a draught of air and swirling towards Janette. She walked quickly behind them, deliberately avoiding a single glance towards the policemen.

And then she was out once more, sun spilling onto the pavement, turning it to the colour of yellowing marula fruit.

As she climbed into the back of the Mercedes, Janette breathed a silent prayer of thanks.

'Everything all right?' Father McGlinchey asked as the taxi set off.

'Yes. I got it,' she said, patting the handbag resting on her lap, her precious visa tucked out of sight.

'Thanks be to God,' she heard the priest murmur as the taxi gathered speed and set off through the city streets.

Father McGlinchey turned back to stare out of the front window. Now came the hard bit, he realised. It was one thing to obtain the correct paperwork and then purchase an airline ticket but quite another to go through Harare airport with the sort of security that involved and board the flight for London. So much could go wrong. And there were many signs that Janette Kohi was still far from safety. Still, the good Lord had led them thus far, hadn't He?

The sound of a siren's whine made them both look back to see a police car not far behind them, its blue lights flashing.

'Father!' Janette gave a scream, her eyes wide with terror.

McGlinchey grasped the taxi driver's arm. 'Get us out of here. Quick!' he implored, as the sound of the police car grew louder.

'Put your foot down! Fast as you can!' the priest yelled.

CHAPTER FIFTY-SEVEN

Wilson Ncube folded his newspaper and leaned back in his chair with a smile. His bribe to that journalist had worked well, his name no longer associated with Sibanda, apart from his public assertions about the dead man's criminality. A line had been drawn under that particular business, he thought, reaching for a cigar. And it was not the only one. Augustus would have to suffer the consequences of his own behaviour. He was finished with his wayward son for good. The old man lifted the gold-plated lighter towards the end of his cigar, preparing to enjoy a few blissful moments, wrapped in satisfaction that he could still enjoy such small luxuries.

'Welcome back!' The manager of Meikles Hotel clapped his hands in evident glee at the sight of the tall white man and his attractive wife. 'Your rooms are ready and await you.' Then, clicking his fingers, he motioned the bellboy to take the Lorimers' luggage upstairs. 'You would like to book dinner tonight in our restaurant?' he asked.

Once they had agreed a time, Maggie and Lorimer took their keys and headed for the lift.

'Different room this time,' said Lorimer, frowning. 'Wonder why.'

Maggie turned away to hide a smile, anticipating his reaction when they stepped into the suite of rooms she had secretly booked for their last few days in Harare, a special treat for her husband's birthday.

'Good lord!' Lorimer took a few steps into the spacious room then looked at Maggie. 'Did you plan this?' He waved a hand towards the vases of flowers and the ice bucket with a bottle of champagne. 'And, my goodness, look at this bedroom!'

Maggie followed him from the lounge into a bedroom that had the biggest bed she had ever seen, its gold silk awnings sweeping down from a tall frame and richly embroidered crimson coverlet like something from a child's fairy tale. It was a little excessive, perhaps, that huge silver bowl spilling with fruit, more flowers on the highly polished dressing table, but she only had herself to blame, asking for these special extras.

The bellboy gave Lorimer a small bow as the tall gentleman handed him a generous tip, no doubt imagining this white couple to be famous in their own country, not just a Scottish policeman and his teacher wife.

'How on earth . . . ?' Lorimer caught Maggie by the waist, whirling her around till she began to giggle.

'I've been given a rather generous advance,' she told him. 'A four-book deal for my wee ghost-boy stories.'

'You didn't tell me!' he protested. 'This is a time for champagne, right enough!'

'I wanted it to be a surprise,' she insisted. 'And this was for you, for your birthday. Felt it was time you were spoiled, Detective Superintendent,' she added, laying her head on his chest.

Later, after half the champagne had been quaffed, Lorimer heard a ping on his mobile as a message came through. Lifting the phone, he searched for the sender, only to see that it was from the ranger.

Sitting up, he read the words on the screen, nodding silently to himself. So, the Zimbabwean media had spoken, or at least that organ of the state that had run the news item about Sibanda.

We are free from that oppressor now, Richard had written, above the newspaper attachment. And so it must seem to many, Lorimer thought, though perhaps he was one of the few people who would ever know the truth about what Nelson Sibanda had been planning to do before he had met with his gruesome death. But he had failed to do anything about the death of that young guide, thwarted by a system that existed to cover up corruption.

He heaved a sigh. Would crime always shadow his footsteps, no matter where in the world he went? Back home there would always be cases to be solved, criminals to apprehend.

Was that his destiny? Perhaps. But for these last few days here in Zimbabwe he owed it to Maggie to put these events behind him and try to enjoy their holiday.

Breakfasting in these sumptuous rooms seemed appropriate, Lorimer thought with a sigh of satisfaction as he folded the linen napkin and laid it to one side, happy to see Maggie enjoying a plate of exotic fruits.

'A little bit of luxury will do us no harm,' Maggie said, waving her fork and giving him a grin. 'After all, we both work hard, don't we?'

Before he could reply, the telephone on a side table began to ring.

'I'll get it.' Lorimer rose and strode across the room. 'Hello, Lorimer speaking.'

Maggie looked up, clearly curious as to who was calling.

'Oh. Who did you say? Who?'

Maggie could hear an edge to her husband's voice, a note of steely caution that was second nature to a man in William Lorimer's profession. Then she saw a smile tugging at his mouth and heard his voice change completely.

'Oh, a friend of ... really? Well, of course, please send him up.'

'Who was that?' Maggie asked, her curiosity demanding satisfaction.

'A total stranger,' Lorimer replied. 'But friend, not foe. A man of the cloth, apparently, a Father McGlinchey. He has news of Daniel's mother and wants to talk to us.'

Maggie's lips parted in astonishment. 'Is she here? In Harare?'

Lorimer shrugged. 'I think that is what we are about to find out.'

Soon he was opening the door to their suite to find a small, chubby man with white hair and twinkling blue eyes, beaming up at him.

'Father McGlinchey,' the priest told him, his Irish accent

clearly discernible. 'And you two will be Daniel's friends, am I right?'

Lorimer introduced Maggie and invited the priest to sit down in one of the easy chairs.

'How did you know where to find us?' he asked, taking a seat on a couch next to Maggie.

'Where else would you be but Meikles Hotel.' The priest laughed. 'One does not have to be trained in the art of detection to work that out!'

'We're just back from a safari trip,' Maggie said. 'Arrived here last night.'

The priest nodded and smiled at her. 'I know that too,' he chuckled. 'Janette's friends, the Mlambo family, have kept me informed ever since you encountered Richard.'

'The ranger?' Maggie's eyebrows rose.

McGlinchey nodded once more. 'We have a sort of underground network, ye see. Priests and pastors helping to allow people to flee from their oppressors.'

'Like Daniel?'

'Yes, and now we are trying to help Janette to fly out of Harare and onwards to be with her son in Glasgow.' He looked at Lorimer. 'That's where you come in,' he continued. 'Why I'm here.'

CHAPTER FIFTY-EIGHT

Their last days in Harare flew past with visits to the zoo, a trip out to Lake Chivero to see some lion cubs and cheetah being reared in captivity as well as a return visit to Larvon Bird Gardens, which Lorimer had decided was one of his favourite places. The priest had not returned to Meikles Hotel but there was no need, his verbal instructions to the Scottish couple sufficient. They had experienced a scare after Janette had collected her visa, the priest had told them, mistaking a police car screaming to an emergency for more bad cops hunting them down. Meantime, Janette was safely back with the nuns, and it was best that the Lorimers did not meet with her just yet, lest anyone was watching the Scottish couple's movements.

'I'll be a bit sad to go, in spite of all the trauma we've been through,' Maggie admitted, as they boarded the coach that was to take them to Harare airport. 'I wonder if we'll ever return to Africa.'

Lorimer did not look back as they drew away from the front of the hotel, his mind very much on what was waiting for them. If McGlinchey was right, then there should be no trouble. But the death of Nelson Sibanda had eliminated only one bad apple in a barrel that was swilling about with rottenness. There might still be an impediment to their safe passage out of Zimbabwe.

Janette Kohi clutched the handle of her suitcase anxiously, glancing around from one side to the other, the check-in queue bringing her closer and closer to the desks where smartly dressed young men and women waited to process passengers' baggage and issue boarding cards. She felt shabby by comparison, her old skirt and blouse in plain shades of brown and cream chosen to help her merge into a crowd. She started as a bored-looking, unsmiling girl motioned her forward and thrust out her hand for Janette's passport. For a moment Janette felt hot, a trickle of perspiration under her collar, and then she was being handed a slip of white paper in her passport and being ordered to lift her suitcase onto the conveyor belt. The young woman flicked some baggage tags onto it and then Janette watched as it slid away out of sight.

'Where do I go now?' she asked timidly.

'Security!' the girl snorted in derision. 'Over there. Follow the signs, Grandma!'

Blushing, Janette murmured her thanks and turned in the direction the girl had pointed. She had little for the journey, a Bible and some sweets the nuns had given her, their gracious prayers and hugs a small comfort as she had set off from the sanctuary that had been her home these past weeks. She'd also folded her favourite shawl neatly in her carry-on bag as well as the folder containing her airline tickets, passport and enough money to see her all the way to her journey's end.

Just as she began to look for a sign for Security, she heard a familiar voice calling her name.

Janette whirled around, mouth opening in astonishment as Campbell, his father and grandfather walked towards her.

'What on earth . . . ?'

'We had to come and see you off, dear friend,' Joseph told her.

Campbell nodded in agreement. 'And Dad's got something for you,' he said, grinning.

'I did not want you leaving without these,' Richard told her. 'Campbell managed to sneak into your house to find them.' He handed Janette a package wrapped in brown paper.

'I made them into this book at school for you,' the lad said, glancing proudly up at his father.

Janette unwrapped her gift to find an old school jotter, similar to ones that she had used as a teacher so long ago, a precious rarity now that children had so little paper and few pencils in their classrooms. Inside, Campbell had stuck several photographs, images that she'd thought were lost to her for ever – her wedding picture, images of Daniel as a baby, his graduation picture as a police cadet and several more.

'Had to take them out of their frames,' Campbell said apologetically. 'Dad said they would be too much to take on the plane.'

Janette let the tears slide down her cheeks as she tried to utter a husky thank you.

'We'll miss you,' Joseph told her, his own eyes full of tears.

She hugged them all in turn and then they walked with her as far as the entrance to Security where other families were hugging loved ones as they departed.

Then she was on her own, a small figure walking in and out of a cordon towards the place where she could see several uniformed police officers watching the line of passengers.

'Dear Lord, be with me,' she whispered, lifting a plastic tray and putting her bag into it as she had seen others doing in front of her.

She tried hard to ignore those watchful eyes as she was beckoned to walk through an archway and then, she was out on the other side, gathering up her bag and heading for the area marked Departures. Father McGlinchey had told her to go straight to the departure lounge and wait at the furthest screen that was showing the times of flights. Slowly she went past shops selling all manner of stuff that she would never afford, things that only rich tourists might purchase as souvenirs of their visit to Zimbabwe. Now she could hear the muffled roar of aircraft engines out on the tarmac as they began to taxi towards the runways, the noise rising above the chatter of so many excited passengers in family groups.

Janette walked to the far end of the lounge, glancing at the screens telling of departure times and gates. There was her flight to London, the words *on time* making her breathe more easily.

'Janette? Mrs Kohi?'

Janette looked around, fearful for a moment that she was about to be apprehended by one of those armed officers, but the accent she had heard was different.

'Hello, is it really you?'

A tall white man and a dark-haired lady dressed in white slacks and a matching jacket were standing there smiling at her.

'I'm Maggie Lorimer and this is my husband, Bill. We're friends of your Daniel,' she explained. 'And I believe we're going to be on the same flights as you.'

'Father McGlinchey . . . ?'

'He arranged it all,' the man with the melodic voice told her. Then he looked up and nodded. 'That's our departure gate announced now. Shall we go, ladies?'

Then, picking up a rucksack and slinging it over his shoulders, he offered Janette Kohi his arm.

CHAPTER FIFTY-NINE

'The whole plan really began with my neighbour, Kristine. She's blind and has mobility issues,' Janette explained, 'but she has great strength of character.' She paused for a moment to take a sip of tea then shook her head. 'But, of course, young Campbell came to warn me before that.'

They were seated together on the big plane, Janette between the Lorimers, enjoying a cup of tea while the Scots sipped rock shandies. Maggie had asked Daniel's mother how she had evaded capture by Sibanda's hoods and now the whole story was coming out.

'Never thought I'd be disguised as a nun,' Janette chuckled. 'Me a staunch Presbyterian! It's a very ecumenical community, mind you.'

'We met your neighbour,' Lorimer said. 'She hinted something to Maggie about a pastor.'

Janette smiled. 'Pastor John is overseas right now so it was Kristine's priest, Father McGlinchey, who took care of me.'

'We met him, too,' Maggie exclaimed. 'Lovely Irish man with twinkly eyes.'

'That's Father,' Janette agreed. 'I think the nuns adore him in their own way. Each time he came to visit they would flutter around him like so many butterflies.'

Then she began to chuckle. 'Oh my, I won't forget the fright he gave me the day he came to bring me away. Poor man knocked over a plant pot by the back door and sent it crashing to the ground. Nearly gave me a heart attack! I thought it was the men who'd attacked Joseph Mlambo who had come for me. But once we had left, all I felt was such relief to be in safe hands.'

'He takes a lot of risks helping people escape from difficult circumstances,' Lorimer remarked.

'They all do,' Janette replied, her face serious for a moment. 'If anyone had found out how Pastor John had helped Daniel . . . ' She shook her head. 'It doesn't bear thinking what might have happened to that good man.'

Bit by bit Janette Kohi's story emerged, her flight from home, the long weeks living with the nuns and the anxiety she had suffered wondering if she would be found and taken away.

'But you're safe now,' Maggie said, patting the older lady's hand. 'And we're taking you home to see Daniel.'

'And Netta,' added Lorimer. 'I think you're going to be great friends.'

Janette nodded, her eyes too full of tears for any more words.

'God is good,' Maggie whispered, seeing the old lady's sudden emotion.

Outside, darkness was falling and it would be a long night's journey to reach their journey's end. But tomorrow would bring a new day and the promise of brightness filling the skies.

Darkness came early in those cold winter afternoons, his warm cell almost a relief after the exercise yard. Augustus sat down heavily on the edge of his bed. It was over, the prison governor had told him that morning when he had been summoned to his office. McGregor's associates, Lafferty and Dobbie, had confessed to their part in the plot to hunt down Daniel Kohi and how it had all come from the big Zimbabwean currently detained at His Majesty's pleasure. Everything that could go wrong had gone wrong, the men in whom he had put his trust turning on one another over the desire to find a stash of stolen money from an armed robbery many years ago. And Kohi was still out there, a cop in this city, free to go about his life.

Sibanda was dead and with him any hopes that he might have had of carrying out his revenge on Kohi's mother. The old lady's house remained empty, it seemed, so she had got away before any of Sibanda's men could track her down.

He put his head into his hands, remembering the prison governor's words. He could expect many more years added to his sentence and there would be no question of repatriation for Augustus Ncube. *It is what you deserve*, the governor had told him severely as Ncube had tried in vain to reason with the man. The law here in Scotland would decide on the terms of his imprisonment but he should not expect to see the world outside these walls until he was quite an old man. Revenge was not the answer, the prison chaplain had told him. There were other ways to live his life. And now, facing a future here within this dark place, Ncube began to wonder if he was right.

CHAPTER SIXTY

Netta was first to the door when the bell rang, then she hesitated and took a step back as Daniel came beside her.

'I think it's them,' she said, biting her lower lip in excitement. 'You go first, son. Go on.'

Daniel unlocked the door and opened his arms to the small woman standing on the doorstep of their close, Lorimer and Maggie behind her.

'Mum!'

He felt her bones as he hugged her, this woman who had given him so much in his life and who had made so many sacrifices, old now and no doubt worn out after the journey.

'Daniel, it's really you!' she whispered, looking up into his face.

Then they were all indoors, the mother and son holding on to each other as their friends watched their reunion, Netta dabbing her eyes with a clean handkerchief.

'Mum, this is Mrs Netta Gordon, your penfriend,' Daniel

said, turning at last to introduce them. For a moment he saw his old friend's lip tremble as she stood gazing at the small African woman.

And then, just as if it was the most normal thing in the world, he heard Netta ask, 'Anyone for a pot o' tea?'

ACKNOWLEDGEMENTS

Where to begin my thanks? With Donnie, who brought me all the way to a beautiful country that was then known as Rhodesia to be his bride. Some of the adventures we had in those early days of our marriage and subsequent visits to Zimbabwe have found their way into this story, the country itself unchanged as far as its bountiful wildlife and landscape are concerned, many other aspects of life sadly quite altered.

I owe a debt of thanks to the police officers, current and retired, who so willingly give of their time to help me: former chief constable Sir Iain Livingstone, Bob Frew, Mairi Milne, Chief Inspector Pauline Thompson and Superintendent Rob Hay. It has been a learning curve for me to find out more about the early years for a probationer in Police Scotland as I try to demonstrate the sort of work that Daniel might carry out. Thank you, Pauline, for my visit to Cathcart office in Aikenhead Road. Expect me to be calling on you often!

Thanks to son, John, for permission to use his property in Nithsdale Drive where Daniel and Netta now live in my fictional world. I am sure the residents there have no idea of the adventures happening in that alternative universe!

Thanks to my editor, Rosanna Forte, for her patience as I struggled to write this book at times through spells of ill health. So nice to be treated like part of a family and not a commodity by my lovely publishing house, Little, Brown. (I was not at all like Douglas Adams who said he loved the sound of deadlines whizzing past him!)

Thanks to all the staff who see this book through its various processes with special mention to Sean for his amazing cover, and Jon and Liz who help so much. The whole Sphere team continue to be marvellous as do Emma Dowson and her colleagues for all their tireless work in marketing the books. You are all superstars.

To my agent, Dr Jenny Brown, for your unfailing support, encouragement and friendship, my dearest thanks. You are the best!

Alex Gray, 2023